DAIRY QUEEN DAYS

A Novel

ROBERT INMAN

LITTLE, BROWN AND COMPANY
Boston New York Toronto London

ALSO BY ROBERT INMAN

Old Dogs and Children
Home Fires Burning

First Edition

The characters and events in this book are fictitious. Any similarity to real persons, living or dead, is coincidental and not intended by the author.

Library of Congress Cataloging-in-Publication Data

Inman, Robert.
    Dairy Queen days : a novel / Robert Inman. — 1st ed.
      p.   cm.
    ISBN 0-316-41873-0
    I. Title.
    PS3559.N449D35   1997
    813'.54 — dc20   96-26258

10 9 8 7 6 5 4 3 2

MV-NY

Published simultaneously in Canada by Little, Brown & Company
(Canada) Limited

Printed in the United States of America

For Chris and Larkin Ferris

I am leaving, I am leaving
But the fighter still remains.
— From "The Boxer"
Simon and Garfunkel

Life can only be understood backwards;
But it must be lived forwards.
— Søren Kierkegaard

DAIRY
QUEEN
DAYS

ONE

TROUT MOSELEY WAS a day shy of sixteen when his father, Reverend Joe Pike Moseley, ran away.

Most people thought it started with the motorcycle. Maybe even before that, when they sent Trout's mother off to the Institute. But people thought Joe Pike had been handling that unpleasantness reasonably well — "keeping his equilibrium," as they said — until he showed up with the motorcycle.

It was an ancient Triumph, or at least what had once been a Triumph. Joe Pike found it in a farmer's barn, in pieces, and brought it home in the trunk of his car. Trout was standing at the kitchen window when he saw Joe Pike back the car down the driveway to the garage behind the parsonage. By the time Trout got out there, Joe Pike had the trunk open and was standing with his arms crossed, staring at the jumble of wheel rims, pitted chrome pieces, engine, handlebars, gasoline tank.

"What's that?" Trout asked.

"A once and future motorcycle."

"What're you gonna do with it?"

Joe Pike uncrossed his arms and hitched up his pants from their accustomed place below his paunch. "Fix it up. I am the resurrection and the life. Yea, verily." A trace of a smile played at his lips. *"Up from the grave He arose!"* he sang off-key. Joe Pike sang badly, but enthusiastically. In church he could make the choir director wince. He referred to his singing as "making a joyful noise."

"You know anything about motorcycles?" Trout asked.

"Not much."

"Need some help?"

Joe Pike stared for a long time at the jumble of metal in the trunk of the car. Trout wondered after a while if his father had heard the question. Finally Joe Pike said, "I reckon I can manage. It ain't heavy."

"I mean . . ." But then he saw that Joe Pike wasn't really paying him any attention. His mind was there inside the trunk among the parts of the old Triumph, perhaps deep down inside one of the cylinders of the engine, imagining a million tiny explosions going off rapid-fire. Trout studied him for a minute or so, then shrugged and turned to go.

"It's a four-cycle," Joe Pike said.

Trout turned and looked at him again. Joe Pike's gaze never left the motorcycle. "What?"

"You don't have to mix the gas and oil."

"That's good," Trout said. "You might forget."

When Trout looked out the kitchen window again a half hour later, the trunk of the car was closed and so were the double doors of the old wood-frame garage. But he could faintly hear Joe Pike singing inside: *"Rescue the perishing, care for the dying!"*

Over the next two months, Trout stayed away from the garage when Joe Pike was out there. But he followed the progress of the motorcycle by sneaking looks when Joe Pike was gone. At first it was a spindly metal frame propped up on two concrete blocks like a huge insect. Metal parts bobbed like apples in a ten-gallon galvanized washtub filled with solvent to eat away years of grime and rust. Before long, with the metal sanded smooth, the motorcycle began to take shape on the frame. Joe Pike took the fenders, wheel rims, gasoline tank, and handlebars to a body shop and had them repainted and rechromed. Replacement parts — headlamp, cables, speedometer — began to arrive by UPS.

Trout remained vaguely hopeful at first. Fifteen years old, almost sixteen, fascinated by the thought of motorized transportation. But he came to realize that Joe Pike had no intention of sharing the motorcycle.

Joe Pike worked on it in the garage deep into the night, showing up for breakfast bleary-eyed, smelling of grease and solvent, grime caked thick under his fingernails. That was uncharacteristic. Joe Pike was by habit a fastidious man. He took at least two baths a day — more in the summer because he was a prodigious perspirer — and changed his underwear each time. But this present grubbiness didn't seem to bother him. Neither did the state of their housekeeping, which got progressively worse. After Trout's mother went off to the Institute, the church had hired a cleaning woman to come once a week, but she was no match for the growing piles of dirty dishes and laundry. Trout finally took matters into his own hands and learned to operate the dishwasher and the washing machine and dryer. After a fashion. At school he endured locker-room snickers over underwear dyed pale pink from being washed with a red T-shirt. Joe Pike's underwear was likewise pale pink, but he didn't seem to notice, or at least he didn't remark upon it. Joe Pike's mind seemed to be fixed on the motorcycle, or whatever larger thing it was that the motorcycle represented. There was a gently stubborn set to his jaw, almost a grimness there. On Sundays his sermons were vague, rambling things, trailing off in mid-sentence. He didn't seem to be paying the sermons much attention, either. In the pews, members of the congregation would steal glances at one another, perplexed. *What?*

"How's it going?" Trout would ask.

"Okay."

"Don't you get cold out there?" It was March, the pecan trees in the parsonage yard still bare-limbed and gaunt against the gray morning sky.

A blank look from Joe Pike. "No. I reckon not." Then he would stare out the kitchen window in the direction of the garage, and Trout would know that Joe Pike wasn't really there with him at all. He was out there with the Triumph.

It worried Trout a good deal. It brought back all the old business of his mother's long silences, the way she went away somewhere that nobody else could go, stayed for days at a time, and finally just never came back. With Irene's silences, he had felt isolated, left out, wondering what of it, if anything, was his fault. Now, Joe Pike's preoccupation with the motorcycle gave him the same old spooked feeling. Joe Pike, like Irene, seemed unreachable. And Trout finally decided there was really nothing he could do but watch and wait.

So he did, and so did the good people of Ohatchee, Georgia — in particular, the good people of Ohatchee Methodist. They watched, waited, talked:

"What you reckon he's gone do with that thing?"

"Give it to Trout, prob'ly. Man of his size'd bust the tires." (Hearty chuckle here. Joe Pike stood six-four, and his weight ranged from two hundred fifty to three hundred pounds, depending on whether he was in one of his Dairy Queen phases.)

"Well, it gives the Baptists something to talk about."

"Yeah. That and all the other."

"Damn shame."

"Was she hittin' the bottle?"

"Don't think so. Just went off the deep end."

"Poor old Joe Pike. And little Trout. Bless his heart."

Long pause. "Don't reckon Joe Pike had anything to do with it, do you?"

"Course not." Longer pause. "But it does make you wonder."

"Reckon they'll transfer Joe Pike at annual conference?"

"Prob'ly not. He's only been here two years."

"Hmmm. But folks sure do talk."

"Yeah. 'Specially Baptists."

They talked among themselves, but they did not talk to Joe Pike Moseley about his motorcycle. No matter how gracefully he seemed to have handled the business of his wife, there was in general an air of disaster about Joe Pike. People were wary, as if he might be contagious. Then too, a motorcycle just didn't seem to be the kind of thing you discussed with a preacher. At least it didn't until Easter Sunday.

Ohatchee Methodist was packed, the usual crowd swelled by the once-a-year attendees, the ones Joe Pike referred to as "tourists." They were crammed seersucker to crinoline into the oak pews and in folding chairs set up along the aisles and the back wall. It was mid-April, already warm but not quite warm enough for air conditioning, so the windows of the sanctuary were open to the spring morning outside and the ceiling fans went *whoosh-whoosh* overhead, stirring the smell of new clothes and store-bought fragrances into a rich, sweet stew.

When everyone was finally settled into their seats, the choir entered from the narthex singing "Up From the Grave He Arose!" They marched smartly two by two down the aisle, proclaiming triumph o'er the grave, and the congregation rose with a flurry and joined in, swelling the high-ceiling sanctuary with their earnestness. The choir paraded up into the choir loft, everybody sang another verse, and then they all sat down and stared at the door to the Pastor's Study to the right of the altar, expecting Joe Pike to emerge, as was his custom. They sat there for a good while. Nothing. They began to look about at one another. *What?* After a minute or two, they heard the throaty roar of the motorcycle, faintly at first, growing louder as it approached the church and stopped finally at the curb outside. Trout — seated midway in the middle section with his friend Parks Belton and Parks's mother, Imogene — looked around for a route of discreet escape. Joe Pike had spent all night in the garage. He was still there when Trout left for Sunday school. And now he had ridden the motorcycle to church. *Maybe if I crawl under the pew.* But he sat there, transfixed. They were all transfixed.

After a moment, the swinging doors that separated the sanctuary from the narthex flew open and Joe Pike swept in, huge and hurrying, his black robe billowing about him, down the aisle and up to the pulpit. He stopped, looked out over the congregation, gave them all a vague half-smile, and then settled himself in the high-backed chair behind the pulpit. He slouched, one elbow propped on the arm of the chair, chin resting in his hand, one hamlike thigh hiked over the other, revealing a pair of scuffed brown cowboy boots. Trout stared at the boots. Joe Pike had bought them in Dallas years ago when he played football at Texas A&M, but they had been gathering dust in various parsonage closets for as long as Trout could remember. He had never seen Joe Pike wear the boots before.

The choir director, seated at the piano, gave Joe Pike a long look over the top of her glasses. Then she nodded to the choir and they stood and launched into "The Old Rugged Cross." As they sang, Joe Pike sat staring out the window, the toe of his boot swaying slightly in time to the music, his brow wrinkled in thought.

The last notes faded and the choir sat back down. Joe Pike remained in his seat, still staring out the window, out where the motorcycle was. The choir director gave an impatient cough. Then Joe Pike looked up, shook himself. He stood slowly and moved the two steps to the pulpit. He picked up the pulpit Bible. It was a huge thing, leatherbound with gold letters and gilt edging and a long red ribbon to mark your place. Joe Pike held it in his left hand as if it weighed no more than a feather. He opened it with his right hand, flipped a few pages, found his place, and marked it with his index finger.

His eyes searched the words for a long time. Then his brow furrowed in dismay, as if someone had substituted a Bible written in a foreign tongue. He looked up, his gaze sweeping the congregation. His mouth opened, but nothing came out. Sweat beads began to pop out on his forehead. He opened his mouth again and made a little hissing sound through his teeth.

Trout had known for a good while that Joe Pike was really two people — the big man you saw and another, smaller one who was tucked away somewhere inside. Trout didn't know who the small man was. Maybe Joe Pike didn't either, actually. But he gave little evidences of himself in tiny movements of eye, hand, mouth — such as this business of hissing through his teeth — mostly when agitated. You had to be quick to catch it. Most people didn't. But Trout had formed the habit of watchfulness. You had to be watchful in a house where your mother said nothing for long stretches and your father was two people. So now, watching Joe Pike carefully, he saw this hissing through the teeth and read it as trouble, pure and simple.

"What's he doing?" Parks Belton whispered to Trout.

Trout shrugged. "I don't know."

Imogene Belton glared at them. "Shhhhhh!"

Suddenly, Trout felt a great urge to get up from his pew, go up to the pulpit and take the Bible from his father's hand, take him by the arm and say, "It's all right." He felt that the entire congregation, every last one of them, expected him to do just that. But he sat, as immobilized as the rest, all of them like morbid onlookers at the scene of a wreck. Finally, Joe Pike gave a great shuddering sigh and put the Bible back down.

There was a long, fascinated silence, a great holding of breath, broken only by the throb of the ceiling fans. And then Reverend Joe Pike Moseley said, "I'm sorry. I've got to go."

He closed the Bible with a thump. He drew in a deep breath. Then he walked quickly down from the pulpit and up the aisle, the black robe flapping about him, and out the door, looking neither left nor right. Not a soul inside the church moved. After a moment they heard the motorcycle cough to life out front. Joe Pike gunned it a couple of times, then dropped it into gear and roared away. They could hear him for a long time, until the sound finally faded as he topped the rise at the edge of town, heading west. They sat there awhile longer and then one of the ushers got up and went through the swinging doors into the narthex. He returned, holding Joe Pike's black robe. "I reckon he's gone for the day," the man said. With that, everybody got up and went home.

Trout woke the next morning in an agitated muddle, and for a moment he couldn't think of what was wrong. Then he remembered Joe Pike and the motorcycle.

Trout had slept badly, what little he had slept at all. He had assumed Joe Pike would return, certainly by nightfall. Apparently, so had the good people of Ohatchee Methodist, because none of them inquired, in person or by phone, during the afternoon. Whatever was going on at the parsonage or in the tortured soul of Reverend Joe Pike Moseley — best to let it marinate until Monday.

By dark Trout was getting worried. He pictured Joe Pike stranded somewhere, sitting morosely on a deserted roadside with a flat tire or a blown cylinder. Or worse. He thought at one point of sounding some kind of alarm. But two things deterred him and gave him some ease.

The first was the physical image of his father, massive and fearless. Joe Pike had played football for Bear Bryant. He was the only Georgia boy on the Texas A&M team when the Bear went there in 1954 and piled sixty of them onto buses and took them out in the desert to a dust-choked, heat-blasted camp and tried to kill them. Most gave up, some of them sneaking away in the night, dragging their weary bodies and their cardboard suitcases to the bus station at Junction so they could escape crazy Bear Bryant. But twenty-seven of them survived to ride the bus back to College Station, including Joe Pike Moseley. Trout had never been able to fully understand and appreciate why otherwise sane people willingly endured things like that, but it was enough to know that Joe Pike did. Joe Pike weighed two hundred fifty pounds at Texas A&M, even when Bear Bryant got through with him. He was very slow, but immovable and also brave. The Bear stuck him in the middle of the line and made the rest of the game take a detour around him. He once played three quarters against Rice with a broken wrist, until he finally fainted at the bottom of a pileup. All that was back before he became a preacher and a gentleman, of course. But even now — powerful of body, thunderous of voice — there was no question that Joe Pike was still immovable and brave. The good people of Ohatchee Methodist might think that Joe Pike was fleeing from something yesterday when he swept down out of the pulpit and roared off to the west. But Trout suspected just the opposite. He knew the look on Joe Pike's face, had seen it often enough before. Joe Pike was going to do battle. With what? The answer to that would have to wait for Joe Pike's return.

The other thing that kept Trout from calling for help was sheer embarrassment — both for Joe Pike and for himself. He imagined that by now, Joe Pike had probably fought whatever battle he was looking for and was laying low somewhere, considering how he might return to Ohatchee without the congregation or the Bishop doing anything drastic. Joe Pike was not a man to hurry to trouble. And for Trout's part — well, there would be snickers and whispers enough at Ohatchee High School tomorrow without sending out an alarm Sunday night.

So Trout fretted and kept his own counsel and finally drifted off into troubled sleep in the small hours of the morning. When he awoke, the house was still empty and quiet. Joe Pike, wherever he had gone, was still there.

As Trout lay in bed wondering what the hell to do, he could feel something else besides Joe Pike Moseley nibbling at the back of his brain. Then he remembered: it was his birthday. Sixteen years old. This was supposed to be something really special, wasn't it? But there was nobody here singing and prancing around, the way Joe Pike loved to do on birthdays and Christmas and Confederate Memorial Day and any other excuse he could find to be celebratory. For such a gentle man, he loved nothing better than a good celebration.

It occurred to Trout that maybe a lot of Joe Pike's celebrations had been an attempt to fill up Irene's silences. A kind of pitiful denial that never really worked. Since they had taken Irene away, Joe Pike had simply stopped trying. A final admission of defeat. And now, on what should have been the most celebratory occasion of Trout's young life, Joe Pike had gone away.

Trout mulled it over for a while longer, feeling a little brain-fevered. Then finally he got up and padded barefoot to the kitchen, where the clock on the stove read 8:30. Late for school. Nobody here to write him an excuse. What to do? He decided, for the time being, on inertia. He poured himself a glass of orange juice, sat down at the kitchen table, drank it slowly, and listened to the silence. In truth, he decided after a bit, the empty quiet was something of a relief after all that had happened. You could only put up with so much ridiculousness. Considering that, he felt better.

Then he thought, *I am alone in the house and I can do anything I want to do, as long as it's not permanent damage.* So he got up, took off his pajamas, dropped them in the middle of the floor, and stood there feeling the silence on his bare skin. He wandered buck naked through every room in the parsonage, ending up in the living room, where he checked to make sure the front door was locked; then he sat down in Joe Pike's favorite chair and finished the orange juice, celebrating the utter novelty of it.

Even when his mother had been here, mute and withdrawn, it hadn't been like this. A Methodist parsonage was a public accommodation. Church people would drop by at all hours of the day or night and march right in without knocking, as if they owned the place. Which, in fact, they did. A preacher might fill up the drawers and closets with his clothes and tack doodads to the wall, but he didn't own the place. The congregation considered the parsonage not so much the preacher's residence as an extension of the church itself. So there was always a lot of noise, coming and going, and you didn't wander around in your pajamas, much less buck naked. Over the years Irene had shrunk from that. Her own silence seemed in part a protest against invasion, the only way she could get any peace and quiet.

Now, as Trout sat doing what he darned well pleased, he considered that this, too, was a form of protest over being at the mercy of other people's silences and preoccupations. But enough of protest. Empty silence or not, it was his sixteenth birthday. Nobody could take that away from him. Even if he got run over by a truck at midmorning, the obituary would still read, "Troutman Joseph Moseley, 16 . . ." It was a marvelous thing, like having Christmas and the Fourth of July and Easter and Confederate Memorial Day all rolled into one. And even more marvelous was the fact that he was sixteen on a Monday, the only day of the week the state driver's license examiner would be in

Ohatchee. Trout Moseley didn't need anybody singing and prancing to get a driver's license.

He drove Joe Pike's car downtown himself and parked it across the street from the courthouse. He was waiting, first in line, when the examiner arrived at ten.

"Ain't you supposed to be in school, son?" the examiner asked.

"My daddy said it would be all right to skip this morning," Trout lied without blinking. "I've got band practice after school this afternoon, so I couldn't come then." *Band practice?* He admired his own inventiveness. The closest he got to music was church on Sunday and the Atlanta oldies station on the radio. But at five-ten, one hundred thirty pounds, he looked more like a band member than an athlete.

He produced his birth certificate and took the written examination. Trout had been studying for more than a year, had every word of the manual committed to memory. He sat quietly while the examiner checked his answers, and then they walked across the street to the car for his road test.

"How'd this car get here?" the examiner asked as they climbed in, Trout behind the wheel, the examiner holding a clipboard in his lap with a stub of pencil stuck under the metal clip.

"My daddy brought me and then walked home."

"Who's your daddy?"

"Reverend Moseley."

Eyebrows up. "Joe Pike Moseley?"

"Yes sir." Had the examiner heard about Joe Pike's Sunday escapade? Apparently not.

Wide grin. "I used to play football against Joe Pike. Lord, he was a grain-fed young'un. And rough as a cob." The examiner laughed, showing stained, uneven teeth. "Him and a long tall drink of water named Wardell Dubarry. Wardell would hit you low and then Joe Pike would get up a head of steam and come in high. They near about ruined our quarterback one year. You had to watch Joe Pike, or he'd take your head off with an elbow."

"Well, he's still grain fed," Trout said. He put his key in the ignition, started the car.

"Played for Bear Bryant."

"Yes sir. Texas A&M."

"Folks never could figure why Joe Pike went all that way to play football. He could've got a scholarship at Georgia. Or Georgia Tech." The examiner shook his head. "And then made a preacher to boot. You just never know about folks."

"No sir. I guess not."

"He doing okay?"

"Yes sir," Trout said. "He's just fine."

"Well, you tell him Will Dobbins from Thomson asked about him."

"Yes sir. I'll do that."

The examiner put his hand on the door handle. "Hell, turn the car off, son. I imagine you know how to drive just fine. You made a hundred on the written test. No sense in us wasting gas. Just make the Arabs richer. Come on in and I'll write you out a temporary license."

Trout drove out the highway a good way toward Valdosta with all the windows rolled down, filling the car with warming April and the smell of fresh-turned earth and blossom, feeling the novelty of being alone in the car, sixteen years old, legally licensed. It was heady stuff. Someday, he thought, he might drive the car buck naked. That would be about as ridiculous as you could get. He thought fleetingly of going on to Florida. Decided against it. Thought about going to school. Decided against that, too. And then he thought suddenly of Joe Pike and the motorcycle and his spirits sank. He turned around and headed home.

It was nearly noon when he got back to the parsonage. The phone was ringing, jarring the emptiness.

"Hello."

"Trout, it's me."

"Where are you?"

"Hattiesburg, Mississippi."

"What are you doing in Hattiesburg?"

"It's on the way to Junction."

"Junction what?"

"Texas. Listen, there's some chicken pot pies in the freezer."

Trout sat down at the kitchen table and stared at the refrigerator. Over the telephone line, he could hear the faint roar of traffic, the bleat of a semi's air horn.

"Trout?"

"Yes sir."

"You can fix 'em in the regular oven or the microwave. Directions on the package. Poke some holes in the top with a fork."

"Are you all right?"

"Yea, verily," Joe Pike said. "A little minor problem with the wiring, that's all. I got it fixed." There was a long silence from Joe Pike, broken by the dinging of a bell on a gas pump, a woman fussing at a child. Then he said, "I need you to hang in there with me, Trout. Something I've gotta do . . ." His voice trailed off. "Just hang in there, okay?"

"Okay."

"Love you, son."

"Love you, too."

Then there was a click on the other end of the line, and Trout was left with the silence and, after a moment, a dial tone. He hung up the phone, heard the rattling of the front door. He peered down the hallway and saw Imogene Belton through the door glass. She had a key and she was coming right on in.

Trout thought, *He didn't say anything about my birthday.* And then he thought, *But I didn't ask him when he was coming back, either.*

The Bishop came on Friday, after Trout had spent the week at the Beltons' house, clucked over by Imogene until he was sick to death of it.

"I feel like a freak," he told Parks.

"Well, what do you expect?" Parks answered.

What he did not expect was the Bishop. But he was waiting in the Beltons' living room when Trout and Parks got home from school. He was a trim, gray-haired man, about sixty, and he wore a black suit and clerical collar. He had good, strong gray eyes and a nice smile and a firm handshake. But Trout thought of what he had heard Joe Pike say one time: "When the Bishop shows up all of a sudden, it's most likely either death or embezzlement."

The Bishop politely but firmly shooed Imogene and Parks out of the living room, sat down on the sofa next to Trout and leaned forward, his elbows on his knees. Then he said, "Trout, your father's had a breakdown."

Trout shrugged. "It's an old motorcycle. He said he was having a problem with the wiring."

"You've talked to him?"

"Monday. He called from Hattiesburg."

"Did he sound all right?"

"Yes sir. I reckon so."

"Well," the Bishop said, "it's not just the motorcycle."

Trout sucked in his breath. "Is he okay?"

"Resting. A few days in the hospital . . ."

Trout stood, his schoolbooks clattering to the floor. "Where is he?"

The Bishop pulled him gently back to the sofa. "He's all right, Trout. I talked to him myself this morning. Joe Pike has . . ." — he fanned the air with his hands a bit, searching for words — ". . . he's been under a lot of pressure, and I think something just got out of kilter."

They sat there for a moment, Trout imagining Joe Pike huge and pale in a hospital bed . . . tubes and breathing apparatus . . . Trout felt sick. Orphaned at sixteen. Both parents gone batty.

Finally the Bishop said, "Your father needs a little time and space, I think. I've got some friends near Lubbock, and he's going to stay with them for a few days. And then" — he pursed his lips, musing — "I'm sending your father home, Trout. To Moseley. Maybe with his family, familiar surroundings, he can get his legs back under him. Your uncle Cicero will go out to Texas and fetch him and take him directly there. He and the minister at Moseley will simply swap pulpits. I think this is best for everybody concerned."

Trout thought about the Easter congregation at Ohatchee Methodist, staring slack-jawed as big solid Joe Pike Moseley, the most substantial of men, unraveled before their eyes. And then the curious stares of everybody at school, the hovering Imogene Belton, the half-whispers. He thought, with a rush of despair, *It won't do to stay here.*

The Bishop put his hand on Trout's knee. "I know this isn't easy for you, Trout. Moving, right here at the end of the school year."

Not just that. Unfair. Not just moving, but the whole business. Why should he, at sixteen, have to be the sane one in the family? At sixteen, you were supposed to be flaky, irresponsible, hormone-driven. Unfair. But there it was.

"No," Trout said. "It's okay. We'll manage."

The Bishop sat there for a moment, then rose from the sofa, smoothing the creased front of his black trousers. "Of course, there's the other thing, too. Moseley's just two hours from Atlanta."

Atlanta. The Institute. Irene. That's what the Bishop was getting at, of course, but he wouldn't come right out and say it. Nobody, including the Bishop, wanted to talk about Irene, not directly. When you got anywhere near the subject, folks started acting like boxers, bobbing and weaving and staying out of reach of a good left hook. Joe Pike had bobbed and weaved as long as he could, and then he lit out for Texas. Well, all right. Trout would pack up bag and baggage and move, unfair as it might be. But before long, somebody was going to have to sit still and talk to him about his mother.

TWO

HOME. MOSELEY, GEORGIA. Trout supposed it was as much home as anyplace else. He had never lived there, but compared with a series of four-year stays in various parsonages, Moseley was the one geographic constant in his life. It was a place of holiday visits, a day or two at a time in the big house across the street from the Methodist church. Never on the holiday itself, because a preacher had to be in his own pulpit for Easter or Christmas, but usually in the days after, when there was still the lingering smell of a roasting turkey or a spray of Easter lilies on a front hall table. Trout was never there for a long enough time to get much sense of the town. But you didn't have to be there for long to know that to be a Moseley in Moseley was something special. Trout remembered what Joe Pike had said in a moment of particular earthiness: "When a Moseley farts, everybody smells it."

It began with Trout's great-grandfather, Broadus Moseley. And it began with great promise in 1885 when Broadus moved with his wife and family from the North Carolina piedmont to what was then nothing but a quiet rural Georgia crossroads with a scattering of ramshackle houses. There had been some sort of unpleasantness in North Carolina, a family falling-out, the details of which remained murky. The family settled some money upon Broadus, but that was not its most important gift. Rather, it was an inbred business acumen and a knowledge of the burgeoning cotton mill industry.

There were three things to recommend the site he picked for his venture: it lay along the road from Augusta to Atlanta; the tracks of the Georgia Line were nearby; and the farm economy thereabouts was flat busted. It was exactly the combination Broadus was looking for: decent transportation, cheap land, hungry people. First he bought a great deal of land, far more than he needed for a mill. Then he built a railroad spur from the Georgia Line and erected a nondescript two-story brick building, powered it with coal-fired steam, and equipped it with looms, the latest European design. And the people came, ragged from the hardscrabble farms — reluctant to give up their independence, but desperate to survive.

Broadus intended it to be more than a mill town. He used the mill as a magnet to draw commerce. And since he owned the land, he shaped the growing town as he wished — parceling out tracts for business ventures and homes, laying out the streets to suit him. He named the town Moseley and the main street Broadus Street. ("Broad Street?" visitors would ask. "No, Broadus," the natives would answer, enjoying the quirk.) When it had progressed to a village of several hundred souls, he saw to its incorporation. And as its patriarch and principal wage payer, he saw to its politics. Broadus was a staunch Democrat who nevertheless admired certain Republican principles — chiefly, that men with sense enough to have money ought to call the shots.

By the time Moseley's main thoroughfare had become U.S. Highway 278, paved all the way from Atlanta to Augusta, the town was a thriving commercial center with a variety of retail businesses, a bank, schools, a newspaper, and a water and sewer system. The agricultural economy enjoyed something of a revival, and the town served as its hub and meeting place, its chief source of feed, seed, fertilizer, and loans. And Moseley Cotton Mill was the anchor, supplying steady employment and an economic base for the community. Broadus was careful not to repeat the mistake of so many in the southern textile business: getting too big in boom times and then having to scramble to stay afloat in bad. He kept the business prudently in check and kept plenty of reserves in the bank. He boasted of never having laid off a worker for economic reasons. Moseley Mill employees would never make a great deal of money, but as long as they behaved themselves, they wouldn't find themselves out on the street, either.

By the end of World War II, about a thousand people lived in Moseley in a residential area that radiated north and south along Broadus Street.

At the Augusta end of town was the mill building, and beyond it, a spiderweb of unpaved streets and small white frame houses — owned, tended, and ruled by Moseley Cotton Mill. Broadus kept the mill and mill village outside the city limits. It was his domain.

At the Atlanta end of town, separated from the mill end by the business district, the Moseleys and others of a certain stature lived. There were sidewalks here, canopied by oak trees that grew to great girth over the years. The houses were gracious if not particularly imposing, with wide banistered porches and a good deal of ornamental ironwork. Broadus Moseley's house was the only one with columns, but they were modest columns, one story high, supporting the porch that wrapped around the front and both sides of the house. Broadus believed in status but not ostentation.

As a buffer between the business district and his neighborhood, Broadus laid out and landscaped a small park — an acre of Saint Augustine grass and oak trees with a band shell in the middle.

There might be two ends to Broadus Street, but both were simply part of U.S. 278. In its best days, the mill end and the money end of town shared a certain vibrancy — the commonality of diesel fumes and the steady rumble of traffic that eased into town, stopped fitfully at the one traffic light at the center of the business district, and then ambled on. The Koffee Kup Kafe became a favorite lunchtime stopping place for Atlanta-to-Augusta travelers. *Southern Living* magazine lauded its sweet potato pie. And no right-thinking politician seeking statewide office would pass up the opportunity for a rally at the band shell in Broadus Moseley Park. It was unstated, but understood, that only Democrats were welcome. A Republican seeking the governorship ventured by in the late sixties, but only five people and a stray dog came to hear him, and three of the people were out-of-towners who wandered over after lunch at the Koffee Kup.

That was Moseley, Georgia, in its heyday. By the time Trout Moseley came to call it home, it had changed considerably. Now, most folks knew Moseley as a name on a big green sign on Interstate 20, which paralleled U.S. 278 a couple of miles from the center of town. Now, you could stand on the sidewalk in the middle of the business district at midafternoon and not see a car move for five minutes.

On one side of the street were City Hall and the next-door police station along with a few businesses that clung hopefully to life on the strength of local trade — a small grocery, a women's and men's ready-to-wear, the post office, the bank, and a former dry cleaners now occupied by the County Welfare Department.

The other side of the street was less fortunate. It boasted a hardware operated by Trout's uncle Cicero, who was also the police chief, and next door to Cicero, a struggling feed-and-seed. It sold more lawn and garden fertilizer and bug spray than farm supplies, most of the farmers in the county having given up on row crops and planted pine trees in the wake of the latest agribusiness downturn. Next to the feed-and-seed was a large weed-grown vacant lot where a furniture and appliance store had burned to the ground not long after the Interstate opened. People had taken it as an omen. It gave the business district a gap-toothed appearance. Beyond the lot were the Koffee Kup Kafe and a row of vacant storefronts. One had been home to the newspaper until it had gone out of business shortly after the opening of the Interstate and the furniture store fire. As business dwindled, there were no longer enough advertisers to support the weekly. And people who lived beyond the city limits didn't give a hoot about what happened in Moseley.

One thing that had not changed about Moseley was its reputation as a church town. There were six churches in Moseley proper, not counting the AME Zion for the black folks, which was two miles outside the city limits toward Augusta.

In the general vicinity of the mill were a Church of God, a Free-Will Baptist, and a Pentecostal Holiness. In his day, Broadus had referred to them as "sect" churches, full of shouting and carryings-on that kept his mill workers up all night during revival week. But he co-opted them all by subsidizing their physical facilities and their preachers' salaries, in return for which the preachers espoused thrift, hard work, loyalty to the Moseleys, and a disdain for liquor and unions.

Adjacent the business district at the Augusta end of town was a sturdy brick Baptist with a stubby white steeple, and on a back street a block away, a modest Presbyterian.

But the other end of town was reserved for Broadus Moseley's church. Moseley Memorial Methodist was directly across the street from Broadus's home, where he could keep an eye on it. Broadus built it as the mill and town grew and prospered. It was constructed of dark red brick with a cedar shake roof. It had twelve stained-glass windows — four on each side and two at the front and back — each depicting one of the Twelve Disciples. The parsonage was next door to the church so that Broadus could keep an eye on it and its occupants, too.

In the town's most prosperous days, it was a thriving church with a reputation and influence among Georgia Methodists far beyond its size. Young preachers who were marked by the Bishop for great things often pulled a tour of duty in Moseley on their way up the ladder of the church hierarchy. Back in the fifties there had been some talk about expanding the sanctuary, tearing down the parsonage next door and extending a wing in that direction. But the Moseleys vetoed that. Broadus Moseley was long in the grave by then and his son Leland, Joe Pike's father, was running Moseley Cotton Mill. Yes, Leland saw the need for more space. But it was the church Broadus Moseley had built, and his shadow still cast long across the community and the congregation. He had never taken kindly to folks' questioning his judgment. And he would not now, Leland said, take kindly to folks' meddling with his church and his stained-glass windows. Instead, they added an early-morning service, which became quite popular and was at the time a novelty among Georgia Methodists. That lasted until the early seventies, when I-20 took the starch out of the town. Not long thereafter, Moseley Memorial Methodist retreated to a single eleven o'clock service. It was all that was necessary.

Trout would learn all this over time. At the beginning there was only Aunt Alma, Joe Pike's older sister. She was enough.

Alma took care of everything. She sent a Moseley Cotton Mill truck and two men to the Ohatchee parsonage on a Friday morning, a week after the Bishop had broken the news to the congregation about Joe Pike's transfer. By noon the men had packed up and loaded everything Joe Pike's family owned. Imogene Belton had seen to the packing. There wasn't a great deal — hanging clothes on a bar the men had rigged across the back of the truck; a stack of boxes, including several from Joe Pike's study at the church; a few odds and ends, like Trout's bicycle and his mother's sewing machine and his father's old mahogany bookcase. Most of the furniture and furnishings in the parsonage belonged to the congregation, right down to the pots and pans, mostly bits and pieces donated over the years by its members as they updated their own homes.

The chairman of the Official Board of the Ohatchee Methodist Church came by at midmorning and stayed while the men from Moseley Mill packed and loaded. He tried to appear helpful, but Trout knew he was there to make sure the Joe Pike Moseley family didn't make off with anything they weren't supposed to. Trout decided not to take offense. After all, it was an altogether strange business. An air of doom hung over the parsonage and everything in it.

The last thing was the statue. Trout wrapped it in an old blanket and put it in the front seat of the car. Then he went back to the house and made one last check before the chairman of the Official Board locked up.

"Trout, I'm sorry things turned out the way they did," the chairman said, pocketing the key and offering Trout his hand. "But the Lord works in strange and mysterious ways, His wonders to behold."

Somewhere in the back of his mind, Trout could still hear the echo of the motorcycle pulling away from Ohatchee Methodist on Easter Sunday morning. Now, *that* was a wonder to behold. But it wouldn't do to say so to the chairman of the Official Board. So Trout said, "Yes sir."

"Your daddy's a fine man. He just needs a change of scene."

"That's what the Bishop said."

"You take care of him now, you hear. And give him my best."

"I'll do that."

Trout followed the truck from Ohatchee three hours north to Moseley, driving Joe Pike's green Dodge. It was midafternoon when they arrived. The May sun was still strong above the oak trees along Moseley's main street as Trout eased the car up to the curb between the church and the adjacent parsonage. He parked next to the Georgia State Historical Society marker dedicated to his great-grandfather: BROADUS MOSELEY. CIVIC VISIONARY AND TEXTILE PIONEER. 1861–1934.

There were several vehicles parked at the curb and in the parsonage driveway. A group of workmen clustered about an opening in the brickwork on one side of the house, peering into the dark underbelly. Another man was clipping the shrubbery in front. And two men

were carrying a floral print sofa from a van with big letters on the side
that read, BUCKLEY FURNITURE COMPANY, AUGUSTA, GA. Aunt
Alma was standing on the porch directing traffic.

Alma was in her midfifties, tall and angular. She was rather attractive in a sharp-featured way, and Trout thought she probably had been
something of a beauty as a girl. But now there was a sort of pinched
severity about Alma. Her graying hair was close-cropped, almost boy-
ish. She wore a plain gray dress with a lot of pleats at the waist, a little
long at the hem, and glasses with plain gold rims. Trout thought she
looked like someone who had stepped out of one of the old issues of
Life magazine that Joe Pike kept in his church study.

She met Trout halfway down the sidewalk and gave him a hug.
"Trout! Welcome home!" She smelled of flowers, something not quite
perfume. Trout's mother, Irene, had never worn scents, or any makeup
for that matter, and it always surprised him a bit when a woman had
the smell of flowers about her.

"Hello, Aunt Alma. You smell good."

"Lilac water," she said. She released him, held him at arm's length,
looked him up and down. "You look more like your grandfather
Leland every day. He was a bit on the thin side, but he had nice blue
eyes and a good chin. I think a good chin is important on a man. Your
grandfather Leland looked like he knew what he was doing. And he
could add columns of numbers in his head. You couldn't fool Leland
Moseley when it came to numbers."

"I'm not much good at math," Trout said.

Alma shook her head and looked at him down the length of her
nose. "You're not *all* Moseley. But I suppose you can't help that, can
you?"

Trout shrugged. "No ma'am. I guess not."

"Well, come on in and let me show you what I've done."

The two men carrying the floral print sofa were in the living room,
still holding it. "Over there," Alma ordered, and they set it against a
side wall. Trout's gaze swept the room and he felt his eyes go wide.
Everything was brand-spanking-new, with the rich smell of lacquers
and pristine fabrics — sofa, two occasional chairs, love seat, coffee
table (with copies of the *Methodist Christian Advocate* and *Southern
Living* on top), fern stand (with artificial fern), knickknack shelf (with
knickknacks, an assortment of porcelain stuff), brass fireplace set,
Persian rug.

"I simply cleaned it out," Alma said with a sweep of her arm. "Took everything to the mill and stacked it outside the gate and told 'em to take what they wanted. It was all gone in thirty minutes, down to the wastebaskets. Then I went to Augusta and went shopping."

Trout looked at their image in the big mirror above the mantel and felt a little unclean, as if he had gone straight from mowing the grass to the Lord's Supper. He imagined sitting buck naked on the big floral print sofa. No. You would take great pains not to even break wind in a room like this. Alma was looking at him. She expected him to say something. "Gee," he said.

"That's just for starters," Alma said, and marched off. Trout followed her down a long hallway past two bedrooms, through the dining room, into the big kitchen, and finally to a third bedroom at the back of the house. Alma gave him a detailed inventory as they went along, ticking off items in her strong, clear voice. She seemed to have committed the bill of lading to memory. Everything was new, right down to the set of Corningware dishes in the kitchen cabinets and the oak seats on the commodes.

Trout's room had twin beds, a desk with a brass study lamp, a low bookcase, a five-drawer dresser — all in maple. The window curtains and bedspreads were a coordinated plaid — deep reds and dark blues, the same colors as the oval braided rug. Above the desk was a large framed picture of Jesus' hands, clasped in prayer. Trout went to the window and looked out at Moseley Memorial Methodist Church next door. This side of the building was shaded by pecan trees, and it appeared that every light in the sanctuary was on. He could see the stained-glass windows clearly, four of them on this side, each one a Disciple, each likeness with a name at the bottom. Simon the Cannanaean, Bartholomew, Judas Iscariot, James the son of Zebedee. Sort of the third-string disciples, Trout thought. He wondered how the artist knew what they looked like.

Trout turned back to Aunt Alma. She stood in the doorway, arms crossed. Watching him. Waiting. "It's real nice," he said. "We never had a place this nice." Then he heard some bumping about under the house.

"Central air," Alma said. "They're finishing up. The place had window units, but I took them all out. I put in a new heat pump, new ductwork. Everything." Trout noticed that she kept saying "I." Not "we" or "the church." She gave another sweep of her arm. She also seemed inclined toward sweeping gestures. "There's nothing," Alma said with a firm smile, "like starting over."

Trout thought about his father. Joe Pike liked to put his feet up on the furniture or throw one leg over the arm of a living room chair. He'd think twice about doing that here. But then, there was a lot Joe Pike Moseley would have to think twice about now. He was, indeed, starting over.

"When is Daddy gonna be here?" Trout asked.

Alma didn't say anything for a moment. Then she pursed her lips as if she were drawing on a straw. "When have you talked to him?"

"Last week."

"How did he sound?"

"Tired."

"Well," Alma said, "he hasn't talked to me. I've just had to handle everything on my own. But I *understand* that Joe Pike will be here tomorrow."

Alma turned around and walked out of the room, leaving Trout standing there staring at her back. He found her a few minutes later on the front porch, directing the men from the Moseley Mill truck who were carrying boxes up the front steps. "Put the clothes in the closets and take all the boxes to the kitchen. We'll unpack them there. Don't set anything down on the new furniture."

"Aunt Alma," Trout said.

She turned to him. "Yes?"

"I can unpack my things, but I think maybe the rest oughta wait till Daddy gets here. He's kind of peculiar about moving."

"Peculiar."

"Yes ma'am."

She nodded. "Yes. I suppose he is. Under the circumstances, who wouldn't be?"

Trout gave her an odd look, but he didn't say anything. Aunt Alma, as Joe Pike would have said, had a burr under her saddle. But Trout figured that until Joe Pike got here, it was best to keep his eyes and ears open and his mouth shut. Or as Joe Pike would have said: head up, fanny down. An old piece of Bear Bryant wisdom. Joe Pike was full of Bear Bryant wisdom. It had the ring of Scripture to it.

While the men emptied the truck under Alma's watchful eye, Trout wandered about the grounds taking stock. There was a single expanse of front lawn that took in both parsonage and church. The parsonage had the same dark red brick and cedar shake roof as the church, making them all of a piece. But the parsonage, being smaller, had room for a nice backyard, separated from the rear of the church by a low hedge. There was a brick barbecue pit, a swing hanging by chains from a big limb of a spreading pecan tree, a birdbath, a small frame garage that doubled as a storage shed, and a plot of broken ground where the previous occupant had been preparing a garden. Joe Pike would like that. He liked to dig, plant things, fuss over them, eat the fruits of his own labor.

For as long as Trout could remember, there had been a garden somewhere on the grounds of whatever parsonage they lived in. When Trout was a small child, Joe Pike had always set aside a corner of the plot where he could dig about, sifting the cool, damp earth through his fingers, while Joe Pike hoed and watered nearby. One year Joe Pike gave him a single tomato plant. It was his to care for. He cared for it too much, poking and prodding and watering and digging about the roots. It died. Joe Pike said the tomato plant was like a young'un. You had to know when to leave it alone.

There had been no garden at the Ohatchee parsonage this year. Joe Pike had been too busy with the motorcycle. But there was still time to plant, and here was the broken ground, waiting for him. If Joe Pike planted a garden, it would be a good sign.

Trout sat down in the swing and pondered that awhile. He was still there when Alma came around the corner of the house and sat down next to him.

"Do you need anything for the night?" she asked. "Toothbrush, pajamas?" Trout gave her a blank look. "You'll have to stay across the street with your Uncle Cicero and me."

"I'll be all right over here," Trout said. "I'm used to . . ." He broke off. He didn't want to say too much. Head up, fanny down.

"Yes," Alma said. "I know all about that."

"Well," Trout said agreeably, "I'll stay with you and Uncle Cicero." He stood up. "I'll just get some stuff . . ."

"Fine," Alma said. "Then I want to show you something."

Trout and Alma drove to the mill in her marvelous automobile, a 1934 Packard that Leland Moseley had bought when he took over management of Moseley Mill after Broadus's death. It was an important car — broad-shouldered and powerful, with gleaming chrome, huge whitewall tires, and a black finish so highly polished that it was like looking into a deep well. For as long as Trout could remember, it had hunkered under the porte cochere at the white-columned house across the street from the church, off-limits to children. As small boys, Trout and his cousin, Eugene, Alma's son, would stand well back and admire the car and talk about what it would be like to get it out on the highway at a hundred and twenty miles an hour. But they never touched it. Trout wouldn't have dared. He was by then an obedient child. Eugene would, but Aunt Alma had put some sort of terror into him about the car. Now, it was understood in the family that since Alma ran the mill, it was Alma's car. She drove it once a week, usually out toward Atlanta a few miles to exercise the engine, rarely to the mill. But on this May evening she said to Trout, "We'll take the Packard." It was the first time Trout had ever been inside the car. It had a cavernous interior and smelled of age and old leather. Like going for a ride in someone's parlor.

Moseley Cotton Mill was still in the two-story red-brick building that Broadus Moseley had built at the other end of town, surrounded now by a high chain-link fence with a padlocked gate. Alma handed Trout a key, and he unlocked the gate and swung it wide while Alma eased the car into the deserted lot and parked it next to the building. "Best lock it back," she called as she climbed out, and Trout closed the gate and joined her.

They went first through a small office area, an open space separated into cubicles by opaque glass partitions, each with a desk and file cabinets. Then down a hallway past a closed door with a brass plaque on it that read: ALMA MOSELEY, PRESIDENT. Finally, through another door and into the mill itself.

It was a long, narrow, high-ceilinged cave, crowded with row upon row of machines stretching back through shafts of late-afternoon light that danced with dust motes filtering through tall dingy windows. The machines were squat gray hulks, each with several small white cones on top, identical except for the bold black numbers stenciled on the side. Trout thought suddenly of war, the staging area for some giant battle. He stood there staring for a long moment, trying to imagine the mill in operation, the machines rumbling and clattering, people scurrying about. But there was only a hollow quietness, a dappled blend of light and shadow. Trout took a step toward the nearest machine, bent to peer at the white cones, saw that they were spools of thread.

"Cotton," Aunt Alma said quietly at his back, startling him. Trout turned with a jerk.

"One day, this will be yours," she said.

"Mine?" Their voices sounded hollow and distant in the great expanse of the room.

"Yours and Eugene's. You're the last of the Moseleys. And I don't believe there will be any more, not of your generation."

"What would I do with it?"

"Make cotton. That's what Moseleys do. You know all about that."

"No ma'am." And he didn't. Joe Pike didn't talk much about the family.

Alma's eyes swept the great room slowly. "Well, you will. Your great-grandfather came down from Carolina and built this mill and this town from scratch. For nearly a hundred years, this place has made the finest cotton yarn in the South." Her voice was soft, reverent. It had the ring of Scripture about it.

"The Moseley men . . ." she paused and gave a tiny impatient jerk of her head. "Well, most of the Moseley men . . ." Then she looked straight at Trout and fixed him with narrowed eyes. "We're going to get things back on track, Trout. At long last. We're going to start all over. Do you know what I mean?"

"Not exactly," he said.

"Well, you will." She started to go, then turned back to him suddenly. "There are three things I want you to remember, Trout. One, don't ever forget who you are. Two, be careful of these wild-as-a-buck young'uns out here in the mill village. And three, stay away from your Great Uncle Phinizy."

Trout woke abruptly in the night. The statue. It was still in the front seat of Joe Pike's green Dodge, parked now in the parsonage driveway. He sat up quickly and remembered that he was in the big four-poster bed in what had been Eugene's room on the second floor of Aunt Alma and Uncle Cicero's house. When they were growing up, Eugene was the only youngster Trout knew with a four-poster. Eugene was a good bit older and lived now in Atlanta. But the four-poster stayed behind. You didn't take things out of Broadus Moseley's house.

Trout swung his legs over the side of the bed, found the floor, flicked on a bedside lamp. He dressed quietly, then turned out the light, opened the door and padded barefoot down the carpeted stairs and out the front door, carrying his shoes.

He sat down on the top step and put on his shoes, then sat there for a moment, elbows on knees. Here, in late May, the night still had a bit of an edge to it, a breeze making the leaves dance, the outlines of objects still finely drawn in the light of the streetlamps — empty street, church and parsonage across the way. Another month and the night would blur with heat and haze, the concrete of the sidewalks warm to the touch long after midnight, the air still and close. In late May you could still feel a sense of expectancy. By late June whatever you were expecting had either come or it hadn't. A month. School would be out, Joe Pike would be settled into whatever he wanted to make of his ministry. *I'll give it a month,* Trout thought. And then . . . And then what? Did a sixteen-year-old near-orphaned preacher's boy have a lot of options? Hah. Anyway, he would give it a month.

He stood and started down the steps, and then the voice from the shadows of the porch grabbed him by the scruff of his neck.

"Where you going?"

"Shit!" He turned with a frightened jerk, the hairs on the back of his neck standing straight up.

"Shit?" the voice asked. "That's a mighty big word for a little old preacher's boy."

Trout stared into the shadows, and as his eyes adjusted, he made out the form slouched in one of the porch rockers, the glowing end of a cigarette. Then the tinkle of ice in a glass and the faint, sweet smell of whiskey. He thought for a moment it might be Uncle Cicero. But Cicero didn't smoke or drink. Out of respect for Aunt Alma, it was said. And besides, Cicero was in Texas, or at least on his way back. "Who are you?"

A low, rich laugh, like a diesel engine rumbling to life. Suddenly, Trout knew exactly who it was. Without ever having cast eyes on the man. And he heard some deliciously . . . what? . . . *wicked* quality in the voice that explained why Aunt Alma had said stay away from . . .

"Great Uncle Phinizy."

"You were expecting Basil Rathbone?"

Trout moved closer. "What are you doing here?"

"Why, I live here."

"I thought you lived in Baltimore."

"I *resided* for some time in Baltimore. There's a difference."

Trout felt his heart rise in his throat, his pulse quicken. Phinizy. The other son. Over the years, Trout had heard bits and pieces from Joe Pike. About the time of Broadus Moseley's death, there had been a falling-out of some kind. Leland took over the mill; Phinizy left. As far as Trout knew, he never came back. Joe Pike was the only one he kept in touch with. When Joe Pike spoke of Phinizy, it was usually with a laugh and a shake of his head. Something akin to awe there, but entirely different from the way it was with Bear Bryant.

Phinizy took a long drag on the cigarette, the end of it glowing bright orange, then flipped the butt into the bushes at the edge of the porch and exhaled a long stream of smoke. "I'm out back. Upstairs over the garage. Drop in when the notion strikes you."

Trout started to speak, but thought better of it.

"Did Alma warn you about me?" Phinizy asked. Trout nodded. "I would have been surprised if she hadn't." He took a long pull from his glass and smacked his lips appreciatively. "I'm rather infamous, I think. Black sheep. Embarrassment to the family, or at least Alma's notion of the family. But I rather like being infamous. If you're a nobody, you're just a nobody. If you're famous, they erect a statue of you and pigeons crap on your head. But if you're infamous, you're somebody without having to put up with pigeon crap."

Trout had a notion why Joe Pike Moseley had stayed in touch with Great Uncle Phinizy all these years. There was, in his raspy whiskey-and-smoke voice, a hint of some kind of hidden knowledge that he might, if he liked you, share. And without a lot of bullshit. Trout had the strange but inescapable feeling that he, too, had known Phinizy for a long time. Or maybe just wished he had.

"Alma's a pickle," Phinizy said. "She can't help it. Too much like her father."

Before he could stop himself, Trout blurted, "And who's my daddy like?"

The raspy laugh rumbled out of Phinizy's throat again. "I don't think he's figured that out yet. We'll see. Now go on about your business, whatever it is at three o'clock in the morning."

"And what's your business at three o'clock in the morning?" Trout asked.

"Waiting."

"For what?"

"To see what'll happen."

Trout stared for another moment, then shrugged, turned, and headed down the steps. He heard the click of the lighter and turned back for an instant to see the gnarled face in the brief flicker of flame, a grimace as Phinizy sucked air around the edges of the cigarette.

The statue was about eighteen inches high, heavy plaster, a boy and girl in peasant garb. They stood close together, the boy's mouth next to the girl's ear. It had a name: *The Secret.* Trout didn't know its origin, but it had been with them for as long as he could remember, as familiar as underwear. It was chipped in a couple of places and the plaster had broken on one of the fingers of the boy's hand, revealing a piece of wire underneath. That had been Trout's doing when he was perhaps three or four. In the parsonage where they lived then, the statue had resided on a tall fern stand, and Trout had reached for it one day and pulled it over. It barely missed his head, landing with a thud on the rug. He screamed with fright and Irene rushed in, grabbed him up, examined him frantically for damage. "What were you doing?" she cried. "You could have been killed!" And Trout blubbered, "I wanted to hear the secret." After that, the statue was always kept out of Trout's reach. When the Moseleys made one of their periodic moves, Irene would wrap the statue in a blanket and lay it carefully on the seat of the car between her and Joe Pike. And when they arrived, she carried it straightaway into the house and found a good spot for it. That meant they had taken proper possession, as much as you could possess a parsonage.

The front door of the parsonage was unlocked, as Aunt Alma's own door had been. Nobody seemed to lock anything around here except for the mill. Trout turned on the living room light, unwrapped the statue, and stood in the middle of the room holding it, looking for the place Irene might have chosen if she were here. He briefly considered the mantel, but it was filled with bric-a-brac, some lacquered plates, a Chinese bowl, a clock — all new stuff. The old statue would look out of place. So Trout took it to his own room and set it on top of the chest of drawers. Not perfect, but it would do. He stood looking at the statue for a moment; then on impulse he leaned close and put his ear next to the plaster girl's. Nothing. He straightened quickly, looked around, felt his face flush. Headline: BOY HEARS SECRET OF LIFE FROM STATUE. VISITS POPE TUESDAY.

Trout looked at his wristwatch. Three-thirty. He was wide awake. Might as well get a few things done. He found the church unlocked, too, and toted several boxes full of Joe Pike's preacher stuff to the study. It was empty except for a mahogany desk, an electric typewriter on a stand, a coatrack on which Joe Pike could hang his robe, two walls of built-in bookcases. Trout left the boxes in the middle of the floor, unopened. When Joe Pike got here, he would want to arrange and rearrange things to suit himself, filling shelves with books, moving furniture about, hanging framed certificates and photos on the wall (including an eight-by-ten of himself in his Texas A&M football uniform, massive and poker-faced in a three-point stance), fussing with everything until there was a comfortable, rumpled feel about it. Joe Pike was very territorial about his office. Church members might barge right on through the front door of the parsonage anytime they pleased, but they (and for that matter, Joe Pike's own family) would never think about entering the pastor's study without knocking. And if Joe Pike didn't want company at the moment, he might boom out, "I've got the Lord in here right now. We're transacting business. Come back later."

So Trout left the boxes unopened, then went back to the parsonage and unpacked his own things, stowing away clothes and books and personal items. He put his tennis racquet on top of the dresser along with his trophy from the Valdosta Junior Invitational. And he took down the picture of the praying hands from over the desk and replaced it with his Jimmy Connors poster. He put the praying hands on a high shelf in the closet. *Go ye into your closet and close the door and pray to the Lord which is in secret . . .*

Finally, he wandered into the master bedroom. The men from Moseley Mill had hung Joe Pike's and Irene's clothes in the two closets and left a stack of boxes on the floor next to the bed. These, too, would wait for Joe Pike.

Trout sat on the bed and began to think about all that had turned his life upside down. Losing both parents to one disaster or another, feeling the hot flush of embarrassment over being an oddity at the very time in life when you wanted to fit in, being uprooted from school and friends, driving up through Georgia into a past he knew precious little about. Standing in the great empty mill building, hushed like church except for Alma's voice. *We're going to get things back on track, Trout. Start all over.* What did that mean? Trout didn't want to pick up where things had left off, when they had suddenly fallen off a cliff. He wanted his father back from Texas and his mother back from the Institute and the Atlanta oldies station playing on the radio in the kitchen and Joe Pike prancing about in some sort of celebration or another. It hadn't been all good back then, but it was better than now, better than empty stillness and yawning uncertainty. Better than all this strange newness, all these rules about who you could and couldn't talk to, all this mystic Moseley-ness. Better than having damn little you could count on. Better than this hollow feeling in the pit of his stomach that had been with him for a good while now.

He sat there for a long time, then looked up to see the bedroom windows beginning to gray with first light. He stared at the cardboard boxes. He wouldn't have opened them if he could. There might be things inside, things about Joe Pike and Irene, that he didn't really want to know. Having them back, damaged or not, would be enough.

THREE

THERE WAS A good-sized crowd gathered at the parsonage by the time Joe Pike got there at midafternoon on Saturday.

The ladies of the Parsonage Committee arrived first, bearing armloads of food and housewarming gifts. They made a big deal over Trout, and then they wandered through the parsonage, making a big deal over Alma's redecorating. Trout overheard one woman mutter, "The living room's a bit garish for a parsonage." And another replied, "She paid for it. She can be as garish as she wants."

The members of the Official Board of the church began trickling in, most of them men. The crowd swelled until there were thirty or so people, spilling out the front door of the house onto the porch and lawn, sipping punch in paper cups from a large bowl the ladies had set up on the dining room table.

They were, Trout came to realize, Joe Pike's distant past.

A man named Fleet Mathis was the longtime mayor and had been Joe Pike's scoutmaster before Joe Pike grew suddenly to great size and gave up the Boy Scouts for football.

"People been asking for years, when's the Bishop gonna send Joe Pike back home?" Fleet Mathis said.

"He'd have been here long ago, but Irene wouldn't stand for it," Aunt Alma said. She seemed unconcerned that Trout was right at her elbow when she said it. Aunt Alma seemed accustomed to saying exactly what she thought, whenever she thought it, and expecting everyone to agree with her.

Mostly, they did. But out of Alma's earshot, they appeared to say what they pleased. They regaled Trout with stories about his father's growing up. Garth Niblock was the barber who had given three-year-old Joe Pike his first haircut. He told how Joe Pike had screamed with indignation as his shoulder-length locks, his mother's pride, fell to the floor under Leland's watchful eye.

Miss Althea Trawick, now retired and shriveled, had been one of his elementary-school teachers in the years before Leland shipped Joe Pike off to Georgia Military Academy. Joe Pike didn't want to go, she told Trout, and later he rebelled and came home and caused a family uproar. Joe Pike, she said, seemed to keep the family in more or less constant uproar.

Charlie Babcock was the dentist who had filled Joe Pike's childhood cavities. Joe Pike had always had a sweet tooth, he said. He laughed and said he hoped Joe Pike would be a frequent customer at the new Dairy Queen, because Charlie sure needed some cavity business.

Tilda Huffstetler was the owner of the Koffee Kup Kafe who made Joe Pike's hand-decorated birthday cakes in her kitchen until he was a grown man. She told of shipping cakes by parcel post to Texas A&M when Joe Pike was off playing football, how he would always make a special phone call to thank her. This afternoon she had arrived with two of her famous sweet potato pies (famous, she said, because they had been featured in *Southern Living* magazine — "If it's in *Southern Living*, it's gospel") and insisted that Trout stop by any afternoon after school for a free slice.

Grace Vredemeyer was the church choir director, somewhat younger than most in the crowd and one of the few who wasn't a Moseley native. She had moved there with her husband twenty years earlier, only to lose him to cancer, and had stayed on. She had brought a copy of the weekly church bulletin for Joe Pike and showed Trout her column on church music entitled "Grace Notes." "I hope you can sing better than your daddy," she told Trout. "That man can't carry a tune in a bucket." To which Trout confessed that he couldn't either, but at least he was aware of the fact.

Judge Lecil Tandy was no longer a judge, but had been some years before and was still called "Judge" in the southern way. The name fit. He was tall and spare, with a lovely mane of soft white hair. He wore a three-piece seersucker suit, sagging a bit with age, and a watch chain from which his Phi Beta Kappa key dangled. Judge Tandy was the longtime Moseley family and Moseley Mill attorney and vice-chairman of the Official Board of the church. Aunt Alma was the chairman.

Trout guessed their average age at somewhere over sixty. They were sweet people, he thought, with soft, gentle rhythms of speech, in no particular hurry to say or do anything. They stood about on the porch and under the shade of the pecan trees on the lawn, drinking punch and trading bits of reminiscence and making Trout comfortable in their company. In their voices he could hear the echoes of Joe Pike's childhood, and he felt a tinge of wistfulness. To have grown up in a single place, to be able to say you were truly "from" somewhere . . . well, that might not be too bad. And he began to see how Joe Pike might find rest here for whatever troubled his soul. It would be, he thought, like drifting off to sleep under a soft, familiar blanket.

Just before three, a GMC pickup truck towing a U-Haul trailer pulled up at the curb in front of the parsonage. Uncle Cicero was at the wheel, Joe Pike riding shotgun. "Here he is!" somebody called out, and they all turned to look as Joe Pike threw open the door and hopped nimbly out of the truck and came hotfooting it across the parsonage lawn. "Good Lordy, looka here!" he called. The crowd surged out to meet him with Aunt Alma in the lead, and they gathered around him, hugging and shaking hands, all talking at once.

Trout hung back a bit, giving Joe Pike the once-over. His face was still ruddy from his motorcycle ride, but he looked fit and rested, big and solid and dependable, nothing like the man who had stood in the Ohatchee Methodist pulpit just weeks before, ashen-faced and sweating like a field hand.

Joe Pike was in his element now, never better than when he was in the middle of a crowd. Trout remembered how it was at Methodist Summer Camp years before: Joe Pike, one of the preacher-counselors, riding herd on a bunkhouse full of second-grade boys, Trout among them. Headed for the lake for an afternoon swim, Joe Pike draped with noisy, clambering kids, hanging from his shoulders, arms, legs. Trout, trotting along behind, watching. Joe Pike was the most popular guy at camp.

He was the most popular guy on the Methodist parsonage lawn this late-May afternoon, working this crowd like a master fisherman with a big bass on the line — reeling them in, drenching them with his smile, lifting them up.

"Lord, Miz Trawick, you ain't aged a day since I was in the second grade. I remember you in Vacation Bible School, saying, 'The Lord wants everybody to sit down and shut up.'"

"You never did," Miz Trawick shot back, hands on hips.

"No ma'am. I'm still on my feet, still talking." Big grin, sweeping them to him with his huge arms. "Mighty good to be back home . . . Mister Fleet, it's good to see ya . . . 'preciate y'all coming over . . . be over next week to get some of your sweet potato pie, Tilda . . . Hooooo-doggies!"

Then finally he looked out over their heads and his eyes lit on Trout and his face went soft. "Howdy, son."

"Howdy yourself."

The rest of them stood back a bit, and Joe Pike reached Trout in three big strides and threw his arms around him. He didn't say a word, just swallowed Trout up and held him for a long moment. Then he released him and held him at arm's length.

Trout looked up into Joe Pike's big brown eyes and saw what you would not see from a distance — a kind of opaqueness there, like a sheer curtain. There was a weariness around the edges, deep crow's-feet that hadn't been there before. He could tell that part of Joe Pike was still off someplace else, maybe out there on the road to Junction. That was the thing about Joe Pike. There was so much of him, he could be two places at once. For such a big man, he was a quick, moving target.

"You okay?" Joe Pike asked.

"Yes sir. How about you?"

Joe Pike worked his jaw for a moment. "I'm still vertical."

Trout thought he might have said more, but Aunt Alma was at Joe Pike's side now, taking hold of his arm. "Well, come on in and see the parsonage."

"Alma's been redecorating," Tilda Huffstetler said.

"I'll say she has," Fleet Mathis chimed in. "You better not let the Bishop see it, or he'll want to move in himself."

That drew a laugh from the crowd, and Joe Pike looked down at Alma. "Alma, what have you gone and done?"

Alma gave a wave of her hand. "Started all over."

Joe Pike nodded, then gave a little hissing sound through his teeth. "Sounds about right."

They started toward the house, and as they climbed the steps, Trout looked back toward the curb. Uncle Cicero's pickup truck was gone. The U-Haul trailer was still there, tilted forward on its tongue. Joe Pike, he realized with an uncomfortable lurch of his stomach, had brought the motorcycle home.

He was alone in the open gun turret, crouched in the bucket seat behind the quad-fifties, peering up into the fog, every nerve ending alive, as if he were wired directly into the ship's power plant. He heard the drone of engines high above. Germans. Or maybe Japs. He stared, trying to part the fog with his eyes, swinging the muzzles of the guns back and forth. They were getting closer, coming at him from every point on the compass, their nasty high-pitched roar closing in. *RUM-UM-UM-UM-ADN-ADN-ADN-ADN-RUM-UM-UM.* "Show yourself, you bastards!" he cried. He squeezed the trigger, and the guns bucked and roared, blotting out everything. A long fevered burst, every fourth round a tracer, evil red blips spitting off into the fog. He released the trigger. And still they came, even more of them now. Whole squadrons. An entire air force. *RUM-UM-UM-UM. . .ADN-ADN-ADN.* Then something about the sound caught his ear and he jerked his head up, straining to listen. *Damn! They're on motorcycles!*

Motorcycles. Trout sat bolt upright in bed. He was drowning in sweat, his pajama bottoms plastered to his legs, the bedsheets soaked. "Uggghhhh," he grunted.

He lay there for a moment, listening, trying to sort through the muck in his head. It was very early. The morning was the palest of gray around the edges of the window shade near his head.

Then he remembered. Moseley. The parsonage. Aunt Alma. The cotton mill. Joe Pike. The U-Haul trailer.

The door to the backyard garage was open and he could see the rear end of the motorcycle and next to it, Joe Pike's big rump. It occurred to him that Joe Pike had put on a little more weight during his trip. A grand tour of the Gulf states' Dairy Queens. He was crouched by the motorcycle, screwdriver in one hand, fiddling with the engine. Every so often he would reach up with the other hand and goose the throttle. *RUM-UM-UM-UM. . .ADN-ADN-ADN. . .RUM-UM-UM-UM.* Trout stood in the open doorway watching for a moment, and then Joe Pike seemed to sense he was there and looked back over his shoulder.

"Morning," Joe Pike said brightly.

"Daddy, for gosh sakes. It's five-thirty." *RUM-UM-UM-UM.* "You're gonna wake the neighbors."

Trout stepped out of the shed, feeling the cool wet grass on his bare feet, looked over at the house beyond the back fence. A light was on in the kitchen window, and a woman in curlers was peering out. She stared at Trout and he gave her a weak, embarrassed wave and she disappeared. He realized she must think he was the one out here playing with the motorcycle. Clad only in pajama bottoms. Crazy preacher's kid. Well, that was better than her thinking that it was the preacher himself over here making a ruckus at five-thirty. Joe Pike didn't need to get off on the wrong foot here.

Joe Pike was sitting on the motorcycle now, legs splayed out to the side, hands on the handlebars. He had on an old grease-smudged T-shirt and a faded pair of khaki pants. And the cowboy boots. He dwarfed the motorcycle, yet the man and the machine seemed to fit together in a strange way. He goosed the engine again, then cocked his head to one side, listening, and gave a tiny nod of satisfaction. He looked over at Trout. "You're up mighty early."

Trout shrugged. "I had this dream about guys on motorcycles."

"I never dream," Joe Pike said. "It's probably not healthy. They say you get rid of a lot of psychic waste matter when you dream."

Trout looked for a place to sit, spied an old Coca-Cola crate, turned it on end, and perched on it. "What're you doing?" he asked.

"Adjusting the idle. I took the carburetor apart and cleaned it and blew out the fuel line. It's been running a little rough. But I think I got it fixed. Must have been a piece of dirt or something." He reached down and turned off the ignition, and the motorcycle died with a cough. Trout crossed one leg over the other and wrapped his arms around his bare chest, huddled there on the Coca-Cola crate, watching, studying. Joe Pike hadn't known diddly about motorcycles when he brought the Triumph home in pieces in the trunk of his car. Didn't know a spoke from a piston. And here he was taking apart the carburetor.

"You been up long?" Trout asked.

"Never went to bed," Joe Pike said. He pulled a grimy handkerchief out of a back pocket and started rubbing on the glass face of the speedometer. "I couldn't sleep, so I've been nesting. Got all my stuff unpacked in the church study, put my name on the marquee out front. And today's sermon topic."

"What's your topic?"

"Bear Bryant and the Holy Ghost."

"Is that what you put on the marquee?"

"Yep."

"Aunt Alma said she planned a service without a sermon. Some extra hymns and stuff."

Joe Pike shrugged. "Preachers preach. Especially new preachers. Everybody wants to see if a new preacher can hold a congregation."

"Haven't you ever preached here before?"

"Not since I was ordained. My ordination service was in this church. You were just a baby. And I preached a sermon, sort of a call to arms, about the Disciples going out to witness. 'Go ye unto all the world . . .'" He smiled, remembering. "Young preachers tend to be full of piss and vinegar."

Trout took note of that. *Piss and vinegar.* Joe Pike's customary manner of speaking was colloquial, down-home, even mildly earthy at times. He had gained a reputation as a preacher whose choice of words raised eyebrows and kept the folks in the pews alert. Like the time in an Ohatchee sermon when he said Christians should get off their fatty acids. But *piss and vinegar?* This was something new. And it rolled easily off his tongue, the kind of thing Joe Pike Moseley the Texas A&M football player might have said. But then, Joe Pike Moseley was just back from Texas, wearing cowboy boots and taking apart a carburetor.

Joe Pike finished with the speedometer, then crammed the handkerchief back in his pocket. He climbed off the motorcycle, knelt on one knee next to it, reached for a ratchet wrench, and started removing the spark plug from the engine.

"How you been getting on with Alma?" he asked over his shoulder.

"Okay."

Joe Pike held up the spark plug, examined it closely. "She give you any instructions yet?"

"She told me not to forget who I am, be careful of the mill kids, and stay away from Great Uncle Phinizy."

Joe Pike turned with a jerk. "Phin?" He blinked, his face all puzzlement. "He's here?"

"Yes sir."

"Where?"

"He's living upstairs over the garage behind Aunt Alma's."

"I'll be doggoned," Joe Pike said softly.

"He says he's infamous."

"Yes, I imagine he is."

Joe Pike pulled out the handkerchief again, wiped off the spark plug, and studied it carefully, a smile playing at the corners of his mouth. Then he looked up at Trout. "Let me tell you about Uncle Phin. When I was playing football at A&M, he was the only member of the family who ever came to see me. We were playing Baylor, and when I walked out the door of the dressing room after the game, there he stood. Drunk as a lord, sucking on one of those Picayune cigarettes."

"Why was he the only one who went to see you?"

Joe Pike didn't appear to have heard the question. He turned back to the motorcycle, tightened down the spark plug, put the wire back on, then put the wrench and screwdriver in a cloth pouch and stored them in a compartment under the seat.

He stood, wiping his hands on his khakis, then finally looked down at Trout. "I'm sorry I missed your birthday."

Trout shrugged.

"It's not every day a guy turns sixteen," Joe Pike said.

"I guess not."

"I haven't gotten you a present yet. Thought I'd ask what you wanted."

"I got my license," Trout said.

"You did?"

"Yes sir. The examiner said he played football against you in high school. You and some fellow named Dewberg or something like that."

"Wardell Dubarry."

"That's it."

"Wardell and I used to do the old high-low on quarterbacks."

"Well, the examiner said y'all near about ruined his team's quarterback. He said y'all were rough as a cob."

"Yeah. I guess we were. Me and the mill kids. Wardell's still here. Still works at the mill. We'll go see him."

"Okay."

Joe Pike slung a leg over the motorcycle and eased down into the seat and reached for the handlebars. And then he seemed to forget for a moment that Trout was there. He stared off into the distance, far beyond the back wall of the storage shed, out past the edge of town, maybe beyond Atlanta. Maybe even all the way to Texas. And Trout realized that in some essential way, Joe Pike hadn't come back yet.

"Daddy . . ."

"You can still get there on two-lanes."

"What?"

Joe Pike turned and looked at him. "All the way from Ohatchee, Georgia, to Junction, Texas, and I never set foot on an interstate. Only a few four-lanes. Mostly just back roads where you can't see past the next hill. Lots of farm tractors and school buses. Folks wave at you when they pass. Figure you must be from somewhere around there or you wouldn't be on their back road in the first place. Never looked at a map, either."

"Didn't you get lost?"

"Hell, I was lost when I started. I just kept the nose pointed west, and I stopped and asked for directions every so often. It took a bit longer, but I wasn't in any hurry in the first place." Trout could hear the pride in Joe Pike's voice. *Hey, Ma! Look what I did!*

Joe Pike sat there for a moment, then shook his head, swung one leg over the motorcycle and sat sidesaddle looking at Trout.

"When is Mama coming home?" Trout asked.

He expected Joe Pike to duck this one, too. But instead, his eyes never left Trout. "Cicero and I stopped in Atlanta," he said. "Your mama's doctor didn't think it was best that we see her. Said she was resting, getting along okay."

"When, then?"

"The doctor was a little vague about that. He was a little vague about everything."

Instead, it was Trout who ducked his head. He thought at first that there was something false about Joe Pike's steady gaze. The appearance of dealing with things. But then he looked back up at Joe Pike and saw that that wasn't the case at all. If anything, it was too much honesty.

"Trout. . ." he said.

"Yes sir."

"I love you, son."

"I love you, too."

"Bear with me. And Mama. Give it all some time. One thing about it . . ."

"What's that?"

"It'll either work out or it won't."

"That's not much to go on," Trout said.

"No. I suspect not. Not much reassurance. But that's life, son."

Trout felt a rush of anger. Damn Joe Pike for leaving, and damn him for coming back empty-handed. He could understand the leaving, at least a little. Irene gone to ground, Joe Pike's faith — in himself and in God — shaken, his ministry gone sour. Okay, so he had gone out to do battle, smote his demons hip and thigh, vanquish devilment, whatever. But somewhere out there on the road to Texas, out on those rural two-lanes with the wind in his ears and the sun in his eyes and the heat phantoms on the pavement ahead, he seemed to have lost heart. And now he had returned from the journey weary and subdued — still vertical, as he said, but whacked off at the knees. And unsure of what was next. Trout, who needed desperately to be reassured about even some small thing, found that Joe Pike was reassured about nothing. There appeared to be no solid ground under either of them. *It will either work out or it won't. That's life.* Oh? Is that what life is? Well, if so, he thought, it truly sucks.

Trout realized that anger would serve no purpose here. It might even spook Joe Pike again. It was not a good sign that he was out here at six-thirty on a Sunday morning tinkering with the damned motorcycle. Better to watch and wait. He was getting quite good at it. So he gave Joe Pike a long look that he tried to shape into something like kindly forbearance. "Okay," he said. "Okay."

Aunt Alma seemed a bit disappointed that Joe Pike wanted to preach. She had indeed planned a Sunday morning service without a sermon — two anthems from the choir, Scripture readings and the like by various lay folk, Fleet Mathis giving a report on his and Eunice's recent trip to the Holy Land. Joe Pike could just take it easy, she said. But he insisted. He put on his robe and marched in behind the choir and sat patiently while everybody went on with the service Aunt Alma had planned.

Aunt Alma said it was the biggest crowd they had had in years, even bigger than Easter. But it truly wasn't very big, nothing like the regular Sunday turnout in Ohatchee. There were a lot of empty seats. And like the welcoming committee the day before, it tended toward older people, some of them downright ancient. There was a scattering of middle-aged and younger couples, only a handful of children. Three other teenagers, a boy and two girls who sat together on a back pew and didn't seem much interested in Trout.

It was a fairly small sanctuary: an arc of oak pews nestled close to the communion rail in front of the pulpit, all the wood stained dark; the cross and twin candles on the Communion table a burnished brass; deep burgundy carpeting on the floor; a sweep of stained glass along the walls where the Twelve Disciples looked down, bathing everything with softly fractured color. They sang old hymns — "Blessed Assurance" and "Rescue the Perishing" and "Take the Name of Jesus With You" — and the singing had a rich mellowness to it, aging voices with the pipe organ flowing beneath like an underground stream.

It was almost noon when Joe Pike finally rose to speak. It was absolutely still and expectant. The congregation waited. So did the Twelve Disciples, looking down from the windows, their bearded faces impassive. Joe Pike stood for a moment, leaning across the pulpit, his gaze taking everything in, resting finally on Trout, sitting with Aunt Alma and Uncle Cicero in the third row, directly in front of the pulpit. Their eyes met for an instant. *Pay attention. I'm gonna give it a shot.*

Then Joe Pike's gaze broke away and he raised up a bit, stood tall behind the pulpit, towering over it. "I've been in a fight," he said. Then he paused for a moment, cocked his head to the side, worked his jaw into a crooked grin. "I never knew but two folks who could whip me. That was Bear Bryant and the Holy Ghost. I ran into both of 'em in Texas."

He paused for a moment and ran his fingers through his hair, slicking it back on his head. There was dead silence in the sanctuary. *What's going on here?*

Joe Pike went on. "I like the phrase 'Holy Ghost.' Now I realize that the church, in its wisdom and an effort to be modern, has changed it to 'Holy Spirit.' But I like the thought, outdated though it may be, of God's ghost lurking about. Something we can't see but sometimes feel. An apparition that oozes through walls and appears in places we'd rather He not be." His eyes swept over the congregation again. "Have you ever been sitting alone in a room and all of a sudden felt there was somebody else there? And you looked up and there wasn't?" He raised his eyebrows, waiting. Trout saw a few heads nod among the congregation. "Well, that's the way I felt a few weeks ago. I was riding my motorcycle to Texas." He said it off-handedly, as if he were describing a trip to the grocery store. "And the Holy Ghost got on in Flatwoods, Louisiana. I had stopped at a traffic light, and when the light turned green and I pulled away, I thought to myself, 'There's somebody on this motorcycle with me.' Well, the Holy Ghost stayed on the back of that motorcycle all the way to Junction, Texas. I couldn't get a good look at Him, but I could feel Him back there, hanging on. And when I realized who it was, I got to asking questions. I'm talking really deep theology here. Everything from immaculate conception to papal infallibility. But every time I'd ask the Holy Ghost a question, He'd say, 'Uh-uh. Not important.' Now, I don't have to tell you, that gets mighty irritating after a while. And by the time we got to Junction, I'd had about enough. So I jumped off the motorcycle and yelled, 'Awright, dang it! Tell me what's important!'" Joe Pike smote the air with a massive arm. "But the Holy Ghost didn't say a word. Even though I couldn't see Him, I could feel Him pretty good, so I grabbed Him in a headlock and threw Him down on the ground, and we wrestled there for a good little while. And the Holy Ghost whipped me."

Joe Pike stopped suddenly, took a half-step back from the pulpit, and stood for a moment staring off above the congregation's heads, lost in thought. Trout stole a glance at Aunt Alma. She was staring at Joe Pike, mouth open. Then she closed her mouth and gave a tiny shake of her head. Joe Pike cleared his throat and stepped up again. "Texas ain't a good place to get whipped. It's hot and dry and you can get a mouthful of dirt when you waller around on the ground. And I did. It felt just like it did when Bear Bryant got through with me. I knew I'd been whipped. But I'm a stubborn fellow. So I asked the Holy Ghost one last time, 'What's important?' And this time, He asked back, 'What do you believe?' I thought about that for a good while, and then I said, 'I believe in the Father and the Son and the Holy Ghost. And beyond that, I'm pretty much open.' And the Holy Ghost said, 'That'll have to do for starters.' And then He told me to rest up and then get on back to Moseley, Georgia, and work on the rest of it. So here I am."

It was rather astonishing, Trout thought. He had sat through years of Joe Pike's preaching, and this was something entirely new. Joe Pike's sermons had always been heavy on Scripture and theology, spiced with anecdotes and snippets of humor — a clever phrase here, a nugget of scriptural wisdom there — all delivered in Joe Pike's rich, rolling voice that cascaded down over the congregation. He was a master of gesture — a quick jab of finger, a sweep of arm, a slow openpalmed beseeching. He was a huge, black-robed conductor, guiding the congregation through the symphony he had carefully crafted in the hours he spent behind the closed door of his study. When it was done, the supplicants might not be able to say in so many words exactly what the point was, but they spoke of Joe Pike's sermons with some satisfaction as "deep."

This, though — his first sermon in sixteen years in Moseley Memorial Methodist Church — was something altogether different. *Piss and vinegar.* Joe Pike looked out across the congregation as if to say, *Any questions here?* But nobody said a thing. Trout cut another quick glance at Aunt Alma. Her mouth was set in a thin, disapproving line. Everybody else looked simply perplexed. Joe Pike sat down.

Uncle Cicero had changed into his police chief uniform by the time they sat down to dinner in the dining room at Aunt Alma's house. Cicero explained that as the chief of a two-man police force, he felt it incumbent upon him to share weekend duty. He would be "on patrol" through the early evening. Cicero was short and a little beefy, mostly bald on top. But his tan uniform with dark blue piping and epaulets fit him nicely, and he wore it well. Little silver eagles were pinned to his collar points. His big leather belt with handcuffs, flashlight, billy club, and holstered .44 Magnum pistol was hanging on a coatrack out in the front hallway.

It was just the four of them, their voices a bit hollow in the highceilinged dining room with its massive mahogany furniture. The black woman named Rosetta who cooked for Alma and Cicero kept coming in from the kitchen with platters heaped with food, and Joe Pike kept taking portions while Rosetta beamed at him approvingly, and he and Cicero carried on a running discourse about the hardware business. Aunt Alma was unusually quiet. Perhaps, Trout thought, still taken aback by Joe Pike's sermon. Perhaps even offended. There was a prim set to her mouth, and she ate with small, precise motions.

Uncle Cicero liked talking hardware and he liked the word *your*. As in, "You've got your sand mix and then you've got your mortar mix and then you've got your concrete mix."

"So what do I need to pour a concrete floor in that storage shed behind the parsonage?"

"Your concrete mix. But before you do that, you'd want to put down your wire mesh."

"You mean like rebar?"

"No, you don't need anything as heavy-duty as your rebar, unless you're gonna keep something real heavy in there."

"Like an armored personnel carrier."

"Or a whiskey still." Uncle Cicero cackled. "Fellow come in my place back a few years ago, bought every sack of concrete mix I had and every inch of rebar. The state boys caught him with a two-thousand-gallon whiskey still in a barn on his proppity. It had your heavy-duty floor underneath it."

Aunt Alma roused herself then and let out a little forced laugh. "Good gracious, Cicero, couldn't you find something more uplifting to talk about at the Sunday dinner table than whiskey stills?"

Uncle Cicero nodded agreeably. "I could. I reckon."

Alma looked across the table at Joe Pike. "If you want a floor in the storage shed, just say so and I'll have the mill superintendent take care of it."

Joe Pike looked right back. "I'll take it up with the pastor-parish relations committee."

"There isn't one."

"Oh? And who takes care of pastor-parish relations?"

"I do."

"I see."

That was when Joe Pike took his third helping of roast beef, after Rosetta glided in from the kitchen and held the platter at his elbow. He took a couple of good-sized slabs and gave Rosetta a big smile. Everybody else passed, and Rosetta disappeared again into the kitchen. Joe Pike cut off a hunk of roast beef, shoved it into his mouth, chewed slowly, and swallowed. Trout picked at his plate, stealing glances at Joe Pike and Alma, waiting.

Finally, Joe Pike said, "I didn't come here to be a kept preacher, Alma."

Alma lifted her napkin from her lap, dabbed at her lips, then folded the napkin carefully and tucked it under the edge of her plate. Took a good deal of time doing it. Then she looked up at Joe Pike. "What *did* you come here for?"

"The Bishop sent me," he said simply.

"The Bishop's trying to save your ministry."

"It's a noble purpose, I suppose."

She shook her head. "Excuse me for saying so, Joe Pike, but you sound a little cavalier about it."

"I don't mean to, Alma. I think we could all use a little noble purpose in our lives."

Trout could hear something gently mocking in Joe Pike's voice, something faintly defensive in Alma's. Some ancient pattern of feint and jab between brother and sister, a ritual of sorts. It was a history Trout knew nothing about. Times past when he had sat at this table, there had always been a crowd — his mother, his cousin Eugene. Until her death ten years previous, Trout's grandmother, Lucretia Moseley. And family friends and retainers. It was a well-mannered crowd, the conversation genteel and polite. Feint and jab were not something you did at the Moseley dinner table.

"Well, I don't know what noble purpose you think you were serving with that business this morning," Alma said.

"You mean my sermon."

"I thought the thing about the Holy Ghost was right interesting," Uncle Cicero chimed in. "You reckon you could tell the Rotary Club about that?"

"Good Lord, Cicero." Alma laughed, and now it sounded even more forced. "The Rotary Club?"

"Well, it's hard to get good programs," Cicero said. "Last week Roscoe Withers got up and told about his trip to Augusta to the chiropractor."

Alma shook her head at Cicero. "Well, the Rotary Club is better off hearing about Roscoe's trip to Augusta than about some" — a flip of her hand — "trip to Texas on a motorcycle."

"Wandering in the wilderness," Joe Pike said. "It's an old biblical tradition." He put another piece of roast beef in his mouth and chewed thoughtfully.

Alma gave him a long, searching look. "I don't know what gets into you, Joe Pike. You've been more or less in a state of rebellion since you were two years old."

"You think maybe it's time I grew up?"

Alma pondered that for a moment. "I think whatever's ailing you, you need to handle it yourself. It has no place in the pulpit."

"Preachers have no right to ask questions?"

Alma leaned across the table toward Joe Pike, hands clasped as if in prayer. "People come to church on Sunday wanting to be told. They want answers. They want something they can depend on. They want some*body* they can depend on. Especially in your case."

Joe Pike looked a trifle amused. "Why especially in my case?"

"Because of who you are."

He gave a great sigh. "Ah, yes. There's always that."

"*Moseley* United Methodist. It wouldn't exist without this family."

A long silence, and then Joe Pike said, "Maybe it ought not to."

Alma flushed. "What do you mean?"

"Maybe the family has done too much. A church that doesn't have any initiative isn't much of a church."

"Initiative? Who's talking about initiative? I'm talking about money. I'm talking about half the budget. Half!"

"They don't have a pot to pee in," Uncle Cicero piped up.

"Cicero!" Alma warned.

"Don't look at me," Cicero said. "I'm Baptist."

"Well, you *attend* the Methodist Church."

"You Methodists are a lot more interesting," Cicero grinned, "running preachers in and out like it was a football game . . ."

"Then join!" she said. "Join, if you think it's so interesting."

"I'm Baptist," Cicero insisted. "What do you think, Joe Pike?"

"A fellow has to do what he has to do, Cicero. Yea, verily."

Alma gave a shake of her head, dismissing Cicero the Baptist. She reached across the table and took Joe Pike's hand. "I don't want to fuss, Joe Pike. Especially over the church. I'm glad you've come. I want you to be happy here, you and Trout. I want us to work together."

"Laboring in the fields of the Lord," Joe Pike said with a thin smile.

"Yes. Of course." She released his hand, then looked over at Trout. "I took Trout by the mill yesterday," she said. "I wanted him to see it. I told him it'll belong to him and Eugene one of these days."

There is something sadly desperate in her voice, Trout thought. If he knew more about her, he might know why. Watch and listen.

"That depends on Trout," Joe Pike said mildly.

"Actually," Trout said, "I've thought about being a tennis pro."

Alma laughed again, and this time there seemed to be a trace of genuine laughter in it. *Silly boy.* Trout felt a flash of irritation, but he kept his mouth shut.

Aunt Alma took a sip of her iced tea, dismissing Trout the Tennis Pro, then looked across the table at Joe Pike again. "Your old friend Wardell Dubarry is still at the mill, you know."

"It's been a good while since I've seen Wardell. We really haven't kept in touch. My fault, mostly."

"He's a troublemaker, Joe Pike."

Joe Pike nodded. "Wardell always did love a ruckus."

"Well, it's more than a ruckus. He's got people stirred up."

"How's that?"

"He's appointed himself as the plant conscience. Always agitating. Safety this, safety that. The temperature's too high, the pay's too low." She waved her hand and her voice rose an octave. "The light's too dim; there aren't enough exits. On and on and on! And I get *no help!*"

"Then why don't you sell it?" Joe Pike asked.

"What?!"

"Find a buyer. People buy and sell businesses all the time."

Alma looked stricken. "I can't believe you said that." There was a long, painful silence, and then she said quietly, "Yes, I suppose I can. You've never taken the slightest interest. Nobody but me."

Cicero chimed in again. "I heard Mister Leland say just before he died that not a damn one of his young'uns did what he wanted 'em to."

Alma's jaw tightened. "I don't believe my father ever used that word."

"What? 'Damn'? Why, Mister Leland was known to offer up your mild expletive every once in a while. Now, I never heard him give anybody what you'd call your dog-cussing, but —"

"HE NEVER USED THAT WORD!" Alma bellowed. The room rang with the echo of her outburst, like putting your head inside a bell while somebody struck it with a hammer. They all stared at her and she flushed with embarrassment.

The door from the kitchen swung open and Rosetta peeked into the dining room. "Y'all want something?"

"You got any more of that squash casserole?" Cicero asked. Alma gave him a murderous look. "Never mind," Cicero said. Rosetta disappeared.

"Papa was not a saint, Alma," Joe Pike said quietly.

Alma turned her gaze on Joe Pike. "I don't believe you have any right to judge," she said. Again, that sadly desperate quality in her voice. And Joe Pike didn't have any response to that.

They all sat there in silence awhile longer, and then Alma composed herself and sat back in her chair. When she spoke again, her voice was quite calm. "I don't expect you to have the same respect for the business I do, Joe Pike. But I don't ever remember you sending back a check." She waited for a response, got none. "And now with your extra financial burden, private care and all —"

"Alma!" Now it was Joe Pike's voice that shattered the air and stopped her dead cold. Trout looked up at his father, massive and bristling beside him, as angry as Trout had seen him in a long time. Then Trout looked across at Alma and saw how she recoiled from his anger.

"I didn't mean . . ." she began, then broke off. They both stared at their plates for a long moment.

And then Uncle Cicero said, "What's for dessert?"

Alma gave him a blank look. "Dessert?"

"I've sort of had a yen for some peach cobbler lately."

"We haven't had dessert in two years, Cicero. Not since your cholesterol flared up."

Cicero thought about that for a moment. "Well, it doesn't keep a fellow from having a yen for peach cobbler."

Alma stared at Cicero and gave a slow shake of her head.

Joe Pike stood up, pushing his chair back with a scrape. "Obliged for dinner," he said. Trout stood up, too.

Alma looked up at him. "I don't want to fuss," she said quietly. "We never used to fuss at this table."

Joe Pike looked down at her. "Maybe we should have. All we did was agree with Papa."

"I just wanted a nice dinner. To celebrate your being home. You and Trout."

"Sure."

"Dinner was real good, Aunt Alma," Trout said. And then something, he couldn't have said what, made him add, "Why didn't you invite Uncle Phinizy?"

Aunt Alma turned beet red. And Joe Pike hustled Trout out of there in a hurry.

As they were going down the front steps, Uncle Cicero called from the front door, "Joe Pike, Rotary Club meets Tuesday at noon in the back room at the Koffee Kup."

They were sitting in the car in front of the Dairy Queen, Joe Pike working on an Oreo Blizzard with crushed pecans on top and Trout, a cone of vanilla. Aunt Alma might not serve dessert with Sunday dinner, but there was always Dairy Queen. It was one of life's certainties. As Joe Pike would say, Yea, verily. They had the windows rolled down, the Atlanta oldies station on the radio. The Coasters: *He's a clown, that Charlie Brown. He's gonna get caught* . . . Trout had been raised on oldies. Most towns where they lived, you could get the Atlanta station. In Bainbridge Joe Pike had installed a special antenna on a tall utility pole next to the parsonage to bring it in. While Trout's friends were listening to Elton John, he got a steady dose of Clyde McPhatter, Elvis Presley, the Shirelles. Joe Pike and Irene danced in the kitchen, something called the Panama City Bop. They were good dancers. Joe Pike, for his size, was nimble and graceful. Tiny Irene whirled like a doll in his hands. Then one day Trout realized that Joe Pike and Irene didn't dance anymore. But Joe Pike kept the radio tuned to the oldies station. *Just in case,* Trout thought.

Joe Pike finished his Blizzard, scraping out the last morsel from the bottom of the cup with his red plastic spoon, reluctantly placing the empty cup on the dashboard. He had a look in his eye that told Trout he might go for another one with the slightest encouragement. Instead, he turned to Trout and asked, "Why did you do that?"

"What?"

"That remark about Uncle Phinizy."

Trout shrugged. "I don't know. It just popped out, I guess. Are you mad?"

"No."

"Aunt Alma likes to have her way, doesn't she."

"Yes. But it's not that simple."

Trout waited for Joe Pike to explain, but he didn't. Finally Trout asked. "What am I supposed to do about Aunt Alma?"

"I guess you'll have to decide that for yourself," Joe Pike said.

He sat there staring at the Blizzard cup while Trout finished his ice cream. Maybe he'll go for a chocolate shake, Trout thought. Or a banana split. Instead, Joe Pike said, "I guess I ought to be shot for what I did."

"What?"

"Running off like that."

Trout didn't know what to say. At a time like this, you could say too much. Or not enough.

"I just want you to know it didn't have anything to do with you, son."

Trout thought about that. He sort of wished it had.

"I'll tell you a piece of truth, Trout. God's got me by the short hairs." A long silence. "Last person did that to me was Coach Bryant."

"What did you do?"

Joe Pike's brow wrinkled, thinking back. When he talked about Texas A&M, about the Bear, he got an odd look at the corners of his eyes. You could see it if you knew where to look. Something like panic there, a nightmare made of heat, dust, agony. And pride, too.

"There were times I wanted to kill him," Joe Pike said finally.

"Why didn't you?"

"I was afraid to."

"You feel that way about God?"

Joe Pike pursed his lips, considering. Then he nodded. "Yep."

FOUR

JOE PIKE DROPPED Trout off in front of the high school shortly after eight the next morning.

"Aren't you coming in?" Trout asked.

"No. Just go to the office and ask for Mr. Blaylock. He's expecting you."

Trout had never started school alone before. Irene had always gone with him on the first day in a new town, even after he reached the age at which having your mother appear at school under any circumstance was something akin to contracting leprosy.

"Do I look okay?" he asked Joe Pike. He was wearing faded jeans, an old pair of Nike running shoes, a plain light blue T-shirt. He carried a half dozen dog-eared spiral binders, crammed with notes from his Ohatchee classes, and a couple of number-two pencils.

Joe Pike put on his mock-Scripture voice. "Give ye heed to the birds of the air and the fish of the sea, for they ask not, what shall I wear or what shall I eat . . ."

"But they weren't sixteen years old."

"You'll do fine, Trout. Play it by ear. It's just a week."

Trout stood at the curb watching Joe Pike's Dodge pull away. *Easy for Joe Pike Moseley to say.* In his day, Joe Pike had belonged here in this aging, nondescript red-brick building with its tall, sun-tainted windows. Joe Pike had never had to walk in cold turkey a week before the end of school with the kind of baggage Trout was toting these days. Trout felt like a man being paraded through town with a dead chicken around his neck.

He walked up the steps, past the squat columns guarding the entrance, into the front hallway. Straight ahead, through open double doors, the auditorium — rows of empty wood-backed seats, a heavy dark blue curtain across the stage with gold letters across the top: MHS. To his left and right, wide hallways — scuffed wooden floors, dingy pale green walls, flaking ceilings, open doorways from which he could hear the faint drone of voices. The place seemed weary.

So did Mr. Blaylock. Over sixty, bald, heavyset, with pale, watery eyes. Trout sat across the desk from Mr. Blaylock while he flipped through the manila folder full of records that Trout had brought from Ohatchee. The top of the desk was bare except for a small note pad and pencil. The pencil was freshly sharpened, the pad empty. Trout thought Mr. Blaylock looked like he wanted to be ready to go home as soon as the bell rang.

The room was sparse — the desk and two chairs, a Georgia state flag on a stand in one corner, a glass-front bookshelf full of old textbooks: *Algebra Made Easy, The American Century, Studies in Good Health.* And perched on the window air conditioner behind Mr. Blaylock's desk, a trophy — a football player in full stride atop four columns, ball tucked under his arm, running to glory; a tarnished brass plate at the base:

MOSELEY HIGH SCHOOL

2-A STATE CHAMPION RUNNER-UP

1953

"Well," Mr. Blaylock said. He closed the folder, opened a desk drawer, dropped the folder in, and closed the drawer. His wooden swivel chair creaked in protest as he leaned back, making a little tent with his fingers under his chin, looking at Trout expectantly.

Trout fidgeted. Finally he said, "I have trouble with math."

Mr. Blaylock gave a small flip of a hand, dismissing math. "Well, I wouldn't worry about it if I were you. Certainly not this close to the end of school. Anyhow, Einstein couldn't balance his checkbook."

"Yes sir."

The window air conditioner droned into the silence. Trout glanced up again at the trophy. Mr. Blaylock followed his gaze, turned with a squeak of the chair, and looked up at the trophy, then back to Trout. "I suppose you know all about that."

"No sir."

Mr. Blaylock gave him an odd look. "Joe Pike hasn't told you . . ." He reached out his hand toward the trophy, an almost reverent gesture. And then Trout understood. It was a sort of shrine.

"An extra point," Mr. Blaylock said.

"What?"

"Twenty-one to twenty. We missed the extra point. Best football game I ever saw in my life — high school, college, or pro. Except for that extra point."

"Well, it's a nice trophy."

Mr. Blaylock looked up at the trophy again, studied the brass plate for a moment, and frowned. "It says 'runner-up.'"

"Was that my daddy's team?"

"Yes. It was your daddy's team. That's exactly what it was. If it hadn't been, we woulda won maybe two games that year."

Then it dawned on Trout. "You were the coach?"

Mr. Blaylock stared up at the ceiling for a long time, and Trout wondered if he had heard the question. Then all of a sudden Mr. Blaylock stood up, banging the swivel chair against the wall. He leaned over the desk toward Trout, eyes lit up, nostrils flaring. "Sometimes you look back on something that happened years before, and you think, 'That was as good as it ever got.' But I knew it right then and there. Damnedest football game in history. Ass-busting, bone-crunching, gut-sucking football, the way it was invented. Kids being helped off the field, coming right back. Halfback from Bainbridge played most of the game with his nose mashed over to one side of his face, dripping blood down the front of his jersey. Coupla my boys didn't know their own names when it was over. I remember standing on the sidelines during that last quarter, thinking, 'Orzell Blaylock, this is it.'"

Then he stopped, blinked, sat back heavily in his chair, gave a huge sigh. "And we missed the extra point. If we'da made the extra point, we'da gone to overtime. And we'da whipped the sonsabitches in overtime. We had the momentum." He stopped, mouth open, breathing heavily. And then he repeated softly, "We had the momentum."

"I'm sorry," Trout said. It sounded pretty lame, but it was all he could think of.

"Yeah," Mr. Blaylock said. "Well . . ." They both sat there for a moment longer, and then Mr. Blaylock asked, "You and Joe Pike see many Falcon games?"

"Who?"

"The Falcons. Atlanta."

"Oh. No sir. They play on Sundays."

Mr. Blaylock nodded. "I reckon Joe Pike being a preacher and all . . ."

"It's not that. It's just that you can't leave Ohatchee after church and get to Atlanta in time for the game."

"Well, you're not in Ohatchee now."

"No sir."

"Moseley's not that far from Atlanta. Maybe you and Joe Pike can see some games this season."

"Yes sir."

"You do like sports, don't you?"

Trout glanced up at the trophy again. "I sure do like sports, yes sir."

"Which ones?"

"Well, actually . . . tennis."

"Tennis?"

"Yes sir." There was a long silence while Mr. Blaylock stared at the blank pad on his desk. Trout wondered if he might pick up the pencil and write something on the pad. But he didn't.

After a moment, Mr. Blaylock looked up at him again. "We don't want any trouble here, Trout."

"No sir," Trout said, feeling his face flush. *What in the hell is he talking about?*

"This ain't a good idea. Especially right now. And I told Joe Pike that. But he insisted. So let's just get through this the best we can, okay?"

"Yes sir."

"Any problems, you come see me."

"Yes sir."

"But I hope you won't have to."

"No sir," Trout said. His eyes went to the blank pad on the bare desk. "I can see that."

Trout vowed to keep his mouth shut and keep a low profile. Head up, fanny down. And by midmorning, he had decided it might be easier than he thought. The teachers seemed nice enough, but wary — as if they didn't quite know what to do with him. And as far as the students were concerned, Trout Moseley might as well have been invisible. They didn't so much ignore him as they looked right through him.

Until midmorning. They were changing classes, the hallway where Mr. Blaylock had assigned him a locker crowded and noisy with students. Suddenly, down the hall a piece, there was an explosion of sound and motion. "Outta the way! Comin' through!" Trout saw the mass of students parting; then she burst through — a flailing windmill of arms, legs, torso, crutches, flying hair, everything galloping off in a dozen directions at once. A big pad of some kind tucked under one arm, books under the other. Trout stared, transfixed. A wreck, happening before his eyes. Incredible.

"Move it! Move it! Comin' through!" She lurched to a halt in front of his locker, screwed up her face in a grimace and looked him straight in the eye. "Who the hell are you?"

"Trout Moseley," he said.

"I knew that."

"Then why did you ask?"

"I just wanted to see if you'd admit it."

"Admit it?"

A bell rang somewhere down the hall. Bodies swirled around them, giving both a wide berth. Invisible Trout Moseley and the human antigravity device.

"Meet me in the football stadium after school," she barked. And she lurched away, leaving him open-mouthed.

At first, he thought she wasn't there. Some kind of trick. The student body, hidden in the bushes next to the stadium, laughing their butts off. It had already been one of the strangest days of his life, ranking not far behind the day they took his mother off to the Institute and the Easter Sunday Joe Pike rode off on the motorcycle.

Then she waved and he saw her sitting in the shade by the concession stand behind one of the end zones. Back to the wooden side of the building, knees bent, the big pad open in her lap, crutches next to her on the grass. He walked the length of the field, feeling sweat trickling down his back and sopping his already-wet T-shirt. The only air conditioner in Moseley High School, it had turned out, was in Mr. Blaylock's office.

As he approached, he could see that she was drawing on the pad, making broad strokes with some kind of pencil, looking up at him and then back down. He stopped in front of her. "Hi. I'm Trout Moseley. I'm new here. What's your name?"

She concentrated on the pad for a moment longer, then looked up at him. "I know all about you."

"Oh?"

"I know your mama's in the Institute in Atlanta, your daddy flipped out and rode his motorcycle to Texas, and you play tennis."

"Well," Trout said, "I guess that about wraps it up." He craned his neck, trying to see over the top of the pad. "What're you drawing?"

She closed the pad with a slap, stuck the pencil behind her ear so that just the tip showed from her close-cropped brown hair. "None of your business. Sit down."

He sat a couple of yards from her, put his books down on the grass beside him and looked out across the hot green expanse of the football field. Twenty-one to twenty. It was just a ball game, wasn't it?

"You can forget tennis," she said.

"Oh?" Had Mr. Blaylock put out a memo to the student body? *This boy plays tennis. Watch him.*

"There's not a single tennis court in Moseley."

Trout thought about the Prince Extender racquet he coveted, hanging on pegboard in the pro shop at Ohatchee Country Club. Black graphite with white binding on the grip. A wicked-looking piece. Walk on the court with something like that and watch your opponent's eyes. *Uh-oh.* Two hundred and fifty dollars. He had been saving up for two years, and he was getting close. If he sent the money, they would ship it from Ohatchee, he was sure of that. It's not every day the pro shop at Ohatchee Country Club sells a two-hundred-fifty-dollar racquet.

"You want to know why?" she asked.

"Why what?"

"Why there's no tennis court in Moseley."

"Okay."

"Your grandfather wouldn't allow it." She waited for some response from him. He shrugged. "He thought it was frivolous," she said with a toss of her head. Trout searched her face. It seemed set in a perpetual scowl. She was rather pretty in a sharp-featured way, but the scowl undercut it. Was it indigestion? Or was she just generally mad at the world? He looked down at her crutches, lying on the grass between them.

"What are you looking at?" she demanded.

He nodded at the crutches. "Is that why you're pissed off? Or is it something else?"

She surprised him by giving him a crooked smile. "Hey, what have we here? 'Pissed off.' Pretty strong stuff for a preacher's kid."

Trout picked up his books, struggled to his feet. "Look. This hasn't been the best day of my life. Mr. Blaylock is fixated on a football game that happened thirty years ago. I've had to check myself several times today to see if I'm transparent, because you're the only kid who's spoken to me and you've got a snotty attitude and I don't even know your name. The lunch meat was inedible. Now you tell me there's no tennis court. I've never lived here before and I don't know what the hell it is about the Moseleys. I just know my dad said one time that when a Moseley farts, everybody smells it."

"Your daddy said that?"

"Yes."

"He's a preacher and he said that?"

"Yes."

She pursed her lips. "Hmmmm."

"Tell me something."

"What?"

"What's with the silent treatment?"

A tiny smile played at the corners of her mouth. But she didn't answer him directly. "Mill kids run this place," she said.

"And the mill kids are just shy, right?"

"No."

"Then what?"

"When you live over in the mill village and your mama and daddy don't make squat for money, there's not much to do for diversion."

"So I'm a diversion."

"You're a Moseley."

Trout looked away, studying the cloudless afternoon sky above the stadium press box, imagining the stands packed with people, the loudspeaker blasting. *Tackle by Joe Pike Moseley.* Joe Pike had made it here. Bet the mill kids didn't give *him* the silent treatment. Was it just Trout? Or had something changed? "What is it with you?" he asked.

"What do you mean?"

"Why did you talk to me when nobody else would?"

"I just don't give a damn."

"Oh. Well, that explains it." He turned on his heel and started walking away.

"Where are you going?"

"Dairy Queen."

He was at midfield before she called out again. "My name is Keats." He didn't look back.

There was a huge pecan tree next to the Dairy Queen, and a concrete picnic table underneath. Trout sat on one side with his Blizzard, Joe Pike on the other with a banana split, two extra scoops of strawberry ice cream.

There was an ancient woman at the window of the Dairy Queen. The man behind the counter was watching her, waiting for her order. The woman scanned the big menu in the window carefully, nodding at each item, silently mouthing their names. It had the appearance of a ritual, and she had the appearance of a regular. Trout could imagine her showing up every afternoon about this time, studying the menu at great length, then ordering the very same item. She never changed, and neither did the Dairy Queen menu. There was something comfortably predictable about a Dairy Queen, Trout thought. The menu, the regulars. The old woman. A couple of guys in an ACE PLUMBING truck with a jumble of pipes in the back. And now Joe Pike and Trout. It was their fourth trip to Dairy Queen since Joe Pike had arrived on Saturday. Joe Pike was working steadily through the menu.

"I've got an idea," Joe Pike said.

"Oh?"

"Jumping for Jesus."

"What's that?"

"An exercise class."

"Where?"

"The church. Did you get a good look at the congregation yesterday?"

"Sure."

"What did you notice about them?"

"Older."

"Moribund. If flies had lit on 'em, the flies would have gone to sleep."

The old woman at the Dairy Queen window finished scanning the menu and placed her order. A fifty-cent cup of ice cream with crushed pineapple on top. The man inside already had the cup ready. He handed it out the window, with a red plastic spoon stuck into the glob of pineapple.

Joe Pike sliced off a chunk of banana and strawberry ice cream from his split, lifted it to his mouth, savored it for a long moment, swallowed. "I stood in that pulpit years ago and delivered my first sermon as a kid preacher. You were one year old, fidgeting in your mama's lap. The congregation . . . It dawned on me this morning. Nothing's changed. The same people, give or take a handful, just fifteen years older. Sitting in exactly the same pews. In a church, when nothing changes, when people don't come and go, that's not good."

"Moribund," Trout said.

Joe Pike concentrated for a while on the banana split. Trout finished his Blizzard, took the empty cup to the trash can, returned to the table.

"It needs shaking up," Joe Pike said. "Something to get the older members' blood flowing, get some younger folks into the church."

"Jumping for Jesus."

"It might be the place to start. You like the name?"

"It has a ring to it, I guess."

"Marketing. Folks nowadays are part of the TV generation. You need a catchy phrase to get their attention. It's a little like selling Alka-Seltzer or Pepsi."

Trout thought about all those old folks, knobby knees and blue-veined legs, paunches and spreading behinds, twisting and bouncing in the assembly room of the education building to a strong rock beat. Maybe a little Four Tops. *Sugar pie, honey bunch . . . Ooga-chukka . . . ooga-chukka . . .* And Joe Pike up at the front, leading the pack. Well, that was a stretch. A test of the structural integrity of the building. Joe Pike in one of his Dairy Queen phases.

"How was it?" Joe Pike asked, interrupting the image.

"What?"

"First day at school."

Trout shrugged. "Okay."

"Just 'okay'?"

"No. Strange."

"In what way?"

"Mr. Blaylock said he didn't want any trouble."

"Was there any?"

"No. He said it wasn't a good idea, my being there. Especially now." He gave Joe Pike a long look, waiting. But Joe Pike didn't say anything. He finished off the banana split, placed the plastic spoon in the Styrofoam boat, wiped his mouth with a paper napkin, wadded it up and put it in the boat beside the spoon. "Will there be any Dairy Queens in heave-n-n-n-n?" he sang off-key, then grinned. "I sure hope so. It is one of life's great pleasures, and I can't imagine the Lord running the afterlife without it. How could you have the Sweet By-and-By without Dairy Queen?"

"Mr. Blaylock told me about the football game."

Joe Pike gave him an odd look. "What about it?"

"Twenty-one to twenty."

A cloud passed over Joe Pike's face then. Not so much pain as . . . what? Embarrassment? "What else?"

"That's about it."

"Well, there's not much more to tell. It was just a football game."

Joe Pike got up from the table and took his trash to the garbage can. Trout sat at the table, watching. When Joe Pike turned back to him, Trout said, "Did you know there's not a tennis court in this town?"

"I never thought about it. No, I guess there's not."

"Do you know why there's not a tennis court?"

"No."

"Grandaddy Leland wouldn't let 'em build one. He thought it was . . ." — Trout searched for the word — ". . . frivolous."

"Who told you that?"

"A girl at school. Where am I gonna play tennis if there's not a tennis court?"

Joe Pike sighed wearily. "I don't know, son."

"The State Juniors are coming up. I haven't practiced in more than a week."

"Maybe we can build a backboard at the end of the driveway," Joe Pike said hopefully.

"It's not the same." Trout knew he sounded petulant, but he couldn't help it. No tennis court, nobody to play tennis with. The only person who even acknowledged his existence all day was crippled. And pissed off at Trout's grandfather, to boot. No, make that pissed off at Moseleys in general. But at least she spoke.

"Yea, verily," Joe Pike said. "Out of the mouths of babes. You speak a profound truth, son. A backboard is not a tennis court."

"What's going on here, Daddy?" Trout asked.

Joe Pike pondered that for a moment, then made a little hissing sound through his teeth. "I'm not sure I know, son."

"When you find out, will you tell me?"

"Sure."

"When do you think that'll be?"

"Maybe tomorrow."

"What's tomorrow?"

"That's when we're gonna see Wardell Dubarry."

Trout woke deep in the night with his brain in overdrive — humming like a high-voltage line with the utter strangeness of it, the incredible twist his life had taken.

He thought of Ohatchee. Even with all that had happened there, it seemed so normal by comparison. He had had friends. A girlfriend. He had played tennis almost every day, even in the winter. He had delivered the *Atlanta Constitution* on his bicycle. He had almost lost his virginity.

The memory of it rushed back in a breath-catching, blood-pounding surge of heat. Cynthia Stuckey. A spring afternoon, the sweet smell of photinia blossoms drifting on the breeze through her bedroom window, parents gone. A flash of white thigh, her breast cool in his hand, her breath like hot wind in his ear. Cool and hot. Hot and cool. He had felt faint, as if he were about to be suddenly plucked from obscurity and made famous. And then . . .

He knew now that she had never entertained the slightest thought of letting him into her pants. She had teased him with breast and thigh and sent him home with an ache in his groin that made it difficult to walk upright, probably laughing her ass off as he limped down her front walk. But he had not known it then, not even suspected it. He had followed her around Ohatchee like a drooling puppy, hoping it would happen again. Just getting close, that was something. If he got close, even if he did more than that, he wouldn't tell his friends. Not even Parks Belton. He would be honorable. No smutty talk about Cynthia Stuckey. He was mad for her. A fool, but a fool gladly.

But then the other craziness had swallowed him — Irene, Joe Pike and the motorcycle, Easter Sunday — and Cynthia had dropped him cold, without warning. Not only dropped him, humiliated him.

Maybe it had been her mother, the chairman of the pastor-parish relations committee at Ohatchee Methodist. Or her father, who was on the school board and had voted to ban *Maggie, A Girl of the Streets* from the school library. They were both tight-asses. Maybe it was Cynthia herself. But she could have let him down easy. Instead, she gathered an audience in the hallway outside Plane Geometry the day he returned to school after Joe Pike's Sunday escapade. Trout could tell by the looks on all their faces that they were waiting for something. He touched her sleeve. That was all. Just touched her sleeve. And she spun on him, a nasty little smirk on her face, and said, "Go play with yourself, Trout. Leave me alone."

That had been two weeks ago, and it still made him writhe with embarrassment. And even worse was the fact that the other memory — breast, thigh, hot breath — could still reduce him to a gasping, fist-pumping pulp. To hell with Cynthia Stuckey! His fist was faithful. Always willing. Never an embarrassment.

So now, lying here in his new bedroom in this new parsonage in his strange new life, he kissed his fist and massaged the hot memory of Cynthia Stuckey from his mind, at least temporarily.

That done, he tried to go back to sleep. He would have to drag himself out of bed in the morning and face another day of near invisibility at Moseley High School. And the thought of that made him even more wide-awake. So he got out of bed and went to the front porch with his portable radio, sat in the porch swing, and tuned in the Atlanta oldies station. And thought about his mother.

Irene knew all the songs. The Shirelles, the Supremes, the Everly Brothers . . . *Here he comes . . . it's Cathy's Clown* . . . Elvis, Ruth Brown, Clyde McPhatter, Dee Clark . . . *Raindrops, so many raindrops* . . . Irene in a dishwasherless kitchen, hips swaying to Little Richard as she labored over a suds-filled sink. Joe Pike and Irene doing the Panama City Bop to Sam Cooke, blinds closed against parishioners who might not appreciate a preacher with rhythm. Big Joe Pike and tiny Irene, bear and bird, gliding and twirling. Watching them, Trout laughed and felt oh-so-fine. They taught him the steps, and they all laughed when he invented one of his own. *We're having a party* . . . The music. Keeping the world at bay, the world outside the parsonage. But then the time came when the music didn't work anymore, when Irene's silences grew and grew until they drowned out everything, even the music.

The Atlanta oldies station was playing Brenda Lee now. *I'm sorrreeee . . . so sorrree . . .* He wondered if Irene might be listening over there in Atlanta at the Institute. Did they allow people at the Institute to be up this time of night listening to the radio? Or did some guy come in at nine and give you a pill? Could you live in the past if you wanted? Or did some therapist keep insisting, "Now! Now!"

Was she lonely? There didn't seem to be much opportunity for company. Joe Pike and Trout were being held at arm's length for the moment. And the Troutmans, her own family back in Texas, were all gone except for some distant cousins. She was the antithesis of Joe Pike. She had no family to speak of. He had too much.

There was so much Trout needed to know from her. And about her. Her silences, and now her absence, had made her a stranger. When he finally got a chance to talk to her, would she know him? Would he know her? And would he even know which questions to ask?

The music drifted out of the radio, hung suspended in the hot quiet of the porch, and settled in that big hollow place somewhere between his stomach and his heart that Trout figured must be his soul.

I'm not gonna cry. Dammit, I'm not. You're not gonna make me cry, God!

But he did, while Brenda Lee sang.

And when she had finished and he had wiped away his hot tears, he looked across the street at Aunt Alma's darkened house. And he saw the light in the window of the garage apartment out back. Uncle Phinizy.

FIVE

THE GARAGE WAS at the back of the deep lot behind Aunt Alma's house, almost hidden from the house itself by pecan trees and a cane thicket, reached by a gravel driveway that curved around the edge of the lot from the porte cochere. There were three open garage bays on the ground floor. In the light of the half-moon, Trout could see the dim outline of lawn equipment and old bicycles in one bay. The other two were empty. The upstairs apartment had two dormers peeking from the roofline, open to the night air. In one of the windows, a light was on. Trout climbed the narrow outside stairs, hesitated for a moment on the small landing, knocked.

"Door's open, Trout."

He pushed the door open and looked inside. Phinizy was sitting deep in a Naugahyde recliner, legs up, floor lamp on at his shoulder, book in one hand, half-smoked cigarette between two fingers of the other. On the table at his elbow were a half-empty whiskey glass and an ashtray overflowing with cigarette butts. Phinizy marked his place in the book with his finger and closed it. He looked up at Trout, studying him. He took a deep drag on his cigarette and released a double stream of smoke through his nostrils that kept coming and coming, the streams breaking apart and curling back around his head, then disappearing as wisps of bluish haze into the lampshade. Trout stared. All that smoke coming out of this little bitty old man. Finally it ended and Phinizy said, "Well, don't just stand there. You'll let all the flies out."

Phinizy reminded him of a shriveled, wizened gnome from one of the folk tales Irene had read to him when he was a small child — leathery skin, beaked nose, gnarled hands. An ancient wreck of a man. But there was something else — a lively snap to the blue eyes, an odd way he cocked his head as if listening for some faint signal. An air of . . . what? Expectation?

"I saw your light on," Trout said, closing the door behind him. "How did you know it was me?"

"Well, Joe Pike left about an hour ago. And Cicero was here a little before that. I figured it was either you or Banquo's ghost."

"Who?"

"Haven't you read Shakespeare?"

"Yes sir. A little."

"Hmmmm. Yes sir. A young'un who says, 'Yes, sir.'"

"My mama taught me," Trout said.

"Ah, yes. Your mama."

"Why was Daddy here?"

"Same reason Cicero was. Same reason you are."

"Why is that?"

"You all think I know something."

"Do you?"

"Not much. Want a drink?" Trout looked at the whiskey glass. "I've got some ginger ale," Phinizy said. "Nobody around here drinks whiskey but me. It'd probably help Cicero and Joe Pike both if they'd tie on a good one every once in a while. But a man's got his obligations, I guess."

Phinizy turned down a corner of the page in his book and placed it on the table. Suddenly, he reached down and yanked the lever on the side of the recliner and sort of catapulted out of it — surprising Trout with the quick movement, the way he bounced on the balls of his feet, catlike — and disappeared through the door to the kitchen, flipping on the light as he went. Then Trout remembered. Rumpelstiltskin. The folk tale. A funny little man, a beautiful girl, gold spun from flax. Trout was struck again by a powerful sense of his mother. He could smell her, feel her. They nestled together on a sofa, the book with the curious illustrations open before them, the rise and fall of her voice reaching deep inside him. *And the little man stamped his foot . . .* It was so immediate, so real, it almost took his breath. Even more than the music from the oldies station.

He heard Phinizy in the kitchen, the tinkle of ice cubes in a glass. He looked around at the room. It was sparsely furnished: recliner, rickety breakfast table with two ladder-back chairs, an ancient sofa. The walls were bare except for one faded picture, an old lithograph — a man and a woman in a rowboat on a lake. He sat down on the sofa and waited.

Phinizy came back in a moment with Trout's ginger ale and a fresh drink for himself. He sat down again in the recliner, lit another cigarette, took a long sucking drag and let the smoke out lovingly, playing with it. Trout took a sip of his ginger ale. It was a little flat. Phinizy probably didn't drink much ginger ale.

"My father built this place," Phinizy said, looking about the room. "He hired a woman from Baltimore to come down here and teach Leland and me the social graces. She was young and rather attractive, and it wouldn't do to have her living in the big house. Father was very big on appearances. So he built this. Called it the guest house." Phinizy took a long pull on his whiskey, held up the glass for a moment and swirled the whiskey and ice around, squinting at it. Then he looked over the top of the glass at Trout. "If you can't hold up your end of the conversation, just say so. I'll try to go it alone."

Trout gave him a blank look.

"Either a question or a statement will be fine, as long as it has some remote connection to what has previously been said. The object here is to generally advance the topic."

"Well, ahhhh . . ."

"That'll do for starters. So, you ask, What am I doing here? Well, why not? I may have spent most of my life in exile, but I remain an heir to Broadus Moseley's vast fortune. I am content to let Alma run it. All I ask is this" — a grand sweep of his arm took in the apartment — "modest abode. I am content to live in the shadow of the big house and bask in its reflected glory."

Trout took another sip of the ginger ale. "Daddy said you've been away for a long time. Why did you come back now?" he ventured.

Phinizy thought about that for a moment. Then he said, "Tell you a joke. Two guys going to truck driving school. Joe and Charlie. Instructor's giving 'em a final oral examination. He says to Joe, 'Hypothetical situation, Joe. You're driving, Charlie's behind you up in the bunk asleep. You're going down a steep two-lane mountain road. Car just ahead in your lane. You suddenly discover your brakes are shot. You're coming up fast behind this car, so you pull out into the other lane. You're going faster and faster. All of a sudden another truck rounds a curve coming *up* the mountain right toward you. Whatcha gonna do, Joe?' And Joe says, 'I'm gonna wake up Charlie.' Instructor says, 'Why you gonna do that?' Joe says, ''Cause Charlie ain't never seen a real bad wreck before.'"

Trout laughed. But Phinizy didn't crack a smile. Trout felt stupid. And he thought that Phinizy was one strange duck. Finally he said, "Is there gonna be a wreck?"

"Ask you a question," Phinizy said. "Are you an optimist or a pessimist?"

Trout thought about that for a moment. "I'm just trying to get through adolescence," he said.

"Ask you another question. Are you a skeptic or a cynic?"

"What's the difference?"

"A skeptic asks questions. A cynic doesn't bother."

"I guess I'm a skeptic, then. What are you?"

Phinizy took a deep pull on the cigarette and held the smoke for a long time, then suddenly started coughing, blasting the smoke from his lungs. He bent double in the chair, shriveled body wracked with deep, wretched spasms. Trout started to get up, alarmed. Phinizy waved him away. The coughing went on for a long time before Phinizy finally began to get it under control. He sat there awhile longer, taking shallow, tentative breaths. He stared at the cigarette still clutched between two fingers, took a defiant drag from it and stubbed it into the pile in the ashtray.

"You oughta quit that," Trout said.

"No," Phinizy said, "I should have quit sixty years ago, right after I started. I was ten years old when I took my first drag off a coffin nail." He took a big drink of whiskey. And then he took off his glasses, pulled a handkerchief out of a pants pocket and wiped his watery eyes. Stuffed the handkerchief back in his pocket. Looked up, finally, at Trout. "Mark Twain used to say the reason he smoked was to have at least one bad habit in reserve, so he'd have something to give up in case of doctor's orders. It's as good an excuse as any, I suppose."

They both sat there in silence awhile, Trout staring at the floor, not knowing what to say.

"You're looking for some answers," Phinizy said quietly.

Trout looked up and shrugged. He didn't even know where to begin. "This place is weird," he said, making a vague gesture that took in town, school, mill, church, and house. And all that had transpired and been said since he arrived. "In school yesterday — nobody spoke to me but this one kid. And the principal said something about not having any trouble. And everybody seems to be ticked off about the Moseleys. But if Aunt Alma knows they're ticked off, she doesn't let on. She just sounds like she's preaching a sermon all the time. Moseley this and Moseley that. You'd think it was a religion or something."

"Did you ask Joe Pike?"

"Yes sir. He said something's going on, but he doesn't know what."

"Well, I don't either," Phinizy said. "I don't have any answers. But I know some history. And I've been around long enough to know that sometimes that's where you find some clues. You want to hear some history?"

"Yes sir."

And that was when Phinizy told him about Moseley, Georgia. About how Broadus Moseley created the town, lifted it up out of red clay and desperation and put his indelible mark upon it. And how he and his heirs, down to the present, claimed it as inviolable territory — a permanent and unchangeable shrine to its creator. It was, for Trout, an initiation into mystery — like Joe Pike in the pulpit, letting the big leather Bible fall open where it wished, reading at random a few verses of profound truth. Clues, portents, an intimation of all the rest. In it, an echo of Aunt Alma's voice: *Don't ever forget who you are.* He knew there was a great deal more, unseen and unknown. But it was a start.

There was the other, of course — the mystery of Joe Pike and Irene Moseley, of silences and escapes, the Institute and the motorcycle. The *why.* But Trout wasn't ready to get into all that with Great Uncle Phinizy. It was a private, personal mystery, and for the time being he would try to puzzle out that one for himself. Later, maybe . . .

And besides, when Phinizy had finished telling him about the town and his forebears, dawn was at the window.

Joe Pike was waiting behind the wheel of the car at the curb in front of the high school at midafternoon, arm slung out the open window. "You look like death warmed over," he said when Trout climbed in.

"I want to go home and go to bed," Trout said. He felt terrible —

drained, stupid with fatigue. All the air seemed to have leaked out of his lungs and puddled somewhere in the pit of his stomach.

Joe Pike started the car. "We've got a stop to make first. How'd it go today?"

"About the same. Where are we going?"

"I told you. To see Wardell Dubarry."

It was the first time Trout had ever been to the mill village. There had never been a reason. And there wasn't much to see. Just past the mill the road curved and the pavement ended and became dirt and gravel, lined on either side by houses, each exactly like its neighbor — white clapboard box on low brick piers, small porch, steep tin roof, door and two windows across the front, red-brick chimney on the right side, short gravel driveway along the left. Patches of grass were neatly trimmed at a uniform height, as if somebody had mowed them all at once. A few trees, an occasional shrub. Here and there, an attempt at individuality — a fern hanging at the edge of a porch, a splash of bright curtain at a window. But it was no match for the overwhelming sameness of the place.

"Why did they build 'em all the same?" he asked Joe Pike.

"They didn't build 'em. Grandaddy Broadus did."

Trout stared, thinking of all Phinizy had told him in the early-morning hours. History. At dawn, when he had finally gotten up to go, Phinizy had said, "Before you can know who you are, you have to know where you came from. Especially you. It's all there, Trout. Go take a good look at it. Then come back and tell me what you saw." The man talked in riddles. Or maybe, Trout thought now as they eased along the mill village street, gravel crunching under the tires, Phinizy just pointed out the riddles.

"They're all white," Trout said.

Joe Pike looked at the houses for a moment. "They get painted every other year whether they need it or not."

"Why?"

Joe Pike shrugged. "Because that's just the way it's always been done."

"Well, why don't they paint 'em something different?"

"Who?"

"The people who live in 'em."

"They don't own 'em."

"Who does?"

Joe Pike squinted at him. "They're mill houses, Trout. The mill built 'em. The mill owns 'em. The mill maintains 'em. Paints, cuts the grass, repairs the roof. Toilet gets stopped up, you call the mill."

"The mill," Trout repeated. "You and Aunt Alma."

Joe Pike shrugged. "I guess so. And you and Eugene and Phin and anybody else who has a stake in the business."

"Uncle Phin didn't tell me that."

"Phin?"

"He had a busy night last night."

Trout stared again at the houses, one after another. Beyond this street, on either side, he could see two more. There must be a hundred houses here. It reminded Trout of the long rows of looms inside the mill.

Then Joe Pike turned in one of the gravel driveways, just behind a faded red Ford, about the same vintage as Joe Pike's Dodge. The rear end was on jacks, hiked up in the air. A pair of legs stuck out from underneath. Faded jeans, almost white with age and washings. Dirty off-brand jogging shoes. No socks. Joe Pike and Trout got out of their car and walked over to the Ford.

"Hello, Wardell," Joe Pike said.

"Hello yourself, Joe Pike," the legs said back. Joe Pike and Trout stood there for a good while. From underneath the car, a clank of metal against metal. Then, "Shit." More clanking.

"Anything I can do to help?" Joe Pike volunteered.

"It ain't a motorcycle, Joe Pike." There was something about the voice that reminded Trout of fruit left on a tree too long, beginning to spoil.

More clanking. "Are you gonna come out and say hello?" Joe Pike finally asked.

"Depends."

"On what?"

"Whether Alma sent you or you come on your own."

"Well, a little of both."

A couple more clanks and then the legs began to wiggle out from under the car. And just kept coming. There was a great deal of Wardell Dubarry, at least lengthwise. When he finally stood up, wiping his hands on a greasy cloth, there was about six feet eight of him, incredibly thin with scarecrow arms and a head that looked like it had been

mashed sideways in a vise — great expanse of forehead, long sweeping jaw, deep-set eyes, unruly shock of gray-black hair.

"There ain't even a goddamn auto parts store in this town," Wardell
said. His voice was a deep, thick drawl, slow like a creek with little
eddies in it where it eased around rocks and roots. Trout stared up at
him, craning his neck. Wardell looked him over.

"This is Trout," Joe Pike said.

Wardell grunted. Trout realized his mouth was open, closed it.
Then Wardell turned to Joe Pike and gave him a long look. "Joe Pike,
you are one big hunk of preacher."

Joe Pike stuck out his hand. "How are you, Wardell?"

It was quick, barely a handshake. "I been better, I been worse."

"It's been a long time," Joe Pike said.

"It's been thirteen years since I laid eyes on you, Joe Pike. This
young'un here" — he gave a nod at Trout — "was still peeing in his
pants."

"Well, he's dry as a bone. And I'm back."

"And cut a deep furrow gettin' here, from what I hear." Wardell gave
a little twist to his mouth, not quite a smile. "How was Texas?"

Joe Pike folded his big arms over his chest. "Which time?"

"Either."

"About the same."

They just stood and looked at each other for a moment. Trout tried
to imagine them playing football together, about the same age as he
was now. Echoes. The driver's license examiner in Ohatchee: *They
near about killed our quarterback . . .* The trophy in Mr. Blaylock's
office at Moseley High: *Damnedest football game in history.* Now here
they were, middle-aged men, one gone to fat and the other to towering emaciation. But yet, oddly enough, almost young in each other's
presence. A bit of teenage swagger, the way they held themselves —
Joe Pike sucking in his massive gut, Wardell standing good and
straight. But there was something wary about both of them, too. They
stood a little back from each other now. Had they been rivals in some
way, back there at Moseley High School? Had they fought over a girl?
Thrown down a great dare? Trout realized with a jolt that Wardell
Dubarry was the first person he had ever met, outside the family, who
shared some sort of history with Joe Pike Moseley. But what of it?

"How's your family?" Joe Pike asked finally.

"Mostly growed," Wardell said. "Darrell's in the Army. Wardell Junior lives in New Orleans, works the oil rigs in the Gulf. Just me and Sue and the girl now."

"That's what you get marrying young," Joe Pike said.

Wardell looked at him for a long moment. "Wadn't nothing else to do. Get a job at the mill, get married. Go to work, raise kids." Something very close to anger there, Trout thought. But it was hard to tell. The drawl covered up a lot, like a coating of thick oil.

Joe Pike uncrossed his arms and stuck his hands in his pockets. "Yeah. I reckon."

They stood there a moment longer looking at each other and then Wardell turned to Trout. "My young'un's in the house. Go on up and say hello. Let me and your daddy talk, since he come on bidness." He indicated the house with a jerk of his head.

Trout looked up at the house, and then he saw her standing at the window, looking out at them.

"Her name's Keats," Wardell said.

"Yes sir."

"Why didn't you say something?" he asked after she had let him in the door.

"Say what?" She stood in the middle of the room, balanced on her crutches. She was wearing a Dairy Queen uniform — red jacket, white cap.

"Your daddy and my daddy . . ."

"So?"

"They went to high school together. They played football."

"So?"

"They played *The Game*."

If it meant a thing to her, she didn't let on. But then, Trout thought, she wasn't the one looking for answers. She seemed to know everything she needed to know. "How old are you?" he asked.

"None of your business."

"So?"

"Eighteen," she said. "Are you just gonna stand there all day? Sit down."

He looked around, spotted an overstuffed chair next to the front window, and sat down in it. She eased herself down on a sofa and laid her crutches on the floor beside her with a clatter. "You asked me if I'm pissed off because I'm crippled," she said. "I thought about that. I woke up in the middle of the night thinking about it. I haven't waked up in the middle of the night thinking about anything for a long time. Do I act like I'm pissed off?"

"You're . . . abrupt."

They sat there in silence for a moment. Trout looked about the room. It was small and cramped, just enough room for the sofa and overstuffed chair, a television set, a knickknack stand filled mostly with small framed photographs. A young man in uniform, another in cap and gown, a school photo of Keats in about the fifth grade, a snapshot of the whole family at a picnic table — Keats, about the same age as the school photo, crutches propped next to her on the bench. On the bottom shelf, a stack of library books. On the spine of one he could make out *Quo Vadis?* The fireplace had been bricked up and an oil heater stood on the hearth, vented with a flue that disappeared into the brickwork. There was an air conditioner mounted in a window next to the fireplace, but it wasn't on. On the opposite side of the room, a closed door. A bedroom, maybe. And through an open doorway at the back, he could see a small kitchen — sink, counter, refrigerator, cabinets, a chrome-and-Formica breakfast table. It was neat, everything spotless. A woman lived here.

"Is your mother home?"

"She works first shift." Trout gave her a blank look. "At the mill." Another blank look. "You know about shifts?"

"No."

"Good God. Your family owns the place."

"Look," he said irritably, "I've been here four days. I've only been in the mill one time in my life, and that was last Saturday." He had forgotten his fatigue for a while, but he could feel its ragged edge wearing at him again. He really ought to go home and go to bed. He looked out the window. Joe Pike and Wardell Dubarry were engaged in heated conversation next to the Ford. Wardell was waving his arms. Joe Pike stood there, red-faced, hands jammed in his pockets.

"The mill has two shifts," Keats said. He turned back to her. "It used to have three. First shift, eight in the morning until four in the afternoon. Second shift, four till midnight. Third shift, midnight till eight. They cut out third shift a couple of years ago. There wasn't enough work. They laid a lot of people off. Those that hung on to their jobs were glad to have 'em."

Trout looked at his watch. Three-thirty. "Your mother works first shift."

"Yeah. And Daddy works second. About the time Mama gets home, Daddy's going to work."

"Why do they do that?"

Keats snorted angrily, "Ask your Aunt Alma. It was her doing."

Trout didn't want to talk about Aunt Alma. So he said, "And you work at Dairy Queen."

Keats got up suddenly with a clatter of crutches. "Not if I don't get my fanny on over there." She headed toward the door, and Trout jumped up from his chair to open it for her. "Don't you dare!" she snapped.

He stopped in his tracks, stared at her, felt the anger scurrying up the back of his neck, whispering in his ear. "Yeah," he snapped back. "You're pissed, all right. You're not just abrupt, you're mad as hell about something. I bet you come home after school and beat your gerbil." He stepped in front of her, opened the door, walked out on the porch, left the door open behind him, stood at the edge of the porch smoldering.

Down in the yard, Wardell Dubarry was saying to Joe Pike, "I am damned tired of regimentation and standardization, Joe Pike!"

"Regimentation and standardization?"

"Ever'body's gotta think alike, act alike, kiss ass alike!" He waved his arms at the house. "Ever'body's *house* gotta look alike, for God's sake! Hell, I oughta paint the place red! And go over yonder and paint Dooley Bledsoe's house blue! And Faye Looney's pink!"

"Fine!" Joe Pike finally exploded. "Paint 'em! I'm not gonna get in the middle of all this, Wardell!"

And Wardell was saying to Joe Pike, "You're already in the middle of it, Joe Pike!"

Then Keats was standing next to him on the porch. "Daddy . . . ," she said. Wardell broke off and looked up at her, and all the anger went out of him. "I got to be at work in fifteen minutes," she said. "Darnella quit and Herschel says I got to be in early."

"Sugar, the car ain't fixed yet."

"Daddyyyy . . . ," her voice rose.

"We'll take her," Joe Pike said.

Wardell gave him a sharp look. "I'll get her a ride."

"Look, it's my fault your car's not ready. It's no trouble."

"No thank you, Joe Pike," Wardell said stubbornly.

Then Keats clambered down the steps, crutches and legs flailing, and the rest of them just watched. It was amazing. She careened off toward Joe Pike's Dodge. "I'm gonna ride with Reverend Moseley, Daddy," she shot back over her shoulder. "Y'all could stand there jawing all day, and I'd be out of a job. Herschel doesn't care how I get there. I can't see why you do."

Wardell Dubarry did a slow burn, but there didn't seem to be much he could do about it. Keats reached the Dodge, opened the front door, threw her crutches inside, vaulted into the seat, slammed the door behind her.

Trout walked down the steps, giving Joe Pike and Wardell a wide berth, and waited by the car for a moment; then he got in the back seat and rolled down the window. Keats didn't look at him.

Out in the yard, the two men stood glaring at each other. Trout wondered what he would do if they started fighting. Call Uncle Cicero? But the mill village wasn't even in the city limits. Never had been, never would be. As Phinizy had told him, Broadus Moseley had seen to that. *Maybe, if it comes to blows, I'll just lean over the seat and start honking the horn.* Or he might just let them go at it for a while. It might be a pretty good match. Joe Pike had a sizable weight advantage, but Wardell Dubarry looked a good deal faster. And he had long arms. But somehow, he couldn't imagine Joe Pike fighting. For his size and history, he was a gentle man. Wardell Dubarry — now there was a different story. He looked like he might fight you at the drop of a hat. Wardell Dubarry, in fact, looked downright nasty.

But they didn't fight. After a moment, Trout heard Joe Pike say, "Wardell, I can't help it if my name's Moseley. Call it a genetic defect if you want." Wardell just glared at him. So Joe Pike shrugged, turned on his heel, and got in the car.

They were halfway to the Dairy Queen before anybody said anything. Joe Pike said, "That's what I want to do when I grow up."

Keats gave him a strange look. "What?"

"Work at Dairy Queen." They rode on in silence a while longer. "Actually, I've always thought of Dairy Queen as a sort of religious experience. Anything that's good for the soul, that's a religious experi-ence. And the taste of a spoonful of ice cream sliding down your throat is good for the soul. It may be what they had in mind when they talked about the Rapture."

"What's your favorite?" Keats asked.

"Oh, just the plain old vanilla. But I hasten to add there is not a loser on the menu. Sometimes I like a little crushed pineapple sundae or a chocolate shake. If you want to talk about a three-course meal, I'll go for two foot-long chili dogs and a banana split."

"Actually, the Blizzard is my favorite. Only sometimes I juice it up a little bit with some extra nuts or maybe even a splotch of butterscotch. You like butterscotch?"

"Yes ma'am," Joe Pike said. "I do dearly love butterscotch. Especially from Dairy Queen."

Good grief, Trout thought. *This is ridiculous. To hell with both of them.* And he put his head down on the seat and went to sleep.

Joe Pike banged on his door at six the next morning. "Trout, time to roll out."

"I'm not going," Trout said.

There was a long silence and then Joe Pike said, "Can I come in?" Joe Pike and Irene had both been good about that, asking before they entered. Especially the last few years. You never knew what a teenage boy might be doing alone in his room. But even if he wasn't doing anything he wouldn't want you to barge in on, it was his space. They both seemed to understand that. In fact, Joe Pike had said to him a couple of years ago, "Whatever you're doing in there, it's okay. You can't do it too much: you won't go blind, you won't grow black hairs on the palm of your hand. Later on, you'll move on to other things. When you're ready to do that, you come talk to me." It was the closest they had ever come to a birds-and-bees talk. It was enough for the time being. It had eased Trout's mind considerably. But later, when it seemed he might get into Cynthia Stuckey's pants, he didn't go talk to Joe Pike. It just didn't seem the thing to do.

"Come on in," Trout said now, "But I'm not going."

Joe Pike eased open the door and peeked into the room. Trout sat up in bed.

"Why aren't you going? Are you sick?"

Trout thought for a moment. "It's a holiday."

"What holiday?"

"Confederate Memorial Day."

Joe Pike shook his head. "Confederate Memorial Day was last month."

"But we didn't celebrate it."

Outside the open window, they heard a lawn mower start up. Joe Pike walked over to the window and looked out. "Morning," he called to whomever was outside. "Can I help you?"

"Miz Alma sent me," said a man's voice.

"That's quite all right," Joe Pike called out. "You tell Miz Alma I cut my own grass." The lawn mower engine coughed and died. "But I really appreciate it," Joe Pike said. "God bless you. And Miz Alma."

He closed the window. "I think we'll turn the air on today. Radio said it's gonna get up to ninety. And ain't even June yet. Of course, that's Atlanta. I was listening to the Atlanta station. Always hotter in Atlanta because of all that concrete. But still . . ." his voice trailed off. He stood next to Trout's bed. "So?"

"I'll stay home and cut the grass," Trout said.

"How about school?"

"I've enjoyed about all of Moseley High School I can stand for one year," Trout said.

"Two days?"

"There's only three left. School's out Friday."

Joe Pike shrugged. "I guess I'm thinking of the principle of the thing. I always like to see a fellow finish what he starts."

"Well, I'm finished," Trout said.

"Hmmmm. Well, come on and eat breakfast. It's on the table. We'll talk about it."

Joe Pike had fixed scrambled eggs, instant grits, slightly burned toast. It was a modest improvement. For a while after they took Irene away, the toast was inedible, the instant grits were watery, the eggs lumpy. So Trout had taken over cooking breakfast. Joe Pike seemed not to notice. He was working on the motorcycle at the time, and there was a lot he didn't notice.

Trout smeared blackberry jelly on the toast, and when he took the first bite, he discovered he was ravenous. He had gone straight to bed after they got home the previous afternoon and slept through the night. Now he cleaned his plate in silence. Joe Pike fixed him two more pieces of toast and he ate those and finally sat back in his chair.

"Is it that bad?"

"It was pretty good."

"No. I mean school."

Trout thought about it for a moment. "Nobody talks to me. They look straight through me, like I'm not there. Everybody but Keats Dubarry."

"Why Keats?"

"I think she thinks I'm some sort of freak. I don't know. She's weird. She's mad at the world."

"Hmmmm. I guess she comes by it honest."

"What's her daddy mad at?"

"The Moseleys. Life. Lack of an auto parts store."

"Was he always that way?"

"Pretty much. It made him a fairly decent football player. Wardell always acted like somebody was trying to take something away from him. He'd fight you. Wardell played left end and I played right tackle. Run one way, there was Wardell. Run the other, there was me. We did some damage."

"Were you friends?"

"I always thought so. With Wardell, it was hard to tell sometimes."

"Did he play football in college?"

"No. Actually, Wardell had an offer. Partial scholarship at a little junior college in Mississippi. But he didn't take it."

"Why not?" Trout asked.

"I don't know. 'Cause he's Wardell, I guess."

"What were you arguing about yesterday?"

Joe Pike's face clouded. "Nothing you need to worry about, son."

"Stop it!" Trout shouted before he could catch himself. Joe Pike's mouth dropped open. Trout couldn't ever remember yelling at his father before. He ducked his head and stared at his plate. But the anger didn't go away. It was a new thing, this anger. Strange and a bit frightening. And it seemed to insist on taking up residence.

"Trout?"

"You won't *talk* to me. Nobody *talks* to me. Nobody *tells* me anything. You all talk in riddles. You tell me what I oughta do, what I oughta think, how I oughta act. But you don't tell me why!" He looked up. "Why? What's going on here?"

Joe Pike took a long time to answer. Trout could see him wrestling with himself, and he realized that there was a lot maybe even Joe Pike didn't know. But dang it, he could tell him what he did know!

Finally, Joe Pike said, "There's trouble at the mill."

"I know that. Aunt Alma said so at dinner Sunday."

"To hear Wardell tell it, they're all riled up over there. Pay's abysmal; they think some of the working conditions are unsafe. Folks working off the clock —"

"What's that?"

"Everybody has a time card. You punch it when you go to work, again when you leave. They call it 'clocking in' and 'clocking out.' Only, some folks clock out and then have to turn around and go right back to work for another hour or so."

"Without getting paid?"

"Yes."

"Isn't that illegal?"

"Yes."

"Why do they do it?"

"Word gets around. Want to keep your job, you put in a few extra hours."

"What does Mister Dubarry want you to do about it?"

"Stop it."

"Can you?"

Joe Pike ran his fingers through his hair, wiggled his head from side to side for a moment, and looked out the kitchen window at the church building next door. Then back at Trout. "I don't run the mill. Alma does."

Then Trout said quietly, "But you're a Moseley."

"Yes."

"Mister Dubarry said you're in the middle whether you like it or not."

"Yes. That's what Wardell said."

They sat there awhile pondering that. And then Joe Pike said emphatically, "I don't need this. I just damned well don't need this."

"Are you sorry we came?"

"We didn't really have much of a choice, Trout."

"Because the Bishop said so?"

"Partly. Circumstances, you know . . ." He waved in the general direction of the storage shed out back. The motorcycle. All it represented.

"What happened in the game?" Trout asked.

"You mean *The Game?*"

"Yes. The extra point."

Joe Pike looked out the window, brows knitted, thinking back. "I fell down," he said finally.

"Fell down?"

Joe Pike looked back at him. "We scored with thirty seconds to go. Twenty-one to twenty. Coach Blaylock sent in twenty-five slant smash for the extra point."

"What's that?"

"A play. Quarterback hands the ball off to the left halfback, he slants across and runs behind the right tackle."

"Why didn't you kick the extra point?"

"In 1953 in Georgia high-school football, kicking an extra point was considered sissy."

"Why do they call the play 'smash'?"

A flicker of a smile played around the corners of Joe Pike's mouth. "Because I'm the right tackle and I'm the biggest, meanest sonofabitch on the line of scrimmage."

Trout was taken aback. He had never heard Joe Pike use the word before. But this was Joe Pike the football player, a person from the past, long before preaching, long before Trout. "And you . . ."

"Fell down. My feet got tangled up and I just fell flat on my face. The halfback climbed clear up my back, but he couldn't get over the top. Linebacker nailed him. Didn't gain an inch."

Trout thought about Orzell Blaylock, sitting there in the principal's office with the trophy gathering dust behind him on the air conditioner. Runner-up. "I think Mister Blaylock's still mad about it."

"I imagine they all are," Joe Pike said. "For most folks, it was the biggest thing that ever happened here, being in the state championship game. But for a Moseley, it might not be such a big deal, you see. The only Moseley in the whole stadium was me. I fell down, but I got up and went on with my life. Went places and saw things. Rest of 'em . . . well, they just stayed here."

"Didn't your mama and daddy come to the game?"

"No."

They sat there and mulled it over in silence. There didn't seem to be much more to say. Then Joe Pike heaved himself up out of his chair with a grunt and busied himself, stacking the breakfast dishes, carrying them to the sink where he added them to a growing pile. Aunt Alma had installed a brand-new dishwasher in the kitchen, but Joe Pike was wary of it. A man who could take apart a motorcycle and put it back together, buffaloed by a dishwasher. He turned to Trout, leaned against the counter. "So, what are we going to do about this incipient rebellion?"

"What?"

"Your refusing to go to school."

Trout shrugged.

"You want me to tell you something? Okay, I'll tell you something I've never told you before." Trout sat quietly, waiting. "You've surprised me, Trout. You were a terror as a little kid. Always into something. Testing the limits. When you were two, we used to sit down at the table for a meal and I'd say, 'Okay, Trout, turn over your milk so we can get started.' And you would. Or maybe you wouldn't. Just sit there and scrunch up your face and look at me." Joe Pike smiled, remembering. "I used to think, this is going to be one pain-in-the-butt teenager. But then all of a sudden you seemed to get over it. And the older you got, the easier you were to handle. It was like the hormones worked in reverse on you. You sort of mellowed out. "

Mellowed out? Damn, he really missed that one. There was no mellowing about it. If anything, just the opposite. There was that point a few years before when he had become aware of the growing tension in the house — of disappointment, dissatisfaction, even anger. He could *feel* it. And he began to feel it at approximately the same time he began to stumble into puberty. The two, he assumed, must at least in some part be connected — a noisy, messy, awkward kid underfoot, body changing alarmingly, voice squeaking, moods swinging wildly. Maybe they had taken a look at him one day and said to themselves, *What is going on here? We wanted a kid, but this little gawky freak?* He wanted to ask questions, but Irene was so quiet and distant, Joe Pike so preoccupied, he didn't know how to approach them. So he did the only thing he could think of. He tried to be good. He picked up his clothes, kept his room reasonably clean, tried not to slam doors or complain about the steady diet of oldies on the radio. When he had a wet dream, he was careful to wash out his pajamas in the bathroom lavatory before he put them in the laundry hamper. He even tried to like math and rutabagas. He was sure, somehow, that if he were truly good, if he made no mess and caused no uproar or embarrassment, Irene would get better and Joe Pike would come to himself and things would be right again. Instead, the silences deepened. So he tried harder than ever. And the harder he tried, the more the silences deepened until finally they took Irene away and left the great emptiness, left Trout baffled and exhausted. No matter how hard he had tried, it wasn't enough. But by then, he had formed the habit of being desperately good. He didn't quite know how to go about being bad. Marijuana made him throw up. Girls with bad reputations scared the hell out of him. The one time he would have willingly sinned, ached to sin, Cynthia Stuckey had stopped him. He was quite sick of all this goodness, but he felt trapped. And too, he was still a preacher's kid and that carried a certain aloneness with it. There was still Joe Pike to think of. But mellow? Horseshit.

"Your mother and I got real worried a couple of years ago," Joe Pike said. "We thought maybe you were on drugs."

"Drugs?"

"Did you ever mess around with drugs?"

"Well . . ." He shrugged, feeling both uncomfortable and irritated. This wasn't what he wanted — a psychoanalysis or a counseling session. He simply wanted to know what was going on. "I'm a preacher's kid," he said.

"Not easy, I know," Joe Pike said. "Not easy being a preacher, either, but at least I've got a pulpit to stand behind."

"Yeah. I guess."

"Well, anyway, we decided you weren't on drugs. You'd just gotten easy to deal with. We decided not to worry about it. Don't look a gift horse in the mouth, you know. But now . . ." He waved his hands and his voice rose dramatically. "Here we have rank disobedience. Open defiance. Rebellion! Anarchy! Domestic chaos!"

Trout considered it for a moment. He gave Joe Pike a careful look. "Why don't you punish me," he said.

"How?"

"Make me learn to ride the motorcycle."

They headed out U.S. 278 toward Atlanta about five miles, Joe Pike wearing his cowboy boots and a battered white helmet that made him look something like the Texas A&M football picture in his church study. Trout rode behind — bareheaded because there was only the one helmet, several sizes too big for him — holding on and craning his neck to see around Joe Pike's bulk. They turned onto a paved rural road, went another mile or so, and pulled off beneath a big oak tree in the bare yard of an abandoned farmhouse. It was a weathered, windowless ghost of a place with a high, sagging porch, vines creeping up the rock chimney, a riot of weeds around the sides and back of the house.

Joe Pike killed the engine. Trout slid off the back of the motorcycle; then Joe Pike let down the kickstand and got off and took off the helmet and tucked it under his arm. Trout climbed onto the seat, put his hands on the handlebars, gripped them, wiggled his fanny. It leaned to the left on the kickstand, so he put his feet on the ground and eased it upright. The cycle felt massive between his legs, warm leather and chrome, heat baking off the engine. He felt a vague stirring in his groin. *Gee. It's like . . .*

"A woman," Joe Pike said. Trout's ears reddened. He looked up at Joe Pike, who wiggled his eyebrows. Then he looked away, across the road to where rows of new corn were pushing up through the brown loam of a plowed field. It struck Trout. *It's been four months. No sounds behind the closed door late at night. What does he . . .* Trout's ears felt as if they might burst into flame.

"Start 'er up," Joe Pike said. He pointed. "Turn the key. Now, that pedal there is the starter. Stomp down on it." Trout stomped. The pedal barely moved. The engine coughed. "You're kinda light. Sort of jump on it." Trout stomped again, using the weight of his body, and the engine fired. "Now a little gas. That's the throttle over there." He goosed the throttle, the way he had seen Joe Pike do. The cycle vibrated under him, through him.

Joe Pike showed him the clutch and brake levers, the gearshift. Neutral and three forward gears. "Ready?"

Trout took a deep breath. It was a little scary. "I guess."

"Kickstand up." Joe Pike used the toe of his cowboy boot to raise the kickstand. "Okay. It's in neutral. Clutch lever in, drop it down into first gear." Trout heard a click as the gear engaged. "Now, it's just like driving a straight-stick car, except you got two wheels instead of four. Give it some throttle as you let the clutch out." Clutch and throttle. He raced the engine a bit, released the clutch. Too quick. The bike jumped a couple of feet, died, started falling to the left. Whoa! Trout struggled, toppling, losing it, panic racing through him. But then Joe Pike dropped the helmet and grabbed the cycle, wrestled it with his powerful arms like a cowboy bulldogging a steer and steadied it. "Okay?"

Trout's heart was pounding in his ears. "I guess."

"Want to call it a day? Try it another time? It's okay if you do."

"No." It was important to do this. It was the first thing they had done together for a long time. If he could pull this off, there might be something in it for both of them. And they both, he thought, needed a little something.

Joe Pike gave him a close look, then patted the handlebars as he would a horse he was trying to gentle. "This isn't a big bike as motorcycles go. Two-hundred-fifty-cubic-inch engine. But still, you got a lot of weight here, son. And it can get away from you in a hurry, like just now. But you can control it as long as you keep moving forward. Momentum helps you keep your balance. A motorcycle's kinda like a person. Gotta keep moving. Stand in one place long enough, and sooner or later you'll topple over."

"Yes sir."

"All right. Try it again."

Trout went through the routine again. Gearshift in neutral. Stomp. *RUMMM-UM-UM-UM.* Clutch in, drop it into low. Throttle. *RUMMMMMMMM-UM-UM.* Joe Pike stepped back and gave him room. Clutch out. He was moving!

"Little more gas! Not too much!"

Joe Pike ambled along beside him, keeping a hand on the rear of the cycle as Trout made a wide turn around the oak tree, wobbling a bit as the bike bumped across the uneven bare dirt. They made several slow, cautious circles of the yard, Trout's heart racing far faster than the engine, but after a while beginning to feel the bike steady underneath him.

"Little more gas," Joe Pike said. "Momentum."

Trout gave it a bit more throttle, and then suddenly Joe Pike wasn't there with him anymore. He was standing next to the steps of the old house, arms folded across his chest, watching. Trout circled several more times and finally eased up toward where Joe Pike stood. He called out. "Clutch in. Brake on. Ease to a stop. Get your feet down. Control it."

Trout stopped the bike and balanced it between his legs, both feet on the ground. He felt giddy. "Okay?"

"You look like you're about to go into labor. Relax."

"Okay."

"Now try the road."

"The road?"

"You wanta ride the thing, don't you?"

"Yes sir."

"Well, you're gonna get pretty bored making ruts in the yard here. Ain't but one way to learn how to ride a motorcycle, son. That's ride it."

"You think I'll be okay? I don't have a helmet."

Joe Pike looked out at the paved road and stared at it for a long moment. Then he looked back at Trout, put a big hand on his shoulder and squeezed ever so slightly. "Just take it easy. Respect the machine, keep your mind on your business, give everybody else lots of room. *Lots* of room. The minute you get cocky, that's when you get in trouble." He smiled. "Take your time. Have fun."

"What are you gonna do?"

Joe Pike picked up the helmet and turned away, walked over and sat down on the sagging bottom step of the old farmhouse, set the helmet down beside him, and hunched forward with his elbows on his knees. He clasped his hands. "I'll be deep in prayer and supplication. Yea, verily." He gave a tiny wave. "Go."

Trout went. Slowly, gingerly at first, keeping it in first gear several hundred yards up the road, getting the feel of the blacktop underneath the bike. Then he held his breath and dropped it down into second gear, gave it some gas and felt a shock of power as the bike leaped ahead. He looked down at the speedometer. Thirty. Then he topped a small rise and a bad thing happened. A small squat house on the left, a pickup truck in the yard. And a dog. Streaking for the road, yapping madly as he approached. "Shit!" he yelled in terror. The dog had an angle on him, a blur of black out of the corner of his eye, almost on him now, going for his leg! Headline: BOY, CYCLE EATEN BY MONGREL. Then — it was a reflex motion, an instinct for survival — he gunned the throttle with a vicious snap of his wrist, and the motorcycle almost jumped out from under him, engine screaming. AIYYYYHHHH! And suddenly he was past the farmhouse and the dog. A quick glance in the rearview mirror. The dog brought up short at the edge of the pavement, staring at his disappearing back, tongue lolling.

Trout flew! There was nothing now but the whine of the cycle, pavement flashing underneath, a rush of brown and green on either side. His heart was in his throat, eyes bugging. Third gear! He dropped it down, felt another jolt of power and then the bike settling beneath him, a marvelous streaking, growling cat gobbling up great lengths of asphalt. Another quick glance at the speedometer. Fifty. It felt like five hundred. The wind roared in his ears, whipped at his hair, teared his eyes. He was scared out of his wits and at the same time thrilled beyond anything he had ever experienced. *Godawmighty!* He leaned into the wind and rode in a state of grace for what seemed a hundred miles before he saw a stop sign ahead where the road dead-ended into another at the top of a hill. He realized it was the road that ran between town and the Interstate. He could see I-20 off to his right, cars and semis barreling along on the concrete. And off to the left, the Dairy Queen.

He rode down that way and turned around at the edge of the parking lot. It was midmorning, slack time. Only a Sheriff's Department car parked in front, a deputy lounging at the window, sipping coffee, talking to somebody inside, paying no attention to the fact that Trout was violating the Georgia Motorcycle Helmet Law. Next to the deputy, a HELP WANTED sign was taped to the plate glass.

He thought about Keats and the rest of them over at Moseley High School. Maybe wondering where the invisible kid was, maybe thinking they had scared him off. Well, to hell with them. He wasn't going back, not this school year. Three months until September. He would think of something. By September a giant meteor might have hit the earth. WHAM! Clouds of dust. A run on gas masks. Anything could happen. In the meantime, he could ride the motorcycle. On a motorcycle, you could outrun a lot.

He turned around and headed back. It wasn't a hundred miles after all. Maybe five. But he rode like a bat out of hell, and when he passed the house with the dog, the cur didn't make it halfway to the road before Trout had roared past.

Joe Pike was sprawled across the steps of the farmhouse, eyes closed. Prayer and supplication. Trout turned in, gunned the cycle, made another quick circle of the yard, stopped in front of Joe Pike, and killed the engine. Joe Pike finally opened his eyes. "Was it okay?"

"Yes sir. It sure was okay." And Trout saw then in Joe Pike's eyes a little of what it must mean to let go of something or someone.

But there was something else, a thing shared, a message passed and

silently acknowledged. Trout understood a little bit about the motorcycle. About Texas. It wasn't so much the getting there as it was the
going. That was the thing.

Joe Pike was gone all afternoon. Trout hung around the house, listened to some James Taylor . . . *in my mind I'm going to Carolina* . . .
read a couple of articles in a tennis magazine, took a nap. Woke up in
a state of excitement, thinking of Cynthia Stuckey. Gave in quite willingly to temptation. He was doing that a lot, he thought. But it was
one of the few things he had much control over these days.

He wandered out to the storage shed in back of the parsonage and
wiped down the motorcycle with the chamois cloth Joe Pike kept
hanging on a nail. Then he threw a tennis ball against the side of the
storage shed. *Thwock . . . thwock . . . thwock.*

He tired of that after a while, sat down in the backyard swing, and
stayed there for a long time thinking about the morning, the motorcycle. He could still feel the tingle through his body — vibration of
the engine, rush of the wind — the precarious strangeness of it.

Then he thought about Joe Pike on the motorcycle, going all the
way from Georgia to Texas with the Holy Ghost riding behind, whispering in his ear. Mile after mile disappearing under the wheels of the
Triumph. One hill, one curve after another. The sun tracking his
movement — rising at his back, setting in his face, disappearing over a
horizon he could never quite reach.

It was a very unpreacherlike thing, riding a motorcycle. Trout knew
of a Methodist minister over in Tennessee who was much sought after
as a stand-up comic, renowned for his religious humor. An oddity, but
not beyond the pale. Several in Joe Pike's own conference were pretty
fair golfers; a good number were prodigious fishermen. Perhaps the
most unusual was the one with the glass eye. He had been a counselor
one summer at Methodist Summer Camp, in charge of a cabin full of
fourth-grade boys including Trout. Bedtime the first night had been a
rowdy affair until the preacher took out his glass eye, placed it on the
window sill next to his bunk, and said, "Boys, I'm gonna be watching
you all night," then turned over and went to sleep, surrounded by
profound silence.

But not a single preacher Trout could think of had a motorcycle.

Joe Pike had always been a little unconventional — awesome in height and girth, a bit boisterous, given to occasionally nudging the limits of preacherly decorum. Nonetheless, a preacher who knew where the boundaries were, the way his son knew what a preacher's kid could and couldn't get away with. But now, Joe Pike had a motorcycle, gave no evidence of being the slightest bit uneasy about it, even after his escapade, and now had taken his hooky-playing son and taught him how to ride the darned thing. In doing so, he had cracked the door — intentionally or not — on an entire beyond-the-limits world. What was Joe Pike trying to tell him?

And how much of all that had to do with this *place* — this Moseley, Georgia, with its own set of strange and unsettling vibrations, undercurrents, mysteries? Its history, as Great Uncle Phinizy had recounted it, much of it bound up in who Joe Pike Moseley was, what he had been and become?

All of this caromed around inside Trout's head as he sat there in the swing, making him a little dizzy with the possibilities. He was thinking too much again, an old sin. He could hear the voice of his tennis coach back in Ohatchee: "Stop thinking, Trout! Just play!"

It was getting late, the shank of the afternoon falling on the backyard. He got up and went in the house, turned on the TV set in time for the six o'clock news from Atlanta. *President Carter, just back from a weekend with his top advisors at Camp David, says the nation is gripped by a great malaise . . .*

Then he heard Joe Pike pulling in the driveway in the Dodge. He turned off the TV and met Joe Pike at the door. He was carrying two boxes. One was white cardboard, rectangular. Trout could tell what was in that. A cake. The other box was square, gift wrapped.

When they had finished dinner, Joe Pike lit the sixteen candles on the cake with a flourish and pranced around the table and sang "Happy Birthday" with great off-key vigor. He was almost like the old Joe Pike Moseley, never happier than at a celebration of some sort, and Trout began to believe that things might turn out all right after all. He laughed until his sides hurt.

Then he opened the other box.

It was a motorcycle helmet. Red with a streak of gold lightning down each side.

SIX

THE REST OF the week passed uneventfully. Trout Moseley didn't go back to Moseley High, which ended the school year without ceremony at midmorning on Friday and graduated a class of thirty-five on Friday night in the football stadium. A lieutenant colonel from the Army post in Augusta gave the commencement speech, in which he espoused thrift, hard work, loyalty, and unyielding opposition to communism in all its forms. None of the Moseley family were in attendance. But when Trout and Joe Pike dined with Aunt Alma and Uncle Cicero on Thursday evening, Alma let it be known that Orzell Blaylock had called some time ago to solicit her opinion of the lieutenant colonel as a commencement speaker, and she had approved. Aunt Alma, on behalf of the family, had awarded a five-hundred-dollar scholarship to the top graduate, a girl who would be attending the Massey-Draughon Business College in Atlanta.

Aunt Alma did one other singular thing. Joe Pike happened to mention Trout's unhappiness over the lack of a tennis court in Moseley, and she arranged with friends in Augusta for Trout to play at the Augusta Racquet and Swim Club. "I want Trout to have every opportunity to fulfill himself," she said. "Papa didn't hold with tennis, and neither do I. But who says we all have to be the same?"

Joe Pike drove him to Augusta on Friday afternoon and Trout spent an hour with the club pro, who worked with him on his backhand.

Then Trout played a rousing match against the club's top sixteen-year-old, summoned especially for the occasion. He was a gangly young man with a wicked serve but little else, and once Trout got over his nervousness and figured out the boy's game, he won fairly easily. It felt good, having a racquet in his hands again, losing himself in the rhythm of competition.

After the match they retired to the veranda of the clubhouse overlooking the swimming pool — Joe Pike, Trout, his vanquished opponent, and the club pro — and talked about the State Juniors coming up. Both boys would be playing for the first time in the sixteen-to-eighteen division; neither would be seeded. But they all agreed that Trout might have a chance to pull off a surprise or two in the opening rounds. He had a decent serve-and-volley game and played the net as if he owned it. The backhand, that was the thing. Sometimes it was passable. Often it was as limp as a wet noodle. Only Trout knew how truly miserable it could be. He knew that if a savvy opponent caught him on a day when his backhand deserted him, he was a dead duck. But the club pro invited him back the next week for another session. They would work on it.

Sitting there at a table under a red-and-yellow-striped umbrella, sipping Cokes, kids splashing about in the sun-dazzled pool below, the *thwock-thwock* of smartly struck tennis balls echoing from the courts beyond, Moseley seemed worlds away. When he and Joe Pike climbed into the car for the drive back, Trout felt again like a pilgrim, going into a far, strange land.

On Sunday morning he awoke early and went out to get the paper from the driveway. That was when he noticed the sign on the church marquee next door: TODAY'S SERMON — THE GOSPEL ACCORDING TO ELVIS. He stood there and stared at it for a long time. *Uh-oh.*

Trout thought the crowd in the pews this Sunday seemed a smidgen larger than last week's. There was a scattering of unfamiliar faces sitting alongside the faithful who had been occupying the same places for years. Maybe the sign out front had something to do with it. Elvis. Dead for about a year now, drawing people into a church, of all places.

Trout sat with Aunt Alma and Uncle Cicero in their accustomed place, front and center. Aunt Alma gave him a curt nod when she and Cicero walked in and sat down, then crossed her legs, smoothed her dress, folded her hands primly in her lap. Cicero gave him a sly wink. Cicero the Baptist. *What are you crazy Methodists up to today?* Trout wondered if he ever attended the Baptist church on the opposite end of town. Probably not, he thought. Cicero seemed to do pretty much what Aunt Alma expected. Just before the choir marched in to start the service, Trout glanced back and saw Uncle Phinizy slip into a back pew. *Wake up Charlie. He ain't never seen a real bad wreck before.* Joe Pike ambled in behind the choir and took his seat behind the pulpit. Trout noted that Joe Pike was wearing plain black lace-up shoes. At least no cowboy boots.

They sang a couple of hymns, mumbled through the responsive reading, took up the collection, and sang the Doxology. Then Joe Pike got up and announced that he was starting a physical fitness group called Jumping for Jesus, in the spirit of keeping the Lord's Holy Temple (the body) fit and pure, starting with his own. He made a little joke about Dairy Queen being a religious experience, which drew a titter of laughter from the congregation. Aunt Alma's expression never changed.

Then Joe Pike delivered a long, rambling Pastoral Prayer and they sang the Gloria Patri and one more hymn. Joe Pike stood tall and massive behind the pulpit, waiting for the congregation to settle in the pews, arranged his notes on the big leather Bible before him. He looked out over the crowd, his gaze moving slowly from one side of the church to the other.

Then Joe Pike made the little hissing sound through his teeth and said, "I've come to realize in the past few weeks that we may find interesting things in unsuspected places if we're open to the possibility of doing that. The word for it, I think, is *serendipity*. It's not in the Bible, but I think it may have a religious connotation in a universe of uniqueness and wonder. Serendipity. A small boy walks along the sidewalk, looks down and finds a dollar bill. Or maybe a toadfrog. They're about the same to a small boy." He smiled, and the congregation smiled with him. "Serendipity. Messages come in all sorts of bottles, washing up on the shore of whatever ocean we happen to be walking along at the time. And there are all sorts of things we might loosely define as Scripture. So — " he took a deep breath " — today's Scripture comes from RCA Victor." He gathered himself up, clasped his hands in front of him like a small boy considering a newly found toadfrog, and sang:

"Are you lonesome tonight? Do you miss me tonight?
Are you sorreeee we drifted apaaaarrrt?"

Trout winced. It was awful. Joe Pike changed keys at least three times before he finished. At Trout's side, Aunt Alma said softly, "Sweet Jesus." Trout would have given a good deal of money to see the look on her face. But he contented himself with cutting a glance at her lap, where her knuckles were turning white around the handle of her purse. Trout expected to hear bodies falling out of pews onto the floor *THUD,* but it was stone-quiet in the church. Sort of like standing on the edge of a sheer cliff, looking off into nothing, your heart in your throat.

"Dear old Elvis," Joe Pike said. "Now, I don't want to appear blasphemous or anything, but have you ever thought about the similarities between Elvis and Jesus?" His gaze swept the congregation. No, they hadn't thought about that, Trout imagined. Not a single one of them had ever considered the possibility. Or suspected that anyone else would.

"Elvis and Jesus," Joe Pike went on. "Both of them born to humble beginnings, both powerfully influenced by their mothers. At a fairly early age, each came to realize in his own way that he wasn't ordinary. There was something special he was meant to do and be. Each became a messiah in his own way. Elvis, for his part, proclaimed a new American music. When he opened his mouth and sang, everything changed. A lot of disciples, a lot of false prophets came along later, but Elvis was the original."

There was some audible shuffling about in the pews now. Trout couldn't stand it any longer. He looked up at Aunt Alma. Her face was drained of color. There was a trace of panic around her eyes. He thought that any minute she might jump up and call out to Joe Pike, "Wait! Don't go there!" Trout looked back at Joe Pike, all alone up there behind the pulpit. All alone, way out on a limb, about to crank up the chain saw.

"I suppose the resemblance ends there. Elvis was a pretty good old boy from what you hear, had a decent raising and all. But fame got him. He couldn't stay away from those pills. Died on a cross of chemistry, and climbed up on it all by himself. But just because Elvis came to a bad end doesn't mean we can't learn something from him. In fact, I think God dearly loves a sinner. If He can't save him, He can use him as an example. We do the same thing: 'Looky there, young'uns. Mess around with that rock-and-roll music, you'll end up like Elvis. Or worse.'"

Joe Pike took a moment, shuffled his notes a bit, looked up again. "Now, what was it old Elvis was talking about when he sang, 'Are you lonesome tonight? Do you miss me tonight? Are you sorry we drifted apart?' Anybody want to hazard a guess?"

It was deathly quiet in the church. *What is this,* Donahue? *Class discussion? Preachers don't carry on a dialogue with the congregation. Preachers preach. Congregations listen.* Joe Pike waited. Trout remembered him standing before the Easter congregation in Ohatchee, sweating and miserable. Trout should have gone to him then. But instead, he had let Joe Pike ride off to Texas. Not again.

"A girl?" Trout blurted. Every head in the place turned to look at him. He could feel their eyes.

Joe Pike gave him a grateful smile. "Probably," he said. "Probably a girl. But" — he raised a finger, held it in midair — "what if he was talking about God. Is that possible?"

"I reckon," Trout said. Too late to stop now.

"Just for the sake of serendipity, let's consider that. Let's imagine that God is out there" — his arm swept toward the ceiling — "wherever it is we put Him. We say, 'God's in heaven.' Okay, heaven. We all know heaven, right? Lots of clouds, choir music, angels loitering about, maybe some biscuits and red-eye gravy for breakfast, a trip to Dairy Queen every evening. Good things happen in heaven. It's a good place to put God. Right?"

Joe Pike looked out across the congregation again and Trout, to his amazement, saw Tilda Huffstetler, in the next pew, nod vigorously. *Good for you, Tilda.*

"So God's up there in this place called heaven, 'cause that's where we put Him. And we can borrow Him on Sunday morning or when we think we need something. Meanwhile, all of us mere mortals are down here on earth. And we're just sort of rocking along. Get up every morning, shave our faces, put on our makeup, bolt down a little breakfast, dash off to work or school. Work all day, stagger to the car and drive back home. Wore out. Frazzled. Get home, the toilet's stopped up, the baby's got the croup, a delinquent payment notice in the mail. Eat supper, watch *Laugh-In* on TV, or maybe listen to a little Elvis on the stereo. Go to bed. Do it all over tomorrow. Most of the time, we just do it. What else, huh? That's life. That's what people do. Right?"

Another pause. This time, Tilda Huffstetler and her husband Boolie both nodded. Trout thought about Tilda down there at the Koffee Kup Kafe all day, making those sweet potato pies, watching folks eat them, making some more. Just feeding their faces, over and over. Pies come and pies go. After you've been in *Southern Living*, what is there?

"We just rock along," Joe Pike said. "But every once in a while, we let our guard down and this feeling creeps up on us. Like there's something missing. I don't know, maybe I'm the only one. But every once in a while, just before I drift off to sleep, I say to myself, 'What's wrong, Joe Pike?' Actually, I've been saying that a good deal lately. What's wrong? What's missing? What is this odd feeling I keep getting? Upset stomach?"

Joe Pike rubbed his ample stomach, felt his forehead.

"Maybe if I take some Maalox, it'll go away." He opened an imaginary bottle, poured imaginary Maalox into an imaginary spoon, drank it down, smacked his lips and made a face. A titter of laughter from the congregation, quickly stifled. "Nope! Still there!" He screwed the cap back on the bottle, set it on the edge of the pulpit and stared at it for a moment. "Then I hear old Elvis sing this song:

Are you lonesome tonight? Do you miss me tonight?
Are you sorry we drifted apart?

This time, he sang it softly, plaintively, and it didn't sound quite so off-key. It sounded . . . what? Small. Scared. *Lonesome.*

"Lonesome," Joe Pike said. "Maybe I'm just lonesome. But you say, 'Wait a minute, Joe Pike! How could you be lonesome? You've got Trout, and he's a fine young man and carries on a good conversation. And you've got the rest of your fine family. And all these good people here in Moseley who helped raise you and who are pulling for you now to get your act together. A whole town full. How can you be lonesome, Joe Pike?' Well, I don't know. Why aren't you" — he waved his arm across the congregation — "enough? Why do I, a minister of the gospel, feel so disconnected from God? Why do those things you taught me in Sunday school when I was a kid, those things they taught me in seminary, not seem to work anymore? Why do I feel lonesome?" He leaned across the pulpit, arms clasped, his gaze slowly sweeping the sanctuary. "And why do you?"

He waited a long time and let that sink in while he searched their faces. Trout looked up at Aunt Alma. Her mouth was ajar, and the look of panic around her eyes had been replaced by something that resembled sadness. Trout stared, unable to help himself. It was something he hadn't seen before, and he understood in that instant that there *was* something sad about Aunt Alma, something she usually kept so private you might never imagine. But here, in the midst of this gathering, it was naked in her face. Joe Pike had unmasked her, if only for an instant. Perhaps it was what he said. Perhaps it was because *he* was the one who said it. Trout could see that for some reason he couldn't yet fathom, it was a terrible burden to be Alma Moseley and that in her most unguarded moments, it made her terribly sad. Just now, was she about to cry? No, he couldn't imagine Aunt Alma crying. But now, and it startled him to know it, he could imagine her going completely to pieces under the right circumstances.

Then Alma looked down at Trout and saw that he saw. Her face flushed. The mask came down again. But Trout thought, *She will always know that I know.*

Up in the pulpit, Joe Pike did not see. He was immersed in his own agony. There was sweat on his upper lip, and he was making the little hissing sound between his teeth. The little man inside the big body, trying to . . . what? Alma and Joe Pike: *they are* both *two people.*

Joe Pike gave a great sigh, like a man who has misplaced something and despairs, for the moment, of locating it. Enough of this muddling about for now, he seemed to say. Out loud he said, "Let's think about all that this week. I don't want to speak for anybody else or put any false notions into anybody's head. Let's just think about it. Are we lonesome for God? With all our praying and hymn-singing and Bible-reading and churchgoing and hallelujah-shouting, do we sometimes in our darkest moments get the suspicion, 'Uh-oh! He ain't here. And He ain't paying attention.' And if He ain't, why?"

Then Joe Pike gathered up his notes and sat down. There was a long, astonished silence. Finally, Aunt Alma cleared her throat. Just that, nothing more. Up in the choir loft, Grace Vredemeyer took it as a signal. She got up and led the final hymn.

Aunt Alma didn't come right to the point at Sunday dinner an hour later, the way Trout had thought she might. They ate — she, Cicero, Joe Pike and Trout — in surprising good humor.

Alma talked about going to New York to shop for clothes. And that surprised Trout, too. He couldn't imagine Aunt Alma shopping for clothes. Everything she wore seemed so severe, plain-cut and solid-colored, unadorned. He tried to imagine her in a floral print with bangle earrings. No.

Uncle Cicero told a long, rambling story about the flimflam artist from Atlanta who had tried to bilk Miz Estelle Collier out of some money the past week. For a thousand dollars, he said, he would spray her roof with a substance that would extend the life of the shingles for twenty years. Miz Estelle Collier had let him get up on the roof with his sprayer, then took his ladder down and called Cicero, who arrived to find the con man hollering from the rooftop. Big-city crime, trying to invade Moseley, thwarted by local savvy. The bumpkins win again. Cicero, as was his Sunday custom, was in uniform, prepared for afternoon patrol. His gun belt was hanging, as was the custom, on the hall rack.

Joe Pike listened to everything, made an appreciative grunt or gave a nod at appropriate times, and ate five pieces of fried chicken.

When they were finished with the main course, Alma had a surprise: dessert. In honor of Trout, she said. Trout started to ask why, but thought better of it. Did he look like he needed dessert? Probably. Even his layoff from tennis, even the daily trips to Dairy Queen, had failed to add a pound to his thin frame. He had his mother's slightness. So, dessert — albeit, a fruit concoction out of respect for Cicero's cholesterol. They were well into it, Cicero holding forth at some length about the unsteady state of the local economy, when Alma broke in and said, "Jimmy's becoming an embarrassment."

Joe Pike looked up at her. "Jimmy?"

"Carter," she said.

"The President."

"We went to the inauguration, you know," Alma said.

Cicero chimed in. "At the inaugural ball, they stuck us in the basement of the Smithsonian right next to the McCormick reaper. With

Guy Lombardo. Some drunk from Delaware spilled his drink down the front of Alma's gown."

"We had nice seats for the parade," Alma said.

"About five blocks from the White House," Cicero added.

Alma's jaw tightened. "And when the parade was over, we went to a lovely reception at the White House."

"With about ten thousand other people," Cicero said. "Everybody that gave more than a hundred dollars."

"It was," she insisted, raising her voice a bit, "a very nice affair. Jimmy and Rosalynn were very gracious."

"You know President Carter?" Trout asked.

"Of course," she said, turning to him. "I've supported Jimmy ever since he ran for governor."

Cicero grinned. "Alma's the kind of supporter who'll give you a hundred dollars and take an hour telling you how to spend it."

"Cicero . . ."

"Yes, dear?"

"Have you ever run for political office or been involved in a political campaign?"

"No, hon. I do hold public office, I guess you could say."

"Appointive. Not elective."

"That's exactly right."

"Then you are speaking from a lack of knowledge."

Cicero smiled at her. "I've always left the politics to you, hon." He looked at Trout and Joe Pike. "It's an old tradition in the Moseley family, supporting worthy candidates. As long as they're Democrats, of course. A hundred dollars and lots of advice. My people, now, they always worked it from the other end. Graft and corruption. Give a politician a thousand dollars and tell him to spend it any way he wants to. And then go back later and help divide up the spoils. Shoot, my people even had truck with Republicans, of all things."

"Your people . . . ," Alma said with an almost imperceptible shake of her head.

Cicero's smile broadened. "We have mostly married above ourselves. With the notable exception of Cousin Flint. He took up with a hooker from Macon."

"Cicero!" Alma cut a glance at Trout.

"I know what a hooker is," Trout said.

"Well, we don't talk about . . ." — she waved her hand in the general direction of Macon — ". . . at the table."

"It is, after all, Sunday," Joe Pike said, taking another bite of dessert.

Alma stared at Joe Pike. "Not," she said after a moment, "that you could tell it by everything that has transpired."

Okay. Here it is.

"Let me venture a guess," Joe Pike said. "You're speaking of my sermon."

"If you want to call it that."

"You took offense, I fear."

"It was an exhibition," she said flatly.

Joe Pike put his spoon down, leaned back in his chair, crossed his arms and waited on Alma. Uncle Cicero helped himself to some more dessert. Methodist trouble. No place for a good Baptist to be.

Trout heard the telephone ring up in the front hall. He hoped nobody would get up to answer it, because things seemed about ready to get interesting here. But nobody at the table seemed to hear it. It rang again and he heard Rosetta pick it up.

"The congregation has just about had enough," Alma was saying.

"Enough what?" Joe Pike asked.

"Enough of your public hand-wringing."

"Is that what I'm doing?"

"First it's the Holy Ghost on a motorcycle. Now it's Elvis as the messiah. My Lord, Joe Pike!"

There was a long silence, and then Joe Pike said, "I take it you're not open to serendipity."

"Serendipity has no place in church."

"And what does, Alma?"

"Scripture. Eternal truth. Godly verities."

"On Christ the solid rock I stand."

"Yes!"

Joe Pike shook his head slowly. "Well, to tell you the truth, Alma, I don't know where the rock is right now. I'm trying to find it."

"Then find it somewhere else, Joe Pike. Not in my church."

"Your church."

"Our church."

"No, I think you had it right the first time. It's not the congregation that's had enough, it's you. Personally."

"Yes I have," Alma said. "I am personally mortified. Embarrassed, to tell you the truth. My brother, making a spectacle of himself in the pulpit of the church his family founded. It's appalling. I am being totally honest with you here."

Joe Pike nodded slowly and thought about it for a moment. Then he leaned toward Alma, elbows on the table. "Did you notice anything unusual about the congregation this morning, Alma?"

"No."

"Did you, Trout?"

"Yes sir."

"What?"

Trout felt himself his father's ally here. "There were a few more of 'em."

"Yes, there were," Joe Pike said. "Out there amongst the vast" — he swept his arm through the air — "reaches of the sanctuary, amongst the empty pews, sprinkled in with the small band of faithful, were a few *new faces*. And there may be a few more *new faces* next Sunday."

"Is that why you put on a show?" Alma demanded. "To draw a crowd?"

"It was an honest effort to be" — he waved his hand again, searching for a word — "honest. And I believe I struck a responsive note with some in the congregation. I saw a few heads nod." He turned to Trout. "Did you see any heads nod?"

"Yea, verily," Trout said.

"Don't mock me, son. I do that well enough myself."

"Yes sir."

Alma gave an impatient jerk of her head. "Well, if what you're after is filling up the pews, I suppose Elvis Presley or Godzilla or any other freak show will do just fine!"

Cicero spoke up. "I think if you'd serve coffee in the vestibule between Sunday school and church, you'd swell the crowd a little. Regular and decaf, and maybe your doughnuts on Communion Sunday . . ."

"Cicero, hush," Alma said. And then as an afterthought, "We Methodists refer to it as a narthex, not a vestibule. *Vestibule* is a Baptist word."

"I don't believe . . . ," Cicero started, then trailed off, deflating. He sat there for a moment, wrinkled his nose, furrowed his brow, stared down at his plate. Good old Cicero, just trying to grease the skids a little. Trout felt a pang of sympathy for him. Alma was drumming her nails on the table, paying Cicero no attention. *Did she pick him, or did he pick her? And whichever it was, why?*

Joe Pike looked at Alma for a long moment, then let out a breath and sat back in his chair. "You just don't see it, do you?"

"See what?"

"The church," he said quietly. "It's dying, Alma."

Now it was Alma's turn to look stricken.

"Those people who always show up," Joe Pike went on. "The terminally faithful. Judge Lecil and Mister Fleet and Eunice, Tilda and Boolie, Grace up there in the choir, all the rest with their perfect attendance records, sitting in the same places year after year until the cushions bear the permanent imprint of their rear ends."

Alma flushed. "Joe Pike!"

But Joe Pike plowed ahead, his voice growing urgent. "Did you ever notice how few cars there are parked at the curb on Sunday? They all *walk*, for God's sake. They all live *here* on this end of town. The Moseley end. It's like a little fiefdom. The Moseley manor house and the Moseley cathedral across the street and all the poor serfs trudging dutifully in the door when the bell tolls."

"They are our people!"

"I love 'em dearly, Alma. But we — our family — we have sucked the life out of them. We have turned them into Christian zombies."

"Stop it!" Alma cried out, banging her fist on the table. The dishes rattled. It scared the hell out of Trout. He jumped an inch or two in his chair. "Christ!" he blurted.

Just then, the door from the kitchen opened. Rosetta stood there staring at them. *My, my. White folks 'bout to come to blows in here. Fightin' over Jesus.*

At the table there was an embarrassed silence. Finally, Rosetta said to the blasphemers, "Fellow on the phone said to come quick. Wardell Dubarry's painting his house."

By the time they got there — all riding in Cicero's police cruiser — Wardell Dubarry was well along. It was a bright red, a shade that reminded Trout of Chinese New Year decorations. Wardell had already covered a good bit of one side of the house and was up on a ladder now at the peak of the roof, brush in hand, paint bucket hanging from the top rung. A middling crowd had gathered. On the other side of the street. *There's all kinds of wrecks,* Trout thought.

Cicero eased the police car to the edge of the street next to Wardell's house, and Alma was out of the car and up the yard before he could get the engine turned off. She stood there below the ladder for a moment, watching Wardell, while the others got out of the car and followed her. Wardell didn't seem to notice a thing. A portable radio, sitting in an open window below the ladder, was playing country music. Merle Haggard. *I'm proud to be an Okie from Muskogee!* Trout looked around for Keats. She was nowhere in sight. Probably working the afternoon shift at Dairy Queen. Did she know what was going on here? Did she care? Probably. Tweaking the noses of the Moseleys. She would get her jollies from something like that. Keats seemed to have a serious burr under her saddle about the Moseleys.

So, apparently, did her father. Wardell was having a grand time up there on the ladder, spreading on the red paint with sweeping flourishes of his brush. He didn't look down, just kept with the work.

"What do you think you're doing?" Alma demanded.

Wardell looked down and gave her an arch look. She could *see* what he was doing, couldn't she? Wardell went back to painting.

So Alma told him what he was doing. "You are painting *my house.*"

"Yes, as a matter of fact, I am. Painting the house," Wardell said.

Alma turned to Cicero. "Arrest him," Alma said.

Cicero looked pretty uncomfortable. He hitched his gun belt. Then he hitched his britches. Trout imagined that Cicero's underwear was probably creeping up the crack of his butt like ivy. "Hon, I can't do that," Cicero said in a low voice.

"What do you mean, you can't do that?"

"This" — he took in the neighborhood with a sweep of his hand — "is outside the police jurisdiction."

"That's ridiculous," Alma said.

"Well, that's what you Moseleys wanted."

"No, it's ridiculous that you won't arrest a man who's breaking the law."

"Which law?" Wardell asked from the top of the ladder.

"Damage to property," she answered.

Trout wanted to be helpful if he could. "You could take down the ladder, like Miz Estelle Collier did with the flimflam man," he said to Uncle Cicero.

"But Wardell's *on* the ladder," Cicero said. "The flimflam man was up on the roof."

Trout nodded. "Yes sir. I can see that."

Wardell added a few more brush strokes while they all watched, at a loss. Merle Haggard sang on: *We don't smoke marijuana in Muskogee.* Aunt Alma finally spoke up again. "Wardell, I'm going to tell you one last time. Stop painting my house and come down off that ladder. If you don't, you are fired. And you'll be out of this house by sundown if I have to put you in the street myself." She speared Cicero with a wicked look. "And given the level of support I'm getting, I may well have to do it myself."

Wardell paused in midstroke, then looked down at Alma. "I'm just doing what Joe Pike told me to do," he said.

"Hey," Joe Pike said, holding up his hands. "Leave me out of this."

"Joe Pike stood right yonder," Wardell said, pointing with his brush at the front yard, dripping red paint, "and said, 'Paint it red if you want to. I don't care.' Young Trout there was standing on the porch. He heard it."

There was a long silence while Alma stared at Joe Pike. "Yeah," he said finally with a shrug of his shoulders. "I did say that. But I didn't mean *paint* the house." He looked at Trout for confirmation.

"That wasn't the way you said it," Trout agreed. "You didn't say *paint* the house. You said . . ."

"Paint the house," Wardell filled in for them. "And I took it to mean 'paint the house.' You're a Moseley, ain't you? And the Moseleys own the house, don't you? And you said *paint* the house." Wardell went back to his painting.

Trout looked at Alma, Joe Pike, Cicero. *This is what a bad wreck looks like.* They all looked a bit dazed and slack-jawed, victims of collision with a man with a bucket of paint. Who wasn't even paying them any attention anymore.

Alma took one more step forward and gripped a rung of the ladder about a yard below Wardell's feet.

Wardell never looked down. "Take your damn hand off my ladder, Alma," he said. "It may be your house, but it's by God my ladder." He kept painting.

And then Joe Pike stepped forward, put *his* hand on the ladder just next to Alma's. He looked up at Wardell, and when he spoke, his voice sounded like barbed wire. "Wardell," he said carefully, "that will be enough of that. If you can't speak to my sister with a civil tongue, I'll come up there and haul your ass off that ladder myself."

Wardell's brush stopped in midstroke. Nobody moved. Nobody looked at anybody else. Nobody spoke. For once, Uncle Cicero seemed not to have the gift of words to grease the skids. It was as if they were frozen in tableau, not one of them having the foggiest notion how to extricate themselves from the situation.

Finally, Wardell said, "I reckon you won't have to do that, Joe Pike." He didn't sound like he really meant it, but he said it anyway.

It was Alma who finally moved. She slowly took her hand off the ladder, then turned and walked very deliberately back to Uncle Cicero's police cruiser. She got in, cranked it up, and drove away. Trout thought she carried it off quite well. The rest of them walked home.

Uncle Phinizy was reading Aeschylus, an old leather-bound volume with yellowed pages. He had found it, he said, in an antiquarian bookshop in Washington — had probably paid too much for it, but with Aeschylus, you wanted the heft of old leather in your hand.

Trout wasn't much interested in Aeschylus. He had come again in the middle of the night seeking answers, and Phinizy didn't seem at all surprised to see him. The door was open, only the screen keeping out the night. Bluish cigarette haze hung just below the ceiling and drifted upward through the shade of the lamp beside Phinizy's chair.

"The usual?" Phinizy asked when he had turned down the page of his book and placed it on the table at his elbow.

"I don't want anything," Trout said from the sofa.

"Well, you sure *look* like you want something."

Trout thought for a moment. "Why are they like that?"

Phinizy lit another cigarette from the one burning low in the ashtray, stubbed out the old one and took a drag on the new. "Did Joe Pike tell you what I did for a living?"

"No," Trout answered, remembering that Phinizy rarely spoke to anything directly. He was oblique. A riddler. It was aggravating, but if you wanted anything from him, you had to put up with the aggravation. He might eventually come to the point. Or he might not.

"I was a spy."

"What? You mean the Russians?"

"Among others."

"Gee."

"Oh," Phinizy said with a dismissive wave of his hand, "nothing glamorous. No parachutes, no submarines at midnight, at least not after the Big War. Most of the time I just read a lot."

"Read?"

"Spent most of my time in a cubbyhole reading newspapers, periodicals, things like that. Amazing what you can learn about people who don't want you to know anything about them, just by reading what they write. Not that they come right out and tell you in so many words. You pick up a piece here, a piece there, and before you know it you've got enough of the puzzle to tell what the whole thing looks like."

"You know Russian?"

"Like it was my mother tongue," Phinizy said.

Trout marveled at that for a moment, then let it go. Interesting, but not at all what he was after. He was bone-tired, head aching from all the space junk spinning wildly inside it, bouncing off one nerve ending and colliding with another. Phinizy was still being oblique. He appeared to tell you something, but he really didn't.

"You don't ever *say* anything," Trout accused.

"Who am I to say?" Phinizy shot back.

"A piece here, a piece there. How am I supposed to figure it out? I don't even know what I'm looking for." He stood up to go, disgusted. "You just want to stand around and watch the wreck. It's your entertainment. You're weird, Uncle Phinizy."

He was halfway down the steps when Phinizy opened the screen. "Trout." Trout stopped, but he didn't look back. Phinizy was seized by a fit of coughing, and Trout waited until he had finished. Then, "I'll come with you. I need some fresh air."

They walked through the downtown together, past the row of vacant storefronts, the Koffee Kup Kafe, the open lot where the furniture and appliance store had been, the feed-and-seed, Uncle Cicero's hardware.

Phinizy ticked off the names of now-departed businesses, ghosts from his youth: Grover's Sundries, where you could get a scoop of homemade ice cream for a nickel on a hot summer afternoon and savor it at a small round oak table beneath a paddle fan (in the back, behind a high counter, Dexter Grover dispensed condoms along with prescriptions, but children weren't supposed to know that); the Freewill Cafe, operated by a jackleg Pentecostal minister who dispensed Scripture with the stew and preached a sermon every afternoon from the sidewalk out front to whatever collection of human beings and stray animals was inclined to gather; *The Moseley Messenger,* a thin excuse of a newspaper that died from lack of advertising and interest; and Bob's Barber Shop, the main attraction of which was a lively penny-a-point pinochle game in the back room.

The town seemed to exist in Phinizy's memory as a vivid fixed point from which the rest of his life proceeded. He, who had lived so long away from it, was a walking compendium of Moseley's history — not just the major occurrences, but the trivia of everyday human commerce that made the place real.

"I loved this place," he said as they passed the last of the empty storefronts and crossed the street. "It was a good place for a boy to grow up."

"Why did you leave?" Trout asked.

"I grew up," Phinizy said. And then, "There was an unpleasantness."

"What?"

"Leland and I had different ideas about things. After our father died, Leland wanted the town to be a shrine to Broadus Moseley."

"And you wanted . . ."

"To let it breathe."

"So you left."

"Ran away, I suppose you could say if you wanted to be uncharitable about it."

They reached the other side of the street and started back in the direction they had come, back toward Broadus Moseley's end of town, past City Hall and the police department, the grocery store and the welfare office. Everything was dark except for a bare bulb dangling from the ceiling at the rear of the tiny police station. There was a padlock on the door. Law enforcement in Moseley went dormant at dark. A lone car with a sizable hole in the muffler rumbled along the street behind them, eased to a stop as the traffic light in front of City Hall turned red, sat there growling in idle for the minute it took the light to turn green, then moved on. Trout stopped and stood at the edge of the sidewalk staring at the traffic light, the street. There was no intersection here.

He turned to Phinizy. "There's no intersection."

"No."

"Why have a traffic light when there's no intersection?"

Phinizy smiled. "To stop traffic. Back in the fifties, Leland got powerfully exercised about traffic speeding through town. So he had the light put up. As you see, it stops traffic."

"But there isn't any traffic."

"No. I-20 took care of that."

"Then why don't they take the light down?"

Phinizy didn't answer. He turned and headed down the sidewalk. Trout followed, glancing back at the traffic light. Green. Yellow. Red. Since the fifties. Everything about the place was like being stuck in a time warp — not just the traffic light, but everything. Including people's lives. Including his own. He half expected a carload of teenagers out of an old black-and-white movie to round the corner — ducktail haircuts, bobby sox, pedal pushers, oldies on the radio. He was beginning to feel like one of them, suddenly thrust backward into a strange and distant and even forbidding time. And held there against his will.

They stopped at Broadus Moseley Park. Phinizy was badly winded by now, though they hadn't walked all that far or the least bit fast. They hunkered in silence for a long time on the steps of the band shell while Phinizy got his breath back. His face looked ghastly in the dim light that filtered through the trees from the lamp out on the street. The night was sultry and close around them, an army of crickets sending coded messages across the grass of the park. *Riddleit-riddleit.* After a while, Phinizy fished a cigarette out of the crumpled pack in his shirt pocket, lit it and sucked noisily.

Trout could feel despair settling in the pit of his stomach. It all seemed so incredibly screwed up and impossible and forbidding. Moseley, Georgia, might be Phinizy's place (or once had been), but it wasn't his. In the series of parsonages that had been home as far as memory took him, there was at least a sense of temporary permanence. A congregation, eager to make you a part of their little community. And inside the parsonage walls, the three of them. Three. But now with one gone, there seemed to be fewer than two. There seemed to be, at bottom, nothing here in this time and place you could count on, maybe even nothing you could really know. It was all smoke and myth.

It was almost as if Phinizy could read his mind. "I wish I had all the answers for you, Trout. But I can't tell you what I don't know," he said. He took another drag on his cigarette and flipped the glowing butt out into the grass. "I'm like you. Looking for bits and pieces."

"What about Aunt Alma and my daddy? At least you know about that."

"Do some thinking on your own, Trout. Form the habit of it."

"How?"

"All right. Alma and Joe Pike. Think about Alma. Try to imagine growing up as Alma. The girl in the family. Your father owns the mill — owns the town, for that matter. What does that mean?"

"Well," Trout said, "I guess you've got plenty of money."

"Money, prestige, social standing. You go off to get finished at a school for proper young ladies up east. You make your debut in Atlanta. The world's just waiting to kiss the hem of your dress. Then there's a younger brother."

"Daddy."

"What does the family expect his role to be?"

Trout thought for a moment. "The good son."

"Yes."

Phinizy waited. Trout searched his memory. "Uncle Cicero was talking about Grandaddy Leland at dinner the other Sunday. Grandaddy Leland said not a damn one of his children did what they were supposed to do."

Phinizy nodded. "And thereby hangs the tale. Joe Pike was supposed to . . ." He waited.

"Take over the business," Trout answered.

"And Alma was supposed to . . ."

"Be a lady."

"But what happened?"

"Daddy played football and became a preacher. Aunt Alma . . ." Trout waved his hand in the direction of the mill. "And she married Cicero."

"Don't sell Cicero short."

Trout thought about Cicero. "He's always saying something. Just when you think the lid's about to blow off."

"Uh-huh. Good work. Now, back to Alma and Joe Pike."

"I think . . ." Trout searched, trying to grab something that made sense. Put the bits and pieces together, enough to imagine what the whole thing looks like. "They both wish they were somebody else, don't they."

"It's a quite common human condition."

"Do you wish you were somebody else?"

Phinizy didn't say anything at first. Then finally, "Show me a man who doesn't have any regrets and I'll show you a man who died at birth. Trick is not to let your regrets run your life. Now, does any of that help?"

Trout shrugged. "Some, I guess."

"But not entirely."

"Is all that . . . what does it have to do with Daddy and Mama and everything?"

"Maybe nothing. I don't know a lot about your mama and daddy, Trout, at least about what went wrong. I'd tell you if I did. And it doesn't do any good to speculate, not on something like that. That's the thing about bits and pieces. Sometimes you put them together and they don't mean what you think they do. Sometimes they don't mean a goddamn thing."

"So what do you do?"

"Keep looking."

"I'm tired," Trout said. "I just want things to be fixed up. I just want to be . . ." He shrugged. What?

"Sixteen."

"Yes sir."

Phinizy looked at him for a moment, and the ancient crevices of his face seemed to soften a bit. Then he put his hand on Trout's knee and gave it a squeeze. It helped, at least a little. Phinizy said, "Something's going on here, Trout."

"What?"

"I don't know exactly. I'm like you. I listen, watch, keep my own counsel. Bits and pieces. But I haven't figured it out yet."

"Something with Aunt Alma and Daddy?"

"More than that. The town. The mill."

"Have you talked to Daddy about it?"

"Not yet. I figure Joe Pike's got his own load to tote just now."

"When?"

"Soon, I hope." Phinizy rose and stood on wobbly legs, gripping one of the posts of the band shell for support. "One piece of advice, Trout." Trout waited. "If all hell breaks loose, don't try to be a hero. Save your own ass."

SEVEN

TROUT LOST IN the first round of the State Juniors. Lost badly to the boy from Augusta. From the first volley, he exposed the nasty little secret of Trout's shaky backhand, and the longer they played, the worse it got. Trout lost the first set 6–4, and by the end of it, he was thoroughly unnerved. The second set was 6–0 and not even that close. Trout felt naked and humiliated, flailing away like a ten-year-old cutting brush with a machete.

When they met at the net at the end of the match, the boy offered his hand and said with a sly smile, "Get a backhand."

Trout shook his hand. "Get a life," he said. And then he thought, *I'm one to talk. He's got both. I've got neither.*

Trout and Joe Pike rode glumly back to Moseley — Trout slumped against the passenger door, letting Joe Pike drive, the hum of the tires on I-20 gnawing at the back of his brain. So much for tennis. After this, he wouldn't dare show his face at another tournament. Not until he got his backhand straightened out. That could take years, if ever.

"Oh ye who labor and are heavy laden," Joe Pike intoned after a while, keeping his eyes on the road.

"Daddy," Trout said, "I just don't need any Scripture right now. Okay?"

"I meant it as comfort. Balm of Gilead, all that stuff."

"He whipped my butt," Trout said.

"That he did," Joe Pike agreed. "Bad luck of the draw, getting the kid from Augusta."

"I wanted to crawl into a hole."

"I've had the feeling. TCU game in 1955 —"

Trout cut him off. He didn't need any Bear Bryant war stories, either. "There's not even a stupid tennis court in Moseley. How am I gonna work on my backhand if there's not even a stupid tennis court?"

"You could go to Augusta. They seem to know your backhand pretty well."

"Hey, come on!"

Joe Pike shrugged, but he didn't apologize. A few months ago, before all the trouble, Joe Pike would have carried on at great length — analyzing, pep-talking, putting a good face on things. Now, he didn't bother. His silence seemed to say, *You blew it, you chew it.*

They rode on. It was late afternoon and traffic had slacked off. They passed Social Circle, Rutledge, Madison. Towns that existed only as green exit signs, bypassed by the oblivious concrete ribbon of interstate in its rush to make Augusta by nightfall. Exit 52: Buckhead. Exit 53: Veazey. Exit 54: Crawfordville. And then Moseley, forced to share a sign with Norwood, insult added to injury. Trout couldn't even summon up the energy for a decent sigh. Air puddled at the bottom of his lungs like swamp muck. Summer stretched ahead of him like an endless, dust-choked road, and he trudged along it toward exile.

Joe Pike hadn't spoken for perhaps fifty miles. But as he flicked on the blinker for the Moseley exit, he said, "Maybe a job. Keep you occupied. Put some money in your pocket. I'll talk to Alma."

They stopped at the Dairy Queen for supper. When Trout went up to the window to place their order, he saw Keats on the other side. She slid the glass open. "I'm sorry," she said.

"About what?"

"The tennis thing."

Trout was stunned. "How . . ."

"Word travels fast."

Trout stared at her. *When a Moseley farts, everybody smells it.* "Want to take a few minutes to gloat?"

She stared back; then the tiniest trace of a smile played at the corners of her mouth. "The whole town was counting on you, Trout. We really had our hearts set on you winning that tournament. It would have put us back on the map."

To hell with her. "I'll have three foot-longs with chili, two chocolate shakes."

The smile faded. "I really am sorry," she said. She slid the glass closed and left him standing there.

The next morning Trout said to Joe Pike, "Maybe I'll go out for football."

"They'll kill you," Joe Pike replied.

"Thanks for the encouragement."

Joe Pike was making fresh-squeezed orange juice. He had sliced a dozen oranges in half and was standing at the kitchen counter, grinding away on a glass juice squeezer, an orange half lost in his massive hand. It made Trout wince, watching him. "Football's not a game for small people anymore." He put down the orange half, drained the juice from the squeezer into a pitcher, and turned to Trout. Joe Pike was huge, deep into one of his Dairy Queen phases now. If he kept going like this, Trout knew, he would pass three hundred pounds by midsummer, drinking fresh-squeezed orange juice and eating Lean Cuisine at home, then fleeing to Dairy Queen for sustenance. If habit held true, he would one day look at himself in horror and launch into grim dieting — salads, popcorn, gallons of water — terrible battles with himself that made Trout fearful. Throughout Trout's young life, Joe Pike had been, in turn, merely big, and huge — two people (at least) at war in the same body. It scared Trout, this going back and forth, kept him wary and off-balance. He wished Joe Pike would just stay put.

"In my day," Joe Pike was saying, "A little guy could play. Coach Bryant liked little guys. 'Agile, mobile, hostile,' he called 'em. But later on, after he'd been at Alabama for a while, he figured out he couldn't win with little guys. They just got busted up."

"Well, I'm not talking about playing for Bear Bryant."

"Soccer. Now there's a sport for a little guy. In fact, it helps to be little if you want to play soccer. Speed. Agility. Endurance." Joe did a little shuffle-step-kick, aiming an imaginary soccer ball through the legs of the table. Trout tried to imagine Joe Pike on a soccer field. No.

"They don't have soccer at Moseley High School. Or tennis."

"Oh."

"Of course, I could go somewhere else."

Joe picked up another orange half, cradled it in his hand and looked out the window for a moment. Then he said, "If you're gonna live in a place, Trout, you gotta *live* in it. Know what I mean?"

Trout didn't say anything. He worked on his scrambled eggs and instant grits, feeling Joe Pike's eyes on him.

"I want you to finish high school here," Joe Pike said.

Want? Or need? Trout thought. He didn't look up. "Like you did."

"Yes."

"Why did you?" No answer. "Miz Trawick said your family shipped you off to Georgia Military, but you ran away and came back home and caused an uproar."

Joe Pike smiled. "Sounds about right."

"Well?"

Joe Pike thought about it awhile. "I guess I just wanted to be regular, you know? Just one of the local kids. And that's what I want you to do."

"I'm not you. And it's different now."

"No," Joe Pike said, "I doubt it's much different at all, son. It wasn't easy for me, and it isn't easy for you. I know that. But it's what you make of it. Everything" — a wave of his hand took in the parsonage, the church next door, Aunt Alma, Moseley Mills, the universe — "is what you make of it."

And what, indeed had Joe Pike made of it — insisting on being one of the regular kids at Moseley High? He might have thought he was, but when he fell down on the extra point try in the state championship football game, it wasn't just a regular kid screwing up, it was Joe Pike *Moseley.* The only Moseley in the stadium, he had said. When a Moseley screws up, everybody knows it. And the stakes, Trout realized, were infinitely higher.

Trout put down his fork, pushed back his chair, stood up, looked down at the instant grits, and made a face. They were really terrible. They sat there in a gray lump on his plate, hardening like cement. Surely, after all these months, he should have the hang of instant grits by now. But they were either too runny or too lumpy. At the motel in Atlanta, the morning before his tennis match, they had had real grits. It was the best thing about the day.

He looked at Joe Pike. "If I'm gonna go out for football, I guess I need to get in shape. What should I do?"

Joe Pike gave him a sly grin, and there was some mischief in it, maybe an echo from Junction, Texas — flinty-eyed and remorseless Bear Bryant looking on as young men beat each other to a pulp in the heat and dust. "Go ye unto the football stadium and cast thine eye upon the grandstand and ascend and descend the steps thereof. Yea, verily."

By the third time he started up the grandstand steps, he had a great deal more appreciation for Bear Bryant. And Joe Pike Moseley the football player.

He could see the shabby wooden press box a great distance away, up there at the top of the stands, and he said to himself that he would never make it because his legs had stopped bending at the knee and his butt was bumping along the concrete steps and he had lost heart. He had passed mere pain on the first trip up, and by now everything was simply sweat-gushing, gut-churning, air-sucking misery. By the time he neared the top, he was barely moving. He thought that he could quit right there and never feel a pang of guilt, but he was afraid that if he did stop, he would tumble back down the steps and bash his head on the concrete. Headline: BOY DIES STUPIDLY IN FOOTBALL STADIUM. So he bent at the waist and gave a heave with the upper part of his body and somehow staggered up the last two steps. Then his legs buckled and he slumped against the wooden side of the press box, flaking paint raking his face. Down on his fanny now, legs splayed, chest heaving, eyes closed, white spots dancing in the grayness.

In his agony, he thought again of Joe Pike. He thought that he had none of his father's genes, that he was in truth too small and timid to play football. But he might try anyway if it would save him from being an invisible curiosity when school started again in late August. Maybe he would break something early in the season and wear a cast and be an object of admiration. Or maybe he would simply remain invisible.

After a while he opened his eyes and looked out across the brown-green sun-baked expanse of playing field, blinking in the great aching whitewashed June noontime. It was quiet except for the singing of crickets in the shady underbelly of the grandstand and the drone of a lawn mower off in the general direction of town.

"Hey!" she called, and he remembered suddenly that she was there, sitting in the shade of the concession stand down at the end of the field.

She had surprised him with her telephone call just before he left the parsonage. He was in his room, putting on shorts and T-shirt, when the phone rang back in the kitchen and Joe Pike picked it up. Trout heard the drone of Joe Pike's voice and assumed the call was church business. Or Aunt Alma. But when he emerged from his room a couple of minutes later, Joe Pike called down the hallway, "Trout. Phone for you."

It must be someone from Ohatchee, he thought. Maybe Parks Belton, inviting him to visit for the summer. Or the rest of his life. He would go, gladly.

"What's up?" she asked, and he recognized the voice immediately.

"What do you mean, 'What's up?'"

"Well, your tennis career is over, you've disgraced the town, school is out, and there's nothing for a rich kid to do in Moseley, Georgia."

God, she is a first-class female asshole.

"Actually," he said, "I was just going to the stable to give my polo pony a workout."

"Your daddy said you're going out for football."

"That's right."

"They'll kill you."

"That's what he said."

"I know. He told me. He's right, you know. Those mill kids, they'd love to get you on the football field."

"Well," he said, "I plan to add fifty pounds and some blazing speed before August, and I will kick their butts from here to Atlanta."

"Can I watch?"

"Sure," he had answered, but he hadn't imagined she meant right now, today, while he committed suicide on the grandstand steps. She was waiting when he got to the stadium. Joe Pike must have told her. Trout wondered if she had brought some of the other mill brats to hide in the bushes and snicker. But she was alone, sprawled in the shade of the concession stand. She gave him a wave, then watched while he made one magnificently vigorous ascent up the steps, bounced back down, started a second, faltered and nearly fell, made it to the top only by the grace of God, lurched slowly down, and damn near died on the third trip up. And now, all courage and fortitude gone from his frail body, he stood on wobbly legs, squinting at her in the brightness. Her aluminum crutches leaned against the side of the small white building. She had her legs crossed beneath her, Indian-style, and her drawing pad was open in her lap. She had a way of wrapping herself around the pad when she was drawing, shoulders slumped, back arched, mothering it, shutting out the rest of the world. But now she looked up at him, up here on the grandstand steps, barely alive.

"Take off your shirt," she called.

"What?" His voice was a dry croak.

Louder. "Take off your shirt."

"Why?"

She didn't answer. She just looked at him, waiting. So he pulled the sweat-soaked T-shirt over his head and stood there holding it, feeling the sun hot on his bare shoulders.

"Put it back on," she said after a moment. "You look like a plucked chicken."

"Kiss my fanny!" he yelled back.

"Show me!"

He turned his back to her, hiked down his shorts a bit, and presented a sliver of bare rump in her direction.

He waited for reaction, got none, pulled up the shorts, and turned around again. She was deep into the drawing pad, paying him no mind. He put on his T-shirt. To hell with her.

Fifteen minutes later they wobbled toward home together in the noon heat, she on crutches, he following on rubber legs — following because there wasn't room for both of them side by side on the sidewalk, and he was afraid if he walked ahead of her she would run over him. From behind, he could get a good look at her incredible, crazy gait — legs, hips, and body galloping off in several directions at once. There was a sort of crazy rhythm to it. Music. It needed music. Something with a strong, solid beat, lots of bass and drums. *Oooga-chuckka, oooga-chuckka.* Fats Domino, maybe. *I'm walkin', yes indeed, and I'm talkin'* . . . She tacked back and forth, taking up most of the sidewalk, and Trout began to get into the beat, doing a little juke motion with his hips, snapping his fingers, making jive sounds with his mouth.

"I hear that."

"Hear what?"

"That stuff you're doing with your mouth."

"What stuff?"

"That's the thanks I get. Sit out there in the hot grass with chiggers crawling up my butt while you run around like a crazy person."

"Hey," he protested, "I didn't ask you to come. I wish you'd stayed home."

"Well, I didn't. So shut up."

The sketch pad was tucked protectively under her left arm, pencils sticking out of her rear jeans pocket. The sketch pad was part of her, lurching along in counterpoint. *Oooga-chuckka, oooga-chuckka.* It bounced around inside his head, vibrating down into his spinal cord. Jive therapy. He could feel some of the strength returning to his legs, but the agony of the grandstand was still strong in his mind. He would have to give a good deal of thought to football.

"Want me to carry that for you?"

"What?"

"Your sketch pad."

"No," she said flatly.

"Aren't you afraid you'll get it sweaty?"

"I'm not afraid of anything," she snapped. And that, he thought, was probably the gospel truth.

A small kid on a bicycle approached, head down, elbows on the handlebars, just lazing along, paying no attention to anything but the cracks in the sidewalk. She waited until he was almost upon them and then she yelled, "Hey! Watch where the hell'ya goin'!" She raised a crutch menacingly, and the kid jerked his head up, eyes wide, and veered into the street, tires bumping off the curb. He struggled with the wobbling bike, almost losing it, finally gaining control. "Damn you, Keats!" He shot them a bird and pedaled off down the street. She launched out again down the sidewalk. The sketch pad had not moved a centimeter.

"You're afraid I'll see what's in it," Trout says.

"It's none of your business."

"Of course it's my business. I'm in it."

"No you're not."

"I saw you down there by the concession stand, watching me and scribbling on that thing."

"It's not scribbling. It's drawing."

"You give me the creeps."

They were at the corner where the street from the football stadium intersected with Broadus Street. She stopped dead in her tracks and turned on him with a flurry of arms, legs, crutches. It was amazing, watching her turn around like that. She pointed a crutch at him, holding it straight out. Her arms were very strong. The crutch didn't waver. "You'd better be nice to me," she said. "I'm the only non-Moseley under the age of eighty in this town who'll give you the time of day."

"Don't bother," he said mildly and made the *oooga-chuckka* sound with his mouth again.

She lowered the crutch and stared at him for a long time, and then her mouth curled in a sneer. "How'd it make you feel when they took your mother off to the loony bin?"

He could feel his jaw drop open.

"And how about when your crazy old man rode off on his motor-cycle?"

"Screw you!" he blurted, flushing with anger.

Then her face relaxed into a smile, all wicked sweetness. "Aw, poor thing. Are you mad? Well, good. I never saw anybody that needed to be pissed off worse than you, Trout Moseley."

Then she turned with a disgusted shake of her head, dismissing him, and lurched away toward the east end of town, toward the mill village. Trout watched her for a moment, tried desperately to think of something brilliantly hateful to shout at her lurching back, and finally gave up with a shrug of defeat and headed west toward the parsonage.

Joe Pike was mowing the grass when Trout got home. He was intent upon it, stalking back and forth across the sun-hardened lawn of the parsonage. The lawn mower bounced ahead of him, rushing to stay out of Joe Pike's way. Joe Pike was clad in an ancient undershirt with the armpits eaten away, a pair of seersucker Bermuda shorts, a battered Texas A&M baseball cap, black wing-tip shoes, no socks. His massive belly cascaded over the frontside of the shorts like an avalanche. He was drenched with sweat, face flushed under the brim of the cap. And smoking a cigar.

He looked up as Trout turned down the walk toward the house, waved, stopped, and cut the lawn mower back to idle.

Trout looked down at Joe Pike's shoes. "You're gonna rub blisters on your feet like that."

Joe Pike stared at the shoes, then took the cigar out of his mouth. "I couldn't find my tennis shoes. I guess they're still in a box somewhere."

"Why didn't you . . ." Never mind. Instead, he said, "You don't smoke cigars."

"I used to," Joe Pike said. "Coach Bryant used to pass 'em out in the locker room after the game. When we won."

"What happened when you lost?"

"We tried to hide."

"Well, it stinks."

Joe Pike took a long look at the cigar. "There is something faintly spiritual about the combination of sweat and cigar smoke. I'll bet the Israelites smoked cigars when they got through smoting the Philistines hip and thigh. I'll bet God passed out cigars and said, 'Y'all went cheek to cheek and jaw to jaw, boys. So light 'em up.'" Then he jammed the cigar back in his mouth and gazed out across the lawn. The path left by the lawn mower looked like a snake, with splotches of uncut grass Joe Pike had left in his wake. When Trout mowed, he tried to keep his lines neat and straight, guiding the wheels of the mower along the indention left in the grass by the previous pass. "Looks like it was done by a drunk Meskin on a blind horse," Joe Pike said around the cigar. Not *Mexican, Meskin*. Something else he had brought back from Texas.

"Yeah," Trout said. Late in the afternoon, when it was cooler, he would get out the lawn mower and repair the damage. Neat lines and all that.

They both stood there and surveyed the mess for a moment and then Joe Pike reached down and cut the lawn mower off, and the engine died with a whimper. "Let's clean up and go get some lunch."

"The usual?"

"Sure."

Joe Pike ordered a foot-long hot dog with chili for Trout, three for himself. They sat in the car in front of the Dairy Queen and ate, watching the lunch crowd ebb and flow around them. When they had finished the hot dogs, Joe Pike went back to the window and brought Trout a huge tub of vanilla ice cream and a red plastic spoon.

"If you're gonna play football, you've gotta put some meat on your bones," he said.

Trout looked into the tub. There must be a gallon of it. The ice cream made a little curlicue at the top where the machine had cut off the flow. "Don't you want some?"

Joe Pike patted his belly. "Not me. I'm trying to watch it."

Trout spooned off a white glob of ice cream and let it slide down his throat, where it came to rest on top of the foot-long hot dog. He remembered the grandstand steps, the merciless sun. He felt sick, a little light-headed. "I can't eat that," he said, and put the tub of ice cream on the dashboard. Moisture beaded on the outside of the tub, trickled down onto the vinyl. They both stared at it for a moment. Then Joe Pike gave a great sigh and reached for it. "Waste is sinful." He looked at Trout and shrugged. "The starving children in China, you know."

Trout watched, mesmerized, as Joe Pike ate the whole thing, working the spoon around the inside edges of the tub where it was beginning to melt, carving like a sculptor and lifting it lovingly to his lips. He seemed lost in the ice cream, as if he were down inside the tub somewhere, an infant in its womb, doing forward flips and backward rolls, surrounded by its rich cold creaminess. He finished finally, scraped the bottom of the tub, licked the last drops off the plastic spoon, smothered a belch. Then he tidied up, gathering all their trash and taking it to the big barrel at the corner of the building. He came back to the car, slid under the wheel, cranked it up, rolled up the window, and turned on the air conditioner. There was a broad dark band of sweat down the back of his shirt and his collar was soaked. He would go home now and take another bath. Joe Pike took lots of baths in the summer. Trout realized they hadn't said a thing for perhaps ten minutes.

All the regulars were there at the Dairy Queen. The old woman ordering her cup of ice cream with crushed pineapple on top. The two guys in the ACE PLUMBING truck. Joe Pike and Trout Moseley in their old green Dodge.

"I got to thinking today, "Joe Pike said, "we should have some theological discussions, Trout. I don't believe we ever have."

"No sir. I don't remember any."

"Imagine that. Me a preacher and you sixteen years old, and we've never gotten beyond 'Jesus Loves Me.'"

"I guess not."

"Divine intervention, angels on the head of a pin, virgin birth — do you ever wonder about any of that stuff?"

"Well, it's not anything I'm worried about," Trout said. "It's not like acne or anything like that."

"If you were to ask me a theological question, what would it be?"

Trout shrugged. "I don't know."

"Come on. Something really profound."

Trout thought about it for a while. He really wanted to go home and take a nap and then sit in the swing in the backyard and think long and hard about this business of playing football. But Joe Pike seemed insistent. Maybe this was a game, too.

"Why are you a preacher?" Trout asked.

Joe Pike hung fire for a long moment, took a deep breath and let it out slowly. "Hmmmmmmm," he said finally.

"Well?"

Joe Pike put the car in gear and started backing out of his parking place, craning his neck and making an intense thing out of looking out the back window of the car.

"Well?" Trout said again.

"Let me sleep on that one."

Trout drifted out of sleep the next morning to hear voices. Joe Pike. A woman. He jerked awake.

Grace Vredemeyer. They were sitting at the kitchen table, each with a coffee mug, the Mr. Coffee burbling on the counter, dripping a fresh pot. Grace Vredemeyer had a thin, tinkly laugh. Like cheap wind chimes. She was wearing a summer dress, bare at the shoulders, lots of flowers and vines. Trout thought of draperies. Her back was to Trout. Joe Pike looked up, saw Trout standing in the door, frowned, and made a little wave with his hand, shooing Trout away. Grace saw him, turned and stared at Trout, then giggled. "Oh, my."

"Trout, don't you think you should put some clothes on?" Joe Pike said.

Trout looked down at himself. Boxer shorts. His face flushed. He started to go, but then something — he couldn't say exactly what — stopped him. "What are you doing here?" he asked Grace Vredemeyer.

She didn't bat an eye. "I brought my column for this week's church bulletin," she said, holding up a sheet of paper. "Grace Notes."

"Trout . . . ," Joe Pike started.

"Can I read it?" Trout asked.

"Of course," Grace Vredemeyer said.

She held out the piece of paper, Trout took a couple of steps toward her and plucked it out of her hand.

GRACE NOTES
by Grace Vredemeyer
CHOIR DIRECTOR

You may have asked yourself from time to time how the hymns for each service are chosen. Well, there's more to it than just selecting a few numbers at random out of the hymnal willy-nilly.

First of all, I like to get the service off to a sprightly start with a good upbeat number. Something to get you "Jumping for Jesus," to borrow a phrase from Reverend Moseley's new aerobics program (Wednesday afternoons at five).

I like to think the second hymn should be slower paced, reverent and prayerful, coming as it does right after the Pastoral Prayer and just before the Offertory.

And then the third hymn, which precedes the sermon, should . . .

Trout handed the paper back to Grace Vredemeyer. "I'm going out for football," he said.

"Oh, that's nice." She threw Joe Pike a glance. "Another football player in the family."

"Yes ma'am."

He stood there for a moment longer looking at Grace Vredemeyer, definitely *not* looking at Joe Pike. Grace waited him out. She seemed to be a woman of infinite patience. Finally she said, "Have you found a girlfriend in Moseley?"

"Not yet," Trout said. "I'd really like to have one, though. Sometimes" — he took a deep breath — "I wish I were a brassiere." He cupped his hands and held them in front of his bare chest.

This time, Grace Vredemeyer didn't giggle. She snorted.

Joe Pike leaped out of his chair. "Trout!"

"Yes sir?"

"Apologize!" he thundered.

"Sorry, Miz Vredemeyer."

"Go to your room! Put some clothes on!"

"Yes sir."

He heard the front screen door bang shut a few minutes later, and then Joe Pike stood filling the doorway of his room, breathing hard, color high. "What in the hell was that?" he demanded.

"Grace Vredemeyer."

"Don't you smart-mouth me, buster!"

Trout ducked his head, stared at the floor. He might be pissed off, but he wasn't ready to be pissed off and look Joe Pike Moseley in the eye at the same time. "Why did she come here?"

"This is the parsonage, Trout. You know what a parsonage is. It's an extension of the church. People are in and out all the time."

"She could have taken it to your office."

"I wasn't *in* my office. But I'm going to my office now. And by the time I get back for lunch, I want you to have your attitude in gear. Understand me?"

Trout nodded.

Joe Pike surveyed the room. "Clean up. Put some pants on." Trout nodded again.

"I'm getting a little tired of your moping around, Trout. I can't help it if you lost the tennis match. I can't do anything about where we live. I'm trying to make the best of the situation. And I don't *need* you muddying the water." Trout looked up at him finally and Joe Pike's hard glare softened a little. "Just hang in there with me. Okay?"

And then Trout said, "Mama didn't like people coming to the parsonage all the time. It really bugged her."

Joe Pike looked as if he'd been hit hard in the stomach. Or maybe lower. He stood there for a moment, then turned and left. The back door slammed, and after a couple of minutes Trout heard the motorcycle start up back in the shed. Then it roared around the side of the house and took off down the street, heading out of town.

Trout spent a wretched hour, imagining Joe Pike growling along west on I-20, the nose of the motorcycle pointed again toward Texas. And all Trout's fault, for getting pissed off (as Keats had told him he should) and invoking the name that seemed to be Joe Pike's most implacable ghost-demon. Mention Irene, and Joe Pike went into a psychic three-point stance, the old defensive lineman digging in and waiting for onslaught. What was he so afraid of? She was such a small, quiet thing — especially now, sitting over there in the Institute in Atlanta, deep inside herself. Did she have any idea how she haunted this place and its inhabitants? Did she think of them? Did she think at all? Was she lost forever? Was she lost on purpose?

The silence, Irene's insistent silence, drove Trout out of the house, and he sat huddled in the swing on the front porch for a while. He thought of going to Phinizy's bare rooms. But what to say? *I ran Daddy off.* No, that didn't sound too good for either of them. Big old Joe Pike Moseley, he of stout body and mostly stout spirit, driven from his own home by a sixteen-year-old boy and the specter of a tiny, quiet woman? And Trout — consumed by his own miserable adolescent selfishness? Better to keep that to himself.

Then too, to air out your business was to invite advice, and he didn't think much of the advice he had gotten recently.

Keats: *You oughta be pissed off.* Well, see where that had gotten him just now. Joe Pike was gone and Grace Vredemeyer probably thought he was a smart-aleck pervert.

Alma: *Don't forget who you are.* Well, that's exactly what he'd like to do. She might like being a Moseley in Moseley, but to Trout, it was like having a dead chicken hung around your neck.

Phinizy: *Save your own ass.* Easy for Phinizy to say. He could say anything he damn well pleased, stir up all kinds of ruckus, and then beat a retreat if things got too hot. Trout was stuck, at the mercy of all the rest of them. No escape. He didn't even have a credit card.

So Trout sat there on the front porch of the parsonage, trapped between the dark silence of the house and the hot June morning, thinking despairing thoughts, mourning the loss of his father. Traffic passed in fits and starts: Uncle Cicero in his police cruiser, making his morning rounds, keeping Moseley safe from crime and communism; a Merita Bread truck headed for the Koffee Kup; a few cars and pickup trucks; an eighteen-wheeler loaded with live chickens, scattering feathers in its wake. And then he heard the motorcycle, coming in from the east, the unmistakable throaty rumble as Joe Pike geared down and stopped for the traffic light at the center of town. Trout stood, walked down the steps and waited in the yard next to the driveway. After a moment, Joe Pike turned in and stopped next to Trout, the engine throbbing beneath him. His hair was windblown and there were crinkly lines around his eyes from looking off into the distance, down the highway he had perhaps considered but not taken.

"You forgot your helmet," Trout said.

Joe Pike ran his hand across his head. "Yeah. I reckon I did."

"It's not safe, riding without a helmet. You said so."

"Yeah. I know."

"You get hurt, and I'm up a creek."

Joe Pike shrugged.

"I'm sorry," Trout said.

Joe Pike nodded. "It ain't easy."

"No sir. It ain't."

Joe Pike dropped the motorcycle down into first gear and eased off toward the backyard. Trout could almost see the rider on the back behind Joe Pike. Almost, but not quite. But he could see enough to realize that it wasn't the Holy Ghost at all. It was a tiny, quiet woman who used to love to dance.

At midmorning, Keats called. "Come get me," she said.

"What?"

"I need a ride to work."

"Call a cab."

"In Moseley? Are you kidding?"

"Call a friend."

"I just did."

"Oh? I'm your friend?"

"Not if you don't come get me and take me to work. And hurry up. I'm late."

"Look," he said, "you were truly shitty to me yesterday. And I could care less if you get to work or not."

"I'm sorry about that," she said quietly, sounding quite contrite.

"Oh?"

"Yes. I am. Really. I apologize."

"Okay."

"Now get your ass in gear, Trout. I'm gonna be late."

He went on the motorcycle. He didn't ask Joe Pike; he just went to the shed and cranked it up and took off. Joe Pike must have heard, but he didn't make an appearance at the door of his church office.

He found Keats fidgeting on her crutches next to the dirt street in front of her house, dressed in her Dairy Queen uniform. It was freshly starched and the heat of the morning hadn't taken the creases out of it yet. Very snappy, he thought. The yard was full of cars. One of them had an Avis Rental sticker on the back bumper. The front door of the house was open, and he could see people milling about inside.

"Why can't your Daddy take you to work?"

"He's busy," she said, eyeing the motorcycle.

"Doing what?"

"I don't know. I thought you'd bring the car."

"Well, I didn't."

"I've never ridden a motorcycle before."

"Can you get on by yourself?"

"Of course," she said. "You think I need a crane or something?"

It might have helped, he thought. It took her a while, much heaving of limbs, snorting and grunting, banging of crutches. "Don't look," she ordered. He held the bike steady, feet splayed, until she finally settled in behind him, tucked the crutches underneath his arm with the tips sticking out over the handlebars like twin machine guns. She held the crutches with one hand, put the other arm around his midsection and snuggled against him. "Giddy-up," she said.

Trout sniffed the air. "What's that smell?"

"White Shoulders," she said.

"You're wearing perfume?"

She didn't answer. It smelled very nice.

Herschel Bender was a retired Army sergeant. Keats said he had finished his military career running a mess hall at Fort Gordon in Augusta and used his savings to open the Dairy Queen. He was pasty-faced and paunch-bellied with thick arms and neck, dressed in short-sleeved white shirt and narrow plain black tie with a Dairy Queen cap covering his graying crew cut. He spoke in staccato, like a machine gun.

"Don't touch nothing," Herschel said. They were inside behind the counter, in the chrome and air-conditioned coolness. The Dairy Queen was spotless — machinery gleaming, counters scrubbed, floor pristine.

"Herschel hates dirt," Keats said. "He says if you gotta break wind, stick your fanny out the back door."

"You want a job?" Herschel asked Trout.

"I've never done anything like this . . ." Trout waved his hand.

"He's a Moseley," Keats said.

Herschel ignored her. "Not in here. Out there."

Trout looked out through the plate glass. The parking lot baked in late-morning emptiness. Too early for the lunch crowd.

"The tables need painting," Herschel said. There were three concrete picnic tables at the side of the building.

"I know a kid down the street that'll paint the tables," Keats said, her voice rising.

Herschel turned on her. "Keats, you got a problem?"

"He doesn't need a job," she said. "He's —"

"A Moseley," he finished.

"Yeah."

Herschel nodded slowly, thinking it over. "Okay, so I don't hire anybody named Moseley. And maybe I don't hire anybody on crutches."

She glowered at him, and Herschel raised his eyebrows, waiting for her to say something else. She kept her mouth shut. Trout felt incredibly awkward. "Look, I'll . . ."

"You want the job?" Herschel asked.

Trout glanced at Keats. She wouldn't look at him. "Yes sir," he said finally. "I sure do."

Herschel crooked his finger. "Come with me."

The tables were bare concrete, stained with grease and spilled food. Herschel gave them a disgusted wave. "I come out here every day, wash the damn things off, customers come right back and mess 'em up. Grown-ups as bad as the kids. If this place was a mess hall, I'd kick their butts. But you can't do that with a civilian establishment."

"Yes sir," Trout agreed.

"Word gets around you're kicking butts, it's bad for business."

"I guess so."

"So, we'll paint 'em. Won't stop people from making a mess, but it'll be easier to clean up. Capish?"

"What?"

"It's Italian for 'you readin' me?'"

"Yes sir."

"Had a lieutenant in Korea, little sawed-off Guinea, used to say that all the time. Capish? Capish? He'd roust me outta my fartsack all hours of the night, give me some stupid order. Capish? Capish? Hated his guts."

"Why do you say it, then?"

"Bad habit. Like standing over a hot griddle, cookin' food for people to feed their greedy faces. Shoulda taken my money and bought a boat and gone deep-sea fishing every day."

"Why didn't you?"

"I hate fishing."

Trout nodded, not at all sure he understood.

"Well, get to work," Herschel said.

From the storeroom around back, Trout had fetched, at Herschel's direction, a gallon plastic jug marked MURATIC ACID, a bucket, a stiff-bristled scrub brush and a pair of rubber gloves.

"What . . . how do you want me to do it?"

"Get the hose." Herschel pointed to a length of green garden hose, coiled and hung from a spigot on the side of the building. "Mix the muratic half and half. Scrub the tables with the mixture, then hose 'em down real good. By the time you finish the third one, the first one'll be dry. Then paint. Gallon of green enamel and a brush on the shelf in the storage room. Then clean up. Leave the brushes soaking in turpentine. Capish?"

"Yes sir. Capish."

Herschel turned to go. Then, "What'd you say your name is?"

"Trout."

"Like the fish."

"Yes sir."

"Who the hell named you after a fish?"

"It's short for Troutman. That's my mother's family name."

Herschel grunted, started away again, turned back. "Keats. It's amazing how she gets around like that."

"I guess so."

Herschel shook his head. "Sometimes you just wanna smack her in the mouth."

It took a good bit of the day. The first mistake he made was not using the rubber gloves. He put them on and worked for a while, but his hands got hot and sweaty so he took them off. By the time he had finished scrubbing down the tables, his hands were burning, splotched with angry patches of red, the outer layer of skin peeling off his fingertips.

Herschel brought him a foot-long hot dog and a Coke for lunch. "You ever take chemistry in school?" he asked.

"Yes sir."

"You study anything about acid?"

"Yes sir."

"Well, you'll probably die," Herschel said. "If you don't, you'll be disfigured for life and your children will be born deformed."

Trout's mouth dropped open.

"Not really," Herschel said. "Muratic ain't powerful stuff, but it's acid. Hose your hands down real good and put some ointment on 'em tonight."

"I shoulda kept the gloves on," Trout said.

Herschel left him there to eat his foot-long and drink his Coke.

The second mistake he made was taking off his T-shirt when he finished lunch. He thought he'd get a little sun while he painted the tables. When he finished at midafternoon, he tried to put his shirt back on, but he couldn't. His shoulders and back were scorched.

Herschel came out again and looked over the tables. Trout had done a neat job, taking care not to splatter paint on the concrete apron under the tables. They were a nice bright green, drying quickly in the sun. "Looks pretty good," Herschel said.

"Thanks."

"How much I owe you?"

Trout shrugged. "I don't know." He thought for a moment. "Ten dollars?"

Herschel fished in his pants pocket, pulled out a wad of bills and handed Trout a twenty. "Don't sell yourself short."

"Yes sir."

"You looking for summer work? Or are you spending full time developing your tan?"

Trout looked at his shoulder. It was beet red and it left a little yellow indention when he touched it with his finger. "I think I overdid it," he said. "And yes, I'm looking for a job."

Trout felt like his whole body was on fire. Hands burning from the acid, back and shoulders feeling like somebody was sticking him with a million pinpricks at once. Even the wind on his bare skin made him twitch. Keats sat well back on the seat, trying not to bump against him, holding on to the belt loops of his jeans. She didn't say much until they got back into town and stopped at the traffic light on Broadus Street. Then she said, "He offered you a job, didn't he."

"He told me to come back when I get out of the burn ward."

She didn't say anything else until they made a turn at the high school and started toward the mill village. Then she said, "Let me off."

"What?"

"I said, 'Let me off.'"

He rode on for several yards, and then she smacked him flat-handed in the middle of the back. "Owww! GodDAMN!" he bellowed, and almost lost control of the motorcycle. It wobbled, jumped the curb, crossed the sidewalk and came to a stop on the lawn of the school just short of the flagpole. He kicked down the kickstand with a vicious swipe of his foot, jumped off the cycle, grabbed Keats around the waist, hauled her off and dropped her on the grass with a thump. Then he picked up her crutches where they had fallen beside the motorcycle and shoved them at her.

"What in the hell is wrong with you? What in the living name of mother-of-God hell is the goddamn matter?" He was aware that he was screaming, that his eyes were bulging, but he couldn't stop. Sun-burn and acid burn and tennis burn and general cruddy situation burn took utter control of his brain. "The man offered me a job! What's wrong with that? I need the money and I don't have a god-damn thing to do in this goddamn pissant town and I think I'm about to go fucking nuts! I can't help it if my name is Moseley! I didn't choose it!" He screamed at her like a madman, stomping around the spot where she sat on the grass, flailing his arms even though every movement hurt like hell. "I don't want to be a Moseley and I don't want to live here and I am tired of your smart-ass shitty attitude and your ragging on me and cutting my balls off for something I can't do a goddamn thing about! Do you hear? Do you hear? Go home and torture your goddamn gerbil or something. Just leave me the hell alone!"

The motorcycle was still idling. He turned and aimed a kick at the cycle, caught it in the gas tank, toppled it over. The engine died with a cough. "Shit!" he yelled. "Shit, shit, shit!" Then he picked up the motorcycle and climbed back on it and fired it up again.

"I'm sorry," Keats said. It was almost inaudible.

He looked down at her. "What?" he screamed.

"I said I'm sorry."

He sat there on the motorcycle for a moment staring at her. Then she made a little pained face, scrunched up her nose and looked down at the grass. They didn't say anything for a long time. Trout could feel the wrath draining out of his head, seeping down through his neck and chest and puddling in his stomach. He felt incredibly tired and a little light-headed. It had taken a lot out of him. All of it.

Finally she said, "Let's get out of the sun."

The school auditorium was dim and musty, with a storm of dust motes swirling in the late afternoon sunlight streaming through the tall windows, splashing across the rows of battered wooden seats. Trout hunched miserably, elbows on knees, in a seat down in front of the stage while Keats went looking for the first aid kit in the sickroom. She came back after a while with a can of spray something with a big red cross on it. She sprayed it on his back and shoulders and it felt wonderfully cool, taking the sting out of his flesh. Then she sat down in the seat next to him and propped her crutches against the armrest.

"Why?" he asked after a while. She didn't answer. "Why do you do that? Why don't you just leave me alone if you're so mad? I've never been around anybody who's as mad as you are. And you just turn it on and turn it off. It's like a damned ambush."

They heard the front door of the school building open and Trout froze. It was Mr. Blaylock. He could have looked through the open back door of the auditorium and seen them. *Hey! What the hell you young'uns doing down there? You with your shirt off* . . . But he passed by in the hallway without looking. They heard the door to the principal's office close and the drone of his window air conditioner as it started up. Trout eased his T-shirt on. It still stung, but the burn was a lot better.

They sat there a while longer and finally Keats said, "I got run over by a truck."

"What?"

"That's how . . ." She indicated the crutches. "The guy in the house next door got fired — drinking, I think — so the mill sent a truck and loaded up all their stuff to take it off. Joe and I were playing in the dirt behind the truck. Something slipped. It rolled back. And . . ." She shrugged.

"God," he said. "I'm sorry. I'm really sorry." He sat there for a long time, stunned. He had no idea what to say. He had assumed it was polio or something like that. There was still such a thing as polio, wasn't there? But no, it was a stupid truck. A Moseley truck. "Did anybody do anything?" He gestured at her legs. "I mean, to help?"

"I had a bunch of operations. The mill paid for all of it. The Moseleys."

"But . . ."

"Yeah."

Then he remembered something she had said just now. "Who's Joe?"

"My little brother."

"I didn't know you had a brother."

"I don't." She blanched, and then her face went all dull and lifeless. "The truck . . ."

"My God," he said softly. And for the first time, he truly felt the great crushing weight of being who he was. *Don't forget who you are,* Aunt Alma had said. It sounded so easy, so proud, so comfortable when she said it. Since she had said it to him that first afternoon in the mill, it had been mostly an irritation. People didn't speak to you at school, the principal was still upset because Joe Pike fell down in a football game. Everybody watched you, took careful note of every-thing you said and did, compounding the burden of being a preacher's kid. All that was a pain in the butt. But it wasn't anything he couldn't handle. This, though . . . Sweet Jesus. He could see that he was a product of a great aching history that stretched back farther than he could ever see. People with mills and trucks and money and power over other people's lives.

"I'm sorry," he said again. And he truly was. About more than the truck running over Keats and Joe Dubarry. He felt an overwhelm-ing hollowness, expanding and filling the empty space of the high-ceilinged auditorium and oozing out the doors and windows, sucking in an entire town and everything in it.

"It makes Daddy crazy," Keats said. "Every time he looks at me. Every time he sees these." She picked up the crutches with a clatter that echoed like gunfire in the auditorium's stillness, making the dust motes dance. "It's all I've ever heard. The damn Moseleys."

"I guess I understand —"

"No you don't," she snapped, suddenly angry again. "He named Joe for your father."

"Oh."

She picked up her crutches, planted them solidly on the floor, and vaulted up out of her seat. She had powerful hands and arms. She stood there with her back to him, and then she turned around. Her face was hard and sharp. He had seen it yield a little, every great once in a while. This morning when he picked her up, wearing her White Shoulders. But not now. It was a thing she allowed only in tiny pieces, like sloughing off old skin. Underneath, there seemed to be only the hardness.

"Yeah," she said. "Oh."

"Keats," he said quietly, "I didn't do it."

She just stared at him. Again, unyielding.

"I've got enough shit to tote around without all that."

She stared some more. Then she said, "You sure have a foul mouth for a preacher's kid."

"I don't . . . I try to be careful."

"Except with me?"

Trout heaved himself up out of his seat. *Sometimes you just want to smack her,* Herschel had said. Instead, he walked past her and started up the middle aisle toward the door.

"Aren't you gonna take me home?"

"I guess."

"One thing," she said.

He stopped, turned back to her.

"You finally got pissed off. Feel better?"

"No." He truly didn't. He felt as rotten as he had ever felt in his life. He wanted to go home and close the door and be by himself. Be very still. Not move a muscle. Not let a single sound intrude. He wouldn't even have to wait until dark because he thought you could probably create your own darkness if you let go of yourself. Then suddenly he thought, *Like Mother.* Was that it? Was that how it started? And what did she find when she got deep down inside herself — still and quiet and dark? It must be okay, because she had gotten very, very good at it.

"Keep trying," Keats said.

"What?"

"Being pissed off. It takes practice. Like anything worth doing."

EIGHT

WHEN TROUT PARKED the motorcycle in the shed behind the parsonage, he heard music coming from the church education building next door. Loud boogie music. Fats Domino. *Hello, Josephine . . . how do you do . . .*

He opened the door of the assembly room and peered in. Joe Pike, wearing ancient plaid Bermuda shorts, a faded green knit shirt, and jogging shoes. Grace Vredemeyer in pedal pushers and a loose-fitting upper garment, half-shirt and half-vest that wrapped around her bosom from both sides and tied in the back. *Say, hey, Josephine . . .* They faced each other, about ten yards apart, and they were doing jumping jacks. Trout remembered. Jumping for Jesus. The music thundered from Trout's boom box, set up on a table at one side of the room. All the folding chairs that usually filled the room had been stacked against a wall, leaving the expanse of linoleum floor clear for Jumpers. But it was just the two of them. Joe Pike was sweating profusely despite the air conditioning: hair matted against his skull, armpits and shirt front dark green, arms flailing the air, legs hopping out . . . back . . . out . . . back, belly bouncing up and down. Grace Vredemeyer was doing a pale, dainty imitation of Joe Pike's movements, like somebody making angels in snow. She sweated not at all; her hair and makeup were perfectly in place and undisturbed. She bounced a little under her upper garment, but it was like small animals burrowing furtively. She gave Trout a tiny wave without breaking stride. "Come join us," she called out.

Trout waved back, took a folding chair from a stack near the door, opened it, and sat down to watch for a moment until Fats Domino got through with them.

Jumping for Jesus. He hadn't given it much thought when Joe Pike had announced it from the pulpit the previous Sunday. Maybe he didn't think Joe Pike was really serious. He had never done anything remotely resembling it anywhere they had lived before. He was the sort of preacher who would golf with members of the congregation, have uproarious fun at an Easter egg hunt, dress in drag and dance in a chorus line at the Lions Club Follies. But church, to his way of thinking, had always been for, well, going to church. He hadn't had much truck with Boy Scout troops and sewing circles and literary societies, not in the church buildings. But now, everything was out of kilter. Elvis Presley in the pulpit and Fats Domino in the education building. And Joe Pike himself didn't seem to be having much fun with any of it. Look at him now: mouth set in a grim line, brow furrowed in concentration, arms and legs and belly shattering big chunks of air. *Josephine, Josephine . . .*

It troubled Trout on several counts. For one thing, it had the smell of another Dairy Queen phase coming to an end, the beginning of salad days, a body at war with itself. The little man trapped inside the big man, whoever he was, trying to claw his way to the surface. No, he didn't like it one little bit. And he liked this Grace Vredemeyer business even less. That had a smell to it, too, but nothing he dared try to put a name to. Not yet.

The music ended. Joe Pike gave out a big whooosh of air, arms collapsing at his side. "Lordy! That's too much like work!" He pushed the stop button on the boom box before Fats Domino could crank up again. Trout knew the tape by heart. It was one of Joe Pike's favorites. The next song was "Blue Monday." Only this was Wednesday.

"Jumping for Jesus," Joe Pike said to Trout.

"Sure."

"Thought we'd have more of a crowd. But you've got to start somewhere," Joe Pike answered. "Folks hear about it, they'll come."

"We'll spread the word," Grace said. She did a couple of dainty torso rotations, keeping her eye on Trout. "Have you been exercising, Trout?" she asked.

"No ma'am."

"Your face is red."

"Oh. Yes ma'am. I reckon it is. I've been . . ." What to tell? What would Grace Vredemeyer even remotely understand about his day? Better still, would Grace Vredemeyer do the Christian thing and go away so he could talk about it with his father? He had a lot of questions. "I've been lifeguarding at the pool."

Grace gave him a blank look. It was another thing Moseley didn't have. A swimming pool.

"They needed a substitute. Just for the day," he said.

Joe Pike wasn't paying any attention. He was fumbling with the boom box, putting in another tape. He turned back to Grace. "Some alternate toe touches?"

"Sure," she said. She stood there bouncing lightly from one foot to the other.

Trout started for the door. He didn't want to see any more of this. He was exhausted, and his sunburn and his raw hands were beginning to sting again. He needed . . . What? A big vat of vanilla pudding. Naked.

"Your Aunt Alma wants to see you," Joe Pike said.

"What about?"

"Ask her."

"Now? I'm really tired. I thought I'd take a nap." Trout could hear the irritation in his voice and he didn't care.

"She's waiting for you. Get cleaned up first. She said she'd be at the mill until five-thirty."

Trout turned to go. He stopped, hand on the doorknob. "What's for supper?"

"Thought I'd fix us a salad," Joe Pike said.

"I thought so."

By the time he reached the parsonage, the boom box was thumping away again. The Bee Gees now. *Stayin' alive . . . stayin' alive . . .*

There was only a scattering of cars in the parking lot when Trout got to the mill. Second shift, he remembered, the one Wardell Dubarry worked. Trout imagined him now inside, tending looms and cussing the Moseleys. Alma's car was parked in front of the one-story office annex. It was her everyday car, a late-model gray Buick. Trout hadn't seen the old Packard in use since the day he arrived, the day she had brought him here and told him that one day, all this would be his. He stood beside the motorcycle for a moment, looking at the mill building: dull red brick, tall windows so sun-mottled, they looked like stained glass with the late-afternoon light hitting them just so. *Like a church*, Aunt Alma's other church. It had once operated twenty-four hours a day, six days a week, so Uncle Phinizy had told him. And the other church, the one where they were Jumping for Jesus just now, had had two services every Sunday morning to accommodate the crowd. What happened?

The door to the office annex was open. Trout stuck his head in, looked around, didn't see anybody. It was after five, the office staff gone for the day, their tiny cubicles with the wavy-glass partitions empty, desktops bare. Back in the mill area, he could hear the steady hum of machinery. He called out: "Aunt Alma?"

"Back here."

She was at the mahogany desk in her office, a big green-sheeted ledger spread open in front of her. "Be just a minute," she said, waving him into a chair. He sat, hunched a little forward. He had showered gingerly, found a tube of first aid ointment and smeared it on the places he could reach, then dressed in short-sleeved cotton shirt and khaki pants. If he didn't do too much moving around inside the shirt, it was bearable. He waited, trying to be still and quiet.

Aunt Alma looked up at him and frowned. "Do you have hemorrhoids?"

"What? Oh, no ma'am. I just got a little sunburned."

"It runs in the family."

"Sunburn?"

"Hemorrhoids. All the Moseley men have them."

"Well, I never have, ah, had the problem."

"Your father had a terrible case when he was a teenager. Football aggravated his hemorrhoids."

"Maybe that's why he fell down," Trout said. Could you trip over a hemorrhoid?

Aunt Alma gave him an odd look and went back to her ledger. She consulted a pile of papers at her elbow and made entries in the book with a pencil, flipping pieces of paper as she went. "I'm almost finished," she said after a while.

"No hurry," Trout said. And waited some more.

She reached the bottom of the stack of papers, put them aside, then started to work with an old crank-handled adding machine — the index finger of her left hand moving down a column of figures on the ledger, her right hand jabbing keys, hauling on the crank. The paper tape curled out of the top of the machine, longer and longer, almost reaching the floor. Alma was very deft. She never took her eyes off the column of figures until she had finished and given the adding-machine handle a final pull. She squinted at the last figure on the tape and sat there for a long moment staring at it. She closed her eyes, opened them, looked again. Her lips moved silently. Then she ripped off the tape and started wadding it up until the long streamer of paper was just a small hard ball. She dropped it into a wastebasket at the side of the desk.

Trout stared. Alma looked up at him. Her eyes narrowed; then she broke into a perfectly hideous grin. "Now. How's it going?"

"Okay, I guess."

"I heard about your tennis tournament. That's too bad. I know you're disappointed."

"I played pretty badly," he said with a shrug. "I have this problem with my backhand."

She gave him a blank look. "I never played tennis."

"You know" — he demonstrated, wincing a little when the fabric of his shirt scraped across his back — "when you reach across your body to hit the ball. Backhanded. I don't do it very well."

"I see," she said.

"I have a pretty good serve," Trout went on. For some reason, it seemed important to explain this to Aunt Alma, who had grown up in a town where tennis was considered frivolous. Moseley could have used a little tennis, he imagined. Or maybe a drug culture. "In fact, my serve has been referred to as 'wicked.' Like a rocket. WHOOSH!" He made a rocket gesture with his hand, sending a ball screaming across Aunt Alma's desk. She flinched a little. "Usually, I can groove the sucker in there and knock the other guy back on his heels and never even have to bother with my backhand. I get a lot of aces."

"Aces?"

"Yes ma'am. That's where your opponent can't return your serve. But this kid from Augusta, he was *returning* my serve. Every time.

To my backhand. I had one ace the whole dad-burned match, Aunt Alma." Trout shook his head, remembering. "It was horrible. I feel like I let the family down. The whole town, in fact."

She shook her head, sympathetic. "It was just a tennis match, Trout."

"The State Juniors."

"Well, it's not the end of the world."

Trout stared at the floor. "I guess not."

"I'm sorry," she said. "Since I don't play, I suppose I can't fully appreciate what it means to you."

Trout looked up. "You could learn, Aunt Alma. I could teach you to play tennis. Everything — " he shrugged — "but the backhand, I guess."

"Oh no," she said with a dismissive wave of her hand. "At my age?"

"I had a friend in Ohatchee, his grandfather learned to water-ski when he was sixty. You're not that old."

Aunt Alma smiled. "No. Not quite."

Trout imagined Aunt Alma on the tennis court, maybe at the club in Augusta, dressed in a little white tennis skirt with her hair tied back. She had decent legs, what you could see of them. A little hippy, but that was from sitting here at the desk too much. She'd be stiff at first, but once she got the hang of it, she might play decently enough to enjoy the game. If she did, maybe she would build a tennis court. It would be a good way to get to know her better, teaching her to play tennis. If she'd just loosen up a little . . .

"I always wanted to go to Wimbledon," she said. "Not to play, just to watch. No, not even to watch so much as to just *be* there. It has a nice ring to it. Wimbledon. Very British, don't you think? The best people, on their best behavior. Some nice parties, I imagine."

"Well, why don't you go?"

Aunt Alma stared at him for a moment; then something wistful crossed her face. She looked away. "Maybe I should have," she said quietly. "But now? No, I don't imagine so."

Aunt Alma closed her ledger book with a bang, suddenly all business. "Enough about tennis. You've got the rest of your life to think about, Trout, and it's time you started learning."

"About what?" Trout squirmed in his chair. It sounded ominously permanent: *the rest of your life.*

"I'm going to start you off in shipping and receiving. It's hard work and it's not very glamorous, but it's a good point of view. Raw cotton comes in, white goods go out. A few weeks of that, then some time in the spinning and weaving operations. After school starts in the fall, you can work in the office. I want you to know the business top to bottom."

Trout felt his mouth drop open. Here? The mill? It was something he might have to think about in a zillion years, when Aunt Alma was dead from extreme old age and he and Eugene were the only ones left. And then they would hire somebody to run it and send checks every month. But now? Work here in this ancient beast of a building with all that machinery rumbling and growling, waiting to snatch you by the sleeve and chew you to a bloody pulp? He didn't even know how a pencil sharpener worked and didn't want to. He would screw something up horribly and the mill would explode and white stuff would float to earth for days. Headline: BOY PUSHES WRONG BUTTON. Joe Pike should be here. He should be the one running looms and shipping and receiving, maybe even running the whole mill — especially since he didn't seem to know why he had become a preacher. Instead, here was Trout, who had his mother's innate distrust — nay, outright fear — of all things mechanical, contemplating a career in textiles. *Dang it, Joe Pike Moseley, here I am cleaning up after you again.*

"Be here at eight," Aunt Alma said. "Cooley Hargrove is the shipping manager. He'll be expecting you. Now go home and get a good night's sleep. And for goodness' sake, get something for those hemorrhoids."

He was stopped at the traffic light in the middle of town when he heard Uncle Cicero hail him: "Trout! Yo, Trout!" Cicero was standing in the doorway of the hardware store, looking very snappy in his uniform and cap, gun belt circling his waist. "Need to talk to you, Trout."

Trout didn't much want to talk to Uncle Cicero just now. His back and shoulders were stinging again, and he wanted to go home and glop on some more ointment. But there didn't seem to be much of a way out of it. So he pulled over, parked the motorcycle at the curb, and followed Cicero into the store. It was a cavernous, high-ceilinged place, a single big room with shelves rising behind display cases along the walls, aisles lined with bins and more shelves, all filled with tools, nuts and bolts and nails, cans and cartons. Facing the front plate-glass window, a soldierly row of lawn mowers and garden tillers. Hanging from one pegboarded stretch of wall, Weed Eaters and chain saws. From another, brooms and mops. From still another, shovels and rakes and hoes. Along the back wall, sacks of mortar mix, rolls of fence wire, cases of motor oil, cans of paint. Near the front door, a long counter with a cash register and a big roll of brown kraft wrapping paper. It was well lit with low-hanging fluorescent fixtures, everything very orderly and neat, a rich stew of smells — leather and metal, wood and solvent. And color. Orange weed trimmers, green lawn mowers, oak-handled sledgehammers, bright red gasoline cans, even the grays and silvers and blacks of tools. Amazing how colorful hardware could be when you put it all together. Merchandise as decor.

Trout stood just inside the door, taking it all in, while Uncle Cicero leaned against the counter, arms crossed, cap tilted back on his head, lips pursed, watching. It struck Trout that Cicero didn't look at all like a policeman in a hardware store. He looked like a hardware man dressed in a policeman's uniform. The place fit him like a glove. He was perfectly at home. "Gee," Trout said. "It's a lot of stuff."

"I know where every item is, down to the last cotter pin," Cicero said. "Fellow comes in, wants a half-pound of your ten-penny galvanized nails, I take him right to 'em." Cicero pointed down one of the aisles where metal bins held a jumble of nails. "Another fellow comes in, says he needs a lawn mower. How much of a lawn mower? He doesn't know, just enough to cut the grass. How big's the lawn? Oh, about yea-by-yea." Cicero made a lawn with his hands. "What kind of grass you got? Bermuda in the front, Saint Augustine in the back. How often you cut it? Once a week." Cicero walked over to one of the lawn mowers, patted the silver handle. "Okay, what you need is your Lawn Boy Model L-250. Briggs and Stratton two-point-five horse engine, made in the good old U.S.A. Twenty-two-inch cut, self-propelled. On special this month for two ninety-five." Cicero knelt next to the Lawn Boy and pointed to the wheel height adjustment. "For the Bermuda in front, set 'er at one inch. You gotta show that Bermuda who's boss. For the Saint Augustine, pop 'er up to two inches. Cut Saint Augustine too close, you'll damage it. And keep the blade sharpened." He stood, gave Trout a direct look. "In the hardware bidness, you don't sell stuff to folks, you help 'em decide what to buy. And then you tell 'em how to use it. Now" — he stuck his finger in the air — "if the fellow says he's got two acres of zoysia sloping back to front with a stand of pine trees, I tell him to go to Augusta and get him a riding mower. You don't sell a fellow something he can't use, 'cause he'll be back in a week raising hell and you done lost a customer. Got that?"

"Yes sir."

"You come just in the nick of time, Trout."

"What for?"

Cicero tucked his thumbs in his gun belt. "I'm expanding."

"Oh," Trout said, looking around the store. "Where?"

"I've bought out Ezell." Cicero walked past him, out the front door and onto the sidewalk. Trout stood there, not sure what to do, and then Cicero motioned for him to come out. He stood next to Cicero on the sidewalk and followed his gaze to the feed, seed, and fertilizer store next door.

"I've been after Ezell for five years. And just this morning, he walked in here and said, 'All right, Cicero, you can have it.'"

"The store?"

"Yessirreebobtail."

"What are you gonna do with it?"

"Same thing Ezell's been doing. Him and me had sort of a gentlemen's agreement over the years. I didn't stock things like fertilizer and bedding plants and chicken feed and so forth. Somebody come into my store and want your twenty-five-pound sack of eight-eight-eight, I sent 'em to Ezell. Likewise, somebody walk into Ezell's place and want a hoe, he sent 'em to me. Only thing we never could agree on was your tree spikes."

"Tree spikes?"

"You know, those things you hammer in the ground around the base of a tree. Ezell contends that a tree spike is fertilizer. But I contend that anything you hammer is hardware."

Cicero walked back in the store. Trout followed. Cicero pointed to the side wall, the one he shared with Ezell. "I'm gonna knock out part of that wall right yonder, make about a ten-foot opening. And I'm gonna put my tree spikes and Ezell's tree spikes together on a rack right there."

"Sort of like a marriage," Trout said.

"That's it," Cicero laughed, enjoying the image.

"Well, that's nice. I guess."

"That ain't all," Cicero said, and led Trout out to the sidewalk again.

"Yonder." He pointed to the vacant lot just past Ezell's, the place where the furniture store had been. "Auto parts."

"You mean a store?"

"Not a store, Trout, a complex. Cicero's Do-It-All. I got a bulldozer coming in the morning to grade the lot. Then I'll put up a nice little building with skylights and a linoleum floor. And I'll knock a hole in the far wall of Ezell's place." Cicero gave a grand sweep of his arm, taking in the elements of his business empire-to-be. "Hardware. Feed, seed, and fertilizer. Auto parts. All connected."

Trout didn't quite know what to say. It was a little overwhelming. He could feel fatigue thick behind his eyes. He really would like to climb back on the motorcycle and go home and maybe revisit Uncle Cicero's grand design another day. But Cicero waited, beaming. "How about that," Trout said finally.

"It's the best thing that's happened to Moseley in a long time," Cicero said. "It'll draw from all over. Maybe even from Augusta."

"What does Aunt Alma think about it?"

"Well, I haven't told her yet. But anybody can see, all this town needs is a little shot in the arm, Trout. Get folks excited about coming to Moseley again. One-stop shopping." Cicero checked off items on an imaginary list. "Can of spackling paste, box of sixteen-gauge shotgun shells, ten pounds of azalea fertilizer, package of nasturtium seeds, radiator cap for a seventy-one Chevy Caprice, case of Havoline thirty-weight oil."

"And tree spikes," Trout added.

"You betcha." Cicero laughed again. "Don't forget your tree spikes. Then when you get through at Cicero's Do-It-All, go down the street yonder and eat lunch at the Koffee Kup. Pick up a pair of brogans at the dry goods. And shop the produce specials at the Dixie Vittles Supermarket."

Trout looked up and down the empty street. "What supermarket?"

"Oh, it'll come. This here" — he waved, taking in the hardware and Ezell's — "is the catalyst." They both stood there for a while, pondering it. And then Cicero said quietly, "I'd like to be known as a man of vision, Trout. The fellow who turned Moseley around."

Trout gave him a long look. And he saw that in his Uncle Cicero, there was not an ounce of guile or pretense or arrogant pride. Just a sawed-off little hardware man in a police chief's uniform with an honest, open face and the simple desire to do something right, whether it was fixing you up with the right lawn mower or fixing up a town with the right future. Trout liked his Uncle Cicero a great deal at that moment. "I think it's a great idea," he said.

"I hoped you would," Cicero said. "Can you be here at seven?"

"What?"

"First week or so, I want you to just wander around the store and look at things. Read all the labels, see what's where. You got to know your merchandise. I'll make up lists of items, just like I was a customer, and you fill 'em. By the end of the week, you'll pretty much be able to take over."

"Take over?"

"Of course, I'll be close by if you have a question or a problem. Supervising the construction."

Trout felt weak. He wanted to sit down on the curb and put his head between his legs. Cicero talked on, but his voice sounded hollow and far away. "I sure was glad to hear Joe Pike say you were looking for a summer job. But this could be a lot more than that, Trout. It's a chance to grow with the business. Build a career. Who knows —"

"Uncle Cicero," Trout interrupted, "I've got to go home now. I've had a long day. I got sunburned, and my back and neck are killing me. And I'm feeling a little light-headed. So I think I'd better just go."

Cicero looked at him, face scrunched up with concern. "You do look a little peaked, Trout. 'Scuse me for carrying on so and not noticing." He put his hand up against Trout's forehead. "You may even have a little fever there. Want me to drive you home?"

"No sir. I can make it."

"Well, you get a good supper in you, get a good night's sleep."

"Yes sir."

Cicero held out his hand. Trout stared at it for a moment, then realized Cicero wanted to shake. He did. Cicero had a nice firm, honest grip. A man of vision. "See you in the morning," he said.

"I can't eat this stuff," Trout said. He got up from the kitchen table, took the bowl to the sink, crammed all the leafy green and chopped-up red stuff and the crunchy little croutons and the imitation bacon bits into the disposal and turned it on. It roared in protest, digesting. Then he turned back to Joe Pike, who was shoveling a forkful of salad into his mouth, chewing it like a cud.

"What don't you like about salad?" Joe Pike asked after a moment.

"It grows in your mouth," Trout answered.

"Oh?"

"You put it in there and try to chew and it just keeps growing and you feel like you're gonna choke on it."

"You used to like salad. Mom fixed it all the time."

"That was different."

Joe Pike nodded. "Of course."

"I mean," Trout said, "she used different stuff."

"Same stuff."

"Well, she fixed it different."

Joe Pike ate some more salad. Trout watched him for a moment; then he went back to the table and sat down. "There's a chicken pot pie in the freezer," Joe Pike said. "And some sweet potato pie that Hilda brought from the Koffee Kup. And some of Grace's Jell-O fruit business."

"I've got three jobs," Trout said.

"Does that mean you don't have time to eat?"

"Uncle Cicero wants me at the hardware store at seven o'clock in the morning."

"And . . ."

"Aunt Alma wants me at the mill at eight."

"And . . ."

"Herschel wants me at the Dairy Queen at ten."

Joe Pike put down his fork and wiped his mouth with his paper napkin, then placed the napkin back in his lap. "Sounds like a full morning."

"Yeah."

"Are the positions incompatible?"

"What do you mean?"

"Well, you don't want to get lint in the ice cream or tacks in the looms."

"Daddy," Trout said angrily, "don't."

Joe Pike sat back in his chair and studied Trout for a while. "I'm sorry," he said finally. "I'm obviously not approaching your dilemma with the sense of gravity it deserves. Let's start over. You have three jobs — or, at least, job offers."

"Yes sir."

"An embarrassment of riches. Could you do more than one?"

Trout shrugged. "I don't think so. They're all the same hours, pretty much."

"Hmmmm," Joe Pike hummed gravely, furrowing his brow, twisting his mouth, and pondering — or at least appearing to ponder — the situation. Then he drummed a little cadence with his fingers on the edge of the table. Then he stared at a spot where the ceiling met the far wall, as if the answer to Trout's problem might be written there: ATTENTION! GO FOR THE MONEY! "How much do they pay?" Joe Pike asked finally.

"I don't know."

"You don't know?"

"Nobody said. That's not the point."

"What is?"

Trout shrugged.

"All right. Let me see if I can put this in perspective here. Preachers are supposed to be good at putting things in perspective. The hours are about the same. Money's no object. Sounds like it gets down to intangibles."

"Like?"

"Work environment, compatibility with colleagues, expectations for emotional and intellectual fulfillment. Coffee breaks."

Trout pushed his chair back with an angry scrape, got up and turned to go. "I can't even talk to you anymore."

"Sit down," Joe Pike ordered in his best no-nonsense voice. Trout sat down. Joe Pike gave him a long look, then reared back in his chair a bit, arms folded across his chest. "You want me to make up your mind for you? You want me to tell you what to do?"

Trout sat ramrod-straight in the chair and stared at his hands.

"What do *you* want to do, Trout? Which job do you want? Any, all, or none?"

"The Dairy Queen," Trout mumbled.

Joe Pike threw up his hands. "Touchdown!"

Trout stared at his hands some more, and then he finally looked up at Joe Pike. "Would you . . ."

"Nope."

"You don't even know what I was gonna say."

"Yes I do. You were about to ask me to square it with Alma and Cicero."

How does he do that? Does God whisper in his ear?

"Right?"

"I don't want to hurt Uncle Cicero's feelings and I don't want to make Aunt Alma mad."

"Well, there's a chance you will on both counts. But that's part of making a choice, son. I can't make your choice for you."

Joe Pike got up from the table, took his plate to the sink and rinsed off the few shreds of salad that were left. "I bought some wheat germ," he said over his shoulder.

"What?"

"I thought we'd have oatmeal for breakfast. With wheat germ on it."

Good grief.

Joe Pike put the stopper in the sink and started running dishwater.

"Daddy . . ."

"Huh?"

"Talk to me."

Joe Pike stood there for a moment longer with his back to Trout, then turned off the water, dried his hands on a dishtowel, came back to the table and sat down.

"Why are you mad at me?"

Joe Pike gave him a long look, his brow furrowing. "Son," he said finally, "I'm not mad at you. What makes you think that?"

"I don't know. You're just . . . not paying any attention."

Joe Pike sighed, rubbed his face with his hands, then folded them in front of him and leaned across the table toward Trout. "Trout, I'm sorry, son. I've got a lot on my plate right now. I'm worried about your mama, I'm worried about Alma and the mill . . ."

"And you're worried about why you became a preacher. You never did answer my question."

"Yes. That, too."

"Well, what am I supposed to do while you worry about all this stuff? I've got stuff to worry about, too."

"Most kids your age don't want their parents telling them what to do and how to think. I didn't. I wanted my father to just leave me alone."

"Is that why you ran away from Georgia Military Academy and went to school at Moseley High?"

"Yes."

"Is that why you went all the way to Texas to play football?"

"Mostly."

"Well, that's fine for you," Trout said. "I don't want you telling me what to do, either. But I want you there when I need you. And you're not there."

"I'm sorry," Joe Pike said quietly, looking at his hands. "I'll try to do better."

There didn't seem to be much else to say, so Trout got up to go. He was almost to the door when Joe Pike stopped him. "Practice one day when we were getting ready to play Baylor. We had wallered around and looked like a bunch of sandlot kids all afternoon, so Coach Bryant just all of a sudden stopped practice and sent everybody to the locker room. And we sat there and waited for him, scared out of our pants. Players, trainer, assistant coaches. Nobody moved. We waited, and the more we waited, the more scared we were. Finally, about a half hour later, Coach walked in. Didn't say a word, just stood there in the middle of the room. Then all of a sudden he hauled off and threw a block on an assistant coach that would kill a mule. Just slammed into this poor guy and knocked him into a row of lockers. Blam! Blam! Blam! Lockers come crashing down, the assistant coach is laid out on the floor half dead, eyes rolled back in his head, blood pouring out of a cut in his scalp. The rest of us just standing there with our mouths open. Horrified. I'm right at Coach's elbow and I'm about to pee in my britches 'cause I'm afraid I'm next. But then he puts his arm around my shoulder real gentle-like and says, 'You know, Joe Pike, sometimes it just helps to get things off your chest.' And he turns around and walks out. And on Saturday, we whipped Baylor pretty good."

Herschel was cleaning up when Trout got to the Dairy Queen about nine o'clock. There were a few late customers. A family in a pickup truck, mama and daddy in the cab, five kids in the back, all licking on ice cream cones. A station wagon with an "Illinois Land of Lincoln" tag towing a pop-top camper. The occupants, a man and woman and two teenage girls, were sitting at one of the concrete tables, munching on hot dogs. An elderly couple in a late-model Buick, the woman watching a small dog pee in the grass next to the parking lot while the man waited for his order at the window.

"Two cupsa vanilla with crushed nuts," Herschel said to Trout.

"What?"

"Don't just stand there. Fix the man's ice cream."

Herschel had stopped cleaning the griddle to take the man's order as Trout came in the back door. He pointed. "Cups there. Ice cream machine there. Just pull the lever down. Crushed nuts in the container. Anybody's eaten as much Dairy Queen stuff as you and the preacher oughta know what a cup of ice cream looks like. And wash your hands first."

Herschel went back to his work while Trout washed up gingerly at the sink in back. His hands were still a little raw from the acid he had used to clean the tables outside earlier in the day. Then he filled two cups with ice cream. He tried to finish them off with a little curlicue at the top, but it didn't work. The ice cream just flopped over. He found the mixed nuts, sprinkled a few on each. He eyed his work. Not bad for a start. He took the two cups to the front counter and slid the window open. Warm night air and the faint rumble of traffic on I-20 drifted in, mingling with the air conditioning.

"Spoons," Herschel said at his back. "Under the counter."

Trout took two red spoons out of a box and stuck them jauntily into the ice cream cups.

"Napkins," Herschel said.

Trout plucked two napkins out of the napkin holder on the counter and laid them beside the ice cream cups.

"Dollar fifteen," Herschel said.

"A dollar fifteen," Trout said to the customer. Then he recognized the man. Fleet Mathis. The mayor.

"Trout, that you?"

"Yes sir."

"Working at the Dairy Queen."

Trout looked over at Herschel. "I guess so, yes sir." Herschel grunted.

Fleet Mathis took a dollar bill out of his wallet and fished a nickel and dime out of his pants pocket, pushed them across the counter to Trout. "I'da thought you'd be working down at the mill with your Aunt Alma."

"Well . . ."

"Family business and all."

Fleet Mathis waited for a moment, but Trout didn't say anything, and finally he picked up his ice cream cups. "Too bad about the tennis tournament," he said.

"Yes sir."

"Your backhand, the way I heard it."

"That's it."

He started to turn away, but then he stopped and looked back at Trout. "Dairy Queen's our newest business."

"Huh?"

Fleet Mathis leaned over and peered through the open window at Herschel inside. "Sign of progress, that's what I tell folks, Herschel."

"Yes sir, Mayor," Herschel said. "A town that's got a Dairy Queen is an up-and-coming place."

Fleet Mathis looked at Trout. "Kind of ironic, Trout."

"What's that?"

"You working here at our newest business." He thought about that for a moment. "Well, good night, Trout. See you in church Sunday, if not before."

"'Night, Mr. Mathis. Hope you enjoy your ice cream."

He stood there at the counter watching Fleet Mathis walking back toward his car with the two ice cream cups. *He'll probably go right home and call Aunt Alma and tell her I'm working at the Dairy Queen. And then she'll have a fit and come storming over to the parsonage in the middle of the night.* Headline: BOY TRAITOR EXECUTED.

"It ain't an air-conditioned parking lot," Herschel said.

"What?"

"Close the window."

Trout slid the window shut. Then he leaned against the counter for a while and watched Herschel as he finished up at the grill. The muscles in his upper arms bulged against the tight sleeves of his shirt as he worked at the griddle with a spatula, scraping away the greasy brown residue of a day's worth of hamburgers and hash browns. He wore a stained apron, and his Dairy Queen cap was pushed back on his head, revealing a thinning patch of steel-gray crew cut. Herschel gave out a little snort. "Sign of progress, the man says. Next thing you know, they'll be announcing a Kmart and a Winn-Dixie. Maybe even a Lord and Taylor's."

"How long have you been open?" Trout asked.

"Two years next month. Before me, I think the last new business was a Laundromat. 1968. Stayed open a year, the way I heard it." He finished scraping, put down the spatula and turned to Trout. "You know what's wrong with this town?"

"The Interstate."

"No. The attitude. Folks just sitting around waiting for something to happen. Capish?"

"I guess so."

Herschel waved in the general direction of I-20. "Hell, the Interstate's no problem. Wasn't for folks coming in off the highway, I'd be a dead duck. You hungry?"

"Yes sir."

"You look it. Thirty years running a mess hall, I can tell a hungry man when I see one."

There were two weiners left on the little rotisserie cooker next to the griddle. Herschel took a foot-long bun out of the bun warmer, put it in a little paper boat, plopped the two weiners end-to-end in the bun and spread chili over the top. Trout's stomach rumbled in anticipation. He felt hollow.

"Tea?" Herschel asked.

"Sure. Great."

Herschel fixed a cup of iced tea and set everything in front of Trout on the counter. "Preacher ain't feedin' you?"

"We had salad."

Trout sat on a stool and ate while Herschel went back to cleaning up. He fought the urge to wolf it down, savoring every bite, filling up the hollowness. The crunch of the weiner nestled in the soft bread of the bun, overlaid with the tang of the chili. A religious experience, Joe Pike called it. Yea, verily.

When Trout finished, Herschel fixed him a cup of ice cream. "Here's how you do the curlicue," Herschel said. "A little twist of the wrist on the hand that's holding the cup, just as you're cutting off the flow. That's about the only trick I know to working Dairy Queen. Other than that, it's dish it up and dish it out. Clean place, good food, fair price."

Trout thought about it while he slowly ate his ice cream. Maybe that was why he chose the Dairy Queen. The thought of the mill gave him a dull, leadened feeling — all that clattering machinery, spinning bobbins of yarn, looms disgorging miles and miles of plain white cotton cloth, all of it going into the big ledger book on Aunt

Alma's desk. And the hardware store. He liked Uncle Cicero, but the idea of all that *stuff*. Nuts and bolts and loppers and tree spikes rattling around in his brain and banging into one another? There was too much rattling around in there already. He needed something cool and not too noisy and short on detail and long on routine. Dish it up and dish it out.

He scraped the last morsel from the bottom of the ice cream cup and let it slide down his tongue. Then he set the cup down on the counter, stood up, fished in his jeans pocket.

"On the house," Herschel said.

"Thanks."

"Ten to two tomorrow."

"Okay."

"Two-fifty an hour to start."

"That's fine."

Joe Pike and Phinizy were sitting on the front steps when Trout pulled into the driveway. The beam from the motorcycle's headlamp swept across them, but neither looked up. They seemed to be deep in conversation. Trout put the motorcycle in the shed and walked around to the front of the house. Joe Pike was wearing a short-sleeved dress shirt and tie. Had somebody died? Then he remembered. Wednesday night. Prayer Meeting. He felt an old familiar lurch in his stomach. There was something vaguely unsettling about the notion of Wednesday Night Prayer Meeting, something ancient and buried like an old bone turning to dust. He could not remember ever going, and maybe that was it. Guilt? Or something else?

Trout sat down beside Phinizy on the steps. "Hello," Phinizy said. He took a last drag off the stub of a cigarette he held between his thumb and first finger, pulled another out of the pack in his shirt pocket and lit it off the end of the stub.

"Hello yourself," Trout said. "Aren't you gonna offer me a cigarette?"

Phinizy sucked noisily on the new cigarette, then blew a double stream of smoke out his nostrils as he said, "No sir, I am not. Cigarettes make your breath smell bad and then you can't kiss girls."

"Don't you kiss girls?" Trout asked.

"Not anymore. At my age and stage, I'd rather smoke cigarettes."

Then he was shaken by an attack of wheezing and coughing, nasty wracking stuff that sounded like it was coming from somewhere down around his feet. Headline: MAN DIES, LUNGS FOUND IN AUGUSTA.

Joe Pike hadn't said a thing since Trout rounded the corner of the house. He sat hunched forward, elbows on knees, hands clasped, a massive silence. It was hard to see either man's face in the dim light filtering through the tree branches from the streetlamp out by the curb, but Trout could smell the aroma of argument in the air mingling with the pungency of tobacco. Phinizy gave a last hack, took a shallow breath, let it out easily. "Ahhhhh," he said. "A gentle habit, smoking." Then he tossed the glowing cigarette onto the walkway at the bottom of the steps and crushed it with his toe. "Your father and I were just discussing dichotomy."

"What's that?" Trout asked.

"Schism."

Trout gave him a blank look.

"Contradiction."

"Oh. That."

Phinizy looked over at Joe Pike. "A sixteen-year-old boy, and he understands the concept of dichotomy."

Joe Pike didn't say anything.

"Reverend Joe Pike Moseley here has been a rare study in dichotomy this evening," Phinizy went on.

"I just said —" Joe Pike started.

But Phinizy cut him off. "They tell me," he said to Trout, "that your father has always been a stickler for tradition when it comes to church business. The old tried-and-true hymns, real wine at Communion, even if it is watered down a bit, no Boy Scout troops or other such folderol. And good old-fashioned prayer meeting on Wednesday night. Praying and singing. A midweek infusion of the Holy Spirit to tide you over till Sunday. None of this 'Wonderful Wednesday' business they have in lots of churches where they study pop psychology and paint china and do book reviews. None of that in Reverend Joe Pike Moseley's church. Am I right?"

Trout fidgeted. He had learned from experience that the best course when a couple of adults got off on a tangent like this was to excuse himself and go to the bathroom. Or if escape was impossible, hunker down and disappear into the furniture. Anything to stay out of the line of fire. He had done a lot of that when Irene was around, when the tension got to critical mass — Joe Pike being excessively polite, Irene lapsing into what became longer and longer silences, but the air thick with conflict that politeness and silence only made worse. If they'd just *yell*. Explosions come and go. Silence creeps up your butt like a parasite and builds a nest.

But he decided to wait it out a bit and see what happened. There might even be an explosion. Joe Pike was the one hunkered down over there on the other side of the steps, keeper of the great silence. And there was a persistent, needling edge to Phinizy's voice. If he kept it up long enough, he might bring a rare burst of thunder and lightning. At least get a reaction, which was something Trout wasn't having much success at. He remembered Phinizy's joke about the two truck drivers. Another wreck about to happen?

"You're right," he answered Phinizy.

"So here you have a preacher conducting a good old-fashioned Wednesday Night Prayer Meeting. And he gets off on deodorant."

"Deodorant?"

A long moment. They all waited. Then Joe Pike's shoulders shook, and he sort of heaved himself into an upright sitting position. Trout held his breath, but when Joe Pike spoke, his voice was even. "I *said* . . ." He chewed on it a moment, then went on. "I said that *what if* the scientists made a mistake. They tested antiperspirant, and they say it's safe. So the FDA approves it and we buy antiperspirant and put it on our underarms every morning and go about our business. But what if there is some minuscule, hidden ingredient in antiperspirant that turns out, after many, many years of use, to be very, very bad. What if we wake up one morning and our underarms are rotting out? That's all I said."

"And that," Phinizy added, "is when Tilda Huffstetler started crying."

Trout stared. "She did?"

"She did." Phinizy nodded. "Tilda said she's been going to Wednesday Night Prayer Meeting for more than fifty years, and it's the first time she ever heard anybody talk about deodorant."

"Tilda's always been a little high-strung," Joe Pike said. "Maybe it's hormones."

"No," Phinizy said, "I think it's more like confusion. Or, to return to my original theme, dichotomy."

"Look," Joe Pike said, his voice rising a little now, "is there anything wrong with me introducing an idea? . . ."

"Which is?"

"Randomness. Uncertainty. The unknown."

Phinizy gave a wave of his hands. "If we can't be sure of our deodorant, what can we be sure of?" Joe Pike didn't say anything. "God?"

Joe Pike nodded. "That's the point."

"That's *your* point. I'm not sure it registered with Tilda Huffstetler." Phinizy pointed up in the trees. "You're up there in the theological stratosphere somewhere, trying to figure out the meaning of life, and Tilda's worried about her underarms. Or perhaps more precisely, she's worried about why *you're* worried about her underarms."

"I'm the preacher," Joe Pike said with a touch of bitterness. "I'm supposed to have it all down pat."

"To Tilda, you are. She wants to believe in God, her preacher, and her deodorant. You threw her a curveball, high and tight, and it near about took her head off."

Joe Pike snorted. "So what am I supposed to do, Phin? If I have doubts about something, am I just supposed to keep 'em to myself? Isn't that dishonest?"

"I don't get it," Phinizy said.

"Get what?" Joe Pike asked.

"First of all, why anybody — make that, why would a preacher — purposely introduce more chaos into an already chaotic existence?"

"Chaos is the essence of existence."

"Maybe the battle *against* chaos is the essence of existence. Else, why do we impose laws, record history, invent myths?"

"Habit," Joe Pike said.

"Self-defense. We blunder about, being as ornery and unreasonable and illogical as possible. But deep down, we want some rules. Something we can put in the bank."

"Okay, Phin. So we're just supposed to obey the rules. Ask no questions."

"I didn't say that, Joe Pike. You asked me why Tilda Huffstetler cried at Prayer Meeting. I'm playing devil's advocate here. Telling you what I think. You know, part of your trouble is that you're a Methodist."

"What do you mean?"

"Catholics got the Pope, Jews got Israel, Presbyterians got reincarnation, Baptists got biblical inerrancy. You Methodists take it all in.

Come on, everybody. Think what you want. Israelites, reincarnation-ists, inerrantists, probably even a few closet Papists on the back row. Inclusion becomes confusion. Then the other part of your trouble is that you think you deserve answers."

Joe Pike shrugged. "I'm just a poor wayfaring stranger."

"Always have been," Phinizy said. "I think you became a preacher because you thought God would whisper in your ear and tell you what it's all about. But He didn't. So you got on a motorcycle and rode off to Texas looking for Bear Bryant. And he wasn't there. If Bear knew you'd done that, he'd probably laugh his ass off."

"Maybe that's what God's doing," Joe Pike said.

"Maybe."

Joe Pike waved his hands, agitated. "But if I don't know, I've got to ask, Phin. And if it upsets folks, maybe it'll get 'em to thinking, get 'em out of their self-satisfied existence."

"Or, it may just bring the Bishop down on your fanny."

"Could be."

Phinizy stood, brushing ashes off his clothes. "Well, you do what-ever you want, Joe Pike. It's your business. I'm going home and have some bourbon and read Heidegger."

Joe Pike looked up at him. "Tell me something, Phin. Why did you come to Prayer Meeting tonight? You never have before. Why this time?"

Phinizy gave Joe Pike a long look. "Same reason I read Heidegger. You know Heidegger: 'Why is there something instead of nothing?' You and Heidegger are both wallowing in cosmic angst, Joe Pike. Chasing your theological tails like Little Black Sambo's tiger. It's inter-esting to watch." He shot a glance at Trout. "But I sure wouldn't want to live around it." He waited, but got no response. A trace of a smile played at his lips. "I am a cynical old sonofabitch. I don't believe in much of anything. But at least I'm consistent."

He turned then and shuffled off across the yard, lighting a cigarette as he went, the flame from his Zippo flickering in the darkness under the trees. Then he crossed the street — a thin, stooped figure in the dim light of the streetlamp — and disappeared into the long shadows cast by Aunt Alma's house.

After a while, Joe Pike said — to no one in particular — "That's what you get with a church that's been spoon-fed all its life. Put a little spice in the menu, everybody gets heartburn."

Since Joe Pike said it to no one in particular, Trout didn't feel any need to respond and wouldn't have known what to say anyway. So they just sat there for a long time. And finally Trout thought of the thing he *did* need to say. He was bone-tired and needed desperately to go to bed, but he had to say this one thing first: "Keats told me about getting run over by the mill truck," he said. "And her brother."

Joe Pike didn't say anything for a while. And then he took a deep breath and made the little hissing sound through his teeth. "Yeah," he said. "Too bad about that."

And that was all. When Trout realized that was all, he got up and left Joe Pike sitting there on the front steps with his theological angst and went to bed.

What woke him in the depths of the night was the sudden remembrance of what made him uneasy about Wednesday Night Prayer Meeting. It came back to him full-blown, as vivid as the replaying of a documentary.

A parsonage kitchen, a bit down at the heels as they sometimes were in small Georgia towns: scuffed green linoleum on the floor, shiny pale green walls, fluorescent fixture overhead, white metal cabinets. A calendar from an insurance company hangs next to the refrigerator with a parade of red X's halfway across the month of July. Each evening, Trout climbs up on a kitchen chair and, while Irene steadies him, marks off another day with a crayon.

Joe Pike stands now in the kitchen door. Short-sleeved white shirt and tie, Bible in hand. Irene at the sink, hands thrust into sudsy water.

"Time to go," Joe Pike says.

A long silence. Irene's hands thrash about under the water, scrubbing away at a skillet. She lifts it out, runs it under the rinse water, sets it aside on a drying rack. "I'm not going," she says.

"Aren't you feeling well, hon?"

"I feel just fine."

"Well . . ."

"I'm not going."

"Well. . ."

"I mean ever."

Trout doesn't know exactly where he is while this is going on, but he must be somewhere in the room because he can see and hear and even smell everything. It has a smell to it, like something left out of the refrigerator too long. And the look on Joe Pike's face — as if he had been slapped with a dead mackerel. And Irene's tiny back, absolutely rigid and unyielding.

"Irene, hon, you have to go."

"No I don't."

"You're the preacher's wife."

Irene doesn't say a thing, but she gives a tiny shudder, as if she's suddenly struck with a chill. After a moment, Joe Pike gives a shrug of his shoulders. "We'll talk about it later," he says.

He has turned and left the room before Trout hears Irene say, in a small but very firm voice, "No we won't."

Then there is a horrible sucking sound from the sink and Trout realizes Irene has pulled the plug. She stands there looking down as the dishwater runs out, and then she turns and walks away. She doesn't look at him, doesn't even seem to notice that he's there. Droplets of water and bubbles of suds drip from her hands, leaving a trail across the kitchen linoleum. Trout hears the door to her bedroom close. He's afraid to follow, so after a while he goes out the back door and around the side of the parsonage and climbs up in the pecan tree in the side yard and looks in the window. Irene is just sitting there on the side of the bed, facing the open window. Nothing separates them but the window screen and several yards of July night. He starts to raise his hand to wave to her, but then he realizes that she can't see him here in the tree, can't in fact see anything. She is so absolutely immobile that he doubts that she could hear him if he called out, or feel him if he climbed in the window and touched her arm. It is like watching a statue of his mother. Across the street at the church, he hears a piano start up and the thin, ragged chorus of the Wednesday Night Prayer Meeting singing "Blessed Redeemer."

That was all he could remember. Being in the tree, watching his mother, hearing the music. He didn't know what he did next, what he felt, even exactly how old he had been at the time. Five, maybe. Six.

What he did know with certainty is that on a July Wednesday, Irene Moseley had refused to go to Prayer Meeting and that she lapsed into what was the first of the great silences that grew and grew until finally she embraced them as she would a lover and disappeared into the void.

Trout thought, *She won. She never went back to Prayer Meeting.*

Then he remembered what Uncle Phinizy had said: "Save your own ass." Well, that was one way to do it.

NINE

TROUT WAS ON the front walk getting the morning *Atlanta Constitution* when the truck growled past the parsonage, belching diesel smoke, towing a big flatbed trailer with a bulldozer on the back. Joe Pike stuck his head out the front door and watched as the truck rumbled on down Broadus Street toward the middle of town. Trout opened the paper and scanned the headlines: AIDE SAYS REAGAN WILL RUN; ATLANTA COUNCIL TACKLES TRANSIT DILEMMA. Forecast: hot, humid, afternoon thundershowers, high 93. The air conditioning in the Dairy Queen would be a refuge. But first there were Cicero and Alma to deal with. An inert lump of dread weighted his stomach.

Down the street, the truck wheezed to a stop with a hiss of its air brakes. Trout looked up at Joe Pike. "Cicero's Do-It-All," he said.

"What?"

"You know about it?"

"No."

"Uncle Cicero's clearing the vacant lot where the furniture store used to be. He's gonna put up an auto parts store."

"Really?"

"And he's bought out Ezell. He's going to knock holes in the walls and tie the whole thing together and call it 'Cicero's Do-It-All.'"

"Alma didn't mention it."

"I don't think she knows. Unless he told her last night."

Joe Pike pursed his lips in a silent whistle. "How 'bout that old Cicero."

Trout gave Joe Pike a look-over. "That tie doesn't match." Joe Pike's belly cascaded over a pair of dark blue pants. The tie he was wearing with his freshly starched white shirt was decorated with green and yellow amoebas on an orange background. "Where did you get that thing?"

"Texas," Joe Pike said, fingering the tie.

Joe Pike had never had the foggiest notion of fashion. Once upon a time, Irene had checked him before he left the house every day to make sure he didn't have on one brown sock and one black one. Often, he did. Lately, cowboy boots and black robe had covered a multitude of Sunday sins. But this was Thursday.

Joe Pike wiggled the tie and fluttered his eyebrows. "Does it not work for you, sweetie?"

"It depends on what you're doing today."

"Visiting the sick and shut-in."

Trout grabbed his throat and stuck his tongue out. "Gaaaahhhh."

Joe Pike pretended to be wounded. He let the tie flop against his belly. "Well, if you don't like the tie, just say so."

"Maybe the dark blue with the red diamonds."

Joe Pike checked his watch. "Are you going to see Cicero?"

"I guess so."

"I'll drop you off. I want to get a good look at Cicero before Alma beats him up."

When Trout and Joe Pike got there, the flatbed trailer was pulled up next to the curb by the empty lot and the bulldozer, a hulking orange Allis-Chalmers, was backing down the ramp. Uncle Cicero, in uniform, was standing out in the street, directing traffic around the flatbed, waving his arms and giving directions to the bulldozer operator, who wasn't paying any attention to him. The operator played the big clanking machine like a church organist, hands and feet moving deftly over levers and pedals. Another man stood by the truck cab watching.

Joe Pike parked his car at the curb, and he and Trout walked over to Cicero. A Merita Bread truck approached and slowed. The driver peered out the window at the bulldozer.

"Keep 'er movin'," Cicero called out.

"What's going on?" the bread truck driver asked.

"Progress! New business coming to town."

"Here?" The bread truck driver gave a snort, moved on down the street and pulled up in front of the Koffee Kup Kafe.

"Morning, Cicero," Joe Pike said.

"Joe Pike. How y'all?"

"Trout told me about your project."

Cicero's eyes danced with excitement. He looked as if he might break into a jig at any moment. "Yessirreebobtail. Profit and progress. Me and Trout are gonna have a busy summer."

Joe Pike looked at Trout. Trout looked at Joe Pike. Joe Pike shook his head. *Tote your own load, Bubba.*

The bulldozer cleared the trailer ramp, then did a neat ninety-degree pirouette and clanked up over the curb and onto the sidewalk. The concrete groaned and cracked under its weight. The operator cut the engine back to a deep-throated idle.

"Is that Grady Fulton?" Joe Pike asked Cicero.

"Yep."

"Hey, Grady!" Joe Pike yelled out.

Grady peered over at Joe Pike, grinned and waved. Then he climbed down from the seat and he and the other man slid the metal ramps onto the back of the flatbed. The other man climbed in the cab of the truck and pulled away, towing the empty flatbed. Cicero, Trout, and Joe Pike joined Grady on the sidewalk. Grady stuck out his hand and Joe Pike took it.

"Heard you was back," Grady said, looking Joe Pike up and down. "I believe you've growed some."

"Lord, Grady. It's been a long time," Joe Pike said. "This is my son, Trout."

Grady Fulton's hand was all callus and muscle. He was a little runt of a man, not much bigger than Uncle Phinizy, about sixty years old, with narrow eyes that squinted out from under the bill of an ancient, soiled Atlanta Braves cap with Chief Nok-a-Homa on the front. He looked Trout over, then Joe Pike, back to Trout. "You sure y'all kin?"

"I take after my mama," Trout said.

"Uh-huh." He gave a backhand to Joe Pike's belly. "I used to pick your daddy up for work every morning, and it'd take most of the bed of my pickup to carry his lunch."

"Grady and I worked construction during the summers when I was home from college," Joe Pike said to Trout.

Grady nodded. "Spent two of them summers four-laning two seventy-eight out of Augusta. That was about the time you was courting Alma, wasn't it Cicero?"

"Yep," Cicero said, giving a tug on his gun belt. "I remember how Mister Leland used to raise Cain every time he'd see that old truck of yours parked out in front of the house waiting for Joe Pike."

Grady Fulton lifted his cap, ran his hand through gray wavy hair and put the cap back on. "Mister Leland had a burr up his ass about that truck. He sure did." He clapped Joe Pike on the shoulder. "But then, Mister Leland always had a burr up his ass about *something* you was up to, didn't he."

"Yeah," Joe Pike said. "I reckon he did."

"Well," Grady Fulton said, "I got to get to work here. Clock's running, Cicero."

"How long you figure it'll take?" Cicero asked.

"Depends." Grady Fulton's gaze swept the vacant lot. It was waist-high in weeds, flourishing in the summer heat. As he studied the site, he pulled a pouch of Red Man chewing tobacco out of a back pocket of his ancient jeans, bit off a plug, worked it expertly into the corner of his jaw, and tucked the pouch away. "Ain't no telling what's in there. As I remember, they didn't do no clearing to speak of when the furniture store burned."

"No," Cicero said, "we was all just glad it didn't take the whole block. We just let it grow up and tried to forget about it."

Grady Fulton gave a short, dry laugh. "You may be digging up some old haints here, Cicero."

"Yeah, I may be."

"Okay," Grady said. "Let's see what we got. I'll scrape it all up; then I got a front-end loader and a dump truck coming next week to haul it off."

Cicero frowned. "Next week?"

"Or the week after."

"I was hoping maybe you could get it all done today."

"Today? Cicero, I got equipment tied up on two other jobs as it is." He pointed down the street where the flatbed had gone. "Kyle's headed over to Norwood now to pick up another dozer so we can do site preparation for a new Kmart in Thomson."

"I know you're doing me a favor . . ."

"What you in such an all-fired hurry for, anyhow?" He waved at the vacant lot. "It's been like this for ten years."

Cicero shrugged. And Trout thought, *Aunt Alma. He hasn't told her yet.*

Grady Fulton spat a well-aimed stream of Red Man juice into the weeds. He turned toward the rumbling bulldozer. And then Joe Pike spoke up. "Grady, you reckon I could . . ." He waved his arm toward the bulldozer.

Grady gave him a close look. "Been a long time, Joe Pike. You remember how? I can't have nobody tearing up my equipment."

Joe Pike grinned. "I was taught by the best dozer operator in the state of Georgia."

"At least," Grady said. "Well, come on."

Trout looked up at Joe Pike. "What . . ."

But he was already in motion, grabbing a handhold on the side of the bulldozer and pulling himself nimbly up onto the seat as Grady climbed up from the other side. Joe Pike settled himself in front of the controls and ran his hands over them, pointing to the black-knobbed levers and foot pedals, talking with Grady, who nodded and gestured. Trout couldn't hear them over the rumble of the diesel engine. He turned to Cicero. "Is Daddy gonna drive that thing?"

"I 'speck he is. Never saw him do it myself, but I hear he got pretty good at it when him and Grady was working together."

The diesel roared, belching black smoke from the stack above the engine. And then Joe Pike hunkered over the controls and pushed a couple of levers and the bulldozer lurched onto the vacant lot, jostling Joe Pike and Grady, who threw up his arms in mock horror. Joe Pike threw his head back, laughing. He pushed another lever and lowered the blade, and the bulldozer eased forward again. Trout stood there transfixed, mouth open in astonishment, as the blade bit into the earth, curling the weeds and laying them aside like a threshing machine, uncovering what the weeds had concealed — slabs of concrete, twisted lengths of rusty pipe, a fire-blackened water heater, a lot of unrecognizable rubble.

Trout pointed. Cicero smiled, winked. *Well, I'll be damned,* Trout thought. Another piece of Joe Pike's history, and this time something totally out of the blue. The Bear Bryant business — well, he at least knew a little about that. When Joe Pike went tearing off on the motorcycle in search of a past he had left in the heat and dust of Texas, it was at least a piece of history that Trout had heard about, however obliquely. But this? He hadn't the faintest idea what it was all about. And it wasn't so much the *thing*. It was the *surprise* of the thing. It was like seeing a rank stranger sitting up there on the high seat of the bulldozer, disguised somehow in Joe Pike Moseley's big body. Or maybe it was that little man tucked away inside the big one who was pushing and pulling those levers and stomping on the foot pedals as the bulldozer plowed through the weeds and debris toward the back of the lot.

Trout thought about Tilda Huffstetler, bursting out in tears at Wednesday Night Prayer Meeting. No wonder. Joe Pike Moseley kept opening his peddler's pack and pulling out stuff nobody suspected was there. Everything except what Trout really needed to know. He wanted to say, *Whoa! Wait a minute! Enough already!* Damn Joe Pike Moseley.

Down at the back side of the lot, the bulldozer clanked to a halt; then with Joe Pike pushing and pulling on the levers, it made an ungainly turn, wheeling on one churning track, and headed back toward the sidewalk, piling up debris and pushing it ahead of the blade. Joe Pike was all concentration. Beads of sweat stood out on his forehead, and the front of his white shirt was darkening with sweat. He had undone the top button of his shirt and slung his loosened tie back over his shoulder. So much for visiting the sick and shut-in.

"Is that Joe Pike yonder?" Trout heard at his back. He turned to see a crowd of gawkers gathering on the sidewalk behind them.

"It's Joe Pike, all right."

"Good Lord."

"Who's that up there with him?"

"Maybe it's the Bishop." Laughter.

"Cicero, what's going on?"

"Progress," Cicero said forthrightly. "The rebirth of Moseley, Georgia."

Beyond the crowd, Trout saw a gray Buick ease to a stop out on the street. The tinted passenger-side window slid down. Aunt Alma. She stared for a long time, taking it all in. Trout looked over at Cicero. Did he see? Yes. Cicero gave Alma a little wave. She didn't wave back. The window closed and the car moved on, heading toward the mill.

"Ahhhhh," he heard Cicero sigh.

"Did you . . . ?" Trout asked.

"Not exactly," Cicero said.

Headline: SHIT HITS FAN. "I've got to go," he said to Cicero.

He turned and started walking quickly down the sidewalk. Cicero caught up with him in front of the hardware store, jangling a fistful of keys. "I'll open up and you can get started," Cicero said. "You know how to work the cash register?"

Trout kept walking. "No sir."

"Well, I'll show you. Anybody comes in and needs something you can't find, I'll be right down yonder at the construction site." Cicero was at the door of the hardware store, putting the key in the lock.

Trout stopped. "Uncle Cicero . . ."

"Yeah."

"I, uh . . ."

Cicero turned and gave him a long, searching look. And then he knew. His face fell. Trout felt a rush of guilt. But then he thought, *No. I've got to get out of here.* "I'm sorry."

Cicero gave a little weak wave toward the store. "I was . . ."

"Aunt Alma offered me a job, too," Trout said. "I appreciate it. Really. But I'm gonna work at the Dairy Queen."

Cicero looked off down the street where it curved just before it got to the mill building. He looked for a long time, turning things over in his mind. Behind them, at the vacant lot, the bulldozer clanked and rumbled, traffic stopped, the crowd kept growing. It was, Trout realized, the biggest thing that had happened in Moseley in a good little while. He waited a while longer. Cicero kept looking down the street, searching for something just beyond the bend in the road. Trout waited. He thought he owed Cicero that much, not to just walk away. If Cicero wanted to yell at him a little, that would be okay.

Then Cicero turned back and Trout could see something in his eyes that looked very close to desperation. It was there, naked, unconcealed, terribly painful but exquisitely honest — more so than anything he had seen from Joe Pike Moseley in a long time, perhaps ever. Trout wanted to look away, but he couldn't do that, either. He saw, he knew for dead certain, that what was going on down there on the vacant lot with the bulldozer was this little chunky stump of a man in his terribly earnest police uniform trying to save his own ass. And knowing he might not be able, no matter what.

"You oughta do what's best for you," Cicero said. "We all got to get on about our lives, Trout. But" — he gestured again toward the hardware store — "it's always here if you want it."

"Thank you, Uncle Cicero," Trout said. He had a sudden urge to hug Cicero's neck. But he hesitated a moment too long, and Cicero turned and walked back down the sidewalk toward his construction project.

Aunt Alma came up like a shot from behind her desk when Trout told her. "The DAIRY QUEEN?" she cried out.

"Yes ma'am."

"That's the most ridiculous thing I ever heard in my life!"

"Aunt Alma —"

"Out there with trash people scooping up ice cream!" Alma's shrill voice shattered the air of the office. She picked up a stack of papers, waved them in the air and smacked them back on the desk. But Trout found himself, to his amazement, staying very calm. He stood before her desk, hands folded in front of him.

Aunt Alma pointed an accusing finger. "You are your father's son."

"Yes ma'am. I sure am."

"Don't sass me, Trout."

"I didn't mean to, Aunt Alma."

"Your father has been rebellious and defiant since he was in diapers, and he has caused this family untold grief and misery! Has and does! And if you keep going like you are, you're going to turn out the same way!" Her voice kept rising. She waved her arms. Her eyes bulged. Trout thought about what he might do if she popped a blood vessel. Pick up the telephone and call 911? Did Moseley even have 911?

"Aunt Alma, it's just a job."

"That's right!" she cried. "It's just a job! This" — she indicated the mill with a sweep of her hand — "is family! It's your future! Our future! Don't you realize that?"

Trout stood there for a long time, thinking about what he might say and do. He felt weariness settle over him. The easiest thing would be to just take the mill job, give himself over to this aging red building with its strange smells and vibrations and its ghosts of Moseleys past. The Dairy Queen, as he had just said, was just a job. It wasn't, despite what Joe Pike said, a religious experience. The mill, on the other hand, did seem like a Holy Crusade to Aunt Alma. There was a kind of come-to-Jesus fervor about the whole business — but not the abiding joy of a sinner saved. There was about her, as there was about Uncle Cicero, a kind of desperation. In fact, he thought now, the whole damn bunch was more than a little desperate: Joe Pike floundering in religious quicksand; Cicero trying just to *be* somebody besides Alma's husband; Alma herself, clutching her Moseley-ness to her breast like a shield against unnamed terror; even Phinizy, hunkered down behind his whiskey and his books, wry and watchful. And yes, he too was beginning to feel a little desperate. All this business about the future was making him a little crazy. He wanted to go away, find a quiet place where he could think and maybe figure out what to do, how to — as Phinizy had put it — save his own ass. And that was what finally made up his mind for him.

"I'm just sixteen years old, Aunt Alma," he said. "I'm going to work at the Dairy Queen. I'm sorry."

She stared for a moment, eyes narrowing. "Then go," she said, flipping her hand, dismissing him. "Go! Just go." She turned away from him with an angry jerk. Then she picked up the telephone receiver and started dialing. As he walked out he heard, "Put Cicero on the phone." He stopped in the hallway, imagined himself turning back, taking the receiver out of Alma's hand, replacing it in the cradle, and saying, *Leave the poor sonofabitch alone.* But of course, he didn't.

The mill village was teeming with midmorning life — women shelling peas on front porches, burning trash in backyard barrels, hanging wash from backyard clotheslines; men tinkering with automobiles; a pack of kids playing basketball on a bare-earth vacant lot. Keats was waiting on her front steps when Trout pulled up on the motorcycle and turned in the gravel driveway. The Avis Rental car, the one that had been there the day before, was still parked behind Wardell's old Ford.

"Your company's still here," he said as Keats danced toward him across the patch of grass.

"It's not company." She held her sketch pad tightly under her arm. She was wearing perfume again.

"What is it?"

She ignored the question. "How's your sunburn?"

"Better. But don't hold on too tight. Want me to hold your pad?"

"Of course not." She struggled onto the seat behind him, thrusting the crutches under his arms and across the handlebars. Then the pad slipped from her grasp, fell onto the ground next to the motorcycle and flopped open. Trout stared, eyes widening. "Whoooo," he said softly. A nude woman. High, arching breasts, narrow waist, slim thighs and legs, all soft lines and curves in thick pencil strokes. Trout felt himself stir.

"Give me that!" she barked.

He kept staring. "You're pretty good."

She rapped him sharply in the side with one of her crutches.

"Ow!"

"Stop looking. Pick it up and give it to me. Right now!" She rapped him again, harder this time.

"Awright! Damn!" He reached over, straining to keep the motorcycle balanced, and picked up the sketch pad by its spine, letting it close. She snatched it out of his hand. He twisted on the seat and looked back at her. Her face was beet red. "What —"

"None of your goddamn business!"

And it wasn't, he kept telling himself all the way to the Dairy Queen. But he couldn't help thinking about it. The nude woman hiding in the thick pages of the sketch pad had Keats's face. But the body was that of a woman who stood upright, proud and unfettered. A woman who had no need of crutches.

They said hardly a word all morning. Herschel showed him how to make a milk shake and a banana split and a Blizzard, how much chili to put on a foot-long hot dog, while Keats tended the window and kept her distance, closed-off and sullen. Then it was noon and the rush began, and it took all three of them to keep up with the crowd. He tried to help, but he was slow. She was impatient, snatching things away from him when he was half finished, fixing them herself. His irritation grew. Finally, she reached for a milk shake he was holding under the whirring blade of the stirrer.

"Give me that!" she barked.

"I can do it myself!" he shot back.

"People don't have all day waiting for you to fumble around!" She reached for it again, and he jerked it away from her, slopping some of it on the floor. "You're making a mess!" she cried. "Get out of the way!"

"Hey!" Herschel yelled. "Cut it out! You wanna fight, take it outside. Draw a crowd and sell popcorn."

"He's . . ." Keats started, but the look on Herschel's face cut her off.

She turned with a huff back to the counter, slid open a window with a jerk. Joe Pike Moseley peered in, taking stock. "Morning. Y'all okay in there?"

"It's Amateur Hour," Keats snapped.

"Keats!" Herschel warned.

"Awright. Awright."

Herschel looked over at Trout. "You gonna fix the milk shake or not?"

"It's fixed," Trout said, seething, trying to keep his voice under control. He felt an urge to kick one of Keats's crutches out from under her. She was maddening. She made him feel like a kid with a wet diaper.

"Well, give it here," Herschel said.

Trout held out the milk shake. "Put a cover on it." Trout fitted a plastic cover over the shake, held it out again. "Straw and napkin," Herschel said. Herschel took the shake, straw, and napkin and passed them through the window to a woman who was waiting.

"Wanna wait on your daddy?" he asked Trout.

Joe Pike had on a fresh white shirt. He smelled like a bath. And he was wearing the amoeba tie again. Trout looked past him into the parking lot. Grace Vredemeyer was sitting in the front seat of Joe Pike's car. She waved to Trout. She, too, looked fresh from a bath, wearing another of her floral print summer dresses with a lot of neck and shoulder showing. "Visiting the sick and shut-in?" Trout asked.

Joe Pike glanced back at Grace in the car. "Grace sings to 'em; I bring glad tidings." Grace waved to Joe Pike.

"Daddy . . ."

Joe Pike turned back to him. "Uh-huh."

Don't you see . . . But he didn't, that was obvious. Finally Trout asked, "You want to order?"

"Two foot-longs, large order of fries, a chocolate shake, and a vanilla shake."

"What happened to salad?"

"Tonight," Joe Pike answered. "You can't visit the sick and shut-in on rabbit food."

"Glad tidings."

"Yea, verily."

Trout got up the order himself, took his time about it while several other customers came and went. He put everything in a cardboard carrier and delivered it to the window. Joe Pike was beginning to wilt in the heat. He pulled out a handkerchief and mopped his forehead. The collar of his shirt sagged. Out in the car, Grace Vredemeyer still looked perky. But she had rolled down both front windows. Trout opened the window and pushed the items through. "Three eighty-nine," he said.

Joe Pike fished in his pocket and pulled out a five. Trout handed it to Herschel, who rang up the cash register. "We're going to Augusta," Joe Pike said. "Grace's second cousin had open-heart surgery yesterday." Trout imagined Grace bursting into song in intensive care. Headline: MAN DIES WITH GRACE.

"Do you accept tips?" Joe Pike asked.

"No sir," he said as he handed over the change.

"See you for supper."

Keats snorted loudly as Trout closed the window. "Maybe he oughta put in tomorrow's order today. So you'll have it on time."

She glared at him, but Trout didn't say anything, and she turned back to the grill, where she was tending several sizzling hamburger patties. He looked at Herschel, who shook his head. Cool it. Trout took a deep breath and nodded. And he thought longingly of the hardware store.

The lunch crowd had barely cleared out when black clouds began to gather and the wind picked up, skittering bits of trash and dust across the parking lot. Herschel turned on the radio — the station over in Thomson — listening for a tornado warning. But it was just a nasty line of thunderstorms, the announcer said, barreling through on its way from Atlanta toward the coast. Marching to the sea like Sherman, the guy on the radio said. *War is hell, but y'all just keep listening to ol' Dan here 'cause we've got more Country Memories and a special on fryers at the Dixie Vittles Supermarket.*

Herschel stood next to Trout at the counter, peering out at the clouds. They were thickening fast — big, black nasty-looking things, boiling over the horizon from the west. A big truck pulling a flatbed trailer eased by on the road, slowing for the Interstate ramp. A blue tarpaulin covered the cargo and a loose corner of the tarp was flapping in the wind. "War," Herschel snorted. "Shit. What does that doofus know about war?"

"Maybe he was in Vietnam," Trout said.

"Naw. I know him. He's been over here trying to sell me some advertising."

"Did you buy any?"

"Hell, no."

"Why not?"

"You don't *advertise* a Dairy Queen. It's just *here*. You either want it or you don't."

Trout thought about that. Maybe Joe Pike was close to the truth after all. "My daddy says Dairy Queen is a religious experience."

Herschel shrugged. "Well, I don't know anything about that. I ain't religious, anyhow."

"What if you advertised and business got better?"

"What am I gonna do with it? Build another Dairy Queen next door? Then I got two of everything."

"You could add a drive-in window," Keats said. She was sitting on a stool over to the side, crutches propped against the wall, working away on her sketch pad. She didn't look up.

"I already got a drive-in window," Herschel said. "Folks drive in, come up to the window."

"Not when it rains, they don't," Keats said. "If you had a real drive-in window with a cover over it, they could order from the car and get what they want without getting wet."

"Rain don't last forever," Herschel said. "People oughta stay home when it's raining. Only doofuses get out in the rain."

"Like the Army," Keats said.

"Oh, hell yes. That's why I became a cook. It don't rain in a mess hall."

Keats sketched away, her hand making broad strokes on the pad. She glanced up and caught Trout watching her. He raised his eyebrows, questioning. Another nude? Keats stuck out her tongue at him, but there wasn't any malice in it. *God*, he thought, *she can turn it on and off. She could drive you plain crazy if you let her.* Keats went back to her drawing. "Is the Army a bunch of doofuses?" she asked Herschel.

"Only the majors."

"Why majors?" Trout asked.

Herschel smirked. "It's part of the job description. Enlisted men do most of the work in the Army. Lieutenants and captains do a little. Not much. Colonels and generals give the orders. And majors just, well . . ."

"Doofus," Trout offered.

"Exactly." He waved at the gathering storm. "Major sits around with his thumb up his butt until it rains. Then he says, 'Hey, it's raining! Let's get all the troops out and go for a hike, whattaya say!' Poor dumb grunts are slogging through the mud in full field pack, rain dripping down the backs of their ponchos. And where's the major?"

"Taking a nap." Trout offered, getting into the spirit of it.

"Going to the Dairy Queen," Keats one-upped him.

Herschel laughed, a kind of cackling explosion. It was infectious — laughing at laughter — and Trout and Keats joined in. Laughter bounced off the chrome and Formica like shards of light and settled about them, keeping the weather at bay. On the radio, ol' Dan was playing Country Memories and selling fryers. The wind whistled at the eaves of the building. An overhead fluorescent fixture hummed contentedly. Trout felt a rush of relief. It had been a tense morning — Joe Pike on the bulldozer, Uncle Cicero's disappointment, Aunt Alma's angry disgust, Keats's snarling impatience. He felt the hard knot in his stomach, the tightness around his shoulder blades, unwind. Then he thought that it had been a good while since he had laughed at anything much, a good long while since he had indulged in lazy, go-nowhere talk that made you feel like a cat stretching into sleep. The Dairy Queen, even with maddeningly unpredictable Keats sitting over in the corner stroking at her sketch pad, suddenly felt almost safe. A haven where laughter was possible. No theological angst, no industrial crisis, no grand plans for progress. A Dairy Queen should be a place that made people happy, if only just for the few moments that a banana split lasted. He could stay here, he thought. Maybe a cot in the back. He wasn't hard to please.

"Well," Herschel said. "I gotta go to the bank. Might as well do it while there ain't no customers."

Keats looked up. "You'll get wet. Doesn't that make you a doofus?"

Herschel took off his cap and apron, opened the cash register, and took a vinyl bank bag out of the cash drawer. "Nope," he grinned. "They got a drive-in window at the bank." He started toward the back door, then stopped and turned back to them. "I don't know what kind of burr you two have got under your saddles, but I want you to work it out while I'm gone. When I get back here, I wanna see smilin' faces. Happy campers. Capish?"

"Okay," Trout said.

Herschel looked over at Keats. She was deep into the sketch pad. Scratch-scratch. "Keats . . ." She waved one hand, kept working with the other. Herschel turned back to Trout. "There's a gun in the drawer under the cash register. If she doesn't get her fanny off her shoulder, shoot her."

The storm broke just as Herschel pulled out of the parking lot in his panel truck. One moment it was just dark clouds and skittering dust, and the next there was a terrible crack of thunder and the rain exploded — sweeping up in a shimmering wall from the Interstate, fierce and wind-driven, splattering the pavement like machine-gun fire, whipping under the overhang out front, spraying the plate-glass window. On the radio, ol' Dan was playing Johnny Cash: "Five Feet High and Rising." *We better get out in our leaky old boat. It's the only thing we got left that'll float . . .*

Trout leaned across the counter and stared out. The rain was so thick now, you could barely see the road. Then there was a brilliant flash of lightning and a thunderbolt so close, he could feel the hair on the back of his neck stand up. He jumped, then backed away from the counter, bumped into the ice cream machine, and felt the cold touch of chrome on his arm, eased away from that. He looked over at Keats. She was hunkered over the sketch pad, pencil poised in midair, looking at him. No, not really *at* him, the way you would look at a person's face if you wanted to make a connection. Her gaze was fixed on some point near his waistline, maybe a bit below. Her eyes were squinched in concentration and she seemed to be totally oblivious to the storm raging outside or to his nervous dancing about. Then all of a sudden she seemed to *see* him, standing there gawking at her. And she blushed furiously, her face turning the color of a ripe watermelon. She turned away with a jerk and looked out the window.

He realized suddenly that she did this a lot — looking at him when she didn't think he saw, head cocked to the side, eyes lingering on odd places. She was . . . she was . . . studying him. No. More than that. *Undressing* him. Good God! He felt incredibly vulnerable, as if he had stumbled naked onto a stage, blinded by footlights and hearing a sudden murmur of people out beyond in the darkness. Pointing.

Laughing. Blood rushed to his face and neck, pounded in his ears, swelled in his groin. He fought the urge to double over, covering himself.

The wind howled, the rain pounded the roof, the air exploded with one peal of thunder after another. There was a great yawning space between them there in the fluorescent-lit sanctuary of the Dairy Queen. And this sudden, unnerving knowledge that froze him in place and made escape impossible.

He took a deep breath. "If you're gonna draw pictures of me, the least you could do is let me see."

"They're not . . . they're not you," she stammered. He could see that she was rattled. Caught red-handed, like some Peeping Tom looking in his bedroom window. "You saw . . ."

"Just one," he said. His voice was a hoarse croak. "It was . . ."

"Yes."

"But there's lots of stuff in there. You're messing with that thing all the time. Looking at me. Like I'm on display or something." He took a step toward her, holding out his hand.

"No!" she cried, clutching the sketchbook to her. "I told you, you're NOT IN THERE!"

"Then why do you keep *looking* at me like that?"

There was a long, painful silence. She stared at the floor, wrapped around the sketchbook. Then she looked up at him. "I can't do men."

"What do you mean?"

"I don't know what men look like."

He laughed. "What the heck, Keats. Half the people in the world are men."

"I mean . . ." She shrugged. "Without any clothes on."

He stared at her. "What are you, some kind of nut?"

"No. I'm an artist."

"Naked men?"

"No. I just told you, I can't do men. I can't get it right." She rushed on in a torrent of words. "I know what a woman looks like. I can stand in front of a mirror and, ah, you know. See everything. The" — she caressed the air, making a curve with her hand — "way the lines go and all. But I've never seen a man. Without his clothes on."

"For God's sake, go to the library. They got pictures of statues."

"It's not the same."

Trout held his breath, then let it out with a whoosh. "Sheeez." He slumped down on a stool, looking at her huddled over there in the corner. She looked very small and a little desperate, not very dangerous now. He could imagine how it must be with her. She had some talent. She wanted to be an artist, maybe go off to school and study. But there were too many reasons why she never would. Never could. It just wouldn't ever happen, because there was just too much she couldn't escape. One part of him wanted to feel sorry for her. But another part was angry and indignant because of her foul attitude in general and what she was doing to him in particular. So she hunkered over there in the corner, looking a little pathetic and — he knew — hating that because she hated being thought of as pathetic.

Trout felt, for the very first time with her, that he had the upper hand. It gave him a sense of power, a feeling of being in control. And he hadn't felt that way in a good while. About anything. It was like a narcotic. "You give me the creeps."

"I'm just trying to imagine —"

"It's sick."

"No it's not! There's nothing sick about the human body."

"It's sick when you sneak around trying to undress people who don't want to be undressed."

"Look," she protested, holding up the sketchbook, "this isn't some filthy little girlie magazine like you guys hide under the mattress. It's art. This isn't the Dark Ages, for God's sake. And besides, I'm not sneaking."

"It's like you're stealing something from me. It's like . . . like . . . rape."

"Oh come off it, Trout," she said, her voice thick with disgust. "So, I imagine what you look like with your clothes off. What's the big deal!"

And suddenly she was in charge again, putting him on the defensive, making him feel like a naughty puppy. But she wasn't finished. "You could . . ." — she paused for a moment, and a smile flickered at the edges of her mouth — "you could pose for me."

"You mean . . ."

"Sure. Take all the mystery out of it."

"Oh, shit," he said softly. "You are truly nuts." This was, he thought, about the weirdest thing he had heard in a long string of weirdness. Not the idea of being naked with a girl. He had almost been back in Ohatchee with Cynthia Stuckey. But sitting there naked while she drew a picture of him? And that's all? That was entirely different. Interesting, maybe even more than that. But definitely different. It made him squirm with heat and strangeness all at once. He had no idea how to proceed from here.

And then, oddly, rescue came from the most unexpected source.

A car pulled into the parking lot, lights on, windshield wipers flapping furiously, and eased to a stop at the side of the lot near the picnic tables. The lights and wipers stayed on.

"Your Aunt Alma," Keats said.

Trout peered out. A gray Buick. The rain was beating against the windshield so hard, the wipers couldn't keep up with it. Then Aunt Alma rolled down the window about an inch and peered out. She and Joe Pike had the same eyes, he thought.

"I think she wants you to come out," Keats said.

He was thoroughly soaked in the few seconds it took him to dash from the back door around the side of the building to the car, snatch open the door, slide into the front seat and slam the door behind him. The engine was running — powering lights, wipers, air conditioner. Trout shivered as cold and wet collided with the confused knot in his belly. Aunt Alma didn't seem to notice. Her face was puckered up in thought, lips set in a grim line, hands gripping the steering wheel. The wipers went *thwock-thwock-thwock*. The rain was fierce, great driving sheets of it blowing against the car and making it shake. Trout stuck his hands between his legs and hunched forward, trying to stop the shivering, wondering what kind of craziness would bring Alma out in a driving rainstorm to the Dairy Queen. He doubted she had ever set foot on the Dairy Queen property before. It was not an Aunt Alma kind of place. Had she come to shanghai him and take him back to the shipping department? Right now, he didn't really care.

They sat there for a moment and then she said, "Trout, I'm sorry."

It was the very last thing on earth he expected. He opened his mouth, but nothing came out. *What is going on here?*

"I shouldn't put pressure on you," she went on. "I know you've had a tough time the past few months. Your mother, your father . . ." She shook her head. "It's not fair to put any extra burden on you, and I just want you to know I regret that I did."

"Aunt Alma . . ." He shrugged, still at a loss — in fact, astonished. This was Aunt Alma? Ten seconds ago, he would have doubted that she had ever apologized for anything in her whole life. And here she was, doing it as simply and easily as if she were ordering ice cream.

"I want your summer to be nice. Relaxed, no pressure. Is there anything I can do?"

He shivered again. "Could you turn off the air conditioner?"

"Oh," she said. She turned off the air but left the engine running. The wipers *thwock-thwocked.* Trout looked out through the windshield, saw Keats inside the Dairy Queen, up on her crutches now, peering out the window, watching.

"I didn't mean to rush. There's plenty of time for you to learn about the business." She turned toward him in the seat and pressed her hands together. "This is all going to work out." There was a bright snap to her eyes, something almost feverish. "It will work out just fine," she said earnestly. "I'm sure of it."

Trout's head spun. What on earth was she talking about? His future? Uncle Cicero's business expansion? Joe Pike's theological angst? Or was there more? Overpopulation? Air pollution? Headline: EVERY-THING TURNS OUT OKAY.

"All of it." She gave a little flip of her hand, bestowing all-rightness on the world.

"Look, Aunt Alma, if you want me to work at the mill . . ."

"No," she said firmly. "I think you've made the right choice, Trout." She waved at the Dairy Queen. "Enjoy yourself. No pressure. A little spending money in your pocket and nothing earthshaking to worry about."

No, he thought, *nothing but a girl trying to take my clothes off.*

"That's the Dubarry girl, isn't it?" She was leaning over the steering wheel, looking at Keats.

"Yes," Trout said weakly.

"Is she a friend?"

She said it very casually, but Trout was suddenly alert and wary. "Not really," he said.

"Just somebody who rides on your motorcycle."

Trout shrugged. "I've taken her to work a couple of times, I guess."

"Today?"

"Yes ma'am."

Alma looked at him now, very directly. "Did you notice anything unusual over there?"

"What kind of unusual?"

"Activity. Anything out of the ordinary."

He wanted to be careful. But he wanted to be helpful, too. After all, Aunt Alma had come all the way out here to tell him she was sorry. And she had let him off the hook about the mill. And he darned sure didn't owe weird Keats Dubarry anything.

"There was a rental car parked in the Dubarry's driveway," he said. "Yesterday and again this morning. The same car."

"Did you get a good look at it?"

"Pretty good."

"What kind of car?"

"Green. A Ford, I think. It had a rental car sticker on the back bumper. Avis."

"You didn't happen to get a tag number, did you?"

"No ma'am."

"Are you taking the girl home after work?"

"I guess so."

"If the car is still there, get the tag number."

"Okay."

The rain was letting up now. Aunt Alma turned off the windshield wipers. A few drops splattered on the glass, streaking it as they dribbled off. "I need you to keep an eye on things for me, Trout."

"Yes ma'am," he said. "I will."

When Trout dropped Keats off at home, the rental car was gone. "I see your company's left," he said as she struggled off the back of the motorcycle.

"Are you going back tomorrow?" she asked.

"Of course."

She shrugged, turned and started toward the house.

"Would you rather I didn't?" Trout asked.

"I don't care what you do," she said over her shoulder.

"I turned down two other jobs," Trout said.

That stopped her. She turned and looked back at him. "What?"

"Uncle Cicero's hardware store and Aunt Alma's shipping department."

"So what?"

"Aren't you going to ask why?"

"I don't care why. Maybe you're going through a late adolescence,

Trout." She turned again and headed back toward the house, bouncing along on the crutches across the grass. Then she froze suddenly, stayed stock-still for a moment, and turned back to him. To his great surprise, she looked sad. Small and sad and a little vulnerable. "I don't like being angry, Trout," she said quietly. "I see what it does to Daddy. Sometimes I can't help it."

"Does my working at the Dairy Queen make you angry?"

"I guess so," she said. "Up to now, it's been just mine. But it's okay." She paused, then added, "You're okay." And she gave him a tiny smile. She had a nice smile when she let herself, he thought.

"Thanks," he said.

She turned again toward the house. "Maybe I'll come to work naked tomorrow," he called out. She didn't act like she heard him.

As Trout headed home, he saw a fair-sized crowd gathered at the edge of the vacant lot downtown, the parking spaces along both sides of Broadus Street filled with cars. Among them, a Georgia State Trooper cruiser, a County Sheriff's Department car, and a plain blue sedan with an official-looking antenna on the back. As Trout passed on the motorcycle, he saw a length of yellow tape stretched across the front of the vacant lot, holding the crowd back. Over their heads, out in the middle of the lot, he could see the big orange bulk of the bulldozer.

He wheeled the motorcycle around and came back and parked in front of the hardware store. The front door was shut and a sign hung behind the glass: CLOSED. Trout walked quickly down the sidewalk to where the crowd edged up against the yellow tape. It was the biggest assembly Trout had witnessed since he arrived in Moseley — far bigger, for sure, than the Sunday morning congregation at Moseley Memorial Methodist. And it was abuzz with excited murmuring and gesticulating.

About half of the lot was scraped bare, down to red clay soil, puddled here and there by the afternoon downpour. There were several mounds of piled-up debris — chunks of concrete, twisted pieces of rusty pipe, charred timbers. The back side of the lot was still weed-grown, and the bulldozer was stopped at the edge of it — engine silent, seat empty, blade down. A knot of men stood around the front of the machine — a couple in uniform, two others in shirtsleeves. They were looking at something on the ground, and one of the men in shirtsleeves was snapping pictures with a big boxy camera. *An accident?* Trout thought with a rush of alarm of Joe Pike up on the bulldozer seat.

"What is it?" he asked a man standing next to him.

"Skeletal remains," the man said somberly.

"It's probably Cash Potter," said a woman, nodding knowingly.

"What makes you think that?" the man asked.

"Cash disappeared about the time the furniture store burned down," the woman answered.

"Naw," another man said. "Cash turned up in Chicago with a waitress from Augusta."

"Well," the woman huffed, "folks *said* Cash was in Chicago, but nobody I'd consider reliable has laid eyes on him."

Another woman spoke up. "Anyhow, what's to say it's somebody that burned up in the fire? Coulda been somebody that was murdered and buried over yonder."

"Best place in town to hide a body," the first man agreed.

"There was a bunch of Gypsies come through a couple of years ago," the other man said. "Coulda been one of them."

Trout edged away from the debate and looked out across the vacant lot again at the crowd around the bulldozer. Then he spotted Uncle Cicero, hunkering next to the blade with another man, pointing, his finger making a wide circle. Grady Fulton, the bulldozer operator, was standing next to him, hand jammed in the rear pocket of his jeans.

"Uncle Cicero," Trout called out. Cicero looked back and saw him. Cicero waved to him to come over. Trout hesitated, but Cicero kept waving, so he ducked under the yellow tape and started across the bare earth of the vacant lot, stepping around the puddles. He could hear the low irritated buzz of the crowd behind him. The freshly scraped dirt had a sour smell to it, like a stomach turned inside out.

Cicero met him at the rear of the bulldozer. "What is it, Uncle Cicero?" Trout asked.

"Skeletal remains," Cicero said. He sounded very official. His color was high. He took a hitch in his gun belt.

Trout looked back at the crowd. "A woman over there said it might be somebody named Cash Potter."

"No, I talked to Cash Potter on the phone last week. He's living in Chicago with a waitress from Augusta. Afraid to come home 'cause Emma Jean might kill him."

Trout peered around Cicero toward the front of the bulldozer. "Can I see?"

"Well, I don't want you to have no nightmares," Cicero said.

"Is it, like, gory?"

"Well, not exactly."

And it wasn't. It was just some bones sticking out of the dirt. The bulldozer had unearthed a large slab of concrete, and as one end of it angled up out of the dirt, it had exposed what was clearly the bones of a foot, mottled and yellow but quite intact.

"This here's Trout," Uncle Cicero introduced him to the circle of men in front of the bulldozer. "Joe Pike's boy." In addition to Grady Fulton, there was a state trooper, a deputy sheriff, two men from the Georgia Bureau of Investigation (one of them the man with the camera). They all seemed to know Joe Pike.

Trout stared at the foot. "Ever seen skeletal remains before, Trout?" the deputy asked.

"Yes sir," Trout said. "Biology class." The skeleton in biology class at Ohatchee High School had dangled from a wire contraption and was affectionately referred to as "Lubert," after the skin-and-bones principal of the school. But this — this bony foot poking through freshly turned earth, rudely disturbed from long, dark, quiet rest — there was something sad, even embarrassing about it. Like stumbling onto some terribly private act. Trout had a sudden urge to cover the foot with something — a sheet, a shirt, Grady Fulton's Nok-a-Homa baseball cap, anything.

"Is it a man or a woman?" he asked.

The deputy raised one foot, balanced on the other, placed the sole of his shoe next to the sole of the skeletal foot. "Man, I'd say. Size ten." The deputy lowered his foot and they all stood there for a moment, considering that.

Then Grady Fulton pulled his hands out of his back pocket, turned his head, and sent an expertly aimed stream of tobacco juice at the ground next to the bulldozer. "Well, God rest his soul and all that. But I got work to do if we gonna finish this up by dark, Cicero."

"You can't move the bulldozer, Grady," Uncle Cicero said.

"What do you mean, 'I can't move the bulldozer'?"

Uncle Cicero stuck his thumbs into his gun belt. "It's part of the crime scene."

"What do you mean, 'crime scene'?" Grady said, waving his hand at the foot. "It's just some poor old dead sonofabitch."

"Skeletal remains," Cicero said evenly. "Of unknown origin. Until I know who it is and how he got here, I have to make a presumption of homicide. And I'd appreciate it if you'd have a little more respect for the deceased."

"Awright, awright," Grady said, his voice rising. "Get Joe Pike down here and let him mumble a few words over the sonof . . . the deceased. But I got dirt to move."

Grady turned toward the bulldozer.

"If you get up on that bulldozer, Grady, I'll arrest you," Cicero said.

Grady turned slowly back to Cicero and stared at him for a moment, his jaw working like crazy on the chew. Then Grady looked at the Georgia Bureau of Investigation man, the one without the camera.

"Don't look at me," the man said. "This is Cicero's jurisdiction."

Grady stood there a while longer, then took off his Nok-a-Homa cap and scratched his head, put the cap back on, looked down at the ground, and scratched at the dirt with the toe of a boot. Finally he looked up at Cicero again and said, "How long?"

"Could be a couple of days," Cicero said.

"Shit," Grady said quietly.

"We got to get the Crime Scene Unit over here and" — Cicero waved his hand over the general area — "process the crime scene. It'll be at least tomorrow because they're tied up in Thomson. After that, it depends on them. Meantime, I intend to secure the crime scene, which includes any" — he waved at the bulldozer — "object in the general proximity which might have a bearing . . ."

"Shit," Grady said again, not so quietly this time. "So in the meantime, you're just gonna hold up my bulldozer."

"And you."

"Me?" Grady's voice rose a couple of octaves.

"To give a statement."

"I was running my dozer and I dug up a skeleton. That's my statement." Grady was yelling now.

"Tomorrow," Cicero said patiently. "I want you here when the Crime Scene Unit arrives. About eight should do it."

Trout marveled, mouth ajar. Cicero was . . . what? Cool, that's what. In charge, unflappable, professional. Talking law enforcement lingo.

Just like a real police chief. Aunt Alma should see him now. They all should see him.

Grady Fulton threw up his arms. "What am I gonna tell Kmart?" He didn't wait for an answer. He turned with a jerk and stalked away toward the crowd on the sidewalk behind the yellow tape.

"I'll write you an excuse," Cicero called out.

Then he looked at Trout. And winked.

TEN

"TELL ME ABOUT Cicero," Uncle Phinizy said.

"He was terrific," Trout said. "He just took charge of things. Like a . . ."

"Police chief," Phinizy finished. He took a long drag from his cigarette, held the smoke inside while he stubbed the butt in an overflowing ashtray, then finally exhaled, aiming at the open window. He picked up the whiskey and water from the table at his elbow, held the glass up to the light, and swirled its contents with a shake of his wrist, tinkling ice against the rim, admiring the amber color. Then he took a sip, swished it around in his mouth, swallowed, and made a satisfied clicking sound with his tongue against his palate. It was an art form, like his smoking.

Phinizy looked awful — the furrowed skin of his face gray, stretched tight and dry like parchment around his skull, white hair thin and wispy. He seemed to have shrunk in the stifling heat of the upstairs garage apartment. It was an oven, even here in the shank of the day with the sun disappearing toward Atlanta over the tops of the pecan trees at the edge of Aunt Alma's yard. The place had baked all morning and then steamed in the wake of the afternoon thunderstorm. A good bit of the storm seemed to have made its way inside through the leaky roof. Phinizy had placed a few pots and pans around to catch the worst of the drips, but there were puddles here and there on the floor. The thick heat assaulted Trout when he opened the screen door and stepped inside to find Phinizy reared back in his recliner, drink at hand, cigarette smoke curling about his head, reading a book: *Hugo Black and the Bill of Rights*. Phinizy paid him no attention. Trout hesitated in the open doorway.

"Damn a fellow who can't make up his mind whether to come in or stay out," Phinizy said from behind his book.

Trout stepped inside, navigated amongst the pots and puddles to the sofa, sat down, waited, sweated. Aunt Alma should fix the place up, Trout thought, at least put on a new roof. It was wretched — dingy, leaky, permeated with the smells of mildew and rotting wallpaper and the rank odor of gasoline and motor oil from the garage below. Alma might not be able to kick him out, but she wouldn't lift a finger to improve the accommodations, either. Phinizy could fix up the place himself, but he wouldn't give Alma the satisfaction. A Moseley stand-off. Industrial-strength stubbornness. It seemed to run in the family.

After a while, Phinizy turned the book facedown in his lap. "Well, tell me about the ruckus." And Trout told him about Cicero and the skeleton in the vacant lot.

"You seem surprised about Cicero," Phinizy said. "How do you think he got to be police chief in the first place?"

"I figured . . . well, Aunt Alma . . ."

"Let me tell you about Cicero." Phinizy fished in the crumpled pack of Lucky Strikes on the table, lit another cigarette and took a drag. "He was a military policeman in the Army. Went to Korea, got shot, won some medals. Then came back here and married Alma." A smile played across Phinizy's face. "They eloped."

"You mean . . ." Trout's imagination conjured up a picture of Cicero climbing a ladder to Alma's second-story bedroom window, spiriting her away. No. Cicero might be the kind of person who would climb *up* a ladder, but Alma was not the kind who would climb *down* one. Still, the thought of Cicero and Alma running off to get married . . .

"Cicero came to the house and got her while Leland was at the mill one day. They stopped in Augusta and got a Baptist preacher to perform the vows, then called from Savannah that night to say they had gotten married."

"What did Grandaddy Leland do?" Trout asked.

"Threw a fit. I think it was the thought of the marriage being performed by a Baptist that made him the maddest."

"What did he do when they came home?"

"He ranted and raved for a while. Made life miserable for Cicero. The boy really put up with a lot. But then Alma went to Leland and told him if he didn't get his fanny off his shoulder, she and Cicero were going to leave. It scared the hell out of Leland. Joe Pike had already hightailed it off to Texas to play football, and Leland could stand just so much orneriness from his young'uns. So he set Cicero up in the hardware business."

"And the police chief job?"

Phinizy smiled again, savoring a thought. "Cicero did that on his own. The old chief, Max Cotter, fell dead as a wedge from a heart attack right in the middle of a town council meeting one night. Cicero was there, and he jumped up and said, 'I'll take it.' So with Max lying there bug-eyed on the floor, they made Cicero police chief. Nobody liked Max anyway."

"Gee . . . ," Trout said.

"Now, about the hardware store. How do you think Cicero's doing?"

Trout shrugged. "I don't know. He's got all these plans. Knocking out walls, clearing the lot and stuff."

"Uh-huh. And how do you think he's gonna pay for Cicero's Do-It-All?"

"Aunt Alma?"

"Why do you think that?"

"He acts kinda nervous about it. I don't think he told her what he was gonna do."

Phinizy nodded thoughtfully. He picked up the cigarette from the edge of the ashtray, took a drag, exhaled the smoke and studied it as it drifted toward the window. "Things are not always as they seem," he said after a moment.

"What do you mean?" Trout asked.

Phinizy stared at the smoke awhile longer until it was gone. Then he looked back at Trout. And he held up the book he had been reading. "Hugo Black."

"What?"

"You know who he was?"

"No sir."

"United States Senator from Alabama, elected with the help of the Ku Klux Klan. Then Roosevelt appointed him to the Supreme Court.

He became a champion of individual rights. I'll bet those Kluxers in Alabama thought he'd sold out on them. But old Hugo was just biding his time. He needed the Klan to get to the Senate, but when he got to the Court, he cut loose."

Trout stared at him. So?

"You see where I'm headed?" Phinizy asked. His voice was patient, like a teacher with a dull student.

"Not exactly," Trout confessed.

"Things are not . . ." He waited for Trout to finish.

Trout felt blank, his mind sucked dry by the heat. He tried to concentrate. Then the light came on. "Always as they seem."

"Bingo," Phinizy said. "Now, extrapolate."

"What?"

"Hugo Black." He held up the book. "Cicero." He pointed in the general direction of the hardware store.

Trout considered. "Is Cicero going to cut loose?"

"I believe that is exactly what he is doing."

"Can he? On his own?"

"Oh yes."

"Profit and progress." Trout repeated Cicero's mantra.

Phinizy nodded.

"He doesn't need Aunt Alma's money?" Trout asked.

"No."

"Then why is he so nervous about her?"

"Because he's in love with her."

It was an incredible thought, and it did a little ricochet number on the inside of his head. Aunt Alma was . . . Aunt Alma. It was as difficult to think of her as a, well, a love object as it was to imagine her climbing down a ladder to elope. Things are not always as they seem. *How do you ever know what is real?*

It was too much. He stood, propelled upward by confusion.

"You look a bit stricken," Phinizy observed dryly.

"I'm having a brain fart," Trout said. "I've got to go."

He was almost out the door when Phinizy stopped him. "Trout . . ." Trout turned back. Phinizy was lighting another cigarette. He took a short puff, spat the smoke impatiently. "Did you ever think about talking to your mother about any of this?"

Trout stared at him, dumbfounded. "Mother?"

Phinizy looked at him for a long moment, expressionless, then picked up his book and resumed his reading.

Trout lay awake for a long time, thinking about all that had transpired in the brief space of a day, piling in on top of a week, a month, a year, when things seemed to happen so fast that there wasn't time to keep up, much less make sense.

The thing was, people kept surprising him.

He had thought at the beginning that it would be enough to get some answers about his mother and father, and if he at least understood what had happened with them, he could make things right again. But then all these other people came crowding in, loud and insistent, muddling the picture. Instead of his just dealing with Joe Pike and Irene, there was this whole new cast of characters he had never considered, and even the ghosts of some who weren't around anymore. All of them, connected in ways he hadn't completely fathomed. And constantly revealing new quirks and secrets. Moving targets in a funhouse shooting gallery, changing shapes and colors before his eyes.

Aunt Alma. Eloping, for God's sake. With Uncle Cicero. For one thing, he couldn't imagine straitlaced Alma Moseley being that passionate about anyone. Uncle Cicero was a truly nice guy, but not the kind, he thought, that a woman would lose her head over, even years before when she was young and perhaps foolish. But she had. She had had the hots for Cicero. *Good grief. Aunt Alma?* Cicero had wooed her and won her and had spirited her away from right under Leland Moseley's nose. It cast both of them in an entirely new light — especially Aunt Alma. She might hold forth at length on "remembering who you are" and all that stuff, but somewhere deep in her soul there was a spark of rebellion, or there had been for at least one incredibly brazen moment.

It also made Trout smile to imagine Grandaddy Leland having a fit. He would have given a princely sum to have seen it.

Leland had died when Trout was six years old, and Trout's memory was of a tall, spare man with thinning gray hair and absolutely no sense of humor who always wore a vested suit, even when he played horseshoes.

Trout remembered a long-ago summer afternoon, he and Alma's son, Eugene, pitching shoes with Leland at the horseshoe pit Leland had set up. Two metal stakes, each surrounded by a broad bed of sand carved from the neatly trimmed grass of the backyard. Eugene was several years older than Trout, but still a young boy, barely able to toss the heavy iron shoe from one metal stake to the other. Trout couldn't reach the other one at all. Eugene protested: the boys should be allowed to move closer than Leland. But Leland would have none of it. Trout could remember him, all gray-pinstriped and vested, peering down from great height through his wire-framed glasses, saying, "That's the rule. Play by the rules or don't play."

So Eugene, who had a streak of rebellion himself, put down his horseshoe and went in the house. Leland never gave him a look. He and Trout played horseshoes by Leland's rules — Leland flinging the metal shoe with practiced ease, making several ringers; Trout, throwing with all his might but barely able to get his own shoe halfway to the stake. It wasn't much fun, but Trout was not the rebellious type.

After a while the back door opened and Aunt Alma shooed a pouting Eugene off the back porch and down the steps. "Eugene wants to play," Alma said to Leland.

"No I don't," Eugene said. "I don't *want* to play. Mama's *making* me play."

"He'll have to play by the rules," Leland said.

"Of course," Alma said.

And Eugene played. His defiance, at that point, had limits.

That early impression, and all Trout had heard since, added up to this: Leland Moseley was a tight-ass. He had, from all accounts, a rather severe notion of How Things Ought To Be and what it meant to be a Moseley in Moseley. But his daughter had chosen a man who was about as un-Moseley as you could get and, worse than that, run off with him. It was a kind of blasphemy. Trout wondered if it had contributed to Leland's demise. And if it had, did it haunt Aunt Alma? Would that explain a lot?

Aunt Alma was enigma enough. But there was also Cicero, still full of surprises. A successful and savvy merchant with the vision to imagine such a thing as Cicero's Do-It-All rising from the town's rubble. Moseley, Georgia, was dead for all intents and purposes, as dead as the poor soul whose bones had rested for so long beneath the weed-grown lot where the furniture store had once stood. But Cicero had, entirely on his own, decided to dig it all up and strike out boldly, much the same way he had seized upon the police chief's job. Cicero was, more than Trout had ever imagined, very much his own man. That was a very big thing. And more than that, he was — if you could believe Phinizy — still very much in love with Alma. It was bound to be a perilous balancing act for Cicero — being his own man and yet loving Aunt Alma, who seemed so desperately fierce in molding people and things to her expectations. How did Cicero manage it?

But at the very bottom, there was the basic question: What did all this mean to sixteen-year-old Trout Moseley, who was partly the product (through inheritance or influence) of all these people with their stubbornness and defiance and loyalties and visions, their rigidity and angst and despair. Things were indeed not as they seemed. There were all sorts of possibilities where none had seemed to exist. Other people took control of their own lives and saved their own asses, as Phinizy said Trout must do. And there appeared to be all sorts of ways of doing it. What was his?

Funny thing, the one person among the bunch he seemed to understand least was his mother. Fruit of her womb, yet stranger to the secrets of her mind. And odd that Phinizy had invoked her name this very evening in the face of Trout's puzzlement. *Did you ever think of talking to your mother?* What kind of cockeyed comment was that? Heck, they wouldn't even let him close to his mother. She could be a hostage of terrorists, for all the good it was doing Trout Moseley.

Trout sighed wearily. For the moment, it was too much. He was very tired — from all this thinking and from the long, eventful day. So he raised up and fluffed the pillow under his head and settled back into it and began to will himself to stop *thinking* and go to sleep.

He had just about drifted off when he heard Joe Pike prowling the house. He had on his cowboy boots. *Clump. Clump. Clump.* Out of his room, down the hall and into the kitchen. It was a noisy house, plaster walls and ceiling and hardwood floors. You could hear everything, especially if you were trying to go to sleep. After a moment, the refrigerator door slammed. *Clump. Clump. Clump.* Joe Pike strode back up the hall to the opposite end of the house, into the living room. The sofa creaked. Trout heard the tinkle of silverware against ceramic. Joe Pike was eating ice cream. A huge mound of vanilla, he imagined (vanilla was all they had in the fridge, and Joe Pike never ate a small portion of ice cream) topped with Hershey's chocolate syrup. After a while, the sofa creaked again. *Clump. Clump. Clump.* Back down the hall to the kitchen. Water running in the sink, rinsing out the ice cream bowl. Had he put the ice cream back in the freezer? He was as likely to leave it out as not. They lost a lot of ice cream that way. Should Trout get up and check? He threw back the sheet, considered, re-covered himself. To hell with it. A grown man who couldn't re-member to put the ice cream back in the freezer . . . *Clump. Clump. Clump.* Back to Joe Pike's room. The door closed. The bed creaked. Did he still have on his cowboy boots? Then the radio, tuned as always to the oldies station in Atlanta. The Platters: *Yoo-hoo-hoo've got the magic touch . . .* Trout thought of Joe Pike and Irene dancing in the kitchen on some past evening when the Platters weren't quite as "oldie" as they were now. Perhaps Joe Pike thought of it too. He switched off the radio. A long silence. And then the bed creaked again. *Clump. Clump. Clump.* The door opened; Joe Pike walked back down the hall to the kitchen. But this time he didn't stop. The back door slammed. Trout waited, anticipating the rumble of the motorcycle's engine. Would Joe Pike remember to check the gas tank? There hadn't been much left in it when Trout arrived home in the early evening. He meant to gas up in the morning. If Joe Pike went out riding tonight, he would likely run out of gas and have to call Trout to come get him. Trout reached for the bedsheet again. But there was no motorcycle sound. Perhaps Joe Pike had gone for a walk. Where would he walk to this time of night? Oh, shit.

Trout waited for a long time, imagining the worst. He waited for perhaps fifteen minutes. *Long enough,* he thought. Then he got up and padded to the kitchen. The ice cream container was on the counter, beginning to ooze around the bottom, a puddle of melted vanilla spreading across the Formica. Trout wiped off the bottom of the box with a dishrag and put it back in the freezer. Then he picked up the telephone and dialed. She answered on the third ring, and she didn't sound like someone who had been asleep.

"Leave my daddy alone," Trout said. And he hung up.

Trout didn't sleep. He lay staring at the ceiling for another hour or so until he heard the back door open and Joe Pike came in. *Clump. Clump. Clump.* The door to Trout's room swung open, light spilled in.

Joe Pike stood there, massive, filling the doorway. His face was shaded by the hall light behind him, but Trout could tell that Joe Pike was powerfully agitated. He seemed to vibrate. Trout felt a sudden rush of dread. Headline: FATHER BEHEADS SON, BLAMES PHONE CALL.

"Think about the Second Coming," Joe Pike said, his voice a couple of octaves higher than normal.

Trout's mouth dropped open. He had no idea what to think about the Second Coming. So instead he asked, "Where have you been?"

"Over at the church," Joe Pike answered.

Trout turned on his bedside lamp. Even in its weak light, Joe Pike looked flushed and fevered. His hands gripped the door frame. Samson holding up the pillars of the temple to keep it from crashing on his head. "What about the Second Coming?" Trout asked.

"Imagine this," Joe Pike said, the words rushing out. "Imagine that someday we discover something really big out there." He swept one hand toward the heavens. "Some concept so complex and yet so pure and simple that it explains everything. What's smaller than small, what's beyond beyond. What if we wretched little human beings with our muddled minds and corrupted spirits suddenly stumble onto the big answer. And at that very instant of discovery God says, 'Okay, that's what I was waiting for. Curtain down. Come on home.' And that's the Second Coming. Not God coming to us, but us coming to God."

Good grief, Trout thought with a rush of something near panic. The Second Coming? It was something Joe Pike needed to talk to the Bishop about. Trout threw back the sheet and swung his legs over the side of the bed, then realized as his feet hit the floor that he really did, for a moment there, intend to call the Bishop. *Mister Bishop, sir, this is Trout Moseley. Could you hop in the car and run over and talk to my daddy about the Second Coming? I'll try to keep him calm until you get here.* But he didn't stand up; he just sat there on the side of the bed staring at Joe Pike, whose forehead was dotted with sweat, who made hissing sounds through his clenched teeth. No, the Bishop probably shouldn't see this after all.

Joe Pike released the door frame and took a big step into the room. The floor shook a bit under his weight. "Don't you see how logical it is?" he demanded. He was almost shouting now. His voice, his presence, filled the room, squeezing all the air out, making it hard to breathe. "What separates us from the rest of creation?" He rapped on his skull again. "Our minds! We can think! We can imagine! So doesn't it stand to reason that we can figure out the secret of creation and what the dickens we're all doing here?"

"I suppose," Trout said, not knowing what else to say.

"Yea, verily!" Joe Pike exploded. And then all the air seemed to suddenly go out of him with a whoosh. His arms fell to his sides, his shoulders slumped. He stared at the floor. "I'm failing," he said. He waved a hand weakly in the direction of the church building next door. "I've got all these questions. And when I ask 'em, folks just panic. They're good people. Good, Christian people. But they just want me to tell 'em everything's okay. And I can't do that. It's just playing games." He shook his head and his voice was heavy with despair. "Just playing games."

Trout could see that his father was in pain, real pain, and that he needed, at the least, acknowledgment. Back on Easter Sunday in Ohatchee, Trout should have gone to the pulpit and put his arms around Joe Pike. But he didn't. And Joe Pike had ridden off to Texas. It could happen again, Trout thought. And he just couldn't stand that. So he stood up and walked quickly to Joe Pike and put his arms around him, at least as far as he could reach. He held on for dear life, and he felt true fear for the first time. Not just unsettledness or uncertainty, but cold gnawing fear that what little he had left that was halfway sane was about to come completely unraveled.

On top of the dresser next to the door, Irene's statue stood still and mute. The boy, whispering in the girl's ear. The secret? *Hell,* Trout thought. *That kid doesn't know jack. Nobody does.*

Trout woke to the ringing of the telephone. It jangled several times, tugging him up from a deep well of troubled sleep. Then it stopped and he heard Joe Pike's rumbling voice, unintelligible, in the kitchen and he wondered if his father had ever gone to bed. He began to drift off again and then he jerked awake and looked at the clock on his bedside table. 6:15. Who would be calling at 6:15? Then he knew.

He heard the clack of the receiver as Joe Pike hung up, and he lay there, expecting to hear the clump of footsteps up the hall toward his bedroom. *Come on. Get it over with.* But he didn't. Trout stayed in the bed a few more minutes, examining the cold knot of dread in his stomach. And then he got up and went to face the music.

The back door was wide open, letting all the air conditioning out into the fast-warming day. Trout looked through the screen door and saw Joe Pike sitting at the bottom of the steps, his great shoulders hunched forward over the piece of sweet potato pie he was having for breakfast. Joe Pike heard the squeak of the screen door spring as Trout opened it, turned and looked up at Trout, then went back to his pie. Trout closed the door behind him. He sat down beside Joe Pike, stretching his legs and letting his toes wriggle for a moment in the grass. Joe Pike went on eating, finishing off the pie, wiping his mouth on his shirtsleeve. He sat there holding the plate, looking out across the backyard toward the garage where the motorcycle sat.

After a moment he said, "I understand you were busy on the phone last night."

Trout didn't say anything. He didn't look at Joe Pike, either, not directly. But out of the corner of his eye he could see the tiny movement as the muscles along Joe Pike's jawline tightened. His father was pissed. It didn't happen very often. He tried mightily to maintain an air of felicity, compassionate concern, even-tempered ministerial grace. Usually, he succeeded. But his eruptions, when they came, could be downright cosmic.

There was the indelible memory of Joe Pike flinging a cat out the second-story window of the parsonage in Moultrie, where they had lived before Joe Pike had been assigned to Ohatchee Methodist. Trout was ten at the time. The cat had climbed onto Joe Pike and Irene's bed in the middle of the night, pounced suddenly upon Joe Pike's face and dug in its claws. In his own room next door, Trout was blasted from sleep by Joe Pike's anguished bellow: "Sonofabitch!" Then an awful ruckus as Joe Pike sprang from the bed, dashed to the window and threw it open. And finally the howling screech as the cat flew through the air and landed in the backyard. For a long time, Trout could hear Joe Pike stomping and growling about the bedroom, wounded and mad. Trout huddled in his bed, terrified — both at the raw anger and at the thought that Joe Pike might bust his gizzard and fall dead on the floor.

Joe Pike's face was raked with angry scratches when he appeared at the breakfast table the next morning. He seemed fairly well composed, but there was a tightness around his eyes. Trout, at ten, had learned to look for the little signs, to watch and wait, sniff the breeze. He took a long look at Joe Pike, saw the tightness, remembered the explosion of his father's indignant rage that had shattered the night, the awful howl of the cat. And Trout started to cry.

Joe Pike softened. "Hey," he said, patting Trout on the shoulder, "I'm okay. Just a few scratches."

"Did you kill Lester Maddox?" Trout blubbered. The cat was a scrawny stray that Trout had befriended and named in honor of Georgia's governor.

"Good Godawmighty," Joe Pike thundered. "The damn cat almost killed *me!*" Then Joe Pike blanched, a flush of embarrassment spreading across his face, and ducked his head.

Irene had taken it all in, watching Joe Pike, expressionless. "Lester Maddox is just fine," she said to Trout. "I gave him some milk at the back door a few minutes ago." Then she turned to Joe Pike and looked at him for a long moment.

"Sorry," he said, chagrined. "I didn't mean . . ."

"Of course you did," she said. "The cat clawed the hell out of you."

"Irene . . ."

"Why shouldn't you be mad? Curse the cat. Curse God for making a cat act like a cat. Go downtown and stand on the corner in front of the newspaper office and yell, 'I hate cats!' Get really, truly pissed off, Joe Pike. It would do you a world of good."

Trout could feel his eyes widen. He had never heard his mother use a word like that before.

Joe Pike cut a nervous glance at Trout. "Irene, honey . . ."

"Stop trying to be Jesus," she said, her voice flat, tinged with disgust. And weariness. "It's exhausting."

Joe Pike stared at her for a moment; then he rose from the table and left the room.

Trout remembered it all clearly now as he sat with Joe Pike on the next-to-bottom step and felt his displeasure filling up the morning. Trout drew his legs up to his body, wrapped his arms around his knees. What to do? He could say he was sorry, but that wasn't really the case. He was sorry Joe Pike was pissed off; especially sorry that he, Trout, was the object of the anger. It was just not something he needed right now, not with all the other. But he wasn't sorry he had made the phone call. Okay, so Joe Pike hadn't been over there. But he could have been.

"Just who the dickens do you think you are?" Joe Pike asked. Trout didn't say anything for a few seconds, and Joe Pike turned and glared at him. "Huh?"

"She's always hanging around," Trout said.

"Grace Vredemeyer is the choir director," Joe Pike said stiffly. "I am the preacher. The preacher and the choir director are in business together. Church business. The Lord's business. That's all there is to it. Grace Vredemeyer is a fine Christian woman."

"Jumping up and down in the education building with her titties hanging out," Trout said, not making the slightest effort to hide his sarcasm.

"Watch your mouth, mister!" Joe Pike barked.

Trout felt a little thrill of perverse pleasure, and it emboldened him further. "And riding around all over the place in your car."

"Visiting the sick and shut-in," Joe Pike said.

Trout could hear a note of defensiveness creeping into Joe Pike's voice. He bore in. "There aren't any sick and shut-in at the Dairy Queen."

"No, just a smarty-pants young'un," Joe Pike shot back.

"People are talking," Trout insisted.

"Who?"

Trout shrugged.

"Well, they can dang well mind their own business." Joe Pike looked away, and his shoulders gave an angry shudder. He sat there for a while, fuming. Finally he said, "I've made all kinds of fool of myself at one time or another. Been an absolute damned fool on occasion. But" — he turned back and looked Trout straight in the eye — "I've never made a fool of myself over but one woman. Your mother."

Trout said, "I wish you'd make a fool of yourself over her again."

Joe Pike stared at him for several seconds and then his shoulders slumped. He seemed weary with the effort of argument. Joe Pike squeezed his eyes shut, shook his head slowly, opened his eyes again. When he spoke, his voice was dull, the fight gone out of it. "I can't, Trout." There was the same despairing resignation of the man who had clumped into his room in the middle of the night, ranting about the Second Coming and then saying how he had failed.

Again, Trout felt the grip of fear. And on its heels, a rush of anger. "I want her home, Daddy."

"So do I," Joe Pike said earnestly. "More than anything. I think if she were here, I could . . ." His voice trailed off.

What? Recover your faith? Lose weight? Comfort your son? Save the town? Come up with the answers? Stop lusting in your heart after Grace Vredemeyer?

"But she's not ready yet," Joe Pike finished.

"How do you know? Have you talked to her?"

Joe Pike thought about it for a moment, his brow furrowing. "No. They still don't want her to talk to us for a while."

"Why?"

"I believe she sees me as part of the problem." Joe Pike shrugged with resignation.

"How about me? Am I part of the problem?"

"No. Of course not." He shook his head, stared at his hands for a moment. "Just me."

Trout could hear in Joe Pike's voice a plea for sympathy. But Trout didn't sympathize. Not at all. His anger grew, like a headstrong animal straining at a leash, and he just let it go. "What *is* the problem? What's wrong with Mama? Nobody'll talk to me about what *is* the problem."

"She's depressed, son. I've told you that. I've told you everything the doctors have told me. I'm not trying to hide anything."

"Yes you are!" Trout cried. His voice rose an octave, and he knew he sounded like some shrill little kid, but it didn't matter. "You won't tell me what's really wrong! You won't tell me why!"

Joe Pike didn't say a thing. Maybe that was the great unanswerable question. Maybe even the great unaskable question. Why?

Suddenly, Trout felt himself smothering, as if Joe Pike had thrown his great bulk on top of him, every pound of it, squeezing the breath out of him. He wanted to scream, *Get off! Get off!* But the words wouldn't come. He felt a rush of panic. He had to break free or be crushed. Now! He gave a mighty heave and stood up with a jerk, took a couple of steps into the yard and spun back toward Joe Pike. His chest heaved as he gasped for breath and he felt his eyes bulging.

Joe Pike stared at him, alarmed. "Son . . ." He stood and held his hands out, reaching for Trout.

But Trout backed away another couple of steps. "What did you do to her?" he cried.

Joe Pike flinched, as if he had been slapped. "Do?" he said dully. "I didn't *do* anything."

"You . . ." What? What kind of name could you put to all those days and weeks and years of an invisible, deadly gas that filled the house — Joe Pike's forced jollity and Irene's lengthening silences and the growing knot of dread that started in the pit of Trout's stomach and grew like a cancer until it *became* him. They didn't yell, didn't fight, didn't even disagree about anything. It would have been so much easier if they had. But this *thing* between Joe Pike and Irene had no name that he knew. At twelve, thirteen, fourteen, fifteen years old, he didn't even know which questions to ask. So he remained silent, watchful, fearful. Toward the end, Irene didn't seem aware of anything, including Trout. And Joe Pike, his great body sagging with despair, grew remote. Both of them exhausted, disappointed, perhaps even ashamed. They hid their faces from Trout. And in doing so, for them — the once-secure center of his universe — he had ceased to exist. Then they had taken Irene away to the Institute, Joe Pike had ridden off to Texas, and Trout had been left alone and dumbfounded.

So now he faced his father here in the backyard of the parsonage and still he didn't know what questions to ask. He knew only that despair was turning to rage. That, too, frightened him. But he was beginning to see it as the only desperate defense he had left, and if he didn't stand and fight, he would sink beneath the same mire that had sucked in his parents.

"I'm sick," he yelled at Joe Pike. "I'm sick of Mama being gone. I'm sick of you being screwed up. I'm sick of being a Moseley. And I'm sick of this one-horse pissant town that doesn't even have a pissant tennis court."

Joe Pike's mouth dropped open. He started to say something, but instead he just made a sort of gargling sound in his throat. Then he closed his mouth and hissed between his teeth. He closed his eyes and nodded slowly, up and down. Then he opened his eyes and took a deep breath. "Well . . ."

Suddenly, the back door of the parsonage flung open with a bang and Aunt Alma stood there in the doorway, wrapped in a floral print dressing gown, hair wild from sleep, bug-eyed and livid. Trout and Joe Pike stared up at her in astonishment. "The sonofabitch is trying to start a union!" she cried.

ELEVEN

AUNT ALMA CALLED it a "war council." And she looked mad enough to fight. She towered over the living room gathering, enlarged by indignation. Joe Pike was there, Trout (she had insisted because "the day will come when you and Eugene will have to deal with subversives"), Cicero, Judge Lecil Tandy, the family's longtime legal retainer ("We'll take this thing all the way to the Supreme Court if we have to"), and even Uncle Phinizy. Aunt Alma must be dead serious, bordering on grim, if she had swallowed hard enough to include Uncle Phinizy.

It was barely seven o'clock. Judge Tandy looked dazed, his eyes watery and his skin sallow, roused unceremoniously from sleep and given no opportunity to bathe, shave, and don a seersucker suit appropriate to the occasion of giving considered legal advice. He was dressed instead in a flannel shirt, much out of season, and a rumpled pair of gray trousers. Between the cuff of one trouser leg and the black wingtip shoe below was a stretch of blue-veined bare skin and knobby ankle. The other ankle was covered by a black ribbed sock.

Joe Pike hunkered as far down as he could get in a stiff leather chair, a quizzical, distracted look on his face. Uncle Phinizy yawned broadly. It was his bedtime. Only Cicero looked fresh and awake. Cicero was habitually an early riser, and besides, he had human remains waiting for him down at the vacant lot. He was wearing a freshly starched uniform, creases razor-sharp, leather belt already strapped to his waist with pistol on one side and portable radio on the other. Cicero sat with his legs crossed, cap perched jauntily on his knee.

From the back of the house, they could hear Rosetta grumbling in the kitchen as she prepared coffee. Rosetta, too, had been rousted early. Metal and china rattled ominously.

They all sat, awaiting Alma's pronouncement. She stood in front of the fireplace, arms folded defiantly, color high. She too was in uniform: a defiant red summer suit, sensible pumps, hair pulled back in a tight bun, an amazing transformation from the wild-haired specter that had appeared at the back door of the parsonage an hour before. Trout thought she looked quite capable of addressing the State Democratic Convention if called upon. Or a White House conference. Perhaps her old friend President Carter would summon her to vanquish malaise. "Jimmy," she would say, "get a grip."

"Well, we can all thank Trout," Alma said.

Trout looked at her in surprise.

"The rental car parked in Wardell Dubarry's yard," she said. "Cicero traced it to the Augusta airport." She looked at Cicero, waiting for him to report.

Cicero fished a slip of paper out of his shirt pocket. He read: "1979 Ford. Green in color. Rented from Avis by one Sylvester DeShon. Washington, D.C., driver's license. Born eight twenty-two forty-three. Five foot eight, a hunnert and thirty pounds." He looked up at the others. "Scrawny fella." Then back down at his paper. "Hair, black. Eyes, gray. Wears corrective lenses. Picked up the car three days ago, turned it in yestiddy. Put on the registration form at Avis that he's employed by the Consolidated Textile Workers of America."

"Cah-TWAH!" Phinizy said suddenly.

"I beg your pardon," Aunt Alma said.

"Cah-TWAH," Phinizy repeated. "Consolidated Textile Workers of America. C-T-W-A. Cah-TWAH."

Alma fixed him with a withering look. Phinizy gave her a little flash of a smile. She didn't return it. "Do you have any information about the Consolidated Textile Workers of America, Phinizy?" she asked.

"No," he answered. "Just the acronym, Alma."

She continued to stare at him, jaw set, breathing rather forcefully through her nostrils. But she didn't say anything. Finally she turned back to Cicero. "Go on," she said.

"Well, that's about it, hon."

"A union organizer," Alma said slowly. "And black to boot."

"Well, that's no surprise," Phinizy said. "A goodly number of the mill workers are black."

"I know that," she snapped.

Trout stole a glance at the others. Phinizy studied Alma, bemused. Joe Pike studied a spot on the Oriental rug where two stylized deer frolicked amidst a leafy glen. Judge Tandy looked as if he might slip into sleep at any moment. Or die quietly.

Cicero folded the slip of paper, stuck it back in his shirt pocket, hitched up his gun belt, and hiked one leg over the other. The toe of his highly polished black shoe bobbed rhythmically.

From the kitchen, the sudden crash of crockery hitting the floor. Then, Rosetta: "Shit."

Joe Pike cut a quick glance over at Trout. They had been skirting each other warily since Trout's eruption in the backyard of the parsonage. It was hard to tell what Joe Pike was thinking. He had a befuddled look, and his face was slack from lack of sleep. But then, that was the way he looked most of the time these days.

"Thank you, Trout," Aunt Alma said.

"You're welcome," he answered without thinking. For what?

"A nice piece of intelligence," Phinizy said. And to Cicero, "Splendid detective work."

"Wadn't nothing to it," Cicero said. "First, I called your Atlanta airport because I figured anybody renting a car in this area had probably flew into Atlanta. Avis at Atlanta's got three green Fords, but one of 'em has a busted radiator, one was gone to LaGrange, and the other to Alabama. So then I called your Augusta airport and they didn't have but your one green Ford . . ."

"Thank you, Cicero," Alma cut him off.

Cicero gave her a nice smile. "No problem, hon." Then he stood up, plucking his cap from his knee, hitching his gun belt. "Well, I guess I'll be getting on downtown."

"Sit down, Cicero," Alma ordered.

"Hon, I got the state crime lab coming in" — he glanced at his watch — "fifteen minutes." He motioned in the general direction of town. Human remains waiting, perhaps even a murder mystery. A bulldozer held captive. Cicero's eyes fairly danced with anticipation.

"Cicero, we have a problem here," Alma said patiently. "Could you perhaps give us a few more minutes of your time?"

Cicero stood his ground. "The way I see it, hon, you got a legal problem. And you got" — he indicated Judge Tandy with a wave of his hand — "the finest legal mind in the state of Georgia here."

Judge Tandy struggled to his feet, gathering himself to emote.

"Just a minute, Judge," Alma said.

Judge Tandy sat, a bit deflated.

"We have a law enforcement problem," Alma said to Cicero.

"How's that?" Cicero asked. He remained on his feet, crossing his arms over his chest. Trout looked at him in surprise. Cicero seemed a little taller this morning. Maybe it was the angle of the light coming in the high window at the side of the room. Or the uniform.

"A subversive element is at work in the community," Alma said, trying to keep her voice even. "An outside agitator has come in here from Washington, D.C., and is attempting to stir up trouble."

"And now he's gone home," Cicero said.

"And left the radical element" — she shot a finger in the direction of the mill and her voice rose — "plotting God knows what. Wardell Dubarry and his crowd want to take over my business." She looked around at the others. "Our business."

"But hon," Cicero said patiently, "the mill and the mill village are outside the city limits. Outside my jurisdiction."

"They'll be marching in the streets!" Alma cried.

"They'll need a parade permit for that." Cicero looked down at Judge Tandy. "Judge, do we have a parade-permit ordinance in Moseley? I should know, but I confess I don't."

Judge Tandy frowned, considering it. "I don't recall," he said. "I don't know that we've ever had a parade."

"Well, get one!" Alma barked.

"A parade?" Judge Tandy asked.

"An ordinance!"

Just then the door from the dining room swung open and Rosetta backed through carrying a tray laden with silver coffee pot, cups and saucers, sugar and cream pitchers, and a crystal container full of spoons. "Y'all ready for coffee?" she asked.

"No!" Alma yelped.

Rosetta stared at Alma. It appeared for a moment that she might do something violent with the tray, but then she took a deep breath. "That be just fine, then," she said pleasantly. And she turned and went back the way she had come. Trout thought they all could have used a cup of coffee, but he didn't say anything.

The silence hung heavy in the room. Alma gathered herself, regained her composure. "All right," she said to Cicero after a while. "Go ahead. I thought you might be interested in the future of the family business, but you go ahead."

Cicero's gaze floated about the room, resting briefly on each of the others. "You're right. This *is* family business. And y'all are the family. Except the Judge here, who's mighty like family." Judge Tandy gave him an appreciative nod. "Besides, y'all got lots more sense than I have. I'm just an old police chief, doing his duty as he sees it. Anybody breaks the law, I'll take care of 'em." He gave a little wave of his cap to Alma. "See you for lunch, hon." And he left.

There was another long silence. Trout realized his mouth was hanging open. He closed it. Something Cicero had said echoed in his head. *Doing his duty as he sees it.* Then he remembered. General Douglas MacArthur, speaking to Congress. They had seen it on an old *March of Time* film in history class in Ohatchee. How about that, Trout marveled. Uncle Cicero quoting Douglas MacArthur. Did he know what he was doing? It was entirely possible. Just about anything was possible.

Finally, Alma said, "All right. We've got to get a handle on this thing."

"Nip it in the bud," Phinizy said.

"That's right. Judge Tandy, what do you recommend?"

Judge Tandy rose again, squaring his shoulders. He was a tall man, slightly stooped, with a shock of white hair, somewhat longish in the back. In his youth, Trout imagined, he had been something of a dandy. Now, well up in his seventies, he struggled to remain courtly and patrician. He cleared his throat. "In my considered opinion," he intoned, "there are several possible courses of action here, none of which are clearly preeminently advantageous and therefore worthy, in my estimation, of recommendation with complete certitude at this early juncture." He stopped for breath, looked around at what remained of the assemblage. Flannel shirt and bare ankle or not, Judge Tandy looked every bit the sage counsel, Trout thought, duly impressed. "We might, of course, consider the injunctive process. And then again, perhaps not." He nodded wisely. "Howsomever," he went on, "one should not in a situation such as this be predisposed to any particular proceeding, nor upon the other hand be prejudiced against any possibility. One should, in a manner of speaking" — he smiled benignly — "keep one's powder dry."

The words hung ponderously in the air. They waited for Judge Tandy to go on, but instead he sat down, folding his hands in his lap. Alma gave him a slightly vacant look.

"Judge Tandy," Phinizy spoke up. "Are you versed in labor law?"

"No sir," Judge Tandy said firmly. "I am not."

"Then perhaps," Phinizy said, "you should consult with someone who is."

"Splendid idea," Judge Tandy said. "I shall indeed do that." He inclined his head toward Alma. "If, of course, Alma approves."

"Yes," she said softly, a trifle disconcerted by Judge Tandy's discourse. Then she roused herself. "We can handle this by legal means, or by God, I'll shoot 'em."

"I don't think Uncle Cicero will let you do that," Trout blurted. They all looked at him. All except Joe Pike, who hadn't taken his eyes off the spot on the rug for several minutes now.

Alma dismissed the thought with a quick jerk of her head. "Moseley Mill will not have a union," she said through clenched teeth. "No matter what."

"I wouldn't be so sure about that," Phinizy said.

Alma glared at him. "Whose side are you on, Phin?"

He ignored the question. "Here's what will happen, Alma. If these people are serious about this, and you must assume they are, they will circulate a petition amongst the employees, calling for a union election. If they get a certain percentage of employees' names on the petition —"

"Damn their petition!" Alma barked. "I won't accept it."

"It's not your place," Phinizy said patiently. "The petition will go to the National Labor Relations Board, which will then set up the formal mechanism for a vote amongst all the employees."

"I won't allow it."

"You won't have any say in the matter."

"The hell you say!"

"Yes, the hell I say."

"How do you know so much?"

"I'm from Washington." He smiled. "Hotbed of unionism."

Alma turned to Judge Tandy. "Is that true?"

"I suppose," he said.

"Before the vote takes place," Phinizy went on, "you will have ample opportunity to make your case to the employees as to why they should reject the notion of a union. And the union will likewise have an opportunity to make theirs."

They all pondered that for a moment, and then Joe Pike looked up, shifting his gaze from the spot on the rug to one of the high windows where the morning was blazing in, the sun climbing above the trees to the east. Trout's gaze followed Joe Pike's, and he noticed for the first time how the windowpanes were mottled and wavy and how the thick curtains that hung at the edge of the window were faded from years of sunrises. He looked down again at the Oriental rug and saw that it was badly worn in several spots, thick brown threads showing through.

Alma said, "Joe Pike, I want you to go talk some sense into Wardell Dubarry."

Joe Pike started to speak, but Phinizy said quickly, "I don't believe that's a good idea. It might be considered tampering." He turned to Judge Tandy. "Isn't that the case, Judge?"

"I suppose," Judge Tandy said.

"They might win," Joe Pike said musingly, almost to himself.

"That's ridiculous. They wouldn't dare," Alma said.

Joe Pike continued to look out the window. "They might win because they're fed up with Moseleys."

"I repeat," Alma said, and there was pure steel in her voice, "there will be no union at Moseley Mill."

"Then," Joe Pike said, "there may be no Moseley Mill."

"You'd like that, wouldn't you," Alma spat.

Joe Pike turned and looked at her. "Why do you say that, Alma?"

Then Alma saw Judge Tandy peering up curiously at her, head cocked to one side, waiting. And she seemed to reconsider. "Let's not get into that now."

"Why not?" Joe Pike's voice had an edge of insistence.

She turned away and started for the door. "Why don't we have some coffee." She opened the door and called back toward the kitchen,

"Rosetta, you can bring the coffee now." She closed the door and resumed her place. "Judge Tandy —" she began.

"Alma," Joe Pike interrupted, "tell me something."

She stared at him. "What?"

"Why didn't Papa ever build a tennis court?"

Alma rolled her eyes, exasperated. "Joe Pike, for goodness' sake."

"I remember one time, sitting here in this very room. It was a Sunday afternoon, I believe, after dinner. I was about twelve at the time. That would make you fourteen. Papa was standing" — he pointed at the fireplace — "right about where you are now. Holding court. Do you remember?"

Alma said nothing. She just looked at Joe Pike, waiting him out.

"You had been reading a magazine article about a tennis player," Joe Pike went on. "I don't recall the name, but she had won at Wimbledon. And you asked Papa, 'Can we have a tennis court?' And do you remember what he said? He said, 'Tennis is not ladylike.' And then I spoke up and said, 'I'd like to play tennis, too.' And then Papa said, 'Tennis is a frivolous game.' Papa's idea of sport was pitching horseshoes." Joe Pike nodded slowly. "Horseshoes," he repeated.

"All right," Alma said after a moment, as if speaking to a dull-witted child.

But before she could continue, Joe Pike stood up abruptly. "Papa was a pickle, Alma. A sour dill pickle. I should have stayed here and told him so. But I ran off. I think I've been paying for it ever since."

He started toward the door, but stopped just for a moment at Trout's chair and touched Trout gently on the shoulder. Trout looked up into his father's face and saw the sadness there — an ancient thing, perhaps as old as Joe Pike himself. Trout opened his mouth to speak, but he couldn't think of anything to say. And then Joe Pike was gone. They heard his footsteps echoing in the hallway, and then the front door closed behind him. Trout thought for an instant to get up and follow, but again he was at a loss. Could anybody follow where Joe Pike Moseley was going these days? He looked over at Phinizy, who pursed his lips and gave an almost imperceptible shake of his head. *Don't ask me, boy.*

Aunt Alma looked unnerved. She was losing her audience and seemed suddenly fragile and vulnerable, standing there in front of the fireplace in her fierce red suit.

"Well," Phinizy said, breaking the silence, "there's nothing to be done at the moment."

"What do you mean?" Alma asked.

"If there is a union organizing effort, the ball's in their court. Don't you agree, Judge?"

"I suppose," Judge Tandy said.

"You mean we have to sit around and wait for that" — she waved impatiently, her voice rising again with indignation — "rabble to do something?"

It was clearly a foreign idea to Aunt Alma. Moseleys didn't wait for anything or anybody. Never had. Never would.

"I believe that is the case," Phinizy said calmly. "Wait, watch, and listen."

They sat there for a long moment — waiting, watching, listening. Smelling. They all seemed to smell it at once: something burning. As one, they all looked toward the dining room door, the one that led to the rear of the house and the kitchen. "Rosetta!" Alma called in alarm.

Trout was the first to reach the kitchen door, and when he threw it open, thick gray smoke billowed out. Alma was right behind him. "My God!" she screamed. "The house is on fire!" Trout took a deep breath and plunged into the room, arms flailing, trying to drive the smoke away. "Don't go in there!" he heard Uncle Phinizy shout behind him. Too late. Trout was lost now in the smoke, which was getting darker and thicker by the second, seizing his throat and stinging his eyes. Then he saw a flash of orange off to his right and stumbled toward it and saw the skillet blazing on the stove, belching the thick greasy smoke, the eye under the skillet glowing angrily. Next to it, a large pot of grits, also sitting on a red-hot eye, most of it already boiled out over the sides and dripping down the front of the stove. And smoke pouring from the open oven. Flames from the skillet were scorching the wall behind the stove, blistering the paint. Another minute, and the fire would race up the wall and reach the ceiling and then the whole house could go. He could hear shouts back behind him — Phinizy calling his name, Alma yelling at Judge Tandy to call the fire department. He reached for the skillet and then snatched his hands back, feeling the heat. He felt panic seizing him, tried to fight it. *Think! Think! Water! No, it's a grease fire! Got to get the skillet out of here!* He groped along the kitchen counter to his left. And then his hand touched a dishtowel. He grabbed it and wrapped it around the handle of the skillet and pulled it away from the stove. Flames leaped and heat blasted his face and grease spattered, stinging his arms. "Ow!" he yelled, and as he did so, he released the pent-up air in his lungs. Involuntarily, he sucked in a breath and with it, a great rush of smoke. He coughed violently, staggering against the counter, almost dropping the skillet. But somehow he held on, tried to force his mind onto getting his bearings. The back door would be somewhere to his left. He headed toward it, the smoke blinding him, filling his body. He retched violently. And he felt a searing pain in his hands, the handle of the skillet burning him through the dishtowel. *I can't hold it! I'm gonna die in here! Shit!* Then suddenly Uncle Phinizy was there, somewhere in front of him, holding the back door open. "Here, Trout!" he yelled. Trout staggered toward the rectangle of light and burst through the door and down the steps, sucking in great incredibly wonderful gulps of air and flinging the blazing skillet into the backyard, where it landed in an explosion of flaming grease and charred bacon strips.

"Rosetta!" Alma screamed from behind them in the house. "Where the hell are you? Rosetttttaaaaaa!"

And then, the fire siren on top of City Hall, beginning in a low, somber groan and growing to a keening wail.

Trout staggered onto the grass below the steps, lungs and throat on fire, legs rubbery, a great roaring in his head. Phinizy was right behind him, coughing violently, his frail body wracked with spasms. Trout grabbed for Phinizy, and they held on to each other for a moment and then sank to the grass. Phinizy lay on his back, hacking and wheezing desperately. Trout was on all fours. Dry heaves shook his stomach and gagged his throat, but nothing would come out.

The roaring noise in his head subsided a little and from inside the kitchen, he could hear Aunt Alma yelling, "The wall's on fire! Get some water!" And just then, Uncle Cicero dashed around the corner of the house, took a quick look at Trout and Phinizy, and then bolted up the steps and into the kitchen. "I'm coming, hon," he cried. In an instant, he was back down the steps, grabbing the garden hose coiled by the side of the house, turning on the water, dashing back up the steps with squirting hose in hand. Trout could hear the splash of water against the kitchen wall.

Suddenly, Phinizy stopped coughing. Trout looked over at him. He lay on his back, eyes closed, face deathly white. "Uncle Phin," Trout rasped, "are you okay?" No answer. Trout summoned enough energy from somewhere to yell, "Cicero! Help!"

It took the volunteer fire department ten minutes to get there and another twenty for the ambulance, which had to come from Thomson. The five members of the fire department who answered the call worked nearby — Fleet Mathis, the mayor; Earl Cobb, who owned the Texaco station; one of the foremen from the mill; Boolie Huffstetler, who helped his wife Tilda run the Koffee Kup Kafe; and Link Tedder, the city garbage collector. Uncle Cicero was also a volunteer fireman, but of course he was already there. Of the others, it was Link who arrived first, pulling up in front of the house in his garbage truck. The fire truck was right behind, siren wailing, Boolie at the wheel with the other three hanging on to the sides. By this time, Trout was somewhat recovered, though still woozy, and was standing anxiously on the sidewalk in front of the house watching for the ambulance. A crowd was gathered along the sidewalk and spilling over into the yards of the adjacent homes, but giving the Moseley place a wide berth.

The fire truck eased to a stop behind the garbage truck and next to a curbside fire hydrant. Count on the Moseleys, Trout thought, to have their own fire hydrant. The firemen scrambled down, dressed out in bits and pieces of uniform — Boolie wearing a helmet, Fleet Mathis a jacket, Earl a pair of rubber boots.

"Where's the fire?" Earl called to Trout.

"The kitchen," Trout called back.

He watched, fascinated, as Boolie grabbed a thick, short length of hose and attached one end to the side of the truck, the other to the hydrant. The engine of the truck rumbled throatily, changing to a deeper pitch as Boolie used a huge wrench to turn the valve on top of the hydrant. Fleet Mathis stood by a collection of gauges and levers on the side of the truck just behind the cab. "Pressure!" he cried out as Earl attached a big chrome nozzle to the end of the hose that lay neatly coiled in the back of the truck.

They were all quick and efficient, and Trout imagined that they had been through the drill more times than they could count. It would, he thought, pass for something to do in Moseley. The truck was a fairly new red pumper with CITY OF MOSELEY lettered in gold on the side of the door, and just below it, MOSELEY MILL.

Fleet Mathis stood by the truck, hand on one of the levers, while the others rushed past Trout, up the steps, and through the open front door, Earl in the lead, trailing hose behind them.

After a couple of minutes, Earl and Boolie came back, lugging the hose out the door and down the steps to the truck. "It's out," Earl said. He sounded disappointed.

"Well, that's good," Trout said.

Earl gave him a close look. "Are you okay, son? You look kinda peaked."

"I'm fine. Just a little smoke. I don't think Uncle Phin's doing too good, though. They've called the ambulance."

Earl got an oxygen bottle from the fire truck and followed Trout around the side of the house to the backyard. Phinizy was sitting in the grass, his back propped against the side of the steps, eyes shut, looking wretched. Cicero was kneeling beside him, fanning him with a folded section of newspaper.

Earl clamped the oxygen mask gently over Phinizy's mouth and nose. "Breathe deep, Mr. Moseley," Earl said. Phinizy took several shallow breaths; then he mumbled something, but they couldn't tell what he said because of the oxygen mask over his mouth. Earl took the mask off. "What's that?" But Phinizy didn't say anything else and Earl put the mask back on.

"Is he gonna be okay?" Trout asked.

"I imagine he'll be fine," Cicero said. "We'll get him over to the hospital at Thomson and get him checked out."

While they waited for the ambulance, Trout climbed the steps and peered into the kitchen. The windows above the sink were open, but the smoke was still thick and Trout felt a rush of nausea. He started to turn away, but then he noticed the peg just inside the back door where Rosetta always hung her coat and hat. She wouldn't have been wearing a coat on a hot summer day, but she never went anywhere without her hat. There was no hat on the peg now. But her apron was hung neatly.

Link Tedder came up the steps then, carrying a large fan. "'Scuse me," he said to Trout, and Trout stepped aside as Link set the fan just inside the doorway and disappeared inside with the plug. After a moment the fan hummed to life, drawing smoke out of the room, and Trout went back down the steps and stood looking down at Uncle Phinizy. Some of his color was beginning to return. And then Trout heard the siren of the ambulance — faint at first as it barreled down the road from the Interstate, and then louder as it turned at the intersection downtown and wailed to a stop in front of the house. Two medics hustled around the corner of the house with a stretcher, and the rest of them stood back as the medics fussed over Phinizy, checking his pulse and blood pressure and listening to his heart and lungs with a stethoscope.

"Is he okay?" Trout asked.

"Stable," one of the medics said. "But his lungs sound like a diesel truck with one cylinder misfiring."

They loaded Phinizy on the stretcher, and Cicero and Earl helped them carry it around front and load it into the back of the ambulance. "Any of y'all want to ride with us?" one of the medics asked.

"I'll go," Trout said quickly.

"No," Cicero said. "You don't look so hot yourself, Trout. You need to stay here and get your legs back under you." He looked around. "Where's Joe Pike?"

"He left," Trout said. "Before the fire."

"I'll go," Earl said. "Y'all come on when you can."

Cicero clapped him on the shoulder. "I 'preciate it, Earl."

Earl climbed into the ambulance with the stretcher and one of the medics, and the other one closed the rear doors and jogged around to the cab and climbed in. Then Cicero got out in the street and stopped traffic while the ambulance pulled into the driveway and backed up and roared away toward Thomson.

Trout and Cicero went inside. The whole house smelled of smoke, acrid and depressing. Alma was sitting alone in the living room, at one end of the sofa with the open windows at her back. She stared at her hands, folded neatly in her lap. "Are you all right, hon?" Cicero asked. She didn't answer, and he went on toward the kitchen.

Alma looked up then. "Trout," she said.

"Yes ma'am."

"Come sit with me."

He sat down next to her on the sofa and she took one of his hands in hers. "You saved my house," she said softly.

"Aw, I didn't . . ."

"Yes you did," she insisted. "Thank you." She looked at his arms then. "You got burned." The bare skin below his T-shirt was mottled with red splotches where the grease had spattered. He felt the stinging then. He hadn't even noticed. Alma rose. "I'll get some ointment. You sit right here."

She came back in a minute with a tube of ointment and sat beside him and spread it liberally on his arms, her fingers cool and gentle. Trout looked into her face. She seemed very close to tears.

"Thank you," she said again when she was done.

"I can't believe I did that," Trout said.

"This is your home," she said. "You saved your home." She put the tube of ointment on the lamp table beside the sofa, then wiped her hands absently on the skirt of her red suit, leaving a greasy mark. Trout stared at it, but Alma seemed not to notice. *My home?* What a strange thing to say. After a forgettable succession of parsonages, the thought of "home" as some specific physical place was foreign to him. Not this house, certainly. This was Aunt Alma's house.

Alma took his hand in hers again and they sat without speaking for a while. Out in front of the house, the crowd had thinned out, the first rush of excitement over, and those who remained talked in hushed tones, as if not quite comprehending that a disaster could actually strike the Moseleys. The engine of the fire truck throbbed on for a while, but then Fleet Mathis turned off the pump, and Trout could hear Fleet and Boolie stringing out the hose along the street, letting the water drain out before they coiled it neatly in the back of the truck. There were noises back in the kitchen, men walking about, the soft cadence of Judge Lecil Tandy's voice, the scrape of a piece of furniture being moved. But it was all a background. Here in the living room, it was still and quiet. And Aunt Alma seemed somehow . . . what? Softer, perhaps.

When she finally spoke, it startled Trout a bit. "Sometimes I feel all alone," she said. He looked up at her face, saw the tiny wrinkles around her eyes and mouth, more of them and deeper than he remembered. He realized it was the first time he had really *looked* at Aunt Alma. There was something about Alma that made you keep a wary distance, look just *beyond* instead of *at*. But now he looked. And he heard something almost childlike in her voice, something sad and wistful. He watched and waited. And listened.

"I didn't want this." She made a wide, slow sweep with her hand. And Trout understood that she meant more than the house. Much more. Perhaps everything. Her hand dropped back onto his. "I wanted . . ." Her voice trailed off and she looked away and shrugged. "But there was no one else. So I did what I had to do. Do you understand?"

"I think so," Trout said.

"It has been," she said, her voice barely above a whisper, "very, very hard. The others, gone. Papa dead, Joe Pike gone to preach, Eugene to Atlanta. And things changing. Beyond my control. I have done the best I could."

"I'm sure you have, Aunt Alma." Trout tried to be helpful.

She turned to him with a quick jerk and squeezed his hand. "And now it's yours."

"Mine?"

"I didn't know if you had it in you, Trout. I confess I had my doubts." Her voice was urgent now. "Until this morning. What you did . . . it was splendid. It's the way a Moseley behaves."

"It is?"

"Yes. Take charge. Get things done. It gives me strength to go on, Trout. To fight this union nonsense. To keep things under control until you're ready." She patted his hand. "I'm very proud of you, Trout." She gave him a lovely smile. "You're my hero."

Trout tried to feel a little heroic, but he didn't. Not in the least. Instead, he felt incredibly weary. It was just too much. He wanted to go somewhere and hide, but he couldn't for the life of him think where that might be. There seemed to be no refuge. Perhaps the best place would be home in bed. A quiet nap before he had to go to work at the Dairy Queen at three. Ah, the Dairy Queen. Whipping up a Blizzard or fetching a Dilly Bar from the freezer. It was so uncomplicated.

Alma sighed, interrupting his thought of sleep. "Good God, what a morning. Rosetta must have panicked when the fire broke out. Why on earth didn't she warn us?"

Trout started to say something about the apron hanging neatly on the peg by the back door, but he thought better of it. There would be plenty of time to get into that. Uncle Cicero would conduct a thorough investigation and no doubt come to the same conclusion Trout already had. *Et tu, Rosetta?*

The firefighters clumped through the hallway on their way out the door, trailed by Uncle Cicero, who stopped and looked into the living room. "Y'all all right?"

"Yes," Alma said. "We're all right."

She and Cicero looked at each other for a long time. Trout tried to fathom what passed between them, but he couldn't. Alma had a look of exquisite pain on her face. And Cicero looked thoroughly in charge of things. There was a firm, even set to his mouth. A reversal of roles? Or a reversion to old roles? Trout thought again of Cicero, spiriting Alma away from under Grandaddy Leland's nose. And again, it made him smile.

And then the portable radio at Cicero's hip crackled to life. "Cicero, this is Calhoun." Calhoun was Cicero's only police department employee, an excitable man in his early twenties with an unruly head of red hair. Just now, he sounded excited.

Cicero pulled the radio out of its leather holster and fingered the button on the side. "Calhoun, how many times have I got to tell you, observe proper radio procedure. What you say is, 'Unit Two to Unit One.'"

"Cicero," Calhoun said insistently, "you better get down here."

"Where?"

"The crime scene."

"Why, Calhoun?"

"The preacher's got the bulldozer."

TWELVE

UNCLE CICERO HEADED for his police cruiser, parked across the street in front of the parsonage, Aunt Alma and Judge Tandy right behind him. Trout set out at a dead run. By the time he covered the two blocks to downtown, Joe Pike was backing the bulldozer out of the vacant lot, ripping away the length of yellow tape Cicero had put up yesterday to cordon off the crime scene. The big orange machine eased between the van from the state crime lab and a Bronco with CHANNEL 5 EYEWITNESS NEWS emblazoned on the side, grinding the concrete of the curb beneath the treads.

There was a good-sized crowd: two men from the crime lab in white coats, the Channel 5 crew, Calhoun, and a lot of other local folk. They lined the sidewalks and milled about in the street — gawking, pointing, talking excitedly — but they were all staying well out of Joe Pike Moseley's way, including Calhoun. He was standing on the sidewalk in front of the police station, walkie-talkie in hand. The reporter and cameraman from Channel 5 were trying to interview him, but Calhoun seemed beyond words, mouth hanging open wide enough to let in a swarm of flies.

Joe Pike was playing the levers and pedals of the bulldozer — backing well out into the street, then wheeling neatly about and pointing the nose of the machine westward. The yellow crime-scene tape, caught on the rear of the machine, streamed out behind like the tail of a kite. Traffic in both directions came to a halt — a line behind the bulldozer, stretching back toward the mill end of town, several other vehicles stopping dead in the street as they approached from the opposite direction. Beyond the traffic in front, Trout could see Uncle Cicero's police cruiser, blue light flashing. And beyond that, in front of Aunt Alma's house, the fire truck and the garbage truck still parked at the curb. There were people on the sidewalk there, too, peering down the street to see what the commotion was all about.

Trout looked up at Joe Pike. He looked feverish and agitated, much as he had looked as he had stood in the doorway of Trout's room last night, babbling about the Second Coming. But there was a difference. Joe Pike looked quite resolute, as if he had come to some fairly significant decision. He had a cigar jammed in his mouth. Trout yelled over the rumble of the bulldozer engine, "What are you doing?"

Joe Pike took the cigar out of his mouth. "Come on up and you'll see," he yelled back.

He held out a hand. Trout hesitated, as he had in the church in Ohatchee and early that morning in Aunt Alma's living room. But then he thought, *Not this time.* He smelled another disaster, and he hadn't the foggiest idea what he could do about it, but he knew that he must not watch from the sidelines with his thumb up his fanny. So he reached up and Joe Pike's big hand swallowed his own and Joe Pike gave a tug, and Trout scrambled up the side of the bulldozer and settled onto the seat. He saw that Joe Pike was wearing his scuffed brown cowboy boots. They seemed to appear like apparitions whenever some kind of storm was about to break.

"Are you going to Texas?" Trout asked.

"Not quite that far." Joe Pike moved a couple of levers and stomped on a pedal. The big diesel engine roared and Trout could feel the vibration through his spine. Black smoke belched from the stack behind the cab. Traffic was piling up in front of them, and Trout could see Uncle Cicero, Aunt Alma, and Judge Tandy getting out of the police cruiser, heading toward them on foot. Cicero and Alma were walking fast, Judge Tandy bringing up the rear.

Joe Pike moved some more levers and the bulldozer lurched into motion. Trout lost his balance and almost tumbled off the seat, but Joe Pike grabbed him by the arm. "Hang on!" Trout grabbed a handhold on the edge of the seat, another on the metal cage covering the cab over his head.

The first vehicle in line just ahead of them was a grimy pickup truck. A woman was behind the wheel, peering through the mud-spattered windshield, her eyes growing wide as the bulldozer headed in her direction. Joe Pike waved, motioning her out of the way. She yelled something, then threw the truck into gear, backed up in panic, and smashed into the front of a Merita Bread delivery van. The bread van driver responded with an angry bleat of his horn, and the woman snatched the pickup into forward and cut hard right, leaping out of the way of the oncoming bulldozer just in time, lurching to the side of the street. The pickup shuddered to a halt with its front wheels up on the sidewalk. Through the window, Trout could see the woman screaming. But he couldn't hear her over the roar of the bulldozer engine. Joe Pike didn't seem to pay any attention. The bread van driver jumped out, surveyed the damage to the front of his truck, then jumped back behind the wheel and pulled over to the left in front of the Koffee Kup Kafe.

The bulldozer plowed ahead. Trout looked back to see the crowd falling in behind, led by Calhoun and the Channel 5 crew. The cameraman was running about, getting shots of the bulldozer and the crowd from all angles. They were all stepping over chunks of broken asphalt. The big steel treads of the bulldozer were chewing up the street. "You're tearing up the street," Trout shouted to Joe Pike.

"Yeah," he shouted back. "A dozer will do that."

Cicero and Alma were there now, Cicero out in the middle of the street, Alma standing on the sidewalk with a look of utter horror on her face. Joe Pike waved to her, but she didn't move a muscle. Judge Tandy came up beside her, badly winded. He saw Alma's expression, put his arm tentatively around her shoulders, then took it away.

"Stop, Joe Pike!" Cicero yelled up at the oncoming bulldozer.

Joe Pike cupped his hand behind his ear. "Can't hear you!" he yelled, although Trout had heard Cicero plainly.

"He said stop," Trout shouted to Joe Pike.

"Yeah. I know."

But he didn't. The bulldozer bore down on Cicero. He reached for his pistol. Trout's heart leaped to his throat as Cicero's hand tightened around the grip. Then he took it away, shook his head and stepped nimbly to the side as the bulldozer went past. Cars were pulling over to the side, backing into alleyways, fleeing in the opposite direction. Down at Aunt Alma's house, Trout could see the fire truck pulling away from the curb with everybody hanging on, turning into the parsonage driveway, backing into the street, and heading toward downtown. But it didn't go far. Traffic snarled, two cars bumped together and stalled. The street ahead was completely blocked. Trout looked at Joe Pike. Joe Pike shrugged.

It didn't matter. Because Joe Pike wheeled the bulldozer suddenly to the left and pointed it at the sidewalk. He didn't slow until it had lurched up over the curb and reached the edge of Broadus Moseley's park. Then he stopped. And lowered the bulldozer blade. *THUNK.* It landed in the grass just inside the sidewalk. Then Joe Pike shoved the bulldozer into gear again and plowed into the park, ripping up a wide swath of Bermuda grass and baring the earth so long ago covered at the behest of Moseley's patron saint.

Trout had a sense of pandemonium on either side of them — people running back and forth, arms waving, a flash of blue police uniform. But he was transfixed by what the bulldozer was doing to the park. He glanced up at Joe Pike, but he was intent on his work, arms and feet in motion as he shifted levers and mashed footpedals. They were headed now for a big oak tree. Trout flinched, preparing himself for impact. But Joe Pike wheeled neatly around the tree and took dead aim on the band shell. *Holy shit.* The blade hit the concrete sidewalk in front of the band shell first, scooped it up and tossed it aside as if it were Styrofoam. Then Joe Pike flicked a lever and the blade rose about a foot and the bulldozer hit the band shell with a crash of splintering timber. This time, Trout didn't even flinch. It seemed suddenly that nothing could stop Joe Pike Moseley and that no harm could come to him or his son sitting up here on the seat beside him. This might be senseless destruction or calculated purpose. Nothing to do but hang on and find out. Beams toppled, the roof collapsed, the flooring buckled and came up in big chunks of wood. The bulldozer never slowed. It crunched through and over debris; then the blade bit into the ground again, gouging up another swath of grass and earth.

Suddenly, Uncle Cicero was up there in the cab with them, hanging on to the metal cage next to Trout with one hand, pointing his pistol at Joe Pike's head with the other. Cicero yelled, "Joe Pike, you're under arrest!"

"No!" Trout screamed in horror.

Joe Pike looked over at Cicero, gave a huge sigh, and stopped the bulldozer. It idled for a moment. "Cut it off!" Cicero commanded. Cicero was mad as hell, face flushed and nostrils flaring.

Joe Pike switched off the diesel and it died with a rumbling cough. The crowd swarmed up around them, everybody yelling at once. "What's the charge?" Joe Pike asked Cicero.

Cicero lowered his pistol, then stuck it in the holster. "Disturbing a crime scene," he said without hesitation. His voice was steel-hard and unyielding. "Malicious destruction of town property. Malicious destruction of state property. Inciting a riot. Theft and unauthorized use of a vehicle. Failure to obey the order of an officer of the law. Failure to yield the right-of-way. Failure to give a proper turn signal. Reckless endangerment. Unauthorized use of a public facility." He stopped, thought for an instant, then added for good measure, "Failure to obtain a parade permit."

"Cicero," Joe Pike said quietly, "there wasn't nothing malicious about it."

"What in the hell do you think you were doing?" Cicero demanded.

Suddenly, Trout knew. He knew exactly. It was so obvious. "I know," he spoke up.

Cicero stared at him. Trout looked at Joe Pike, then back at Cicero. "Making a tennis court."

"That's right," Joe Pike said.

"Did you know about this?" Cicero asked icily. Trout felt as if he might be a candidate for the charge of accessory before, during, and after the fact.

"No he didn't," Joe Pike said. "It was all my idea and all my doing."

"Well," Cicero said between clenched teeth, "you have royally pissed me off, Joe Pike. And by God, you are going to jail."

He felt like a freak at the Dairy Queen as the afternoon wore itself out, the sole survivor of some terrible natural disaster. Herschel and Keats didn't have a lot to say to him, nothing at all about the events of the morning in town. But he could feel both of them cutting glances at him now and again, perhaps expecting him to come unglued and start screaming and throwing things. But he was quite beyond all that. He was simply numb. Burned out, like an electric motor run too long under too strenuous a load. He even imagined (surely, it was his imagination) the acrid smell of melted bearings and wires. It became so strong at one point that he went to the bathroom in back and checked the mirror to see if he had smoke drifting from his ears or a scorched look about his hairline. But there was only his own vacant stare looking back at him — hollow-eyed and slack-faced. But what could he expect? It had been a long night and an interminable day.

Joe Pike was in the city jail, or what passed for a jail — a one-cell cubbyhole at the rear of the police station. Uncle Cicero had hand-cuffed him (proper police procedure) and taken him straight there, leading him away from the bulldozer through the crowd that grew by the minute as word spread of the ruckus, every step dogged by the Channel 5 TV crew, shouting questions at Cicero and Joe Pike, none of which they answered. "No comment," Uncle Cicero kept saying grimly. "No damn comment." Part of the crowd stayed at the park to gawk at the wreckage of the grounds and band shell, but a good many followed Cicero and Joe Pike as they walked — Cicero with a firm hand on Joe Pike's arm — down the sidewalk to the police department and disappeared inside. Trout followed at a distance, not know-ing quite what to do or whom to ask. He looked around for Aunt Alma, but she was nowhere to be seen. He learned later that she had fled back to her house and had driven the Packard to the mill. Uncle Cicero was up to his ears in police business. And Uncle Phinizy was in the hospital in Thomson.

Trout stood for a while at the edge of the crowd that milled about in front of the police station, watching as people took turns pressing their faces against the plate-glass window to peer inside. Nobody said a word to him, but he could feel the breath of their whispers: *That's him. Joe Pike's young'un. Mama's at the Institute and Daddy's in jail.* There were even a few faces he recognized from his brief stay at Moseley High School. They stared unabashedly. Headline: INVISIBLE STUDENT SPOTTED. But they did not speak. After a while, Uncle Cicero came to the door of the police station and leaned out and said, "Y'all go on home. Ain't a thing here to see. Go on, now." As the crowd began to drift away, somebody pointed him out to the Channel 5 crew, and when they started in his direction, he slipped down an alleyway and took a circuitous route back to the parsonage. He locked the front door and took the phone off the hook and sat for a long time in one of the big overstuffed chairs in the living room, waiting for something to come to him. Nothing did.

About two o'clock he got on the motorcycle and headed down-town. The bulldozer was gone from the park, and so were most of the people. Instead, there were two stake-body trucks from the mill and

several men at work, one group sweating profusely in the early afternoon heat as they cleaned up the splintered pieces of the band shell
for hauling away, another group laying slabs of new green sod where
the bulldozer had ripped up the grass. The downtown sidewalks were
all but deserted. Trout parked in front of the police station and walked
up to the door, above which a small air-conditioning unit throbbed,
dripping water onto the sidewalk. Trout stepped around the puddle,
opened the door and went in. Calhoun was sitting on the edge of a
desk, thumbing through a copy of *Motor Trend*. He looked up and
closed the magazine as Trout entered, but he kept his thumb in his
place.

"I'm Trout Moseley," he said.

"Uh-huh," Calhoun answered.

"Can I see my dad?"

"Guess you'll have to talk to Cicero about that." Calhoun didn't
sound unfriendly, just noncommittal.

"Where is he?" Trout asked.

Calhoun looked out through the plate-glass window. "Over yonder." Trout looked and saw Cicero and the two men from the state
crime lab in the middle of the vacant lot across the street. They had
erected an open-sided tent over the crime scene to shade them from
the sun. One of the men from the crime lab was in a shallow hole,
handing up pieces of what Trout took to be skeleton to the other, who
put them into a big plastic bag. Cicero watched, hands on hips.

"Could you ask him?" Trout asked Calhoun.

Calhoun shrugged, put the magazine down on the desk and started
toward the door. "You could call him on the radio," Trout offered,
trying to be helpful.

Calhoun went back to the desk, picked up the microphone of the
police radio, and pressed a button. "Base to Unit One."

Across the street, Trout saw Cicero take his walkie-talkie out of its
belt holster and hold it up to his mouth. "Whatcha want, Calhoun?"
Cicero's voice came tinnily through the radio.

"Trout Moseley's over here. He wants to see the preacher."

"Well, let him," Cicero said. "I'll be over there in a minute."

Calhoun led him through a door and down a narrow hallway to the
single cell where Joe Pike was propped on an old Army cot. It had a
clean mattress but nothing else. It was stiflingly hot. This part of the
police station wasn't air conditioned. And it was badly lit from a single

overhead lightbulb and a small barred rectangle of window high on the back wall. Joe Pike didn't say anything as Calhoun unlocked the cell door, let Trout in, then locked it back and left. The springs of the cot creaked in protest as Joe Pike swung his legs over the side of the cot and made room for Trout to sit down.

"Are you okay?" Trout asked.

Joe Pike nodded at the wall opposite the cot, and Trout looked up and saw a large poster displaying traffic signs in reds and yellows with a word of explanation beneath each. "I've been studying," he said. "Cicero says most of the people he puts in here are charged with a traffic offense of some kind, so he put up the poster as a gesture toward driver education."

"Why did you do that?" Trout asked.

Joe Pike sighed wearily. He looked awfully tired, and the hot, cramped cell seemed to diminish him physically. He didn't say anything for a long time. But Trout waited. This time, he would get an answer if it took until next week.

Five minutes passed, perhaps more. And finally Joe Pike said, "It's your fault."

"What?"

"And I'm glad it is. This morning, sitting there on the steps. Or at least, me sitting and you jumping around yelling about this pissant town and no tennis court."

"Daddy, I didn't mean . . ."

"No," Joe Pike stopped him. "I know you didn't. But I got to thinking, sitting over there later in Alma's parlor, that's what I should have done. Way back yonder when my daddy and I used to get crossed up. I was way bigger than him, but I never thought of it that way. I always felt like a small, runny-nosed kid, especially after he got through cutting me down. He could use his voice like a switchblade." Joe Pike stopped and looked down at his hands, and Trout could see the exquisite pain in his father's face. "There were times," he went on softly, "there were times I should have stomped my foot and raised hell and said, 'Leland Moseley, you are dead wrong.' But" — he shrugged — "I never did."

Trout felt his heart wrench. He had never heard anything quite so nakedly honest from his father. He put a tentative hand on Joe Pike's arm.

"I guess that's what I was doing today," Joe Pike said. He turned and looked into Trout's eyes. "I love you, son. I guess I'm trying to make up for some things. For you, and for me." A wan smile then. "I guess I really tore up the pea-patch, huh?"

"Yeah," Trout said. "I guess you did."

And then Trout felt a flush of anger. It baffled him at first, but then he began to see where it came from. *Dang you, Joe Pike. Easy enough for you to jump on a bulldozer and go settle an old score, just like you jumped on the motorcycle and high-tailed it to Texas. My fault? No sirree. Don't try to put this monkey on my back.*

Trout asked, "When are you gonna get out?"

Joe Pike gave a big sigh. "I don't know."

"Can't you, what do they call it, post bond?"

"I can, but Cicero says I've got to have a bond hearing. Meantime, I guess I'll have to sit here and ponder the consequences of my transgression."

"And what am I supposed to do while you stay in here pondering your consequences? Fend for myself?"

Trout could hear his voice rising. So could Joe Pike. He leaned his head back against the wall and closed his eyes. He stayed that way for a long time, his only movement the rise and fall of his chest as he breathed. Out in the alley behind the jail, Trout could hear voices. Small boys, from the sound of it, giggling. Then a rock hit the bars of the high window with a *clank*. Trout stood up on the edge of the cot and looked out the window. "Cut that out or I'll whip your ass," he said without rancor. And the boys, three of them — barefoot and shirtless — fled. Then he sat back down. "I understand what you're saying about the bulldozer and all. But where does that leave me, Daddy? It may make you feel better to tear up the pea-patch, but for me, it's just one more piece of . . ."

"Shit," Joe Pike finished for him.

"Yeah."

"You need something solid. Something you can count on."

"Yeah."

Joe Pike opened his eyes now. If he took offense, he didn't show it. "I'm not a very practical man," he said. "I always depended on your mother for that."

"If Mama had been here, she would have told you to . . ." *What? Grow up? Stop trying to be Jesus? Something like that.* Big old Joe Pike — a Goodyear blimp of a man, tethered to earth by the firm hand of a tiny determined woman. Even in the months before they took her away, even in the depths of her great blank silences, her mere presence had kept him anchored. It was only when she left that he began to drift, finally fading into the distance on the motorcycle. *It all keeps coming back to Mama.*

Just then, the door down the hallway opened and Cicero walked toward the cell. He peered in. "How y'all?"

"Just great," Trout said.

"Trout, I'm sorry about all this. But I got to do my job. You understand, don't you?"

"Sure."

"Joe Pike," Cicero said, "I'm gonna go get us some lunch. I'll bring you a plate from the Koffee Kup."

Joe Pike didn't answer.

"Want something to read? Maybe something out of your study at the church?"

Joe Pike waved at the traffic signal poster on the wall. "I think I'll just ponder this, Cicero. It's all about figuring out how to get where you're going without running over anybody."

"Uh-huh," Cicero agreed.

"Things calmed down?" Joe Pike asked.

"Pretty much," Cicero said. "Too hot to be loitering around. And the Channel 5 bunch gave up and went back to Atlanta. I think they went over and interviewed Wardell about the union bidness before they left. They got their whole evening newscast out of Moseley tonight."

"Why were they here in the first place?"

Cicero waved toward the vacant lot. "Human remains. Ain't nothing excites your TV folks like human remains. Everything else just fell into their laps." Cicero shook his head, marveling. "Ain't it the damndest thing. Not a thing worth telling has happened in Moseley since the furniture store burned down and now three stories in one day."

"Yes," Joe Pike agreed, "it has been an auspicious day. I feel honored to have been part of it."

Trout and Cicero looked at Joe Pike, and then they looked at each other. Cicero gave a little shake of his head. Was it history or random chaos? They wouldn't know for a good while. Trout had learned that much from listening to Uncle Phinizy. "Where historical significance is concerned," Phinizy had said, "it's hard to tell a volcanic eruption from a fart in the wind until a century or so has passed. A hundred years from now, Moseley, Georgia, may be just a fart in the wind." Thinking back on the events of the past eight hours, Trout understood. It was impossible to make any sense of it. A hundred years would do wonders for perspective. A good night's sleep would help.

Trout rose from the cot. "I've got to go to work. Can I get you anything?"

Joe Pike smiled and licked his lips. "A dollar cup of Dairy Queen vanilla." Cicero opened the cell door, and Trout stepped out into the hallway while Cicero closed it back and locked it. As Trout turned to go, Joe Pike said, "Trout, you may be a little *too* practical. You worry too much. Try to relax a little. Or failing that, try to find you a woman who's got a wild hair up her butt."

He came to himself standing in the Dairy Queen with Keats's hand on his arm. He was at the ice cream machine, hand on the lever, a cup beneath the spout. The cup was empty. Had he been asleep? No, just missing in action for a moment. He was long past fatigue, floating somewhere between wakefulness and a soft twilight.

"Let me do that," Keats said gently. She took the cup from him. "A shake?"

"What?"

"Were you making a shake?"

Trout tried to remember. It was like swimming through yogurt. "I think so."

"What flavor?"

He shrugged. Keats turned to the window, where a man dressed in wilted khaki work clothes and wearing an ACE PLUMBING cap peered in, frowning. Keats slid the window open. "What flavor shake did you order, sir?"

"Strawberry." He nodded at Trout. "Something wrong with that boy?"

"No sir," Keats answered and slid the window closed again. "Sit," she ordered Trout, pointing to a stool. He sat watching while she mixed up the shake, passed it through the window, and collected the man's eighty-five cents. There were several cars in the parking lot, an older couple at a picnic table, but for the moment, no one at the window. It had been a busy late afternoon, and if custom held, it would be a busy evening. Here in the grip of Georgia summer, the

Dairy Queen was an oasis, a moment's relief from heat and boredom for the locals and from road-weariness for the I-20 traffic. Business had never been better, Herschel said.

"Where's Herschel?" Trout asked.

Keats wiped the counter with a washcloth. "Gone to get a TV."

"What for?"

"It's almost six o'clock."

"So?"

"The news, dummy."

"Oh."

"Don't you want to see it?"

"Not especially."

Keats finished with the counter and hung the washcloth on the edge of the sink. She moved so efficiently about the cramped quarters of the Dairy Queen, you sometimes forgot that she was on crutches. "Well, I do," she said. "My daddy's gonna be on."

"So is mine," Trout said, making a face.

Keats leaned against the counter, a smile playing at the corners of her mouth. "Take fame where you can find it." She could really look nice when she smiled, Trout thought. It even made her eyes look softer, as if the smile muscles released a pigment that changed steel gray to a nice blue.

Herschel came in the back door then, carrying a small black-and-white television set. He set it on the counter, plugged it in and raised the rabbit ears. The picture from Channel 5 over in Atlanta was grainy and drifted in and out, sound disappearing with picture in a swarm of static. And just as *Eyewitness News at Six* came on, there was a rush of customers. But Herschel opened the window and called out, "Be just a minute, folks." And through hiss and snow, they watched as Gordon Goodnight, the anchorman, said, "It was quite a day in Moseley," and then showed them.

The reporter who had been in Moseley that morning had decided to take a somewhat lighthearted, tongue-in-cheek approach. He folded the three events — human remains, bulldozer escapade, and union movement at the mill — into two minutes of gee-whiz-you-won't-believe-this. There was Uncle Cicero presiding over the un-earthing of the skeleton; Joe Pike and Trout on the bulldozer as it plowed through the band shell; Uncle Cicero again, escorting Joe Pike to jail. The sound and picture faded just as he started to say, "No damn comment," so that they couldn't tell whether Channel 5 had bleeped out the "damn." But it returned in time to see pictures of Moseley Mill with Wardell Dubarry standing just outside the gate saying how the mill workers wanted "a decent wage and a fair shake" and had just today submitted a petition to the National Labor Relations Board for a union election. All but five of the workers, he said, had signed the petition. The holdouts, he said, were toadies for the Moseley family.

Trout didn't want to watch, but he was powerless not to. And he found himself, as the story unfolded, thinking of it as an out-of-body experience. He had read about such things: a man involved in a terrible wreck, dying but not quite dead, seeming to float above the scene watching medics work feverishly over his own broken body down below. The victim survives and lives on to tell how it was a detached, almost peaceful feeling. And then a sudden urge to return. To see what would happen next. Trout wished for a moment that he was a hundred years older, looking back on all this with historical perspective. Headline: TROUT MOSELEY DIES AT 116; SAYS IT WAS ALL A FART IN THE WIND.

The reporter signed off with another shot of the bulldozer destroying the band shell. It seemed to sum up everything. Then Gordon Goodnight launched into a story about a woman in Alpharetta who had set her husband on fire as he slept, and Herschel turned off the TV set and they went back to work.

At nine-thirty, when they had served the last customer and cleaned up and Herschel had turned off the red-and-white Dairy Queen sign on its pole out by the highway, Keats asked, "Can you take me home?" Trout hesitated. "It's okay if you don't want to. I can call Daddy."

"No," he said. "I'll take you."

They all left by the back door, and Herschel locked up and got in his car and headed for town. Then Keats said, "Want to talk?"

He hesitated again; but then he realized that he really did, that talking to somebody approximately his own age might be the sanest thing he would do this day. Everybody older seemed to have lost their minds.

They sat at one of the picnic tables beside the Dairy Queen and for a long time they didn't talk at all. It was warm and muggy, especially after having spent several hours in the air-conditioned Dairy

Queen, serving up frozen treats. Out on the Interstate, traffic barreled through the night. A carload of teenagers came up the road from town and turned into the parking lot. The windows were rolled down, the stereo throbbing with some Janis Joplin . . . *Oh Lord, woncha buy me a Mercedes-Benz* . . . Girls and boys inside, laughing. Then, disappointed to find the Dairy Queen closed, they made a quick U-turn in the lot and sped back toward town with a flurry of flying gravel. If they had seen Trout and Keats sitting at the picnic table, they paid no attention. The night settled back into stillness. Out on the Interstate, an air horn bleated. Maybe a regular customer, unable to stop tonight but sounding a howdy anyway as he passed the exit.

"Do you love your daddy?" Keats asked.

She was sitting about two feet away from him, but it was difficult to tell much about her face. The only light was a single bulb left burning inside the Dairy Queen.

"Sure," he said.

"I love my daddy too, but sometimes I think he's crazy as hell."

Trout didn't know what to say. Probably a lot of people thought Wardell Dubarry was crazy as hell. But he had never expected Keats to say it, much less think it. She seemed to be such a fierce defender of all that Wardell stood for. She seemed so sure of what she believed, while he, Trout Moseley, felt mostly baffled.

She read his silence for what it was. "You didn't expect me to say that."

"No."

"Neither did I."

"Why did you?"

"Because I had to say it to somebody."

He nodded wearily. "And I was convenient."

"No, I figured you'd understand. About a parent being crazy and all."

True, he did. Well, not crazy. Did clinical depression and acute theological angst qualify as mental illness?

"I wish he'd just walk away from it," Keats went on. "There's plenty of other jobs Daddy could do. We could move to Augusta, and he could go to work at the Army post. He's really good with his hands."

"A helluva painter," Trout said, then regretted it. Now was not the time for smartass remarks.

Keats let it pass. "I want to go to college and study art."

"Well, no reason why you can't do that. There's all sorts of loans and scholarships if you need 'em."

"It's not the money," she said bitterly, "it's this *place*." She stabbed angrily in the direction of town with one of her crutches. "It's like a big black hole with the mill and that pitiful little house and Daddy's anger. It's like it swallows you up, you know?"

"Yes," he said. And he did. She had put her finger precisely on the *problem*. Being swallowed up. Being sucked down by everybody else's circumstance, feeling that you had no power whatsoever to climb out on your own because you were weak and ineffectual and just a kid and at the mercy of people who should know better, act better.

"Your daddy's angry about" — he indicated her crutches — "what happened. I can understand that. I guess I would be, too."

"Maybe it started with that," she said. "But now, I don't know if he even knows anymore. He's all caught up in this union thing, like if he wins and the union comes in, he'll get his revenge."

"On Aunt Alma?"

"On the world. For shitting on him."

They sat for a while letting all that float in the warm sticky air, listening to the sounds of crickets in the high weeds at the edge of the parking lot and the bass rumble of traffic on the highway.

Then he said, "A couple of weeks ago you told me I ought to be pissed off. Are you pissed off?"

"Yes," she said. "No. I mean, you aren't supposed to be pissed off at your daddy, are you?"

"No, I don't think so. You can get" — he paused, searching for the word — "upset. But really pissed off? I don't think God would let you get away with that."

"God," she snorted.

"Don't you believe in God?"

"Sure. But I don't think He *lets* you get away with anything. Or *doesn't* let you. I don't believe all this crap about God running every little thing."

"When even a sparrow falls . . ." Trout remembered a verse from Sunday school.

"Yeah, I think He knows. But He doesn't worry with all the details. That would run Him nuts."

Trout laughed, but there wasn't any mirth in it. "You ought to talk to Joe Pike Moseley."

"Is he nuts?"

Trout considered again the concept of craziness. "No," he said thoughtfully, "just confused, I think. About himself. About Mama. But mainly about all the God business."

"But he's a preacher," Keats said.

"Yeah. That's the problem. He thought he knew, but now he's not sure."

"And where does that leave you?" she asked.

"About the same place it leaves you, I guess."

She reached out then and took his hand and the shock of her skin on his almost took his breath away. He realized that it had been a great long while since he had felt the soft, smooth touch of female flesh. It was part of that other life, eons ago, that had once been his. His fingers intertwined with hers, and she gave his hand a little squeeze. She didn't say anything for a long while, and neither did he. There didn't seem to be anything that particularly needed saying at the moment, and at the same time, everything to say and all of it with just the touch. He half expected to feel a rise of sexual excitement, but this was different. This was . . . He couldn't find a name for it, but it was at the same time both comforting and painfully sad. Sad to feel such a great, aching need that you couldn't even identify because you were too young and unformed and unwise.

Finally, she took her hand away and rose with a clank of her crutches. "I guess I better go home."

"Yeah," he said. "Me too. I need some sleep. I haven't had much lately."

She turned on him suddenly, a fierce edge in her voice. "Don't you think for one minute I'd do anything to hurt my daddy."

"Sure," he said. "Me too."

"It's just . . ."

"Yeah. I know."

She hesitated for a moment, then said, "I guess things have been pretty rough for you."

"A little." Then, "Maybe more than a little. I've found out it's not easy being a Moseley in Moseley. At least not right now."

"Because of the mess at the mill?"

Caution held his tongue. She was, after all, Wardell Dubarry's daughter. And Wardell Dubarry appeared to be on a rampage just now.

"I'm not trying to pump you or anything," she said, reading his mind. "I don't care if they have a goddamn union or not. They either will or they won't."

"Aunt Alma thinks that one of these days, I'm going to take over the mill. Run it. Me and Eugene."

She gave a snort. "You? Running that mill?"

"Well," he said defensively, "I guess I could if I had to."

"But you don't want to."

"No."

"What do you want to do?"

He sighed. What did he want? At sixteen, were you supposed to have the foggiest idea beyond food, drink, shelter, sex (in just about any form), and a new tennis racquet? "I kinda want to go hide."

"Well, you can't do that here. Not you."

"Then maybe I'd just like to have somebody tell me what to do. You know? I mean, that's really weird, isn't it? I always thought I wanted people to *stop* telling me what to do. But then they did, and . . ." He shrugged. "I guess they're all too busy trying to figure things out for themselves. Daddy's wrestling with God, Uncle Phinizy's sick, Uncle Cicero is busy, and Aunt Alma's pissed off." And scared, he could have added, but didn't.

"What about your mother?"

What a stupid thing to say, he thought. Maybe even mean, considering the circumstances.

But Keats wouldn't drop it. "Why don't you just pick up the phone and call her and ask her what to do?"

"She's sick," he said, spitting out the words.

"I know that. Everybody knows that. She's in the Institute in Atlanta."

"Yeah."

"Well, people call sick people all the time. Or go visit."

"Not there. Daddy says the doctors don't want her to talk to anybody for a while."

"Daddy says," she said with a touch of sarcasm.

Trout could feel the heat rising in his face. This was getting out of hand, and it made him angry. She was treating him like a little kid again. Damn her.

She waited. "Well?"

"It's none of your goddamn business," he said stiffly.

"Probably not," she said quietly. "But I hate to see you just sit there and take it. I keep thinking you'll get pissed off enough to hitch up your britches and do something for yourself."

It dawned on him that she sounded a lot like Uncle Phinizy. *Save your own ass.* But what did she know? Or Phinizy, for that matter? It wasn't their ass to save. "What about yourself?" he asked finally.

"What about me?"

"You don't sound like you're deliriously happy, either. Are you pissed off enough to do anything about it?"

"Not yet. But I'm working on it."

They sat for a while longer on the picnic table, but there didn't seem to be much else to talk about. So they got on the motorcycle and went home.

It was an hour or so later, as he teetered on the edge of sleep, that he thought of the dollar cup of vanilla ice cream Joe Pike had asked for. He thought of his father, sitting in the dark, hot, cramped little cell, knowing at this late hour that Trout had forgotten his one request, that there would be no ice cream this night. It might not be the greatest disappointment in his life, just the latest.

Trout began to cry, and at first he tried to stifle it, but he found that he could not. So he buried his face in the pillow and let the sobs come without struggle or protest. They were bitter tears and there was no comfort in them. Then he wondered, *Why this?* After all that had happened in the long hours since the sun had risen this morning, why was he crying over some stupid ice cream?

THIRTEEN

THE TELEPHONE WOKE HIM. He thought if he lay there long enough, it would stop, but it didn't. Someone pretty damned persistent was on the other end. So he gave up and padded back to the kitchen and answered it.

"Trout, can you come down here?" Uncle Cicero asked.

"Down where?"

"The police station."

"What's the matter?" Trout asked, suddenly alarmed.

"He won't leave."

Trout looked at the clock on the kitchen wall. It was nearly eight. "What do you mean, Uncle Cicero?"

"Your Aunt Alma got a judge out of bed at six o'clock this morning and posted bail for Joe Pike."

"She did?"

"Yes she did. And him a Republican, too. The judge, I mean. I reckon being a Moseley transcends party politics, huh?"

"Well, that's good," Trout said. "He needs to come home." Then what?

"But he won't leave," Cicero repeated. "He refuses to come out of the cell."

"Did he say why?"

"No, he just sits there. Staring at that damned traffic chart on the wall." There was a long pause. "I thought maybe you'd know what to do," Cicero said finally.

"Yes sir," Trout said. "I'm the practical one in the family."

True to Cicero's description, Joe Pike was sitting on the cot, his gaze fixed straight ahead. The cell door was wide open. Trout entered and sat down on the cot next to Joe Pike. Then he joined his father in studying the poster for a while, wondering if Joe Pike had perhaps found some answers up there among all those do's and don'ts. Stop, Yield, No Left Turn, Railroad Crossing. Low Shoulder, Steep Grade, Sharp Curve, Dead End Road. A vehicular minefield. Knowing all this, why would anyone ever drive?

"I'm sorry I forgot your ice cream," Trout said after a moment.

"I really need to stop eating so much of that stuff," Joe Pike said, startling Trout a bit with the sound of his voice. "I need to lose some weight. I have let myself get woefully out of shape and I imagine that I cut an abominable figure. Vanity of vanities. All is vanity, quoth the preacher."

"I saw the TV stuff," Trout said. "You didn't look all that bad."

Joe Pike gave a great sigh. "I suppose you've come to get me out of jail."

Trout didn't say anything.

"Well, I'm not ready yet."

"Why not?"

Joe Pike turned to Trout. "Because I am meditating. I have found a little peace and quiet back here and I am enjoying the contemplative life."

"Looking at traffic signs?"

"You can find all sorts of riches in symbols if you take long enough to think on them."

Trout looked at the poster, picked out one from the top row. "No U-Turn."

"Excellent choice," Joe Pike said. "Start with Thomas Wolfe: 'You can't go home again.' Then consider the lost magic of childhood. And think about the nature of wishes. Children wish for a BB gun from Santa Claus, a dollar from the tooth fairy. Pleasant things, mostly. When grown-ups wish, there's mainly pain involved: take away my arthritis; make my husband stop beating me; deliver me from evil.

Speaking of which, is there something in the nature of evil that is undeliverable? What of the sinner whose life is one dastardly deed after another, crying out with his last breath, 'Lord, I have sinned. Forgive me.' Does the Lord say, 'Of course.' Or does he say, 'Whoa just a minute, bubba. We got to have a little prayer meeting over this business you call a life.'" He paused, thought for a moment. "I could go on. The possibilities are virtually endless, but sooner or later you arrive back at the sign. No U-Turn. I thought about that one a good deal of the night. It's second from the left on the top, right after Stop, which I didn't. I have worked my way to the end of the first row and am ready to start on the second with Deer Crossing. I suspect there may be something there in the nature of nature."

Trout looked over the poster again. There were seven rows of traffic signs. About a week's worth of work at this pace. "Then will you leave?" he asked.

"I haven't thought that far ahead," Joe Pike said. There was something gently wistful in his voice. He seemed calmer than he had in days — a man poking about leisurely inside his soul. There was something to envy about that, Trout thought. Even a practical person could see that.

"Have you been to see Phinizy?"

"I haven't had time."

"Go," Joe Pike said urgently. "I think he's pretty sick."

"All right. Does he have any other relatives? A wife? Children?" Trout realized that for all of Phinizy's relating of Moseley history, he had revealed little of his own.

"No children," Joe Pike answered. "He did have a wife once upon a time. Married her in Italy after the war. But it didn't last. They fought like a couple of alley cats, to hear Phinizy tell it. So there's nobody but us."

Trout got up to go, and he started to say, *Can I bring you anything?* but he thought better of it. He might forget again, and that was so much unlike him, he didn't want to risk it. So he gave Joe Pike a hug and left.

"He won't leave," Trout told Cicero out on the sidewalk. "He seems pretty set on staying. Has he had anything to eat?"

"Oh yeah," Cicero said. "He's got a great appetite. I been toting stuff back and forth from the Koffee Kup since yestiddy."

"Maybe you should stop feeding him," Trout suggested. "Try to starve him out. Or yell, 'Fire!'"

Cicero looked down at the sidewalk. Trout could tell he was terribly tired. He sagged around the edges. "I don't know, Trout," he said, and Trout understood that he meant a great deal more than the Joe Pike problem. They were, all of them, much in need of mercy and grace.

"Maybe everything'll calm down for a while and you can get back to your project." Trout nodded to the vacant lot across the street.

Cicero gave a tiny shrug that didn't use much more than his eyebrows. "Grady come and got the bulldozer. Be a cold day in July before I get it back."

Phinizy looked like cannibals had gotten him. A shrunken head, brown and leathery and deeply creased, displayed upon a backdrop of white, nestled on a pillow with the bedsheet pulled up tight under the chin. A museum piece, that's what Great Uncle Phinizy was. Grotesque, aboriginal. Or maybe just original.

Fifteen minutes, they had told Trout at the front desk, and that only because he was a blood relative. He pulled up a chair next to the bed and sat watching Phinizy, noticing after a while the almost imperceptible rise and fall of his chest under the sheet, so little air being taken in and exhaled that Trout wondered that it could sustain life. The only sound, a tiny wheezing in his throat. A bedside cart stand held an oxygen bottle and mask, but Phinizy was apparently in no need of it at the moment.

Then all of a sudden Phinizy said in a raspy but perfectly clear voice, "The sonsabitches took my cigarettes and my pants and they won't bring me any whiskey." Nothing moved but his lips. Then his eyes fluttered open and he cut a glance at Trout. "What are you gonna do about it?"

"Me?"

Phinizy made a little farting sound with his mouth.

"I just came over here to see how you were doing," Trout said.

"Well, I'm just damn near dead. And I want to die in Moseley, not Thomson. I ain't got a thing against Thomson, but at least in Moseley I can smoke cigarettes and drink whiskey and wear my own pants."

Trout didn't know whether to believe him or not. Dying? From the look of him, that might well be the case. And if it were, Trout knew that it would make him indescribably sad.

"You look a mite taken aback," Phinizy said.

"Are you really . . ."

"Yes," Phinizy said, and there wasn't an ounce of self-pity to it. "They took out one lung five years ago and now the other one is as rotten as a month-old watermelon."

"I'm sorry," Trout said.

"Well, I'm not. Only thing I regret is, I ain't gonna be around to see how it turns out. I'll just have to use my imagination."

The door opened and a young nurse stuck her head in. "Time's up," she said. "Mr. Moseley needs to get some rest."

"Yes ma'am."

The door closed, and Trout got up and moved the chair back against the wall.

"Well?" Phinizy asked. "Are you gonna take me home?"

"Uncle Phin, I can't do that," Trout protested. "I'll go get Uncle Cicero or Aunt Alma." He didn't think it necessary to go into the business about Joe Pike.

"Cicero and Alma are the ones who put me in here."

"Wouldn't the doctors —"

"To hell with them," Phinizy interrupted. "There's not a damn thing wrong with me except that I'm dying, and I've been doing that for months. It could take me several months more. Those assholes just want to watch."

Trout thought of Phinizy as he had most usually seen him — nestled deep in the recliner with glass in hand, smoke curling about his head and disappearing into the pool of light from the reading lamp, holding court with the latest footsore pilgrim who wandered in. The place, for all its scruffiness, fit Phinizy. This place, this plastered and tiled and pasteled sterility with its hospital smells and mutterings, was no place to die.

But what to do?

"Go get your mother," Phinizy said. "She'll get me out of here."

"Mother?"

"She's the only one of the whole goddamned bunch that's got any sense."

"But she's . . ." *What the hell is going on here? All these people sud-*

denly invoking the name of my mother. Have they forgotten? Are they just trying to be nasty?

"Either get Irene or get me out of here yourself. I'm going home. It's your responsibility."

"What if the doctors won't let you leave?"

"Who the hell's gonna ask 'em? I'll just walk out. Go get the car. I'll meet you in the parking lot."

"I didn't come in the car," he said.

They had almost reached Moseley, taking the back way on two-lane roads, when the state trooper stopped them. Trout pulled the motorcycle over to the grassy shoulder of the road next to a thick stand of pine trees. He left the engine running and balanced the motorcycle with both feet on the ground. Not that Phinizy weighed all that much. Not even as much as Keats. The trooper got out of his cruiser and left the blue lights on top flashing and put on his Smokey Bear hat and walked up to the motorcycle. He was about thirty, Trout guessed, lean and crew-cut, creases sharp, leather and brass polished, the hat tilted forward on his head so that it shaded his eyes. A pair of sunglasses hung from one shirt pocket. Above the other was a small brass nameplate: SPENCER. He stopped a couple of yards from the motorcycle, studied things for a while, then walked all the way around and ended up back where he started. Finally he asked, "What in the hell is going on here?"

"I am an escapee from the Augusta Center for the Criminally Insane and Terminally Wealthy," Phinizy rasped. "I have commandeered this vehicle and have wired powerful explosives just under the gas tank. One false move, Officer" — he peered at the nametag — "Spencer, and I will blow all of us into the afterlife."

"He's just kidding," Trout said quickly.

"Try me," Phinizy snapped.

"Really," Trout rushed on, "he's my uncle. Well, my great-uncle. And he's been in the hospital over at Thomson and he's only got one lung and I'm taking him home to Moseley. There's no explosives or anything. Honest."

Officer Spencer didn't say anything for a long time. Finally, he reached out his hand, rubbed his thumb and two fingers together. "Your license."

Trout gave it over.

"What are you doing all the way up here?" Officer Spencer asked.

"What do you mean?"

"The address on here is Ohatchee."

"He's a runaway," Phinizy said.

"Dammit, Uncle Phin!" Trout exploded, turning with a jerk and almost toppling the motorcycle. "Will you just shut up." Phinizy gave a little shrug. Then Trout said to Officer Spencer, "We just moved to Moseley about three weeks ago."

"We?"

"Me and my father. He's a Methodist minister."

Officer Spencer studied the driver's license for a while, making small movements with his lips as he read. Then he nodded. "That one."

"Yes sir." He waited, but Officer Spencer didn't say anything else. "Can we go now? I need to get my uncle on home."

Officer Spencer gave Phinizy a careful looking-over. "His butt's showing."

That was, indeed, the case. Phinizy wore only the light-green hospital gown. Nothing underneath and a fairly wide swath of skin showing down the back. On a younger person, it might have been obscene.

"You can't ride around the state of Georgia like that," Officer Spencer said.

"What if I just take the whole thing off?" Phinizy asked.

"No sir." Then to Trout, "You'll have to cover his butt."

And so it was that Trout rode into Moseley bare-chested and Phinizy had Trout's T-shirt strategically placed at the rear of the hospital gown.

He pulled into the driveway of Aunt Alma's house and kept going to the foot of the stairs of the garage apartment. Then he helped Phinizy up the steps and into some clothes and onto the recliner. He fetched cigarettes and whiskey and volume three of Shelby Foote's history of the Civil War. Phinizy seemed tired but satisfied. "Now go away for a while," Phinizy said.

"Can you get up and down if you need to?"

"Of course."

"I'm going to tell Uncle Cicero," Trout said. "I don't care whether you like that or not."

"Doesn't matter," Phinizy said. "Thank you for everything, Trout.

You are a rather uncommon young man. You just don't know it yet. Come back later and we'll talk."

The rest of the week, to Trout's great surprise and relief, passed uneventfully.

Trout stopped by Phinizy's apartment several times a day, bringing meals from the Koffee Kup Kafe and checking on Phinizy's condition, expecting each time to open the screen door and find him peacefully departed in his chair with a half drunk glass of whiskey beside him and a cold cigarette stub between his fingers. But Phinizy seemed his old self — wry, grumpy, curious. His appetite was good, his relish for tobacco and alcohol undiminished. Trout suggested that perhaps Aunt Alma would be happy to hire a woman to come in occasionally and handle domestic duties. Phinizy wouldn't hear of it. "If I wanted a woman, I'm perfectly capable of hiring one myself. But I don't. I have had a singular lack of success with women all my life," he said. "I don't need to spoil the record now. I am completely comfortable with male orneriness and dissipation." He sent Trout to the library with a list of books, and Trout returned with the only one available, a thin volume of Robert Frost poetry. *And miles to go before I sleep.* They spoke no more of death.

Nothing more was said from either side about the union movement at Moseley Mill. Aunt Alma was silent on the subject, and from what Trout could tell, there was no particular agitation among the work force. Everyone seemed to be waiting on that score. To Trout's relief, Alma made no inquiry about the Dubarry family or goings-on in the mill village. Instead, she threw herself almost totally into cleaning up the house. A construction crew arrived to repair the fire damage in the kitchen. A professional cleaning crew came from Augusta and began to scrub walls and floors and carry off piles of clothing and linens to be dry-cleaned. Alma dogged their every step, making sure they handled the furniture and fixtures with care. She wanted everything back in its place exactly as before. Her greatest anguish was the draperies. They were simply rotten with age and came apart when the cleaners took them down. Alma sped off to Savannah with salvaged scraps of cloth, bent on finding exact replicas, or at least a close approximation. The house was a fixation. Nothing must change.

Alma made no more mention of Rosetta, but Cicero remarked that he had inquired at her house, hoping to learn more about the origin of the fire, only to find that she was visiting a sister in Detroit.

What Cicero did clear up was the mystery of the skeleton in the vacant lot. Dental records identified the remains as that of a wanderer from Birmingham, reported missing by his family several years earlier. As best the state crime lab technicians could determine, the man had somehow reached Moseley on a cold winter night, broken into the rear of the furniture store seeking a warm place to sleep, and had managed to start the fire. When the building collapsed, the body had been buried under the rubble. The initial investigation had blamed faulty wiring, so no one had imagined a human being was involved. Until now, when Cicero started digging up the past. Channel 5 Eyewitness News reported the new developments, but they did not send a crew back to Moseley. They simply replayed the earlier pictures of the crime lab technicians bagging the bones. Moseley's brush with notoriety had passed.

Joe Pike remained in the tiny cell at the rear of the police station. Trout visited daily, but Joe Pike seemed distant and preoccupied. By the end of the week, he was nearly to the end of the traffic signs on the poster, and the more he thought about, the deeper into himself he seemed to slip. Mayor Fleet Mathis came to call, gently suggesting that perhaps Joe Pike was needed elsewhere in the community. Joe Pike demurred. The preacher from the Pentecostal Holiness Church also showed up and spent several hours in prayer and meditation with Joe Pike. At the end, he seemed inclined to join Joe Pike on a more or less permanent basis, but Cicero hustled him out, reminding him that he had another job as night watchman at a poultry processing plant in Warrenton and a family to feed. Cicero brought Joe Pike three meals a day from the Koffee Kup Kafe. Dinner and supper included sweet potato pie. Cicero was keeping a tab, he said, and would present Joe Pike with a bill when and if he finally decided to give up his meditation and go home. The city would not pay to feed a man who wasn't supposed to be in jail.

Trout worked and rested. At the Dairy Queen, he settled into a routine, comfortable and proficient now with preparing any item on the menu. Herschel pronounced him satisfactory, ended his probationary period, and gave him a twenty-five-cent-an-hour raise.

With Keats, what had begun as a sort of truce passed at some point into something a bit more. They talked, stepping nimbly around the subject of their families and the nasty potential for conflict lurking in the background. Instead, they talked as teenagers — about music ("You like all that old stuff," she teased. "The Platters. Yuck. They're about as exciting as an organ recital."), movies (she had been to Augusta once to see a Zeffirelli film and pronounced it high art; his all-time favorite was an old black-and-white with Van Johnson and June Allyson, which turned up occasionally on TV), dreams (portents, she said; entertainment, he countered), and zits. The latter was the only thing they agreed on, but that was okay. Trout found himself lowering his guard, hungering for some normalcy. And so did she. There was no more physical contact, but he could still feel her cool touch on his hand. At night, in the silent dark of his room, he imagined more. In his fantasies, she was strong and unfettered, without limitation. Facing her at work, remembering, he stammered and blushed. There would, of course, be nothing more to it. They were too different in temperament, too bound by circumstance. She could still make him mad as hell.

He had the parsonage blessedly to himself. He ate mostly at the Dairy Queen, making do with orange juice and Froot Loops at breakfast. Nobody came to call. The community, particularly the Moseley Methodist congregation, seemed to regard the situation with the same kind of awed fascination as had the good folk in Ohatchee when Joe Pike replaced his wife with a motorcycle. Another wreck here, obviously not finished. You wouldn't want to get too close for fear of being struck by flying angst. So they stayed away.

Trout fell into the habit of peeling off all his clothes the minute he stepped in the door (though he always took them to the dirty-clothes hamper), remaining unclothed until it was time to leave the house again, except at night when he would sit naked on the back steps for an hour or so, letting the summer air bathe and soothe him. As he sat there on Friday night, thinking about nothing in particular, it began to rain. But it was a warm, soft rain, and he didn't move until it had passed.

He kept the parsonage neat, even spending one morning with the vacuum cleaner. There was something comfortingly satisfying about a simple task that took no thought to speak of and produced immediate results, much the same as preparing a banana split at the Dairy Queen. He mowed the lawn of the parsonage and church on Saturday with the same sense of satisfaction.

He watched TV, slept a lot, felt himself slowly edging up from the black hole of physical and mental fatigue. He found to his surprise that he was now in no hurry for Joe Pike to come home. He tried not to think about it.

He was sitting on the front steps (clothed in shorts and baseball cap) when the *Atlanta Constitution* arrived early on Sunday morning, delivered by a boy on a bicycle who flung the hefty rolled-up bulk from the sidewalk. It plopped with a thud onto the walkway. The delivery boy made a turn when he reached the business district and worked his way back up Broadus Street on the other side, dropping papers at Aunt Alma's house and those of her neighbors.

Trout would have let the paper lay where it landed, but he became curious about the Braves' score from the night before. They had played the Dodgers, and Trout had neglected to check the radio for results before he went to bed. So he barefooted out the walkway and picked up the paper and returned to his place on the steps. He removed the thick rubber band and spread the paper on his knees. And there it was. A large photo dominated the front page: a small crowd, mostly men and mostly young, proceeding along a downtown Atlanta street. GAY PRIDE MARCH, the bold letters above the photo read. And there in the middle of the throng was Eugene. He carried a placard that said, QUEERS HAVE RIGHTS TOO.

Trout studied the picture for a while and read the accompanying article all the way through twice. Then he said, "Oh, shit."

He looked across the street. Alma and Cicero's copy of the *Constitution* lay on the walkway beneath their front steps. Trout thought about going over there and getting it. But did he have any right to meddle? He had no idea what Alma and Cicero knew about Eugene's lifestyle and preferences. They hardly ever mentioned him, except for Alma's occasional insistence that he would one day, along with Trout, be responsible for the mill and the perpetuation of Moseley-ism. If they knew, this might be no great surprise. If they didn't, they soon would, one way or the other. Trout agonized over it for a while longer, and then Uncle Cicero saved him the trouble. He walked out in his bathrobe and fetched the paper with a wave to Trout. He disappeared into the house and Trout held his breath, half expecting an explosion.

None came. After a moment, Trout got up from the steps and put on a T-shirt and shoes and went to the jail.

At precisely eleven o'clock, just as Grace Vredemeyer was lifting her hands to launch the choir into an opening fanfare, the doors to the sanctuary swung open and Joe Pike strode in. Grace's hands froze in midair and she turned and watched Joe Pike (as did they all) as he marched down the aisle and up to the pulpit where Judge Tandy was standing, prepared to lead the service in the absence of the minister. They all saw that Joe Pike was wearing his cowboy boots under the billowing black robe. But it was the only thing even slightly scruffy about him. He was clean-shaven, freshly scrubbed, hair neatly combed. And there was a firmness to his face that Trout hadn't seen for some time — slightly less fleshy, more purposeful.

Joe Pike extended his hand and Judge Tandy, mouth slightly open, shook it. Then he glanced at Grace. "Y'all go right ahead," he said. And he sat down in the big high-backed chair behind the pulpit, crossed his legs, and waited.

Grace Vredemeyer glanced toward Aunt Alma, who was sitting in her accustomed front-and-center pew between Trout and Cicero. Alma had entered the sanctuary five minutes before Joe Pike, followed dutifully by Cicero. She had looked neither left nor right but had proceeded directly to her pew and sat down stiffly, smoothing out her clothing and then reaching for a hymnal. She gave Trout a thin, tight smile. She looked quite attractive, dressed in a navy blue summer suit with white piping on the sleeves and pockets and a simple strand of pearls. Her makeup was faultless, every hair in place. But if you knew what to look for, you could see the strain etched in thin lines around her eyes and mouth. If the sight of Joe Pike marching in abruptly had either surprised or nonplussed her, she gave no evidence of it. At the moment, with Grace Vredemeyer's eyes on her, she moved not a muscle.

Grace turned back to the choir and they sang the introit, and then the congregation rose as one and launched into the first hymn. "Blessed Assurance." Appropriate, Trout thought. He had heard the rumblings about updating the Methodist Hymnal, adding new material that paid respects to changing sensibilities and agitations, referring to God as a woman and all that. But to Aunt Alma, God — as He was represented at Moseley Methodist Church — was unchanging. She sang with a clear, strong voice.

Blessed Assurance, Jesus is mine
Oh what a foretaste of glory divine . . .

Cicero, at her side, chimed in off-key and an octave or so lower. Cicero looked weary and shopworn with bags under his eyes and a rather poor job of shaving. But he sang out bravely.

The sanctuary was packed, the largest crowd Trout had seen since they had moved to Moseley. Those who had not personally seen the front page of the *Atlanta Constitution*, he imagined, had at least heard about it. They had come, like the crowd that gathered uptown at the crime scene days before, to see its effect. Alma, to all appearances, bore it with great, calm dignity. Trout was moved. He was tempted to put an arm around her, but he refrained. She seemed, underneath that granite exterior, to be delicate porcelain.

When the hymn was finished, they all sat down, and for a moment, no one seemed to know what to do. Joe Pike sat musing in his chair, gaze fixed on the toe of one cowboy boot. Finally, Judge Tandy got up from his chair at Joe Pike's side and read some announcements and a few verses of Scripture and then prayed eloquently but vaguely. As he did, a few late arrivals straggled in and, finding no seats, stood self-consciously along the rear wall of the sanctuary. Ushers brought folding chairs from the educational building while the congregation stood and sang again. "Rescue the Perishing," one of Joe Pike's favorites. That, too, seemed to fit the occasion. After the hymn ended, Judge Tandy called the ushers forward and they passed the collection plates. The choir blessed the collection with song, Judge Tandy placed the stacked plates on the altar, and then he looked up at Joe Pike from the Communion railing.

Joe Pike stepped to the pulpit and peered down at the good judge. "Thank you, Judge Tandy. I'll take it from here."

Judge Tandy joined his wife, Myrtice, in his accustomed pew, and the congregation settled in their seats — quiet, expectant. Trout thought of Uncle Phinizy, sunk deep in the bunker of his overstuffed chair, celebrating Sunday with cigarettes, whiskey, and Plutarch. Trout had checked on him at midmorning and found him a bit weak but cheerful. "Ummmmm," Phinizy hummed when Trout showed him the newspaper. He studied the photo for a moment. "He has Leland's nose and eyes," Phinizy said.

"Was Grandaddy Leland gay?" Trout asked, not really knowing why.

"No. He was a prick. That's enough of a burden for a man to carry. Eugene got his only good qualities. The eyes and nose. He's a nice-looking young man."

Trout didn't know what to think about Eugene. He remembered the boy of his childhood, something of a fascination both because he was older and because he possessed a certain spark, a sense of modulated rebellion. He would not touch that sacred family heirloom, the old Packard, but there was a great deal he *would* do, including climbing out on the roof outside his second-story room and drinking black-berry wine filched from Rosetta's supply in the pantry. There had been nothing furtive or odd about Eugene, nothing to indicate he was anything but the most regular of boys. He seemed, even at that young age, to be satisfied with who he was. From the appearance of his smiling, somewhat defiant face on the front page of the *Constitution,* he still was.

Trout had actually never known anyone who was openly gay. There had been talk about the agricultural arts teacher at Ohatchee High School, whose eyes seemed to linger a trifle too long on some of the male students. Trout and his friends antagonized each other with jokes about their own maleness or lack thereof. Gayness was not something any of them personally knew anything about, or would at least admit. It was a condition, it was understood, to be avoided. But this was Eugene. His cousin. Openly and proudly gay. Trout needed some frame of reference other than the snide remarks of teenage boys. But Phinizy was no help. Phinizy went back to Plutarch and Trout went to church.

Where now Joe Pike stood towering over the deadly quiet of the sanctuary. There was not even a cough or the rustle of a petticoat, even among the scattering of children. He reached inside his robe and pulled out a small newspaper clipping. *Good grief,* Trout thought. *He's going to rip right into it.*

But he didn't. Joe Pike cleared his throat. "Maybe you saw this item in the paper a couple of weeks ago. I clipped it out because I thought it was sort of curious. It's about the Salem witch trials." His gaze swept the congregation, lingering now and then on a face. No one moved.

Trout cut his eyes over at Aunt Alma. Her forehead creased a bit, but that was all.

"You've probably heard the story. In Salem, Massachusetts, back in the seventeenth century, a number of young women were charged with practicing witchcraft, tried, and executed. The good people of Salem thought there was ample evidence. The young women had been acting strangely — speaking gibberish and the like. And in that unenlightened time, it was enough to convince the Faithful that the girls' bodies and souls had been possessed by the Devil. So, nothing to do but dispatch them summarily, to keep the evil from spreading and contaminating the entire community. Any reasonable person would do the same, don't you think?"

He waited, but there was no response. The congregation seemed in no mood to engage Joe Pike in Socratic dialogue this June morning. In fact, they seemed in no mood at all, only a state of expectant puzzlement.

"Well" — Joe Pike held up the clipping — "modern scientific thought and method have shed some new light on the Salem witches. In short, researchers have found good evidence that what actually happened was this: the girls ate some bread that was contaminated by a parasitic fungus. They became physically ill, and the illness manifested itself in part in disorderly behavior, delusions, and convulsions. In the Salem of the seventeenth century, that amounted to evidence of witchcraft. Ignorance, you say. How sad that twenty innocent young girls died because they ate bad bread."

Joe Pike folded the clipping neatly and tucked it back beneath his robe. Then he leaned forward on the pulpit, hands gripping its sides, and looked out across the congregation again. "Why do you think God made people who are different?" He waited for an answer. None came. None except from Aunt Alma. She stood up slowly, tucked her purse underneath her arm, and walked out. She had to climb over Cicero to get to the aisle. He sat there for a moment, looking very weary and sad. And he got up and followed Alma out the door.

In the pulpit, Joe Pike waited for a long while until the door to the sanctuary stopped swinging. Then he gave a sigh and plunged ahead. "Why did God make people who are blind or deaf or lame or retarded, people with horrible disfigurations — not because of accident or war, but from birth — little babies who emerge from the sanctity of the womb with arms and legs missing, with brains so ill-formed they have no hope beyond being vegetables. Why? Why?" There was true agony in Joe Pike's rising voice, at once a lamentation and a diatribe. He lifted both hands toward the ceiling. "Why? Why?" he thundered. "What the dickens are You up to?"

A shudder passed through the congregation. They held their breaths, watching Joe Pike's fists clench, seeing the raw, naked anger and grief that contorted his face, expecting the lightning bolt that might consume them all. They all, Trout included, shrank from his rage and blasphemy. But none moved. They were paralyzed, both by fear and fascination.

Joe Pike lowered his arms. "I don't know," he said wearily. "I just don't know. I don't know why the innocent suffer. I don't know why God creates or allows people to be so different that we hide our eyes in shame and shrink from contact and even make jokes to reassure ourselves and prove to the world that THANK GOD WE AREN'T LIKE THAT, and then secretly suffer agonies of guilt because we know in our hearts we've been cruel. I don't know why," he said, his voice sinking almost to a whisper, "God creates or allows a state of mind so bleak that a person cannot see beyond a curtain of despair. I don't know."

There was a long, painful quiet. Trout thought for a moment that Joe Pike might end it there, give a great bewildered shake of his head and retire from the field of battle. It seemed such a final, irretrievable sadness, an abject admission of failure. But he was not finished. He looked out across the congregation again, and when he spoke, they sat and listened in absolute stillness. "I don't know," he said, "and don't expect to. Ever. But there is one small thing I believe, and another that I guess. I believe that God's special grace is upon those who are differ-ent, that whatever temporal, earthly misery they endure is compen-sated tenfold when they stagger and crawl in their wretchedness to the gates of eternity. I believe they will be made whole and that they will sit on the right and left of God's throne and be His elect."

He smiled, and they could see that he took a small measure of comfort and peace from this thing he had come to believe. He went on. "I can only guess at why they have to endure what they endure. But is it possible" — he paused and looked upward again — "that God just wants to see how the rest of us will treat them?"

And with that, he did leave. And after he had gone, the congrega-tion — drained and weak, as if they had been through Joe Pike's valley of shadows with him — got up quietly and went home. There seemed nothing worth saying.

It was a quiet Sunday night at the Dairy Queen. The afternoon traffic had been intense, long lines at both windows stretching out into the crowded parking lot, more people than they had ever seen in one blindingly hot stretch of summer day. Herschel and Trout and Keats worked frantically, filling the orders and passing them through the window and going on to the next and the next and the next. Finally, about seven o'clock, it ended abruptly. Trout shoved a cardboard container with a strawberry shake, two Mister Mistys, three foot-long hot dogs, and an extra-large order of fries through the window, along with change for a ten-dollar bill, and when the man who had ordered it all turned away, there was no one else. They hunkered behind the counter for several minutes like battle-weary soldiers, expecting another assault. But no one came. Finally Herschel said, "Sweet Jesus." It took another half hour of hard work to clean up the mess and litter, indoors and out. At eight, an hour earlier than usual, Herschel turned off the lights and they all headed home.

Trout dropped Keats off at the mill village, both of them exhausted beyond conversation. A minute later, as he passed the mill, he noticed the gate standing wide open, the Packard in Aunt Alma's parking space next to the office door, and the glow of a light from one of the tall windows of the mill itself. He was well past, turning onto Broadus Street toward the parsonage, when curiosity caught up with his work-dulled mind and he turned back.

When he pushed open the door to the weaving room, he heard the splash of liquid somewhere on the other side of the sprawl of silent machines. He followed the sound and found her, walking along the far wall and pouring kerosene on the floor. She looked up, saw him, but said nothing and went back to her work, walking slowly, tilting the can and letting the silver liquid gurgle from the long spout, leaving a reeking trail behind her. The last drops spilled out as she reached the end of the wall and she stopped and put the can down. She straightened and looked at him again. She was wearing the same blue suit she had worn to church that morning. Her hair and makeup were still perfect. But her eyes were now dull and lifeless.

"Aunt Alma . . . ," Trout said tentatively.

"It's finished," she said, her voice mechanical.

"What do you mean?"

"There's nobody left."

"Left to do what?" he asked.

Then she sank slowly down to her knees on the battered wooden floor, pitted and stained from all those years of grime and dust and oil, trod by the weary feet of generations of mill workers who had tended the machines. She spoke softly, almost to herself. "Did you see them today in church? Did you see how they looked at me, all there in their Sunday best, every seat filled to see the Moseleys brought down." Then her face shattered and she began to cry quietly. Trout went to her, stood awkwardly for a moment, then knelt with her. He put a hand on her shoulder.

"I was supposed to be the pretty one," she said. "Daddy said I was so pretty. I was supposed to dance and wear pretty things. Not" — she passed her hand through the stale, close air of the weaving room — "this."

She leaned against him then and sobbed into his shirt, and he held her and let her cry for a long time. And he understood how desperately lonely it had made her, quite beyond Cicero's love and devotion. It was a terrible thing, trying to live up to something, to have your life shackled by your history, or at least your notion of your history.

All of them, it seemed, were trapped in lives they no longer wanted, whether they had freely chosen them or not. Alma didn't want to be the keeper of the Moseley myth. Irene didn't want to be a preacher's wife. Joe Pike didn't want to be a preacher, not in the sense he had originally intended. And Trout didn't want to be sixteen, lost and wretched. Only Cicero and Phinizy seemed to have any peace about them. And even with them it seemed as much resignation as anything.

Finally, Alma pulled back from him. "It's over," she said.

"Why?" he asked.

"There's no one left."

"You've always said you're saving it for Eugene and me."

"Don't speak to me of Eugene," she said.

"Then me." And as he said it, he felt utterly crazy, knowing it was a lie, that if he stayed here that this would all devour him as surely as it had devoured Alma. But he lied to save . . . what? He wasn't quite sure, but he knew it shouldn't end as smoldering ruin and ashes. It had to be worth more than that.

"You?" she said. "You really mean that?"

"Of course."

She started to say something else, but fell silent. He helped her to her feet and took her back to her office. She leaned heavily on him like an invalid. He helped her sit in the chair behind the big desk, where she slumped, dull and vacant-eyed. And then he called Cicero.

An hour later, when he and Cicero had washed down the wall and floor where the kerosene had been poured and Cicero had taken Alma home, Trout went back to Keats's house. It was after nine when he knocked on the door and the porch light came on. He heard the clanking of Keats's crutches inside before she opened the door and peered out. When she saw who it was, she came out on the porch and closed the door behind her. They stood there looking at each other for a moment.

"Will you come with me?" he asked.

"Yes," she said without hesitation.

FOURTEEN

THEY FOLLOWED HIGHWAY 278 as it wandered through farm-land and pine forest and small towns — Crawfordville and Greens-boro, Union Point and Covington — traffic sparse in the towns, lights winking off in the farmhouses as they passed, Georgia drifting to sleep and girding itself for Monday.

Trout avoided the Interstate. It was no place to be late at night on a motorcycle with a girl hanging on behind and two aluminum crutches sticking out over the handlebars. He stuck to the older road because it was mostly two-lane and he knew that it led unerringly to Atlanta. He need only follow the signs. Stars overhead, the air cool but not uncomfortable at fifty miles an hour, the steady drone of the engine, the singing of the tires. There was a kind of hypnotic peace to it, a suspension of time in which the minutes folded back on one another in a rush of wind.

At first he tried to empty his mind of everything but the business of guiding the motorcycle. He was not yet in any sense a skilled rider, though he grew more sure of himself as miles passed without inci-dent. By the time they reached Madison, he was more confident, and his thoughts began to wander. He thought of Joe Pike, riding west on this same motorcycle, fleeing from one set of demons and pursuing another, with the Holy Ghost occupying the seat where Keats nestled now, her arms comfortably about his midsection. It had been less than three months ago, but it seemed a lifetime; and he felt a great deal older, if not wiser, than he had the Easter morning Joe Pike abandoned the pulpit in Ohatchee. Certainly not wiser, because things seemed more muddled than ever, questions more persistent, answers nonexistent. One great difference between Joe Pike's journey and his was that Trout didn't have to go so far. Atlanta might offer refuge, and that was all he asked for at the moment. Joe Pike was proof that you could ride a lot farther and not find any answers.

They stopped at a little crossroads grocery store outside Madison. It was closed, no lights on except a single bulb at the back of the store and a security light on a pole at one end of the building that bathed the small parking area and gas pumps out front in stark bluish white. Trout counted change from his jeans pocket. He had taken everything he had found in Joe Pike's pants while Joe Pike snored, oblivious, in his parsonage bed. He had a twenty and 6 ones in his billfold and enough change for a Pepsi from the soft drink machine next to the front door. They shared it, Trout leaning against a gas pump while Keats lurched about the parking area getting the kinks out of her legs and back, returning to him to take a sip and then clattering off again. There was an awkward grace to it, he thought. He remembered the first time he had seen her, blitzkrieging through the hallway at Moseley High School, blasting everyone and everything out of her way.

"What?" she asked now, catching him watching her.

A week ago he would have stammered and blushed. But things had changed, a subtle shift in wind direction. "How old were you when it happened?" he asked.

"Four."

"Do you remember much before?"

She balanced on the crutches before him. "I used to have a dream all the time. I'd be running across a field with Daddy, both of us holding on to a kite string. Then I'd let go and he would run on, faster and faster with me trying to keep up. And then I'd stop and look up, and the kite would be way up in the sky dancing from side to side. And I would start to dance like the kite. I don't know if it was something that really happened before I got hurt or if I just invented it."

"Do you still have the dream?"

"No. I guess I got over it."

He took another sip of Pepsi and passed her the can. She drank what was left, then tossed the empty can into a rusted oil drum that served for a garbage can. The clatter rang out in the stillness. "We aren't gonna get to Atlanta like this," she said.

Trout stopped again at a Jif-E Mart in Covington and filled up the gas tank. It took all of his one-dollar bills. Inside, he examined a Georgia road map tacked to the wall and saw that Highway 278 merged with I-20 just outside Covington. The thought of confronting I-20 spooked him. But the clerk showed him a couple of back roads he could take until he could pick up 278 again in Conyers.

They set out again, following the clerk's directions until they left the city limits on a narrow farm-to-market road that cut south and west from Covington into the countryside. It seemed that they had fallen off the end of the earth. They went several miles without seeing an inkling of life — only blackness ahead, pierced by the thin, timid beam of the headlamp, and to either side, trees growing close to the roadway, an occasional flash of fence posts, stretches of sheer emptiness. Keats's grip on him tightened.

And then the headlamp went out. They hurtled blindly into the pit of the night and Trout screamed, "Jeezus!" and fought the panic that seized him by the throat and made him want to brake the motorcycle with every ounce of his energy. Keats didn't utter a sound, but her arms were like a vise around him, squeezing his breath, the metal crutches biting painfully into his sides. He let up on the gas and tried to brake with a steady pressure. The motorcycle began to slow. He had no hint of where the pavement was and wasn't until he felt the bike slip suddenly sideways and lurch violently across grass and dirt. He had the sudden impression of a yawning void to his right and he fought to stay away from it, manhandling the motorcycle, almost losing it, summoning a surge of terrified energy and pulling it back to the left until finally it shuddered to a stop and the engine coughed and died.

They sat there unmoving, Trout's feet splayed to either side to keep the bike from toppling. Keats's grip on him eased and his breath came in great gasps. He felt faint. His heart was somewhere up around his ears, pounding like a rock band in heat. After a moment Keats said in a small voice, "That was interesting."

After a while, his eyes began to adjust to the darkness. There was a tiny sliver of moon low in the sky, and it provided just enough light to make out their immediate surroundings. He looked to his right. There was a ditch — not deep, as he had imagined, but deep enough to have caused a nasty spill if the motorcycle had hit it. They might both be dead, or at least badly hurt, lying helplessly in this godforsaken Georgia outback until someone stumbled upon them.

Trout's resolve and bravado — what there had been of it — deserted him. His shoulders slumped in defeat, his stomach churned, a wave of nausea hit him. "I can't do this," he said, his voice quivering.

Keats didn't say anything for a long while. Night sounds bubbled up around them — crickets, an insomniac bird, something small rooting about in the grass along the far edge of the ditch, the faint rustle of a breeze in what appeared to be a field of some kind of low-growing crop beyond the ditch. He felt utterly helpless.

"I've got to go to the bathroom," she said.

"What?"

"Help me off," she commanded.

A flash of rage took him. Damn her! It was all her fault, and if she hadn't said what she said in the first place, he would have never thought of taking off in the middle of the night on a motorcycle for Atlanta, much less with a crippled, tart-mouthed woman hanging on behind, goading him on without saying a word and now, when he was about to crap in his own pants, making him crazy with her goddamn bladder. It was a wonder she hadn't insisted on dragging along her goddamn sketch pad and stopping every now and then to scribble on it. She was maddening.

He lowered the kickstand with a vicious jab of his foot and climbed off and helped her slide off the back, making no attempt to hide his anger. She tottered off down the roadside without a word, and he watched her for a moment and then turned his back and kicked at the grass and heard the rattle of the crutches and then a hissing sound. After a moment she was back.

"Let's go," she said.

He turned on her with a jerk. "Go? Are you out of your mind?" he yelped.

"Yes," she said. "I'd have to be out of my mind to be out here in the middle of East Jesus with you in the first place. I can't believe I let you talk me into this."

"Me?" he yelped. "Talk you?"

"Who knocked on whose door?"

"Who opened it?"

"Why didn't you just take the Interstate?"

"Because I didn't want to get us killed."

They yelled back and forth in the semidarkness and whatever it was scratching about in the grass scurried away in fright.

"Well," she said with great finality, "I don't intend to be here a minute longer than I have to."

"Well, you're stuck," he said flatly.

"No I'm not," she shot back, and she clattered away up the road, putting a steady distance between them.

He stared in utter amazement. "Keats," he called, "don't act like an idiot."

She was perhaps twenty yards away now. She turned and looked back at him — a sturdy, if slightly askew figure, held upright by two thin pieces of aluminum. He could see her quite plainly, even in the weak light. "We can wait until daylight," he offered.

"No," she said, and turned again to go.

He started after her. "All right. Wait up." They wouldn't get far. For all her incredible stubbornness, she would tire quickly, and they would stop and let the rest of the night pass. In the morning he would find a telephone and call Joe Pike. No, Cicero. Somebody would come in a truck and fetch them and they would go back to Moseley and . . . what? The thought of Moseley made him ill. He had fled in panic and darkness, driven out by the sheer accumulated craziness of the place and everyone in it who mattered to him. No, Moseley would not do. But Atlanta? It seemed light years away and, at the moment, unattainable. And walking along a deserted rural road in the middle of the night seemed sheer folly. But what? He couldn't let her go off alone.

He had almost caught up with her when she tossed back over her shoulder, "I'd rather ride."

"The damn thing's broken."

"How do you know? Try it."

He threw up his hands and stalked back to the motorcycle. "All right!" he yelled. "You'll see! You're the most bullheaded, aggravating, two-faced person I've ever met, Keats! Just gotta have things your way! Can't admit for a second you're wrong! Get your jollies out of jerking people around!"

He was still yelling when he stomped down on the starter. The motorcycle roared to life and idled pleasantly. "Shit," he muttered to himself. He flicked the headlamp switch several times. Nothing. But that was all that was wrong. He slipped it into gear and rolled up to where she waited for him in the middle of the road, steadied the bike while he helped her climb on behind him and lay the crutches across the handlebars.

"I'm not two-faced," she said.

"Yes you are. One minute you seem almost normal. And the next you're pulling some kind of weird crap."

"I just know what I want, Trout. And right now I want to go to Atlanta."

He sat there straddling the motorcycle and fumed for a moment longer, then he calmed down a little. "I'll have to take it slow," he said. "I can't see very far ahead."

"Uh-huh."

"Keats, why are you doing this?"

"I'm not doing anything. You are. I'm just along for the ride."

"It's crazy."

"Trout," she said firmly, as if she were speaking to a knotheaded child, "if you don't do this, you might as well go home and dig yourself a hole and get in it and pull the dirt in behind you. Now, I *believe* you can do it. So get your ass in gear."

And so they rode on.

There was, incredibly, a light burning in the small, grimy garage in the tiny crossroads community. He fluttered toward it like a moth, and as the motorcycle drew closer, he could see an automobile inside, its rear hiked up in the air on jacks, and a pair of legs sticking out. The legs became a grease-smeared young man as the motorcycle pulled up to the yawning door of the bay. He sat on the concrete looking up at them, holding a wrench in one hand.

"Hi," Trout said tentatively.

"Evenin,'" the young man said with a little wave.

"Where are we?"

"Pacer," the young man said. "Georgia," he added. "Where y'all headed this time of night?"

"Atlanta."

"Damn. I wouldn't go to Atlanta even in broad daylight."

Trout glanced up at the sign above the garage bay: GLIDEWELL'S AUTO REPAIR.

"Are you Mr. Glidewell?"

"One of 'em."

Keats peered over Trout's shoulder. "Do you fix motorcycles?"

The young man grinned. "I can fix anything that don't eat."

His name was Elmer. He was working late because his daddy had torn the transmission out of the car racing on a dirt track near Macon on Sunday afternoon and needed it to go to work on Monday morning. Elmer quickly found the loose wire on the motorcycle and fixed it and sent them on their way, refusing payment, pointing the way to Conyers.

It was a powerful omen, he decided. But he kept that to himself. And Keats, blessedly, didn't say a word. As they bore on through the night, she nestled her head against his back and slept, keeping a firm hold on him. In an hour or so, the sky to the west began to glow softly with the lights of Atlanta. It was two o'clock in the morning when they reached Decatur and Trout pulled up to a telephone booth and called Eugene.

A shaft of light woke him. That, and the smell of coffee. He stretched his legs and arms and looked up for the source of the strong light. The condo had a skylight, something he hadn't noticed when Eugene had ushered them in. He hadn't noticed much at all, in fact. He was stupid with fatigue, butt gone completely numb. Yet his whole body hummed like a high-voltage transformer with the sensation of riding — the rush of wind and the vibrating rumble of the engine. Eugene had pointed Keats toward the spare bedroom while Trout collapsed on the living room couch. He closed his eyes and rode swiftly off the cliff of consciousness into the bottomless well of sleep, more profound than any he had ever experienced.

Now he was awake, stiff and sore but alert and remarkably rested. He was covered with a light blanket, his jeans and shirt hanging across a nearby chair, shoes tossed on the floor. He couldn't remember covering himself with the blanket or taking off his clothes. When? How? *My God. Did . . .* He searched his memory frantically. He could remember only utter exhaustion and then nothingness. He lifted the blanket gingerly and looked down at himself. Bare legs, Jockey underwear, his usual morning excitement. No sign of . . . what?

"Lost something?" Eugene asked, and Trout made an incredibly awkward attempt to cover himself, jerking the blanket up so that it left his feet sticking out. He looked around to see Eugene standing there with a cup of coffee in hand, barefoot, wearing jogging shorts and a MAKE MY DAY, KISS MY DERRIERE T-shirt, hair tousled, grinning, steam rising from the cup.

"I, ah . . . my clothes," Trout mumbled.

"Over there," Eugene said, pointing to the chair.

"Yeah."

"We thought you'd sleep better without them."

"We?"

"Keats helped me take them off. You were zonked."

Trout smiled sheepishly. "I guess so."

"I called Uncle Joe Pike and told him where you are," Eugene said.

"What did he say?"

"He said, 'I thought that's where he might be.'"

"Did you tell him Keats is with me?"

"Yes."

"What did he say about that?"

Eugene grinned. "Something about a woman with a wild hair up her butt."

"Oh. Yeah."

"Uncle Joe Pike said he'd call Wardell and tell him Keats is okay." Eugene headed for the kitchen. "Coffee's on."

Trout dressed and followed Eugene, who had a cup of coffee waiting for him on the kitchen table. He wasn't much of a coffee drinker, but he dumped in sugar and milk and found that it had a nice warm lift to it. Eugene poured himself another cup and sat down across the table from Trout.

"Keats still asleep?" Trout asked.

"I guess so. We stayed up pretty late talking."

"You did?" He tried not to sound too surprised.

"Keats and I go way back."

"You do?" Surprise won.

Eugene laughed, seeing the look on Trout's face. "I used to sneak over to the mill village and play with Keats and the other kids. Until Mom caught me and shipped me off to McCallie."

Trout realized how little he truly knew about Eugene. He had spent his junior- and senior-high years at prep school in Chattanooga, summers away at camps of one sort or another. When Trout made his infrequent visits to Moseley, Eugene was rarely there. He had gone to college at Vanderbilt, Trout knew that. But he had no idea what kind of job Eugene had or anything about his life. Or hadn't, until yesterday's *Atlanta Constitution.*

Eugene was studying him. "I hear the doo-doo really hit the fan," he said.

Trout shrugged uncomfortably, not having the slightest idea where to go with this. It felt incredibly odd, sitting here and knowing what he now knew about Eugene, knowing that he was supposed to recoil in horror at the thought of what Eugene *was.*

What on earth was he doing here, anyway? Well, admit it, he had been desperate, wheeling into Atlanta at two o'clock in the morning on a motorcycle with a crippled girl on the back and twenty dollars in his pocket, dead tired, no plan whatsoever. They hadn't even worn helmets. They could have been killed. Or, at the least, arrested and thrown in jail for violating the helmet law. Stupid! Stupid! He should have waited until today, found the keys to Joe Pike's car and some more money, left Keats at home. Then he could have driven to Atlanta without dragging along baggage and complicating everything to the point of near insanity. But no, he had to bolt like a frightened colt in the night and do it all wrong. He had damn near spent the night sitting in a ditch outside Pacer. And now here he was drinking coffee with his queer cousin, his asshole tightened up like a prune, and just wanting to get the hell out.

"Okay, let's talk about it," Eugene said.

"What?"

"Come on, Trout." Eugene gave him a long look. "Does it make you uncomfortable?"

"I guess so."

"Do you think I'm going to hit on you or something?"

"I don't know."

"Well, you're not my type," Eugene said with a smile. "And I'm not a pedophile; I'm gay. It's entirely different."

"It is?"

"Yes. So you don't have anything to worry about. Okay?"

Trout nodded. Eugene took another sip of his coffee. "So, ask me. Anything."

Trout went blank. There were a million questions, of course, but none of them in words. This was something you never ever talked about, not in any way but a snide joke, for fear that somebody would think you were . . . *that.* Talk about football, girls, hunting, zits, the Braves, dumb teachers, even jerking off. Anything but *that.* He blurted, "Do you have a roommate?"

Eugene smiled. "Roommate. Well, I *had* a lover. His name is Jason. But we broke up a month ago and he moved out. It was," he sighed, "every bit as painful as your breaking up with a girl."

"Oh." Then he added after a moment, "I'm sorry."

"I'm getting over it. Jason wouldn't pick up his underwear. I try to remember that, not the rest of it."

Trout laughed, and it made him feel a little better.

"I am who I am," Eugene said easily. "I've known for a long time that I'm gay. It's not something I'd have wished for if I'd known how it can complicate your life. But then, it's not something you wish or don't wish. It just is. I am what God made me. And like I heard Uncle Joe Pike say one time, God don't make no junk."

Trout could feel his anxiety easing. This was just Eugene — not much different, really, from the boy Trout remembered. Just older, more mature, but with the same stubborn streak of independence. The same Eugene who had thrown down his horseshoe and walked away from Grandaddy Leland's backyard game years before because he could see that it was rigged and dumb. Eugene seemed at peace with himself. Just playing the hand that he had been dealt.

Trout felt a sudden rush of both envy and self-loathing. He was disgustingly pliable, eager to please, running along behind other people and picking up after them. Especially Joe Pike. He hated that part of himself. And he hated what he believed to be a deep-rooted cowardice that let him simply go with gravity and current. On the one hand, he craved some notion of control over his life, self-determination, self-knowledge. All the things Eugene seemed to have. On the other hand, if and when he truly figured out who he was, it might scare the hell out of him. It may have, he realized, scared the hell out of Eugene at one point in the past. But he had gotten over it.

"Do Uncle Cicero and Aunt Alma know?"

"Dad, yes. God bless him. It was a shock when I told him, back when I was at Vandy. But he got over it. We talk. A lot. He's incredible." He ran his hand roughly through his hair. "Mom? Not, I'm afraid, until yesterday. I tried to drop hints. I even took Jason home with me last Christmas. But she just wouldn't see. Didn't want to see. You know how she is."

"Yeah." And then he told Eugene about the Sunday that never seemed to end, Alma's marching out of church and Joe Pike's sermon and then Alma's trying to burn down the mill. Recounting it, he was struck by how nightmarish it seemed now, by how profoundly the earth had shaken in Moseley, Georgia, in the space of one day. He realized in the telling that it sounded like Eugene had brought down the temple on everyone's head with one photograph on the front page of the paper. But it wasn't so. The fault lines had been there all along. All it took was a nudge.

"I didn't know about the thing at the mill," Eugene said, staring into his coffee cup. "Dad didn't tell me that."

"Aunt Alma talks all the time, or used to, about you and me running it one of these days."

Eugene didn't say anything for a long time. His finger traced a circle around the rim of his coffee cup. His brow furrowed. Finally, he looked up at Trout. "It's all gone," Eugene said quietly. "You realize that, don't you?"

"Gone?"

"The mill hasn't turned a profit in five years," Eugene went on. "Maybe longer. But Mom just kept on running it full-tilt and selling stuff at a loss and using up the cash reserves. She plowed ahead like nothing was wrong, sending everybody in the family their checks, keeping up appearances, holding it all together somehow. Until now."

"The union . . ."

"Wardell and the rest of them are just chasing their tails," Eugene interrupted. "There's nothing to unionize. The cash is gone and the only way to keep going is to borrow. And no Moseley ever borrowed a dime. It's an article of faith. Mama's darn sure not going to borrow money to pay for a union." He paused, then shook his head. "Funny. Wardell wants a union because he thinks things are so bad. Well, they'd be a darn sight worse if Mama hadn't kept the mill running like she has. Wardell's about to find out what 'bad' is."

At first, Trout was stunned. And then lights went on, bells rang, pieces fit. *Watch and listen,* Phinizy had said. Trout had, and he realized that he had known more than he thought. The pained, frightened looks in people's eyes, the fierce clutching at myth and symbol. What it amounted to, he could see now, was desperation — the acts of people trying to save themselves. *Save your own ass,* Uncle Phinizy had said. Well, that's what all the rest of them were doing, whether they knew it or not. Phinizy, Joe Pike, Alma, even Cicero, with their hauntings and agonies and dreams. Maybe Wardell Dubarry and his daughter, too. Everybody scrambling for the lifeboats.

"Who else knows about all this?"

"Dad. Judge Tandy, probably. He does all the legal work."

"My dad?"

"I don't know. Uncle Joe Pike's got his own problems, I suppose."

"Yeah. Uncle Phinizy?"

"Not all of it, I don't think. But he suspects a lot."

"Yeah."

"And now, Keats."

"You told her?"

"Yes."

"What's going to happen?" Trout asked.

"I suppose they'll lock the door and turn out the lights. Mom and Dad will be okay. Dad's done really well. Real estate, stocks and bonds. People have no idea."

No they didn't, Trout thought. He wondered what might happen now to Cicero's Do-It-All, to the notion of economic transformation in weary, down-at-the-heels Moseley, especially with the mill and its wages gone. It seemed the height of futility.

Cicero had obviously known all along what was going on with the mill and the Moseley family money. Had he bought into the charade simply to keep peace? Or had he loved Alma enough that he was unwilling, even unable, to hasten the inevitable. Surely, what Alma had done had been foolish — clutching at blind hope and some terribly warped notion of what it meant to be a Moseley, letting the ghosts of Moseleys past run her life. Surely, Cicero could see it. But he had either ignored or helped stave off the inevitable. To confront it would have meant admitting that the temple was rotten and crumbling. And that would have broken her heart, as Trout had seen it broken last night in the mill. Cicero might be something of a fool for doing what he did. But a man would be a fool for a woman. Trout Moseley knew that. And it stood to reason that a woman might also be a fool for a man. He just hadn't seen that side of it yet.

Eugene stood. "Well, I've got to go to work."

Trout realized he didn't know what Eugene did for a living. "Where?" he asked.

"The studio."

"Are you an artist?"

"Film and video production."

Then he remembered — he and Eugene, playing TV station years before. Eugene organized everything. He combed Trout's hair and put some of Alma's pancake makeup on him. He made a camera from a cardboard box with an old toilet paper tube as a lens. Then Eugene manned the camera while Trout read articles from the newspaper. When Eugene eventually grew up and went off to college, Aunt Alma insisted he major in pre-law. But in the end, Eugene had obviously done what he wanted.

Trout indicated the condo. "I guess you're doing okay."

"I'm having fun." Eugene smiled down at him. "You ought to try it, Trout."

He turned to go, but stopped in the doorway. "Keats is a neat kid. If she has half a chance, she'll make something of herself. She's got a lot of spirit."

"Yeah. She does."

Eugene studied him closely. "She likes you a lot. I guess you know that."

He woke Keats an hour later with a cup of coffee. She was nestled like a burrowing rodent in the double bed in the spare bedroom. She sat up quickly, startled from sleep, and stared at him uncomprehendingly. She was wearing one of Eugene's shirts.

"Hi," he said.

She took the coffee cup without speaking and drank several sips. Then she said, "Hand me my crutches."

He watched as she tottered off unsteadily to the adjoining bathroom. Bare legs, a sliver of white panties showing beneath the hem of the shirt. She came back after a moment and sat on the side of the bed next to him, propping the crutches next to her, looking much improved. She drank more of the coffee.

"I'm a good sleeper and a bad waker," she said.

"Have you called your folks?"

"No."

"Are you going to?"

"No."

"Why not?"

She looked down at her hands. "Because I'm scared." It was, he thought, an incredibly naked confession for someone like Keats Dubarry.

"Scared of what?" he asked.

She looked at him harshly. "Do you know what's going to happen? Do you have any idea of the kind of pain and agony that's coming?" He didn't answer. "No, I guess you don't," she said with a sneer. "You folks up there in the Big House, you'll do just fine. Us po' white trash down in the mill village are out on our butts. No jobs, no place to live, no nothing. Can you imagine what this is going to do to my daddy?"

"But you said he ought to get out of there and find another job," Trout reminded her. "You said he's good with his hands."

"It's losing," Keats said. "That's what he won't be able to stand. Losing to the Moseleys. Every time he looks at me, a little bit of what's good and kind about him dies. And a little more hatred for the god-damn Moseleys takes its place." She turned away from him with a jerk, quivering with rage. He thought for a moment she might cry, but then he knew she would not. She had learned from Wardell Dubarry that anger would keep you going when nothing else could.

"Keats," he said after a while, "I'm sorry. I really am. I don't want anybody to be hurt. Not you, not your family, not my family. I just don't know what to do."

She turned back to him then and gave a weary sigh. "I know."

Impulsively, he put his arm around her shoulders. He didn't know how she might take it, but she looked at him strangely for a moment and then she rested her forehead against his and slipped into the crook of his arm and he put his other arm around her, encircling, protecting. He closed his eyes, and the two of them sat that way for a long time, and there was no sound but their breathing. Then he opened his eyes and saw her legs, bare below the shirt. They were firm and strong and smooth. Whatever damage the truck had done, it was not there. He felt a rush of blood to his face and his breath quickened and his head spun and his stomach did little dipsy-doodles. "I'm really glad you came," he said hoarsely.

Her lips were incredibly soft. He disappeared into them, like falling from a great distance into a cottony cloud, and he only faintly heard the clatter of the crutches as they fell to the floor. He fell and fell and the cloud that was Keats caught him and held him and then they fell together, through rain and then sun, crying out to each other like winged things. And when they landed finally, entwined and enthralled, the earth swallowed them in all its soft, lush greenness.

They huddled together like puppies, sharing warmth and security, not speaking for a very long time. Trout was astonished. That was the only word for it.

So that's what it was. That's what everybody made such a big deal about. Well, he thought with a smile, it was indeed a very big deal. It was not just the joining. That happened so quickly, so awkwardly, it was almost embarrassing. No, it was what the joining meant. You truly stepped out of yourself for the very first time in your life and entered a communal space where you willingly gave up something of your innermost self and were given to in return. It was, he realized, something you could never adequately explain to a friend, even one who had engaged in the same kind of act. Because it wasn't just an act. It was . . . astonishment.

She stirred in his arms, flesh on flesh. He felt immensely tender, almost to the point of tears. He kissed her hair and she raised her head from the crook of his arm where she nestled.

"Did you . . ." he started.

But she put her fingers quickly over his mouth. "No questions," she said.

And they slept.

It was almost noon. She sat up in the bed and moved away from him a bit, and when he finally opened his eyes, she was sitting cross-legged, studying him. Every inch, head to toe and back again, seeming to absorb the minutest detail. Her eyes stopped just below his waist and lingered there and it was almost like a touch. He stirred. She smiled.

"Well, now you know," he said, returning the smile. He should feel incredibly self-conscious, he thought, should make some frantic move to cover himself. But he didn't feel that way at all. He felt freer than he had in a very long time — perhaps ever. He felt that he was letting go of a lot, easing out from under the peddler's sack of stuff he had been carrying around. He reached for her, but she gripped his wrist and stopped him.

"Let me draw you," she said.

"Will it make me feel famous?" he asked.

She smiled again. "Of course."

FIFTEEN

IT WAS A light, cheerful room with the walls painted a pale yellow, bright floral print curtains at the window and a matching bedspread, pictures of birds and woodsy scenes on the walls. There was a nightstand by the bed, a chest of drawers, a small table that served as a desk. The stack of books on the desk included a couple of novels (she was partial to Anne Tyler and Walker Percy), a typing manual similar to the one Trout had used in class at Ohatchee High, and a volume on organic gardening.

The desk also held a portable typewriter and beside it, a thin stack of typed sheets. He thought of reading them while he waited, but decided against it. Whatever she had written, it was private. And in a place like this, your private thoughts would surely be intensely personal and even painful, part of whatever it was they did here to help you save yourself. There was much he wanted to know, but he didn't want to find out that way. It would be, in a way, dishonest. So he stood instead at the window looking out at the shaded grounds, the long oak-lined driveway that led to the main building across the way, where the motorcycle was parked and where Keats waited inside.

Keats. He tried not to think about her, because this — this room and what it meant — was why he had come. But he couldn't *not* think about her. Every nerve ending tingled with the feel and smell and taste of her, and he felt light, floating, helium-filled, strangely abstracted.

He shook his head, trying to rid himself for a little while of the images. There would be plenty of time for that.

Back to the room. She might not come. They had told her that Trout was here, but she might decide not to see him. It wouldn't be because she didn't love him, but because she just wasn't ready yet. And if she did come, what to say? What to tell? What to ask? He was afraid it would all rush out in a great blur of words, all the wrong ones as well as the right ones. He might frighten her. Or bring on one of the great black silences that had so frightened him in the days before they took her away.

It was so quiet, he could hear his heart pounding. He turned on the clock radio on the bedside table. It was tuned to the Atlanta oldies station. Patti Page sang "Old Cape Cod," and he thought suddenly of the beach. He must have been two or three — spooked by the waves that pounded the sand and swirled up around his legs. He cried, and Joe Pike picked him up and held him and then walked into the water to show him it was all right. But every time a wave broke, Joe Pike, unthinking, turned his back and Trout got a face full of salt water that stung his eyes and made him bellow with terror. And Irene had come to rescue him.

He heard the door open behind him, but he was unable to move — stricken suddenly by the fear of what he might see, what she might be. *Oh God* . . .

"Trout," she said softly. He turned slowly and saw that she was small and beautiful and filled with light, even if there were tiny lines etched around her eyes and mouth that hadn't been there before. She was as he remembered, as he had hoped, only different. But not so much that it mattered. And then she took him in her arms and rescued him again, if for just a little while.

"You know? All of it?"

"Yes," she said.

"How?"

"Cicero. He calls just about every day."

Trout was stunned. Cicero had never mentioned Irene except in the most oblique and offhand way. But all the while, he was giving her a link with the world she had escaped.

"And Phinizy calls sometimes," she added. "Mostly just to see how I'm doing and to tell me about something he's been reading."

"They let you talk on the phone?"

"Of course, honey. It isn't a prison."

They sat together on a concrete bench in the shade of a tree just outside her cottage. The afternoon was warm, but her touch was cool as she smoothed his hair and caressed his cheek.

"Dad said the doctors didn't want anybody to come see you."

Her face clouded. "What they tell you here is that you have to take responsibility for yourself. You can't depend on anybody else or blame anybody else. You have to wrestle with who you are and come to grips with that." She hesitated, searching his face for some sign of comprehension. "Do you understand that?"

"I guess so."

"I'm wrestling. And it just seemed better to do it by myself." She smiled. "But I'm glad you came. It was time."

"Are you well yet?"

She pondered that for a moment. And then, without exactly answering his question, she told him about her long pilgrimage — medication, electroshock therapy, a lot of talk, the gradual return of awareness and interest. It was like being a baby chick inside a shell, she said. She hadn't wanted to come out for a good while. The world was too fierce and demanding. But then one day, almost by accident, she had pecked at the shell and a splinter of light had broken through and the journey began. It was painful, often terribly so. "Honesty," she said with a rueful laugh, "really sucks." There were setbacks, days when the old curse returned. But there were fewer and fewer of those now.

"When can you come home?" he asked tentatively.

"I don't know, Trout."

Don't know when? *Or don't know* if? "Can I come stay here with you?"

"No, honey," she said gently. "They wouldn't let you do that." She looked away, out where the sun, almost directly overhead, splattered stretches of grass between the trees with a bright, hot light. It was quiet here, sheltered, the noises of Atlanta beyond the grounds of the Institute only a faint murmur.

"Dad needs you," Trout said tentatively.

She looked back at him. "Dad needs . . ." But then her voice trailed off and she was lost in thought. It dawned on Trout that whatever great chasm of need that existed between them might be unbridgeable, maybe even unknowable. *I am,* Joe Pike had said, *part of the problem. Maybe most of it.* Trout felt a hollow sickness at his core, a dawning awareness that things might never be a great deal better, that she might never come all the way back and that Joe Pike might spin off like a runaway meteor into nothingness. And he, Trout Moseley, sixteen years old and ancient in his battered soul? What? What?

"Mama," he said, his voice small and distant. "I've got to know. Was any of it my fault?"

She pulled him close, pressed his head against her chest and held him for a long time. He could hear the beating of her tiny heart, a bird's heart. He felt hollow. And pointless. She might never tell him. She might not be able.

But after a while she said, "I've had a lot of time to think about what happened, honey. You think about everything, all the possibilities. I wondered if it was just that I didn't want to be a mother, didn't want the responsibility. I wondered if I was a coward. But then I thought of how much I love you. How could I not want to be your mother? You are the most precious thing in the world to me, Trout. No, sweetheart, none of it is your fault. I may have failed as a mother, but you didn't fail as my son."

"You didn't fail, Mama," he protested.

"I left. It's a kind of failure."

He raised up and looked her in the eye. "But why?"

She thought about it for a moment, closed her eyes, sighed, opened them again. "I left because I just couldn't handle things anymore." She paused again, searching for words, for a beginning, perhaps. "Has Dad ever told you anything about his father?"

"They didn't get along. I learned that much."

"Leland Moseley went for an entire year without saying a single word to his son. The year Dad was a senior in high school. They sent him off to the military school, but he ran away and came home and insisted on going to high school in Moseley. And his father refused to speak to him or even acknowledge that he existed."

"Just because Dad wouldn't mind him?"

"I suppose so."

"But that was way back, Mama. What . . ."

"So Dad went off to college in Texas, and that's where he met me. His father showed up, quite unexpectedly, at graduation. And he told Joe Pike it was time to come home and take over the mill."

"But he didn't."

"No. He went on to seminary and became a minister. I think he had God and Leland Moseley confused. He wanted to please Leland, but he couldn't bring himself to go to the mill. So he turned to God, and Leland couldn't argue much with that. Only later, he began to figure out that he turned to God for the wrong reasons."

"And you?"

"I never wanted to be a preacher's wife. It's very hard. People are always watching you, pulling and tugging on you, asking for things and expecting things you can't give. Your dad" — she paused, again trying to find the right words to describe something that may be indescribable — "wants people to love him."

Images flashed through Trout's mind: Joe Pike on the parsonage lawn, surrounded by the remnants of his distant past, pulling them to him, enveloping them with his smile and his great arms, soaking them up hungrily; and Joe Pike at summer camp, lumbering to the swimming beach draped with laughing kids.

"I love him," Trout said tentatively. He waited.

"So do I, honey. But that wasn't enough. And there came a time when I began to ask myself, 'Why am I putting myself through this? Why is he?' And I suppose that's when I started to run away."

Trout could see the pain of it in her face, and he realized that it was pain, as much as anything else, that had permeated their lives all these years. That was the worst thing about the silences. The pain. For all of them. Pain, disappointment, and finally exhaustion. Bending under the great weight on your shoulders, the weight of being who you were, or at least who you were supposed to be. Eventually, you might have only two choices: run or die. *Save your own ass.* But in doing so, it was an admission of failure. It was a word Joe Pike had used, and now Irene. They had all lost a lot. Much of it was irretrievable.

He crumbled then. "I miss you, Mama." She searched his face and then put her arm around him while he cried unashamedly, burying his face in her lap, a lost and bewildered little boy, for one last moment the child he would never be again.

It was midafternoon when Trout called Joe Pike and told him they were leaving Atlanta. They got on the motorcycle and headed out, finding Highway 278 in Decatur and retracing the route they had traveled the night before. The towns and crossroads — Conyers,

Pacer, Covington — and the ribbons of winding rural road that connected them seemed strange and unfamiliar in the daylight, like territory fought over and conquered in some long-ago night battle, filled with sound and fury.

They said little to each other until they stopped for a foot-long hot dog and a shake at the Dairy Queen in Covington. It had a small covered patio that shaded several picnic tables, and they sat alone and ate ravenously.

"I'll bet Herschel's mad as hell," Trout said.

"Yeah. We should have told him, I guess."

"Do you think he'll fire us?"

"Probably. Then hire us back. At least me."

"Why you?"

"Well, he can't do without me."

The Dairy Queen seemed somehow strange and distant, something he had known long ago. Everything was changed now. What to do? Who could tell him? It was still only mid-June and the summer stretched ahead like an unending highway, the horizon shimmering with heat phantoms. There was, at least, Keats.

When they had finished, Trout took all their trash to a nearby can and then sat down again across from her, and they looked at each other for a long moment.

"I don't know what to say," he said finally.

"About your mother?"

"About anything. Us."

She looked away from him.

"I didn't mean to . . . I mean, I wasn't trying to . . . it just happened."

She looked back. "Look, Trout. Let's don't spoil it, okay? Let's leave it where it is."

"Damn it!" he said. "Stop making me feel like a little kid!"

"If you feel like a little kid, that's your problem."

"I love you!"

Her eyes softened then, and she reached for his hand and held it. "It was the sweetest thing that ever happened to me," she said gently. "I want to keep it that way."

"But what about . . ."

"I don't know. That's all I can say. I don't know." She raised his hand to her lips and kissed it lightly. "Right now, I just want to go home."

It was late afternoon when they reached Moseley. And as they rolled in from the west, Highway 278 becoming Broadus Street, he was struck by how small and dowdy it looked. Even Aunt Alma's house seemed to sag under its own weight and he noticed, for the first time, that paint was beginning to flake from the fascia board above the front porch. The Packard was parked under the porte cochere, but the Buick wasn't there. And across the street at the parsonage and church, there was no sign of life at all.

The park looked almost normal, except there was no band shell. You had to look closely to see where the gash the bulldozer had made was now sodded over.

The rumble of the motorcycle engine echoed hollowly off the downtown buildings as they rode through. It was mostly deserted, everything except the Koffee Kup Kafe closed for the evening, long shadows swallowing the storefronts and making them even more somber and drab than ever. The vacant lot where the furniture store had been was an open red sore. The slab of concrete that had un-earthed the skeleton was a dirt-covered scab at the middle of the lot. Across the street there was nobody in the police department, or at least not visible in the front room. Trout wondered if Joe Pike had gone back to his cell, back to contemplation of the rules of the road. Then he remembered that Joe Pike had answered the telephone in the parsonage when Trout called. But where was he now? Maybe at the Dairy Queen.

They passed the city limits sign on the east side of town, and that's when he got his first glimpse of the commotion in front of the mill. As the motorcycle drew closer, he could see that the gate was closed and a big crowd was milling about in front of it. A couple of hundred people, men and women, black and white, a sprinkling of kids. It looked like the entire population of the mill village. Joe Pike's car and Cicero's police cruiser sat at the curb, well back from the crowd. As he turned onto the mill street, he could see Alma's car parked inside the fence next to the office door. The crowd at the gate seemed agitated, and as he got nearer, he could hear its angry buzz and he could see Wardell Dubarry towering over the rest of the mill workers, one hand on the gate, shaking it furiously. It was padlocked. Then he saw Joe Pike and Cicero and Calhoun standing next to the police cruiser. The driver-side door was open, and Cicero was standing next to it, talking on the radio, while he kept an eye on the crowd.

"Damn!" Trout said. Why couldn't they all just be quiet for a little while?

He could feel Keats craning her neck to see around him, seeing what he saw, her body tensing. About the same time, Joe Pike spotted them. His eyes and Trout's met and Joe Pike shook his head vigorously, warning him away. Trout turned to give the crowd a wide berth, and then Keats yelled, "Stop!" He kept going. "Stop, Trout! Dammit, stop!"

"I'm taking you home," he yelled back. "You might get hurt."

"Let me off!" she bellowed. "Let me off!" She started beating on his back with one of her fists, holding on to him with the other hand and digging her fingers painfully into his side. At the rear of the crowd, people turned to look at them. And then Keats stopped hammering on his back and began to slip backward off the motorcycle. Damn! She'd kill herself! He slammed on the brakes and she lurched hard against him, and then as he fought to keep the cycle from toppling over, she scrambled off, an incredible flurry of crutches, arms, and legs. She left him there struggling with the bike and plunged into the crowd, disappearing in the general direction of Wardell.

Trout got the motorcycle under control and turned around and headed for Cicero's police cruiser. As he pulled in behind it, Joe Pike pointed a no-nonsense arm toward the parsonage. "Go home, Trout."

Trout glanced at the crowd, pressing up hard against the locked gate. Wardell was rattling the gate furiously and the noise level was rising. This was not a placard-carrying crowd, not some well-organized protest. It was a nasty-looking spur-of-the-moment mob. And Keats was somewhere in the middle of it. Trout killed the engine, kicked down the kickstand, climbed off the motorcycle and headed toward Joe Pike and Cicero. "Did you hear me?" Joe Pike barked.

But just then there was a roar from the crowd, and they all looked and saw Aunt Alma emerge from the mill office. "Open up!" Wardell bellowed. Alma paid them no attention. She got into her Buick and sat there for a moment.

Cicero turned to Joe Pike. He looked grimly alarmed. "I told her we should have called the state folks an hour ago!"

"What's going on?" Trout demanded.

"Go home!" Joe Pike ordered again.

"No!" he shot back, standing his ground. "What happened?"

"Alma closed the plant."

Another roar from the crowd. Alma was backing out of her parking space now, turning and easing toward the gate. The noise was deafening. Cicero turned and said something to Joe Pike, but Trout couldn't hear what it was. He handed the radio microphone to Calhoun and yelled something to him. Then Cicero headed toward the crowd, hitching up his gun belt as he went, Joe Pike close on his heels. Trout followed, slipping in behind them as Cicero lowered his shoulders and waded into the crowd. They edged along the fence, Cicero and Joe Pike shoving people out of the way as they struggled toward the gate. Trout was bumped and jostled. He almost went down, but he grabbed on to the back of Joe Pike's belt. Joe Pike whirled angrily, then saw who it was. "Get outta here!" But it was too late now. Bodies pressed in around them — yelling, pushing, pressing toward the gate in a heaving mass. "Hang on!" Joe Pike yelled, and pushed on.

Through the fence, Trout could see Alma's car stopping, Alma getting out, walking up to the gate, unlocking it. "The plant's closed!" she cried. "This is private property! Get off!"

"Well, if we ain't coming in, you ain't coming out!" Wardell yelled back. The noise exploded, drowning out everything for a moment until the gun went off. POW! Then bedlam. A panic in the other direction. Joe Pike staggered, almost losing his feet, and Trout was bounced roughly against the wire fence. He held on and suddenly they burst free and he looked around Joe Pike's great bulk and saw Cicero and Wardell, faced off like two bulls, Cicero's arm holding his police revolver high in the air. Cicero kept his eye on Wardell, but he yelled through the fence to Alma, "Get in the car!"

"Yeah!" Wardell screamed at her back as she retreated from the gate. "Get in the car, Alma! Turn tail and run! Go see that faggot young'un of yores in Atlanta!"

Joe Pike lunged forward and Trout lost his hold on the belt and almost fell. He grabbed the fence to steady himself, just in time to see the powerful movement of Joe Pike's right shoulder and hear the sickening crunch as his fist collided with Wardell Dubarry's face. Suddenly, all sound ceased — except for the sound of Wardell's body slamming backward into the gate and dropping with a thud to the ground. Nobody moved. Cicero stared at Joe Pike, then Wardell, an astonished look on his face, his gun still high in the air.

Joe Pike stood over Wardell, massive and unmovable. "Get up, Wardell," he said. "Get up and apologize to my sister."

But Trout could see that was quite impossible. Wardell was out cold.

Then from somewhere off to Trout's right there was a horrible scream and then an explosion of motion as Keats came slashing through the crowd, yelling incoherently, scattering people with her crutches. She lurched up to where Joe Pike stood over Wardell, her face contorted with rage. "Goddamn you!" she screamed. "Get away from him!" She smacked Joe Pike's shin with a crutch. He didn't say anything, but he backed away a couple of steps, and Keats collapsed on the pavement next to Wardell, covering him with her body. She sobbed against his ashen face while they all stood, stunned and un-moving, watching her. It was pitiful. Trout took a step toward her, but she looked up and saw and stopped him with her savage voice. "God-damn you! All you goddamn Moseleys!"

And Trout knew that she was quite beyond comfort.

He tried, just once. It was just after six the next morning when he knocked on the door of the Dubarry house. After a moment, Keats opened it and stood there, staring at him as if he were an apparition. She was calm, but there was a fierce hardness to it. After a moment she said, "You're crazy, coming over here."

"Can I see your daddy?" he asked.

"No," she said, and started to close the door. But then Wardell was there, standing just behind her and peering out. When he saw who it was, his eyes bulged with rage and he made a ragged gargling sound through the wires that held his jaw together.

"Mr. Dubarry," Trout said, "I came to ask you to drop the charges against my daddy so he can get out of jail and preach Uncle Phinizy's funeral."

Wardell just glared at him, stunned at the audacity of it, then turned away from the doorway in disgust.

"You'd better leave," Keats said.

Trout heard a screen door slam somewhere behind him and turned to see a shirtless, barefoot man standing on the porch across the way, arms folded across his chest, eyes narrowed. Then he saw more people on other porches, some of them drifting down into their yards, moving slowly in the direction of the Dubarry house. The hostility hit him like a hot wave.

"Don't come back, Trout," Keats said. Her voice was absolutely flat and emotionless. "Ever."

He was stunned. "Keats. Don't. After what happened . . ."

"Nothing happened," she said.

"Yes it did!" he cried.

"You're just like a little puppy. You want somebody to hold you so you'll stop whining. Grow up, Trout."

"No," he cried. "Don't do this, Keats." It was something he had to hold on to, something that was just his. She couldn't take it away. She couldn't.

"Forget it," she said. "It doesn't matter."

"I'll never forget it," he said, his voice barely a whisper.

"Okay, don't. But leave me alone. Don't ever come back here. If you do, I'll hang pictures of you all over the high school. Use your imagination."

He knew, with a sickening sense of helplessness, what she could do if she wanted. She knew every line and angle of his body, had committed them to paper and memory, and she could bend them into any shape or act her imagination could conjure up.

He felt helpless. Betrayed. But then he looked into her eyes and saw that it was the same with her, only worse. She was a small wounded animal, snarling at the thing that had hunted her down and cornered her. It was not really him. It was all the other. And she had only her crutches and her anger to hold her upright. That, and the gift of her talent. Maybe she would use it to find her way out. But if she did, it would be on her own. She was beyond his reach, perhaps always had been. There had been one brief, exquisite moment when he had thought there might be such a thing as grace and redemption and, yes, love. But it existed now only in his memory. Another loss, perhaps the most profound of all.

He sat on the back steps of the parsonage in the twilight waiting for the sun to dip below the treeline so it wouldn't blind him as he rode west. The motorcycle leaned on its kickstand at the edge of the house, the small duffel bag strapped to the passenger seat with a piece of rope he had found in the garage.

As he waited, he looked about the yard. The grass needed mowing. The storage shed needed painting. Next to it, the small plot of plowed-up ground was becoming clotted with weeds. Joe Pike had never gotten around to planting a garden. It was too late now.

Joe Pike still languished in the tiny cell at the rear of the police station, guarded by Calhoun, the new police chief. Joe Pike appeared somewhat at peace. But with him, it was hard to tell. It might be just exhaustion. They were all exhausted. He hadn't had much to say to Trout. Things were a trifle uncertain, he said. The Bishop would be in Moseley tomorrow to see to things at the Methodist church. And then there was the judge to consider. Joe Pike was reading Aeschylus now. And Heidegger. Trout had brought him the books from Phinizy's apartment, along with an enormous tub of Dairy Queen ice cream.

At graveside, there had been just the family — Trout, Alma, Cicero — and two fellows from the funeral home in Thomson. The four men carried the casket from the hearse. It didn't weigh much.

It was early, before nine, and the June sun angled through the tall pines that shaded the Moseley family plot. It had rained during the night, and the grass underfoot was spongy and the freshly dug earth was soft and ripe-smelling. There was the faintest of breezes, just enough to make the pines whisper.

Aunt Alma looked rather pretty. She was dressed in a mint green summer suit, silk maybe, something that clung to her figure. She had a nice figure. She, too, looked at peace. Or at least relieved.

The four men placed the casket on the metal stand over the open grave and then they all stepped back and stood there for a moment, no one quite knowing what to do next.

Then Cicero cleared his throat and spoke up. "Phinizy was a good listener," he said. "People went trooping in and out of his place at all hours of the day and night with all manner of baggage, and he always had time to listen. He had what some folks might call some bad habits, but I don't think they really amount to much in the big picture."

They pondered that for a moment, then Trout opened the Bible he had brought and read the passage from Job that Joe Pike had suggested. *"With the ancient is wisdom; and in the length of days understanding."*

"Amen to that," Cicero said. Then he turned to Alma. "Anything you want to say, hon?"

"I wish I had known him better," she said simply. "I wish I had . . ." Then her voice trailed off.

They all stood there for a while longer and then one of the men from the funeral home said, "Y'all want to stay while we finish up here?"

"No," Cicero said. "We've got a plane to catch."

"I'll stay," Trout said.

As he walked home later, he found himself thinking about Great Uncle Phinizy and smiling. Phinizy had seen the wreck and it was a doozie.

Cicero and Alma would be in Bermuda by now. They would probably stay for a good while, Cicero had said. Would Trout be okay while they were gone? Of course, he assured them. He was used to fending for himself. There were chicken pot pies in the freezer. And of course there was the Dairy Queen. He didn't want Cicero and Alma to worry.

When he returned to the parsonage from the cemetery, he changed into jeans, packed a few things, and made his call.

"Sure," Eugene said without hesitation. "Come ahead. For as long as you like."

It would be dark again as he rode. But that was all right. This time, he knew the way.